nickelodeon

BiG NATE

DESTINED FOR AWESOMENESS

Inspired by the comics and
book series by Lincoln Peirce

Based on the episodes written by
Mitch Watson, Elliott Owen, and Sarah Allan

Andrews McMeel
PUBLISHING®

Andrews McMeel Publishing
a division of Andrews McMeel Universal
1130 Walnut Street, Kansas City, Missouri 64106

www.andrewsmcmeel.com

Book design, layout, and lettering by The Story Division
www.thestorydivision.com

Editor: Lucas Wetzel
Art Director and Cover Design: Spencer Williams
Designer: Niko Dalcin
Production Editor: Dave Shaw
Copy Editor: Amy Strassner
Production Manager: Chuck Harper

Special thanks to:
Jeff Whitman, Alexandra Maurer, and Jarrin Jacobs at Nickelodeon
Steffie Davis, Steve Osgoode, and Niko Dalcin at The Story Division
And special thanks to Lincoln Peirce for editorial guidance throughout this project.

22 23 24 25 26 SDB 10 9 8 7 6 5 4 3 2 1

ISBN (paperback): 978-1-5248-7560-2
ISBN (hardcover): 978-1-5248-7806-1

Library of Congress Control Number: 2022935046

Made by:
King Yip (Dongguan) Printing & Packaging Factory Ltd.
Address and location of production:
Daning Administrative District, Humen Town
Dongguan Guangdong, China 523930
1st Printing — 5/16/22

CONTENTS

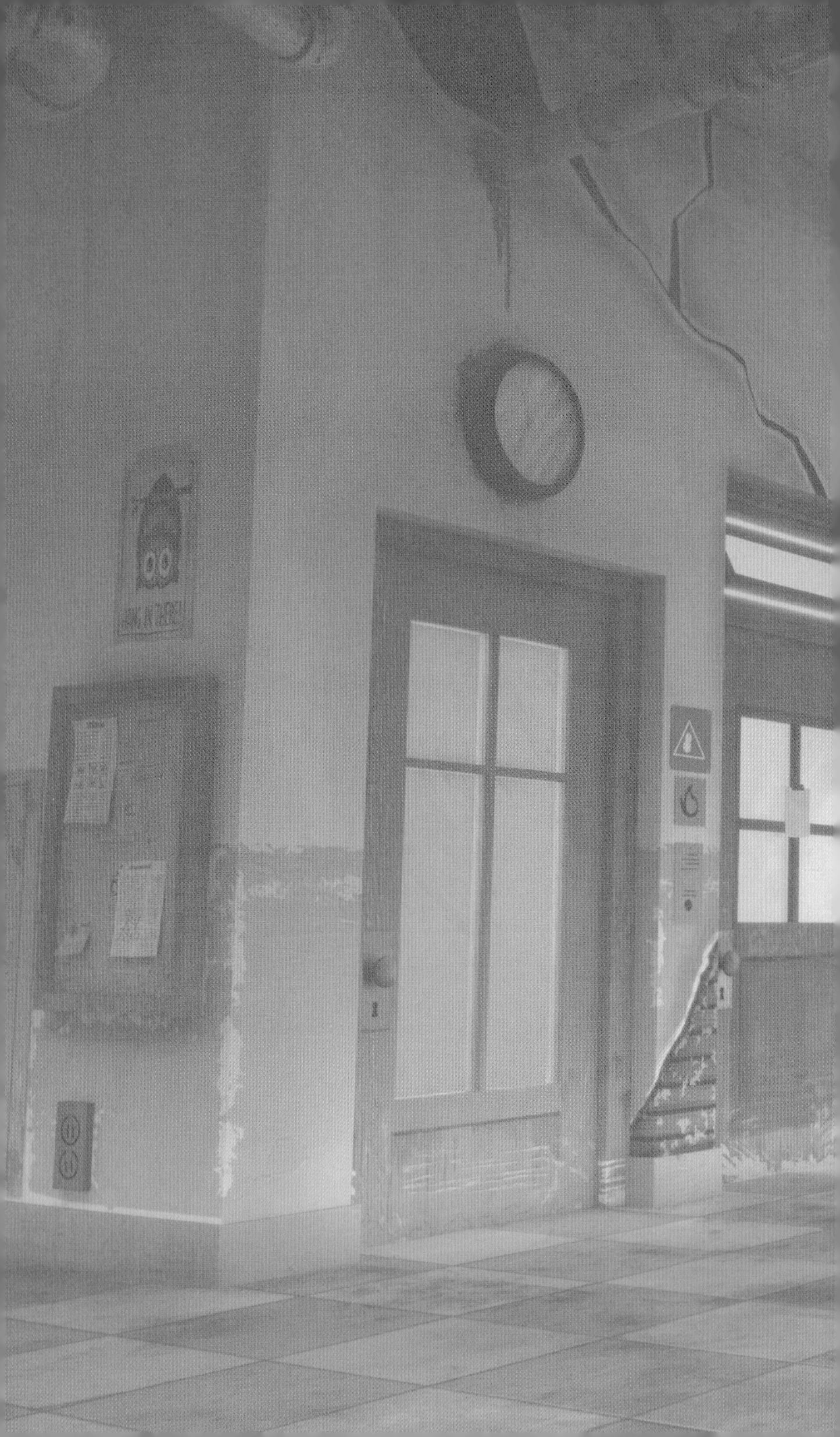

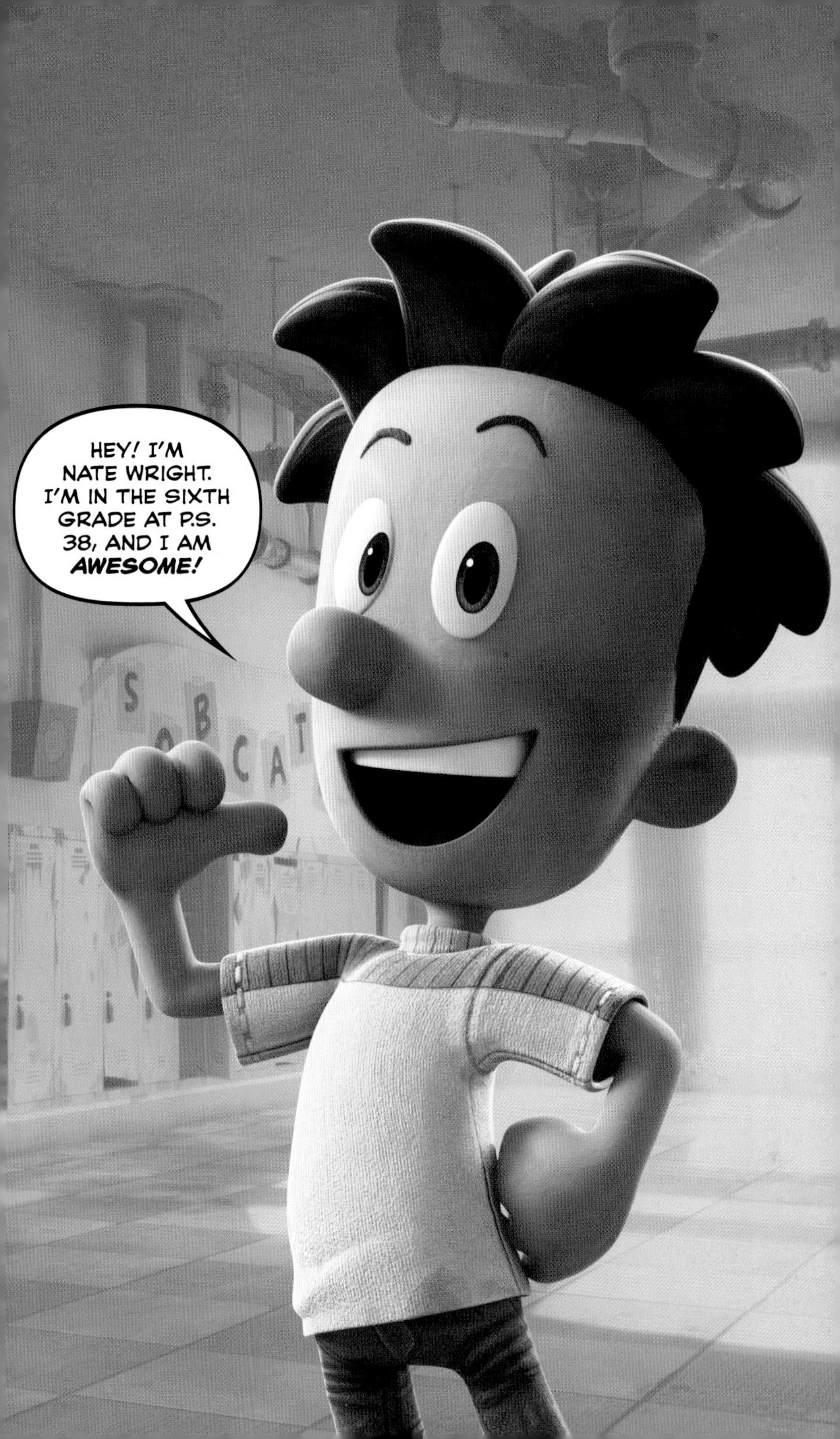
HEY! I'M NATE WRIGHT. I'M IN THE SIXTH GRADE AT P.S. 38, AND I AM ***AWESOME!***

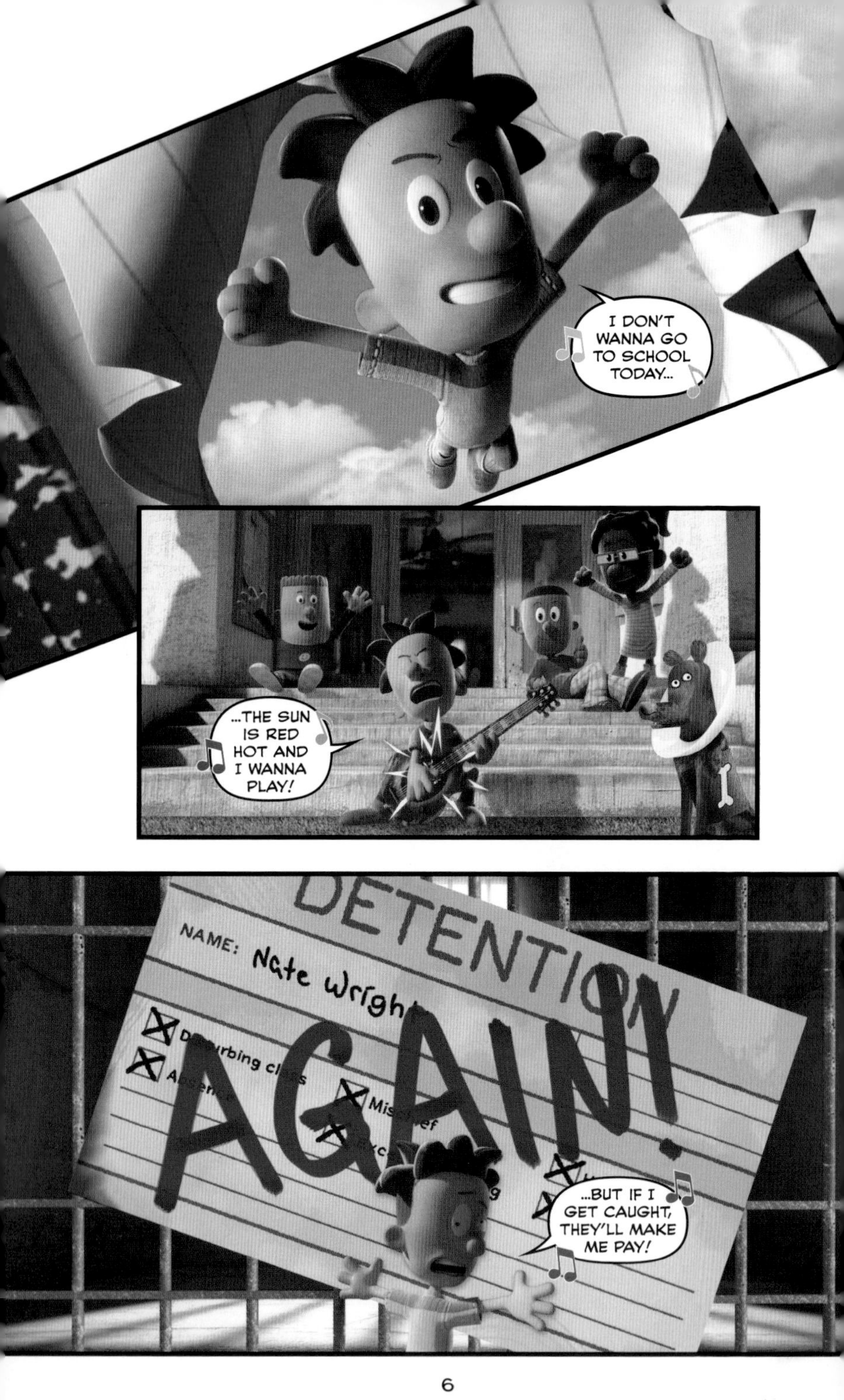
I DON'T WANNA GO TO SCHOOL TODAY...
...THE SUN IS RED HOT AND I WANNA PLAY!
DETENTION
NAME: Nate Wright
AGAIN!
...BUT IF I GET CAUGHT, THEY'LL MAKE ME PAY!

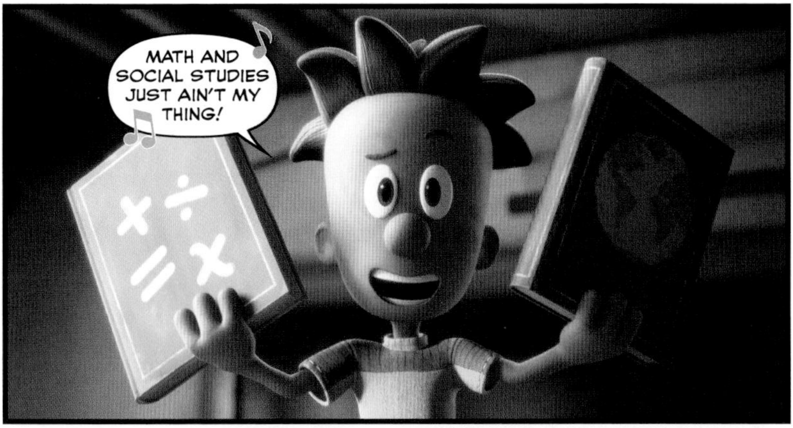
MATH AND SOCIAL STUDIES JUST AIN'T MY THING!

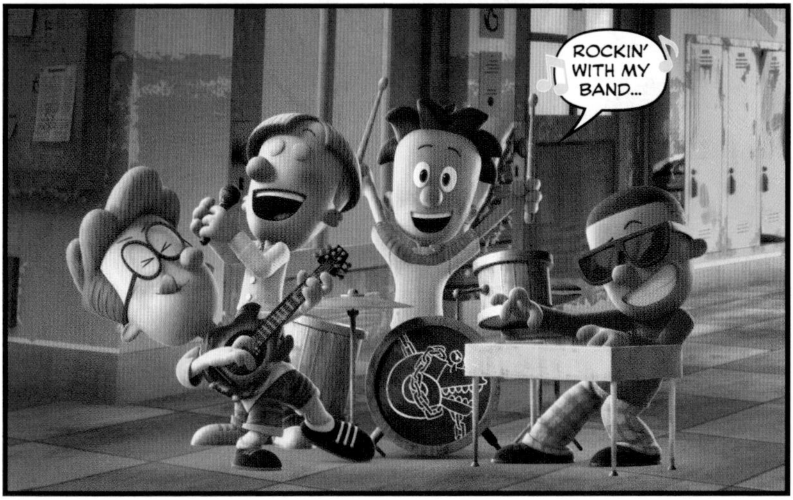
ROCKIN' WITH MY BAND...

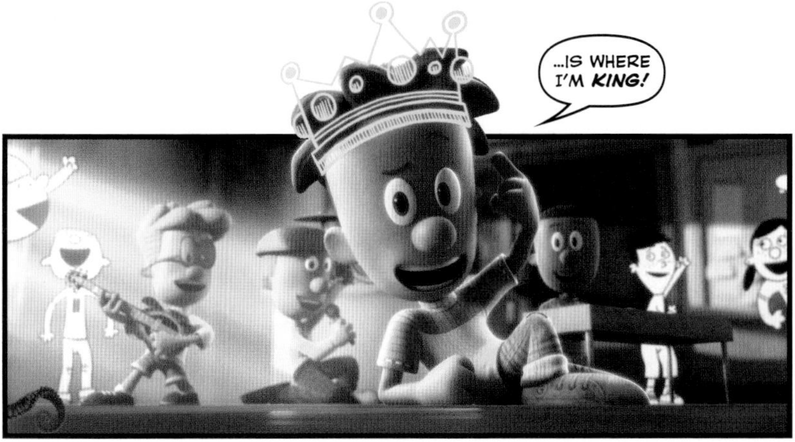
...IS WHERE I'M *KING!*

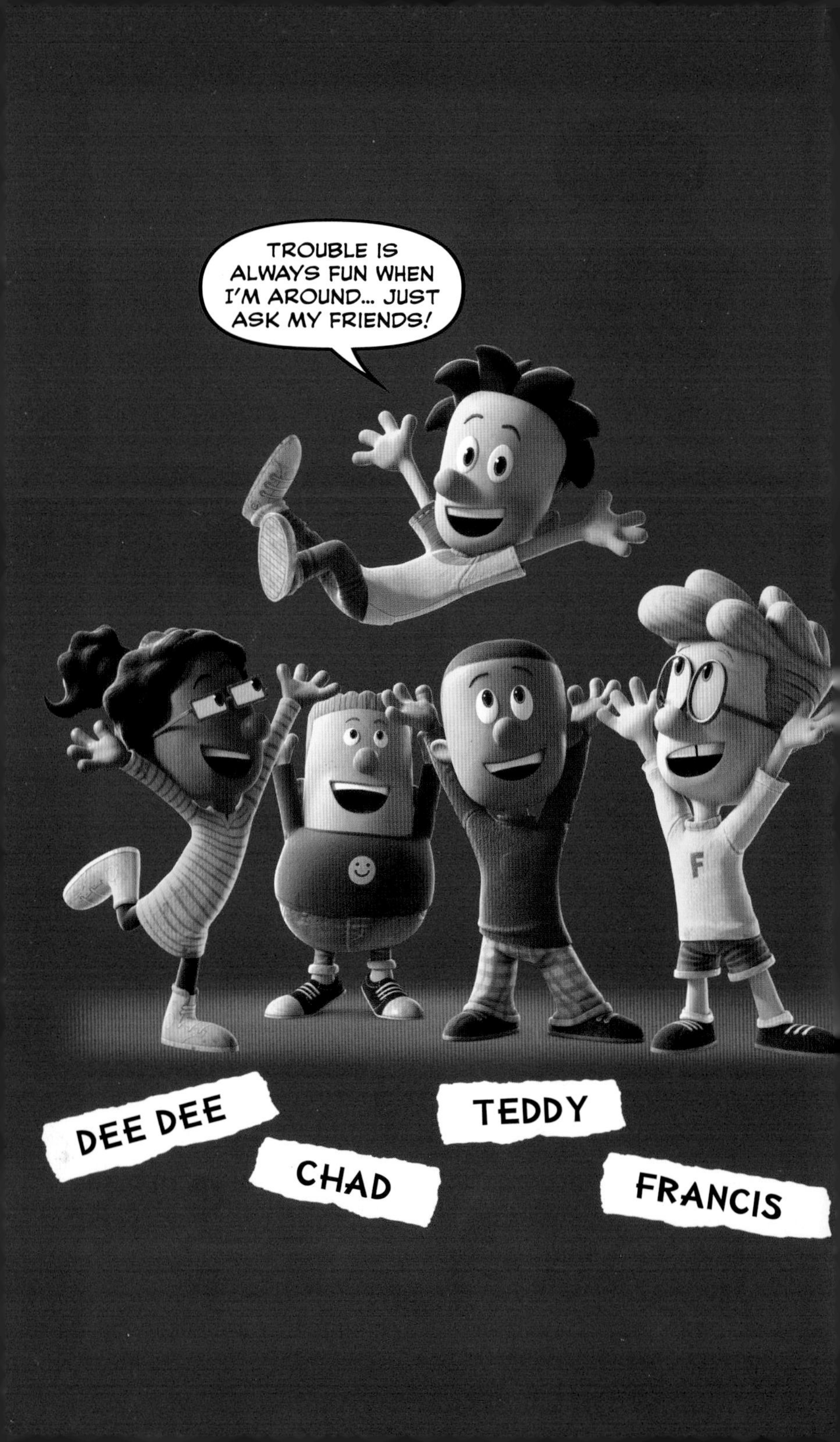
TROUBLE IS ALWAYS FUN WHEN I'M AROUND... JUST ASK MY FRIENDS!
DEE DEE
CHAD
TEDDY
FRANCIS

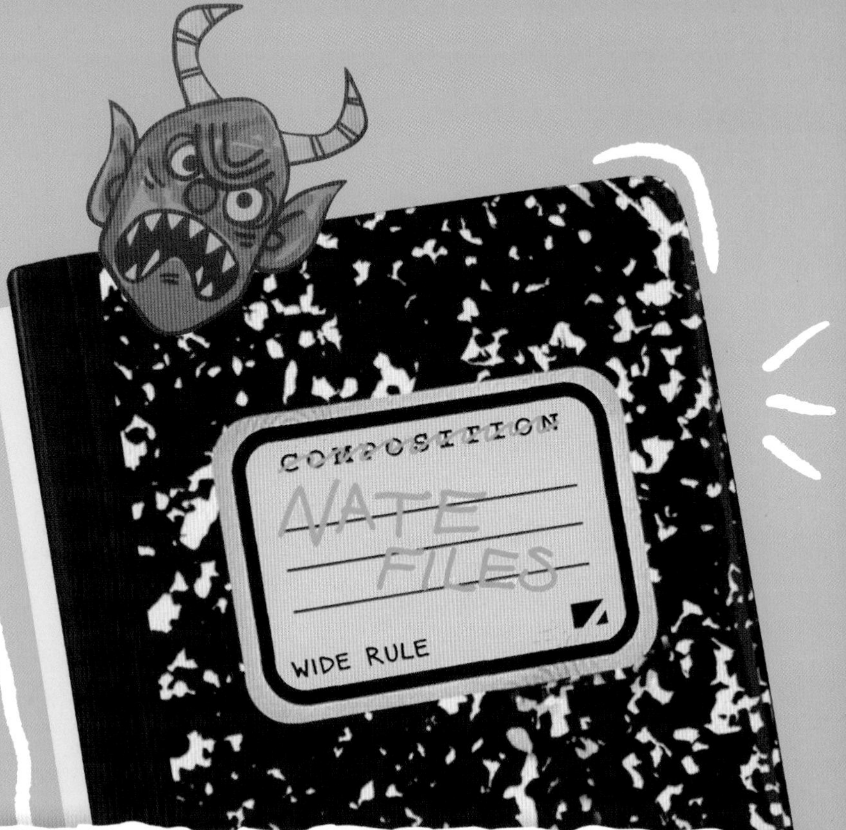
COMPOSITION
NATE FILES
WIDE RULE

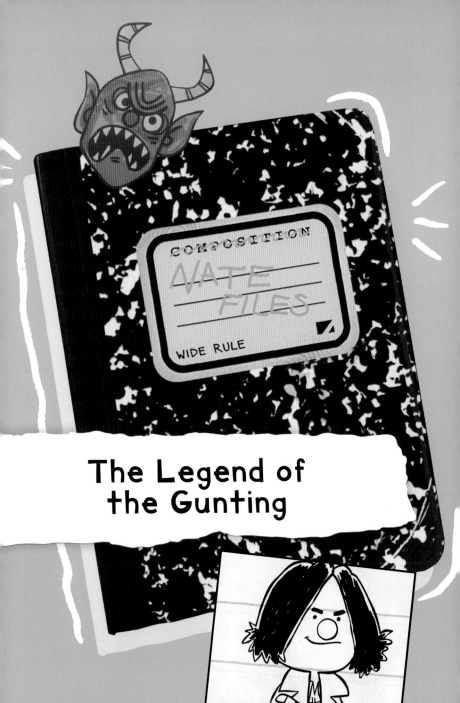

The Legend of the Gunting

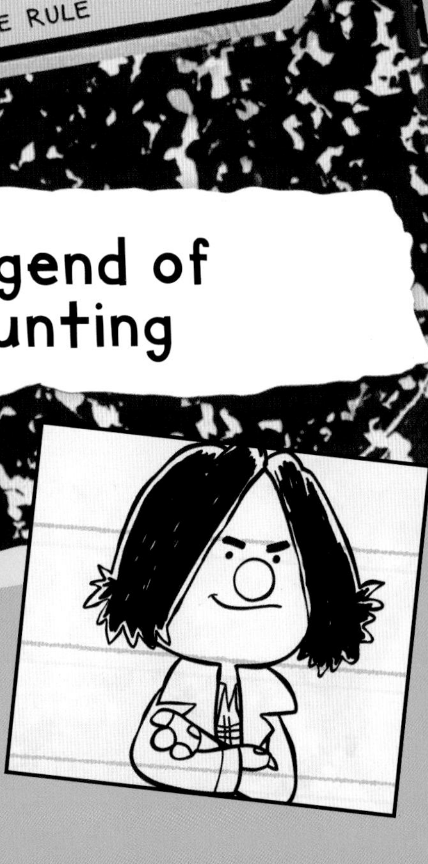

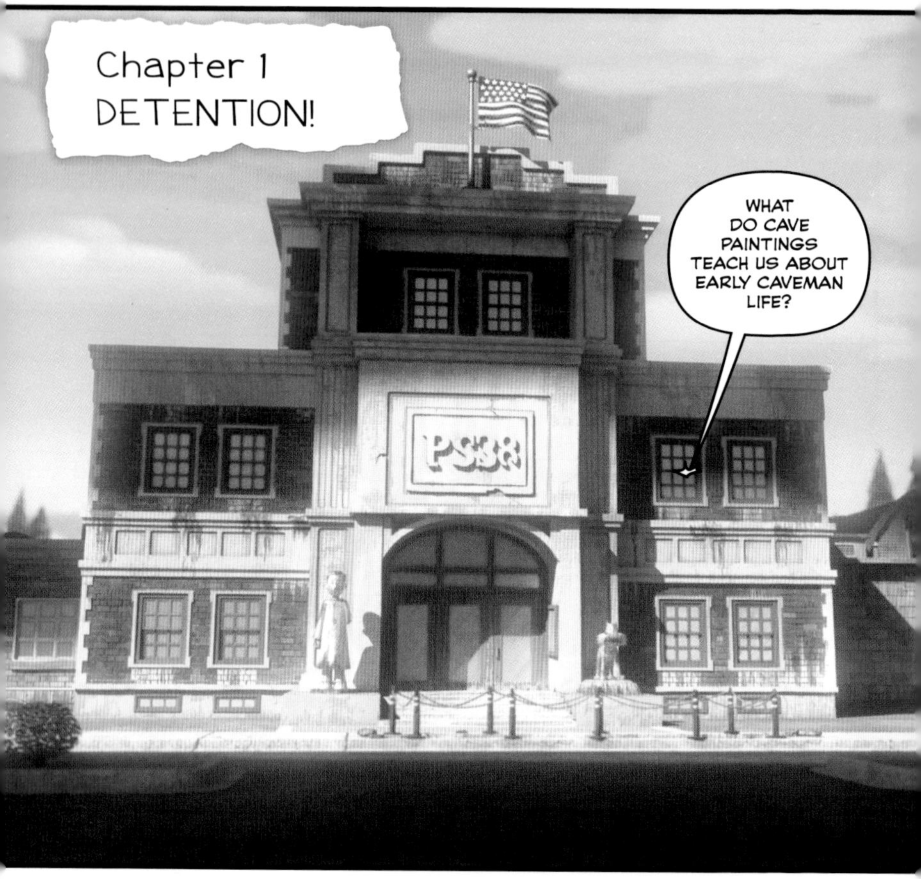
Chapter 1
DETENTION!
PS38
WHAT DO CAVE PAINTINGS TEACH US ABOUT EARLY CAVEMAN LIFE?

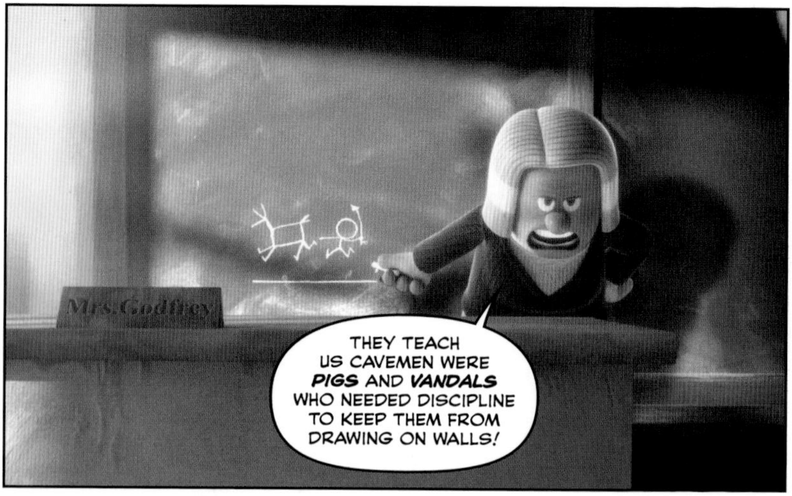
Mrs.Godfrey
THEY TEACH US CAVEMEN WERE *PIGS* AND *VANDALS* WHO NEEDED DISCIPLINE TO KEEP THEM FROM DRAWING ON WALLS!

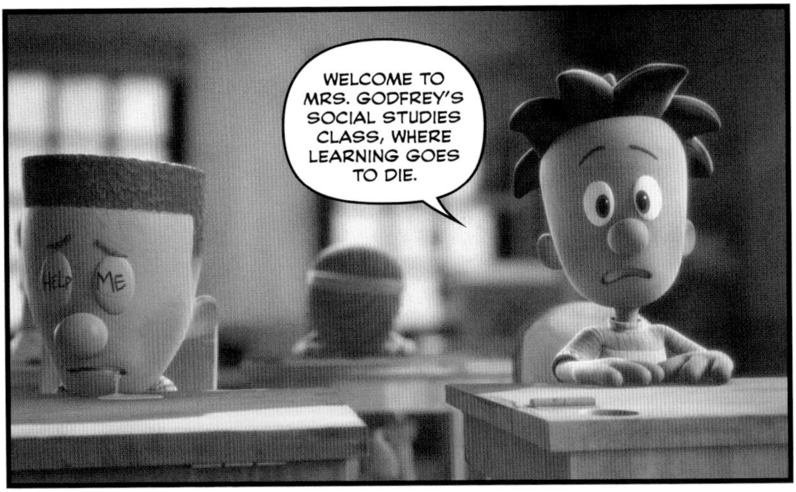
WELCOME TO MRS. GODFREY'S SOCIAL STUDIES CLASS, WHERE LEARNING GOES TO DIE.
HELP ME

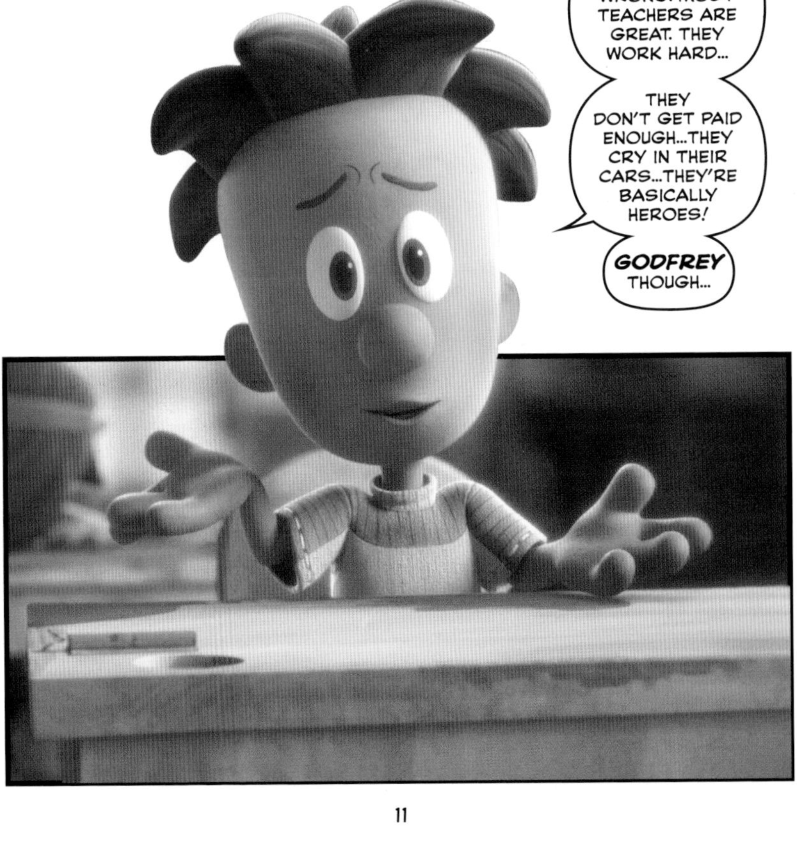
I MEAN, DON'T GET ME WRONG. MOST TEACHERS ARE GREAT. THEY WORK HARD...
THEY DON'T GET PAID ENOUGH...THEY CRY IN THEIR CARS...THEY'RE BASICALLY HEROES!
GODFREY THOUGH...

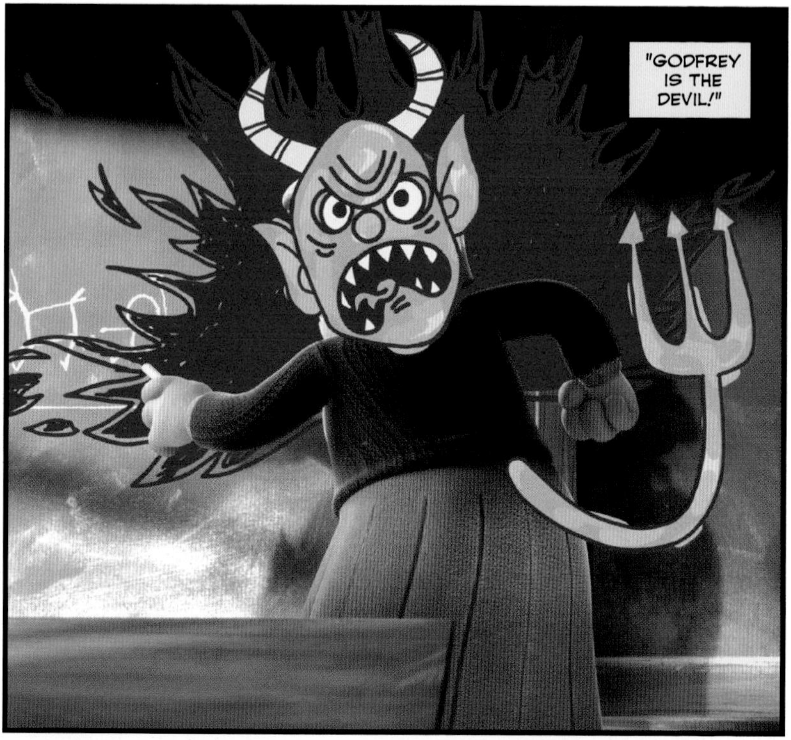
"GODFREY IS THE DEVIL!"

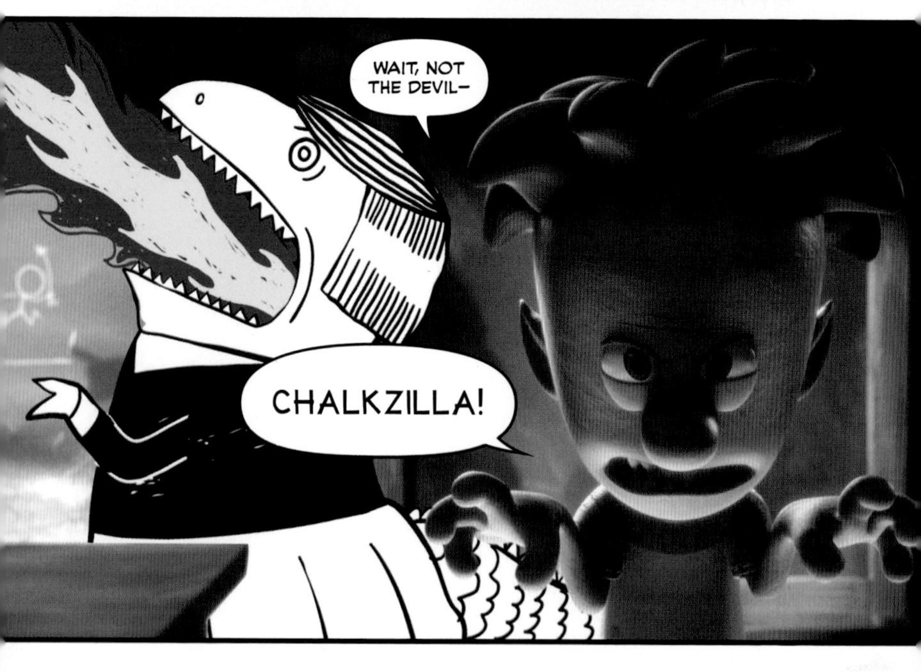
WAIT, NOT THE DEVIL–
CHALKZILLA!

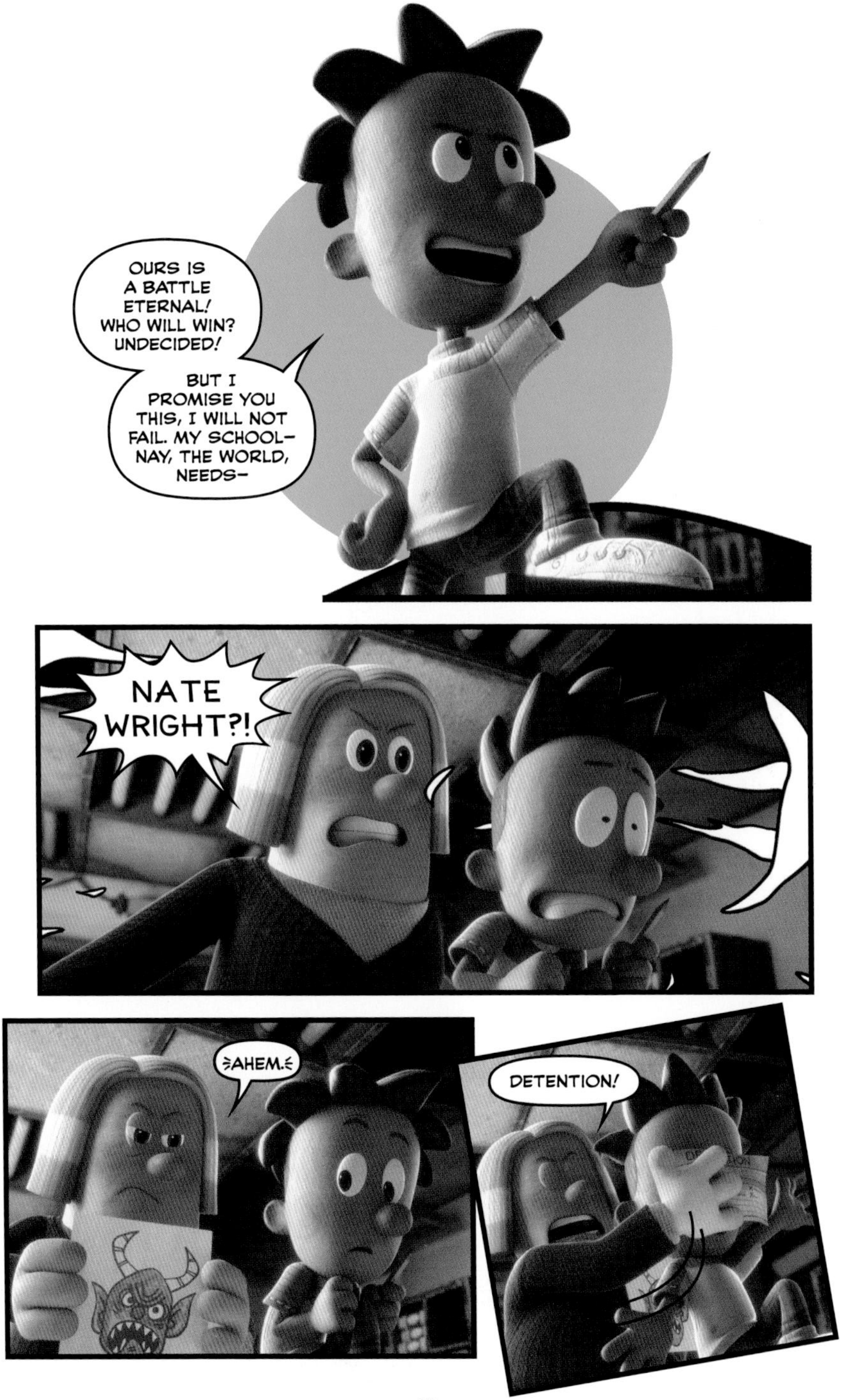
OURS IS A BATTLE ETERNAL! WHO WILL WIN? UNDECIDED!
BUT I PROMISE YOU THIS, I WILL NOT FAIL. MY SCHOOL– NAY, THE WORLD, NEEDS–
NATE WRIGHT?!
AHEM.
DETENTION!

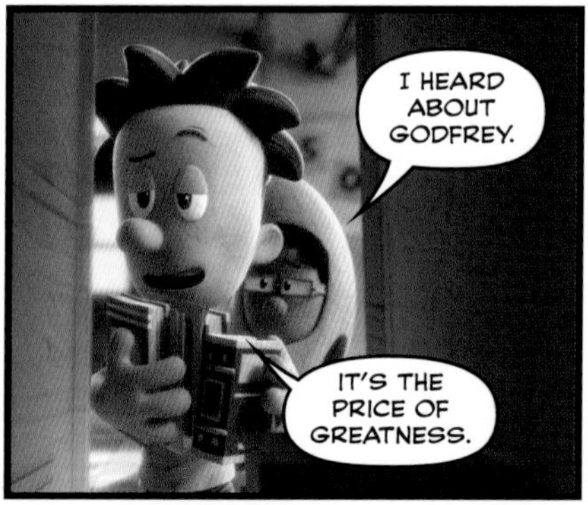
I HEARD ABOUT GODFREY.
IT'S THE PRICE OF GREATNESS.
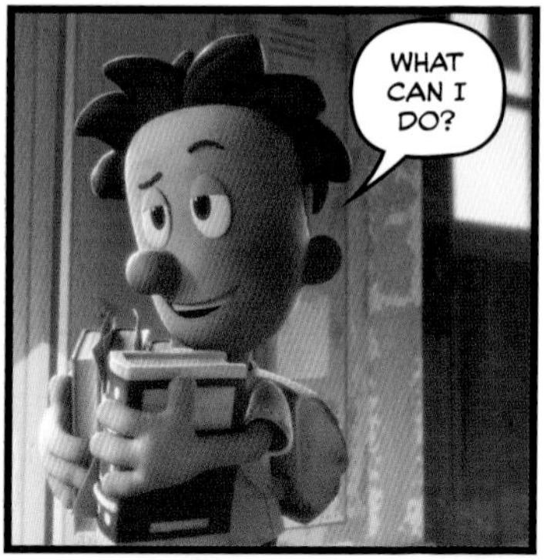
WHAT CAN I DO?
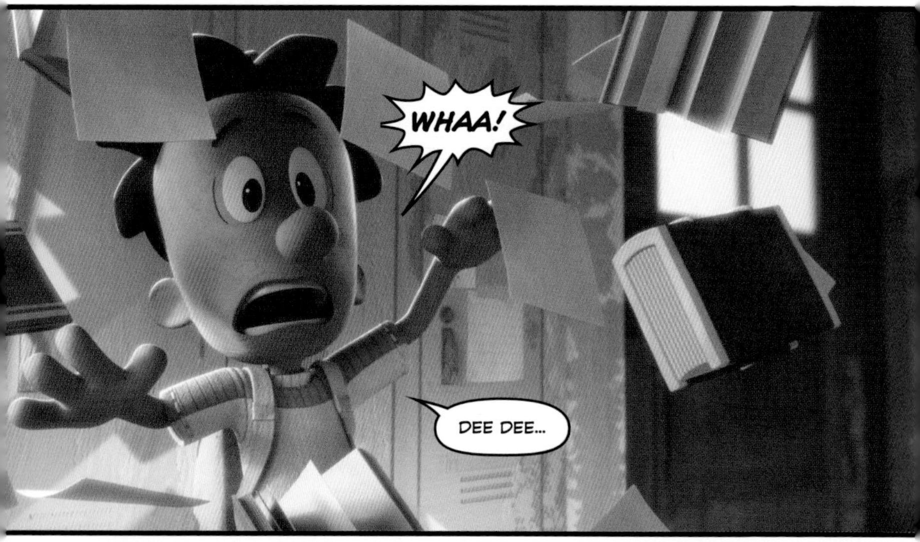
WHAA!
DEE DEE...
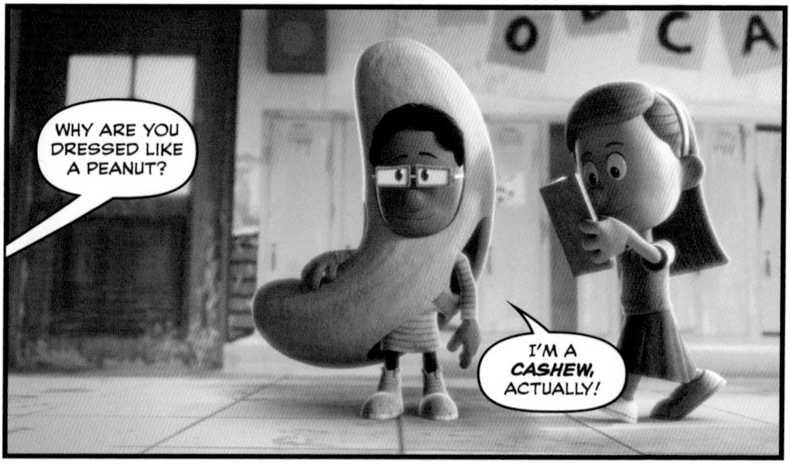
WHY ARE YOU DRESSED LIKE A PEANUT?
I'M A CASHEW, ACTUALLY!

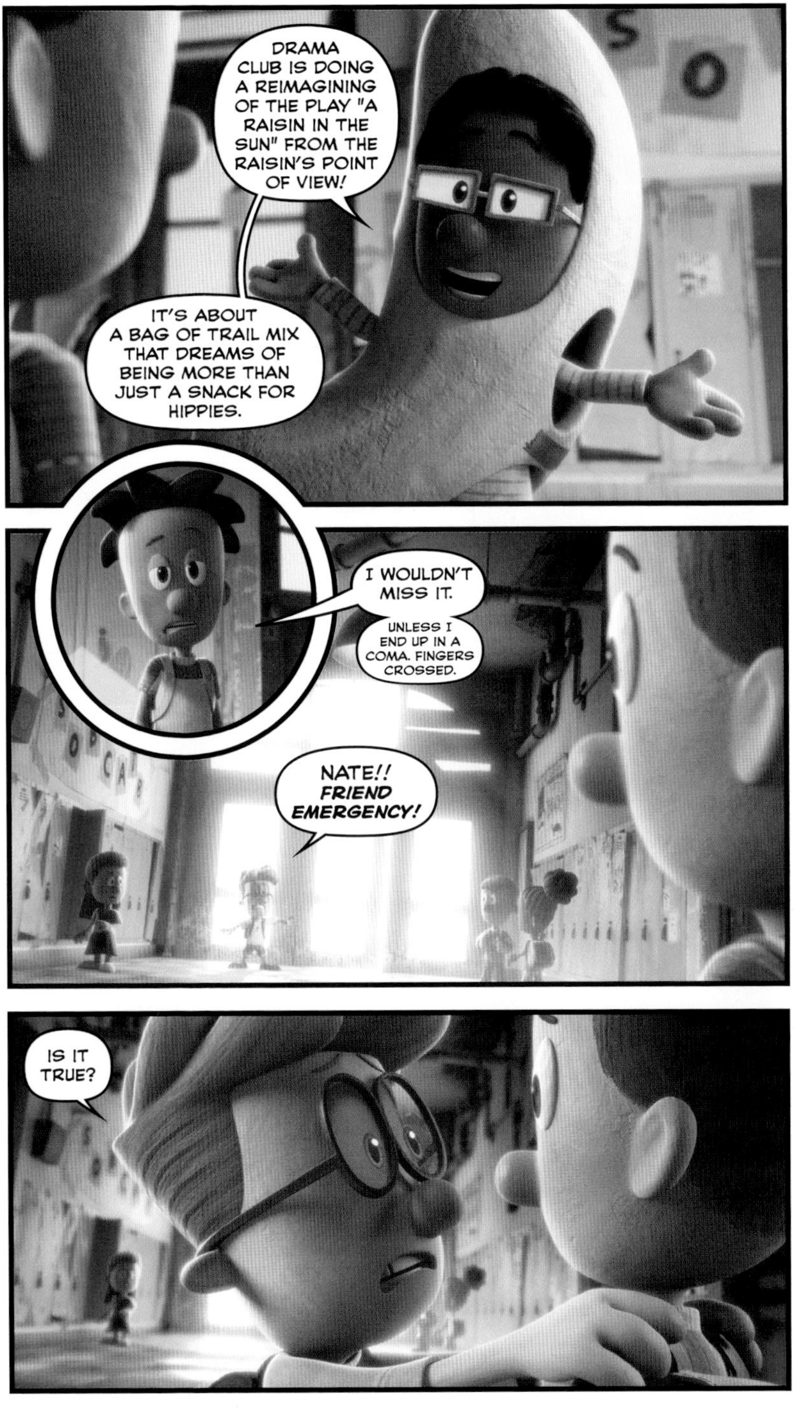
DRAMA CLUB IS DOING A REIMAGINING OF THE PLAY "A RAISIN IN THE SUN" FROM THE RAISIN'S POINT OF VIEW!
IT'S ABOUT A BAG OF TRAIL MIX THAT DREAMS OF BEING MORE THAN JUST A SNACK FOR HIPPIES.
I WOULDN'T MISS IT.
UNLESS I END UP IN A COMA. FINGERS CROSSED.
NATE!! *FRIEND EMERGENCY!*
IS IT TRUE?

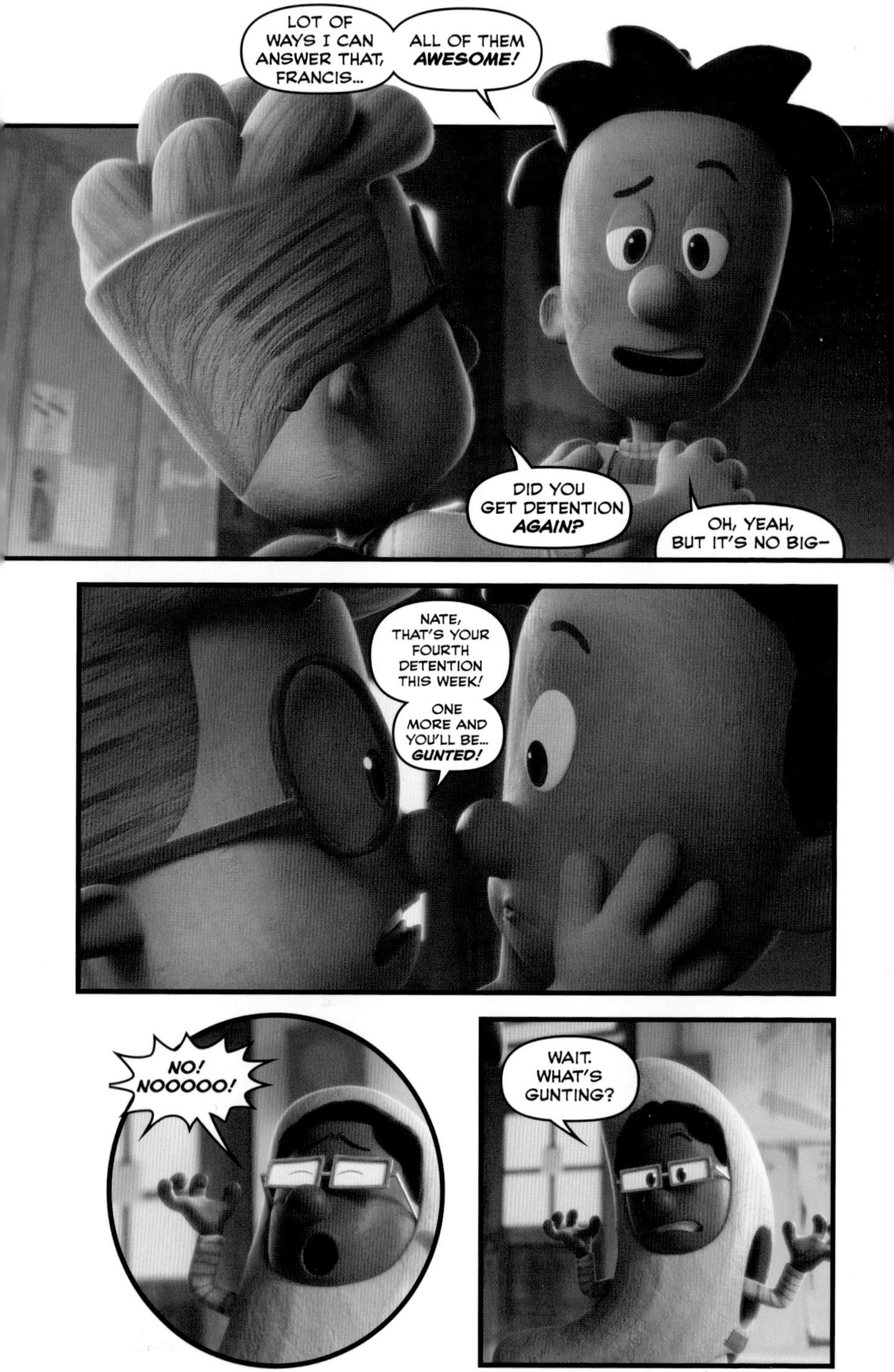
LOT OF WAYS I CAN ANSWER THAT, FRANCIS...
ALL OF THEM AWESOME!
DID YOU GET DETENTION AGAIN?
OH, YEAH, BUT IT'S NO BIG–
NATE, THAT'S YOUR FOURTH DETENTION THIS WEEK!
ONE MORE AND YOU'LL BE... GUNTED!
NO! NOOOOO!
WAIT. WHAT'S GUNTING?

 "LET ME TELL YOU ABOUT...

THE ➡ LEGEND OF THE GUNTING!

"BRAD GUNTER WAS THE MOST NOTORIOUS KID AT P.S. 38. A *LEGENDARY PRANKSTER* AND MY PERSONAL HERO.

"HE REPLACED EVERY FRISBEE IN SCHOOL WITH HUNKS OF BALONEY...

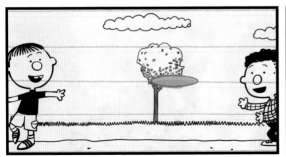

17

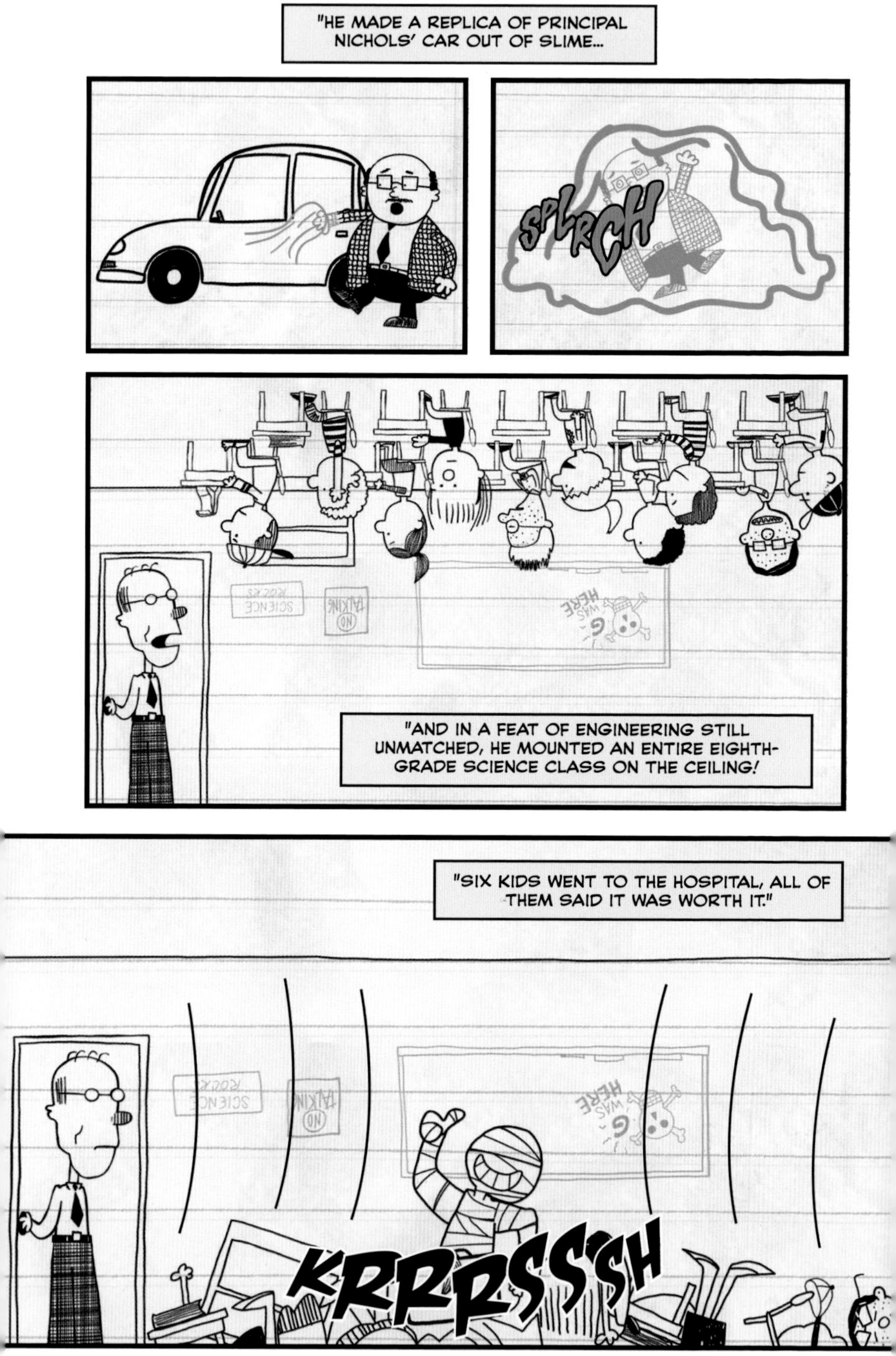
"HE MADE A REPLICA OF PRINCIPAL NICHOLS' CAR OUT OF SLIME...
SPLRCH
"AND IN A FEAT OF ENGINEERING STILL UNMATCHED, HE MOUNTED AN ENTIRE EIGHTH-GRADE SCIENCE CLASS ON THE CEILING!
"SIX KIDS WENT TO THE HOSPITAL, ALL OF THEM SAID IT WAS WORTH IT."
KRRRSS'SH

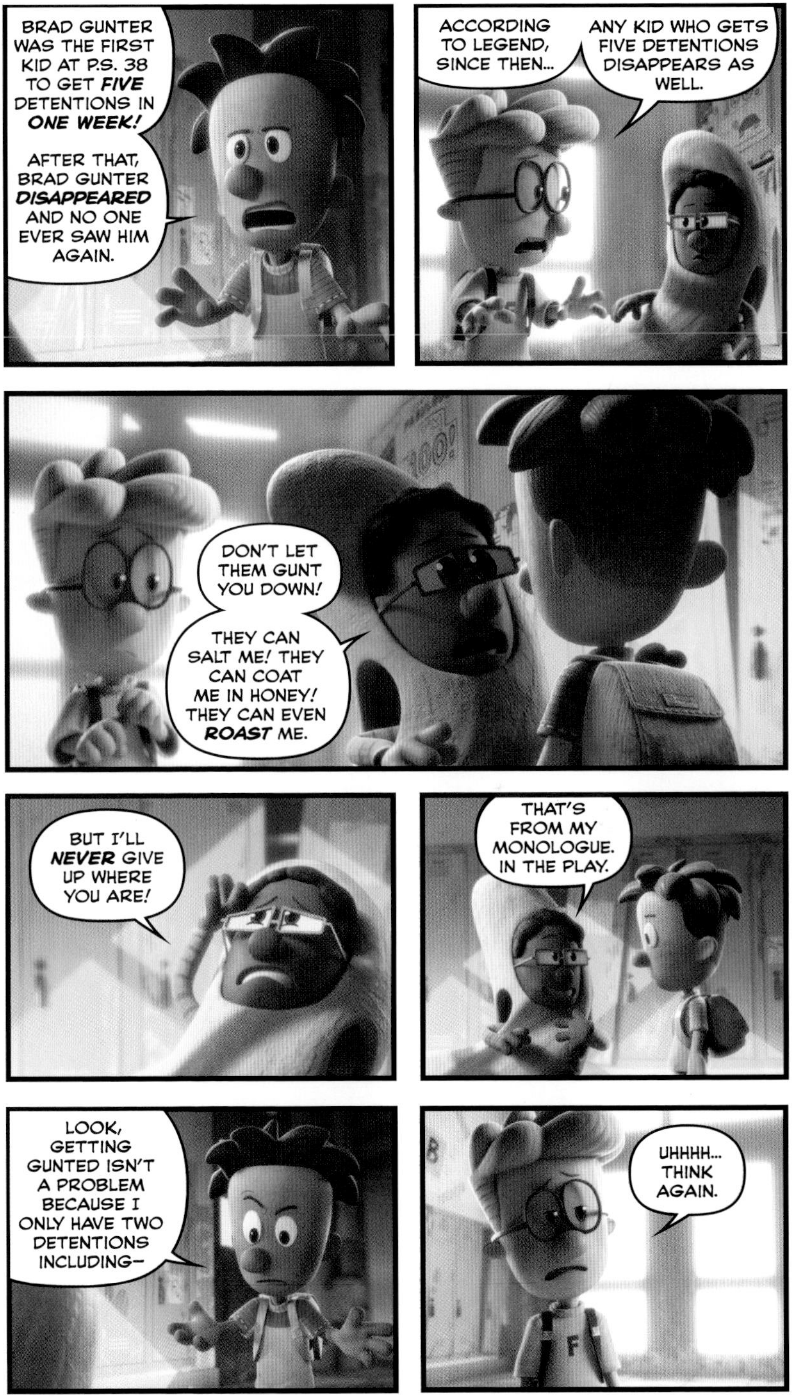
BRAD GUNTER WAS THE FIRST KID AT P.S. 38 TO GET ***FIVE*** DETENTIONS IN ***ONE WEEK!***
AFTER THAT, BRAD GUNTER ***DISAPPEARED*** AND NO ONE EVER SAW HIM AGAIN.
ACCORDING TO LEGEND, SINCE THEN...
ANY KID WHO GETS FIVE DETENTIONS DISAPPEARS AS WELL.
DON'T LET THEM GUNT YOU DOWN!
THEY CAN SALT ME! THEY CAN COAT ME IN HONEY! THEY CAN EVEN ***ROAST*** ME.
BUT I'LL ***NEVER*** GIVE UP WHERE YOU ARE!
THAT'S FROM MY MONOLOGUE. IN THE PLAY.
LOOK, GETTING GUNTED ISN'T A PROBLEM BECAUSE I ONLY HAVE TWO DETENTIONS INCLUDING—
UHHHH... THINK AGAIN.

DETENTION 1

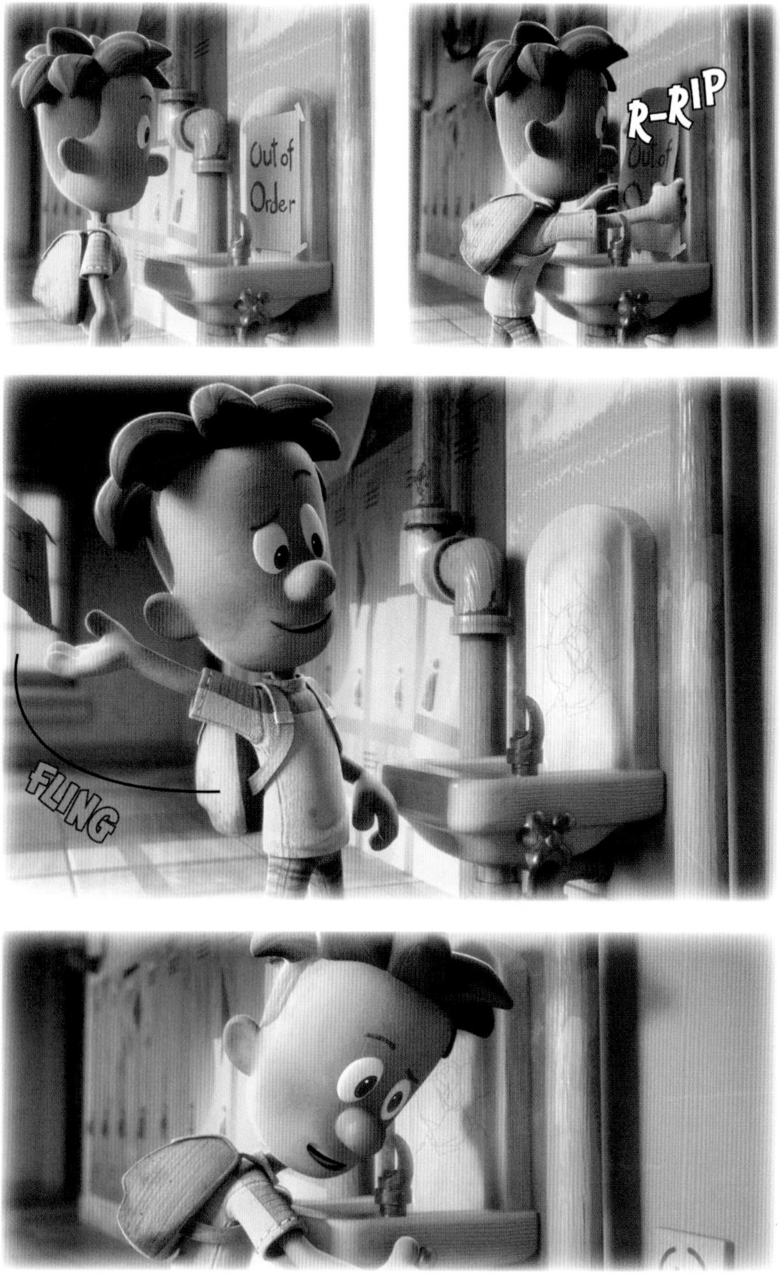

Out of Order
R-RIP
Out of
FLING

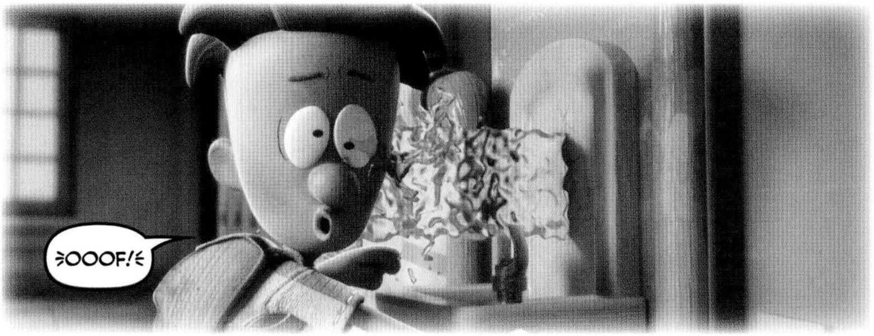
OOOF!

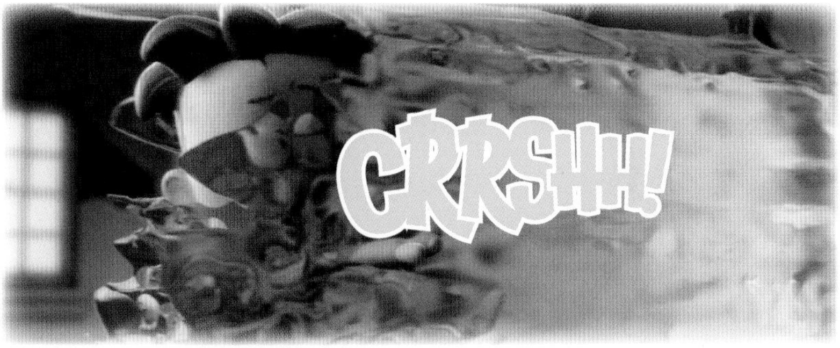
CRRSHHH!

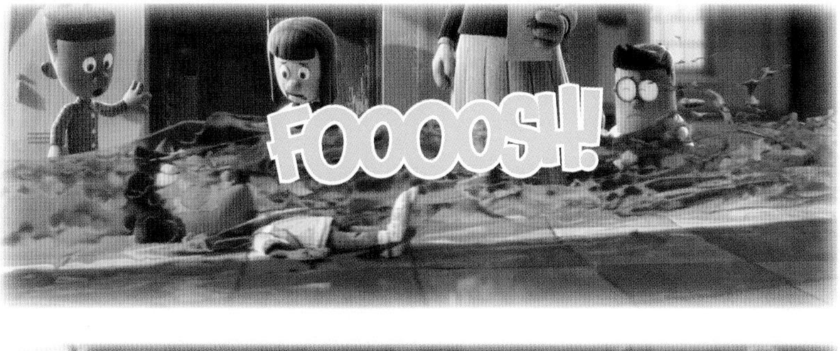
FOOOOSH!

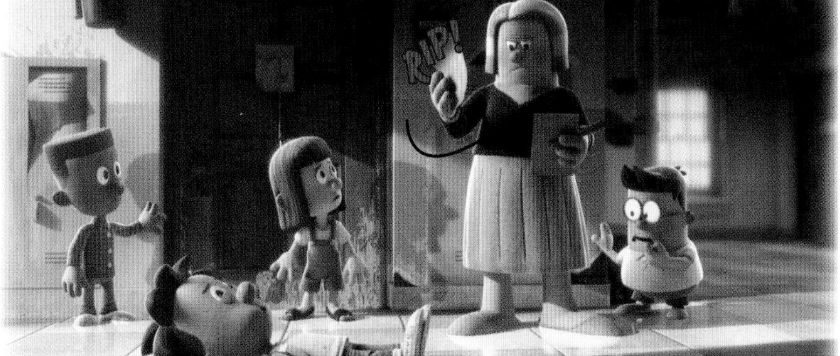
RIP!

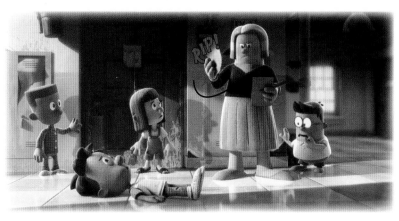

DETENTION 2

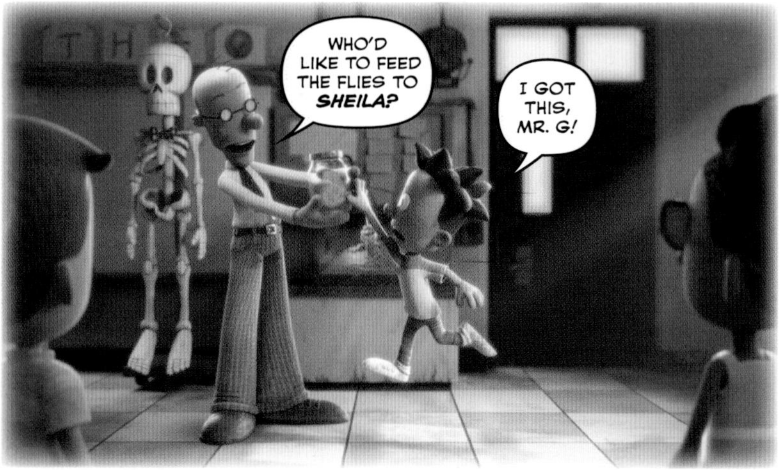
WHO'D LIKE TO FEED THE FLIES TO *SHEILA?*
I GOT THIS, MR. G!

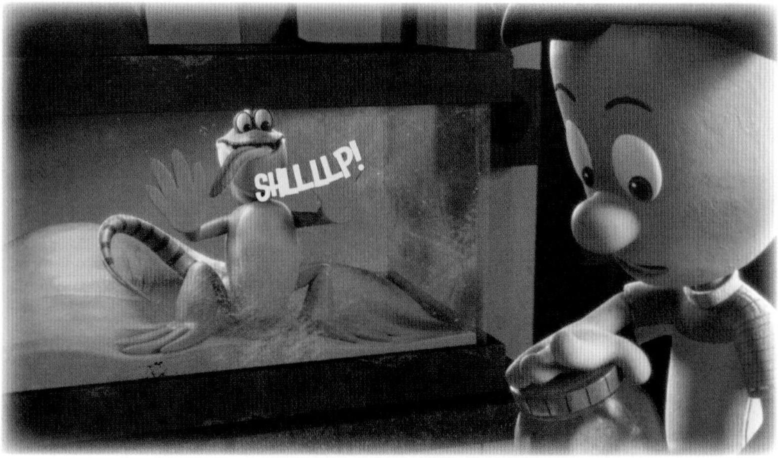
SHLLLLP!

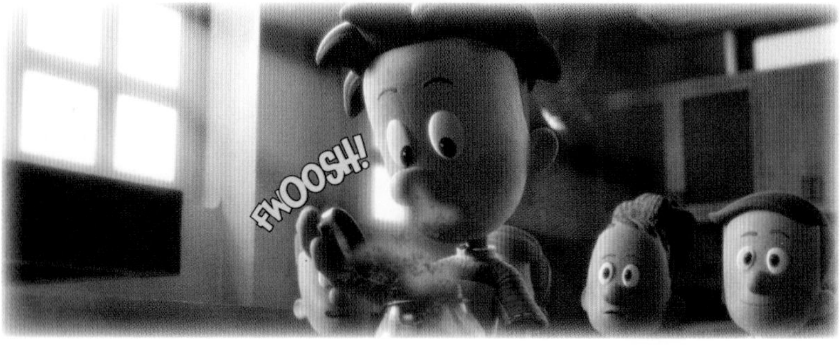
FWOOSH!

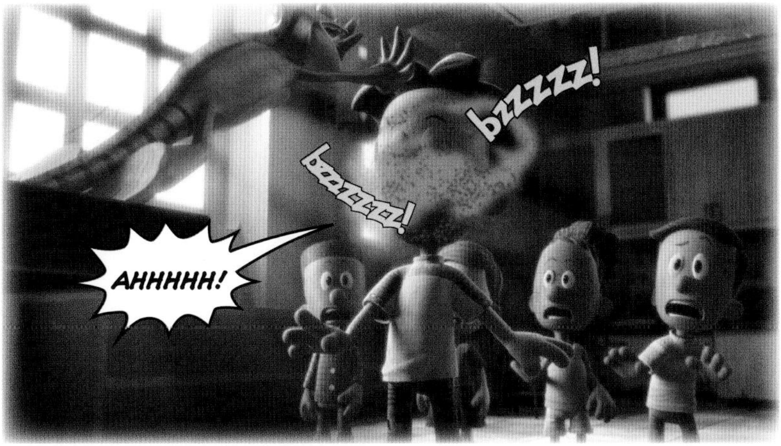
bzzzzz!
bzzzzzz!
AHHHHH!

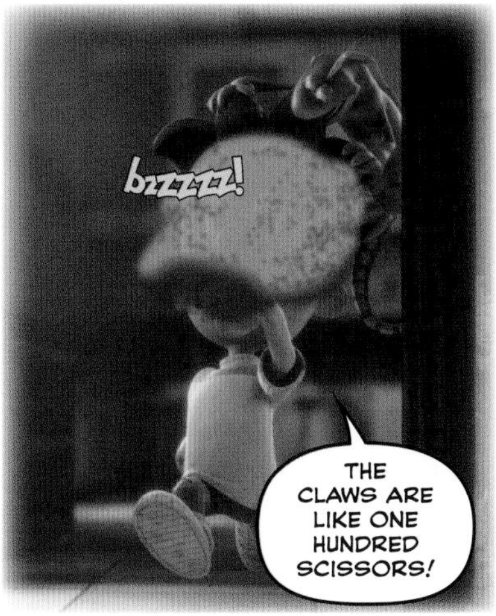
bzzzzz!
THE CLAWS ARE LIKE ONE HUNDRED SCISSORS!

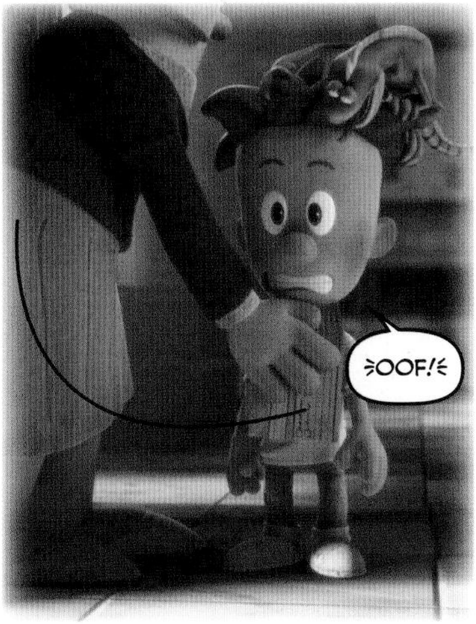
OOF!

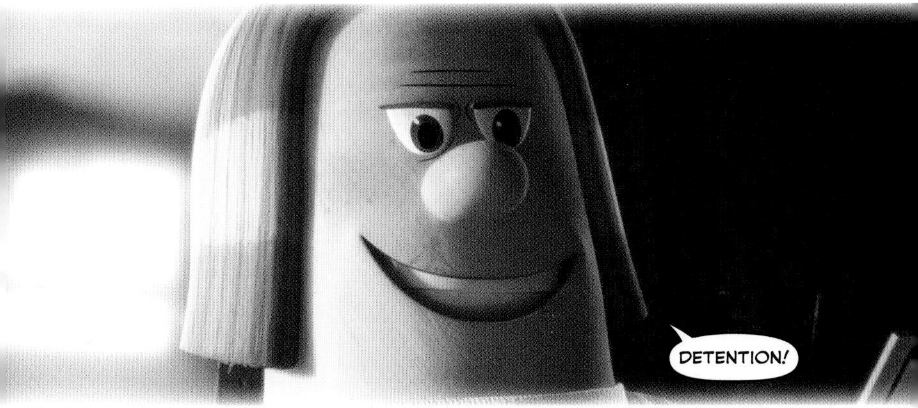
DETENTION!

DETENTION 3

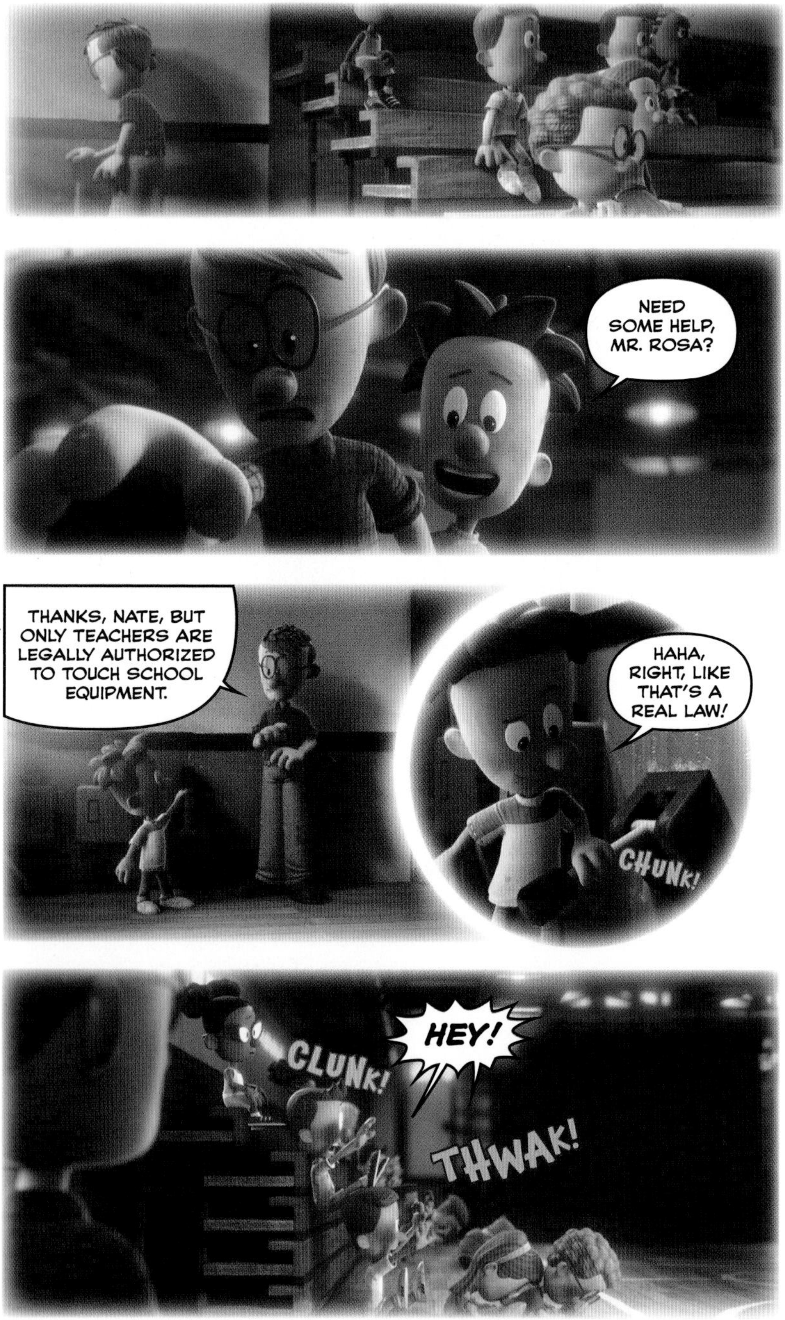
NEED SOME HELP, MR. ROSA?
THANKS, NATE, BUT ONLY TEACHERS ARE LEGALLY AUTHORIZED TO TOUCH SCHOOL EQUIPMENT.
HAHA, RIGHT, LIKE THAT'S A REAL LAW!
CHUNK!
HEY!
CLUNK!
THWAK!

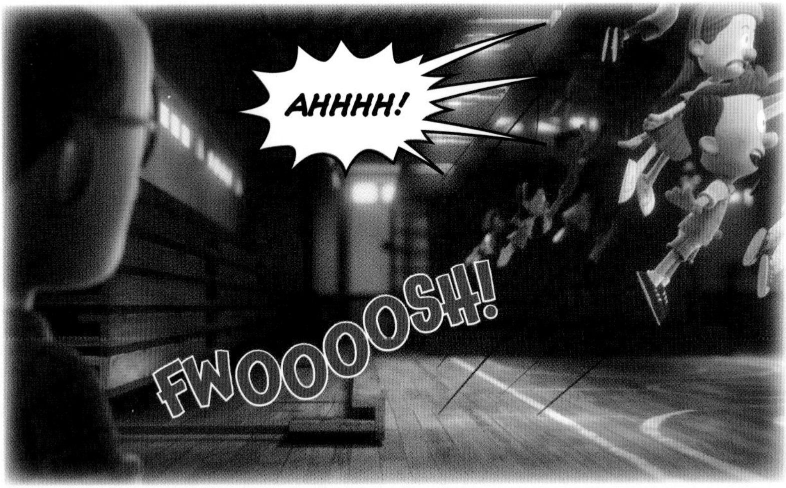
AHHHH!
FWOOOOSH!

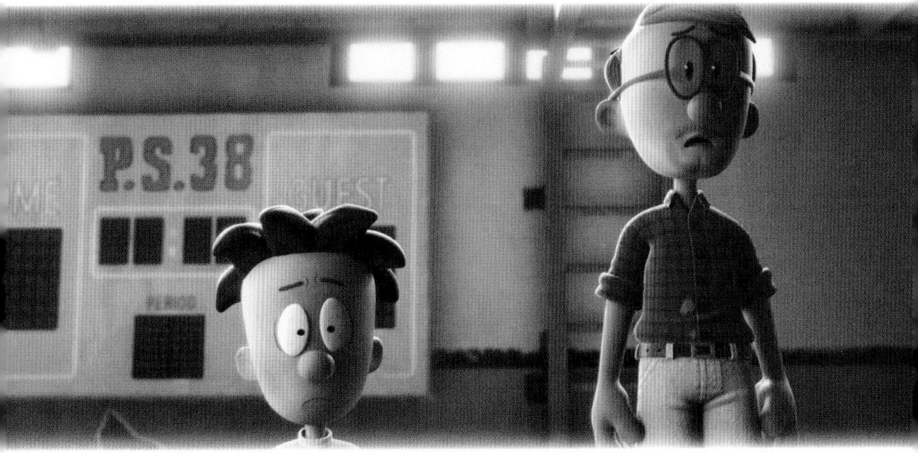
P.S.38

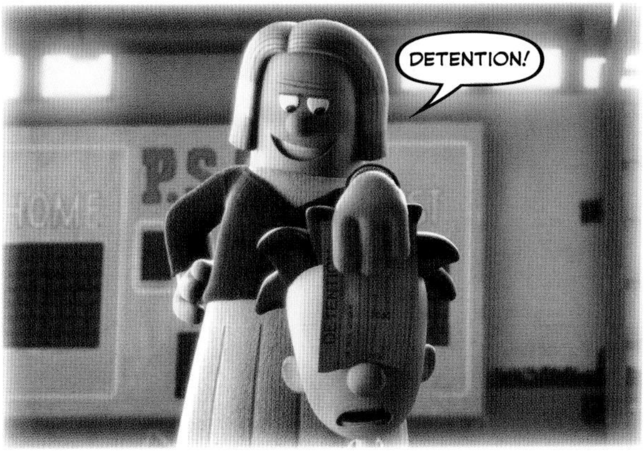
DETENTION!

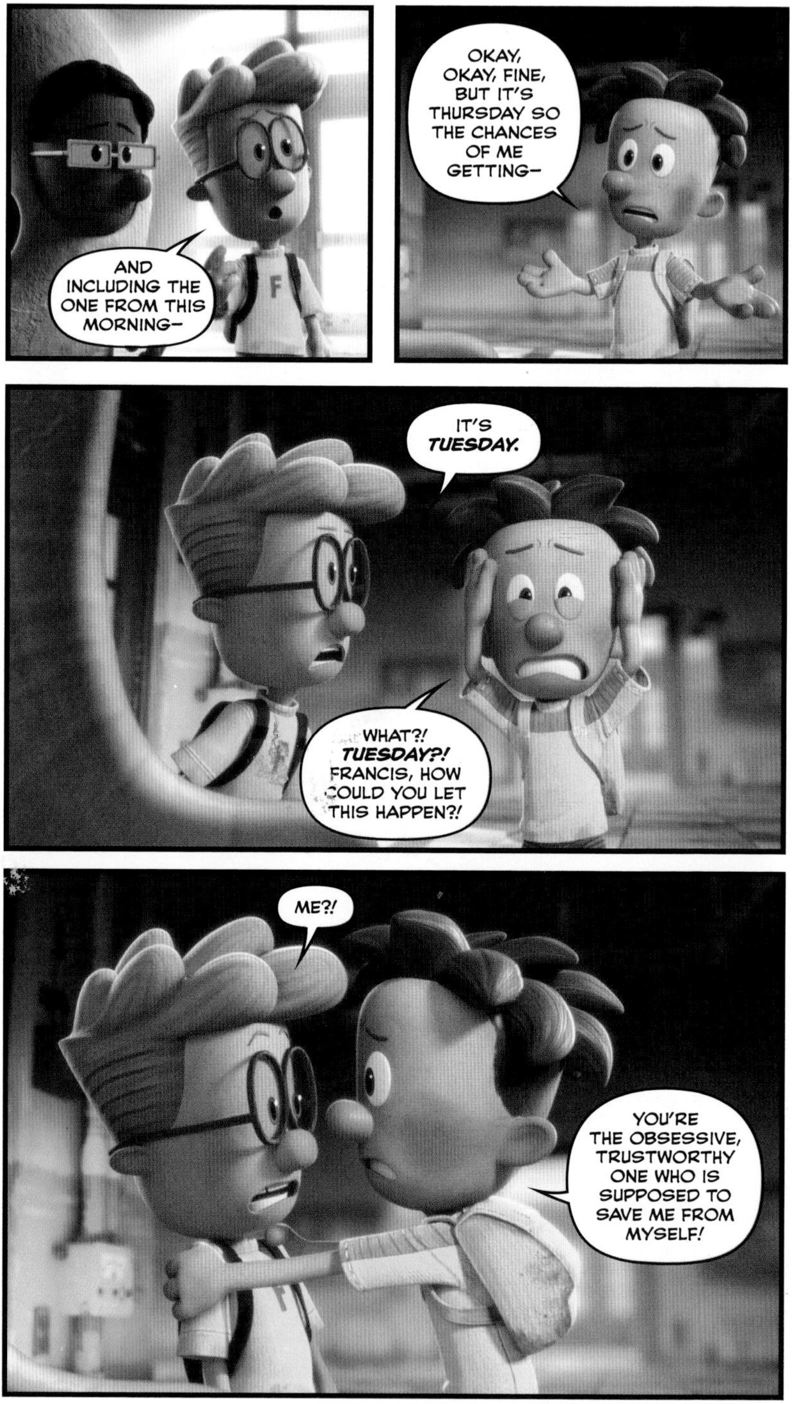
AND INCLUDING THE ONE FROM THIS MORNING—
OKAY, OKAY, FINE, BUT IT'S THURSDAY SO THE CHANCES OF ME GETTING—
IT'S *TUESDAY.*
WHAT?! *TUESDAY?!* FRANCIS, HOW COULD YOU LET THIS HAPPEN?!
ME?!
YOU'RE THE OBSESSIVE, TRUSTWORTHY ONE WHO IS SUPPOSED TO SAVE ME FROM MYSELF!

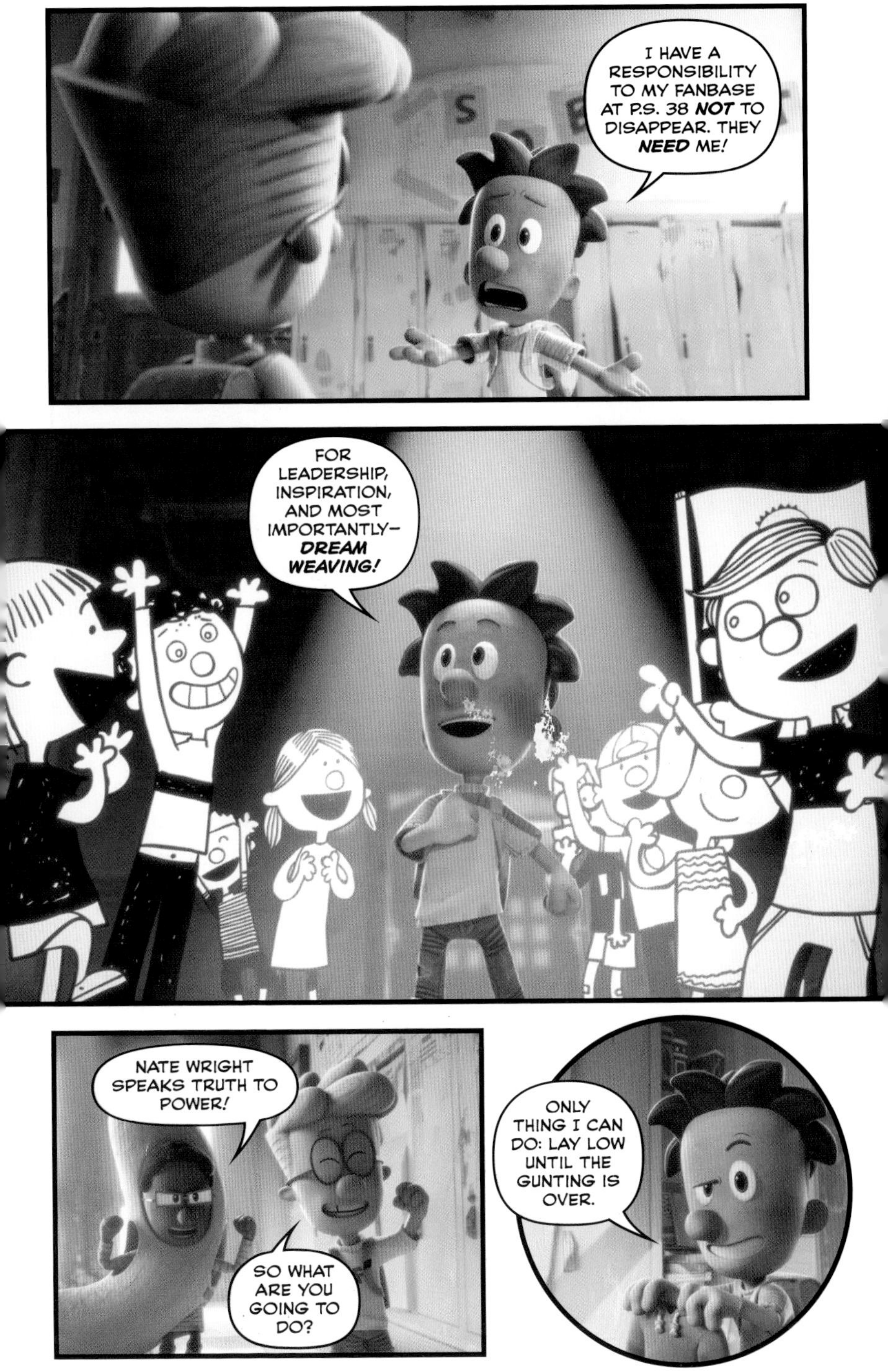

I HAVE A RESPONSIBILITY TO MY FANBASE AT P.S. 38 **NOT** TO DISAPPEAR. THEY **NEED** ME!
FOR LEADERSHIP, INSPIRATION, AND MOST IMPORTANTLY— ***DREAM WEAVING!***
NATE WRIGHT SPEAKS TRUTH TO POWER!
SO WHAT ARE YOU GOING TO DO?
ONLY THING I CAN DO: LAY LOW UNTIL THE GUNTING IS OVER.

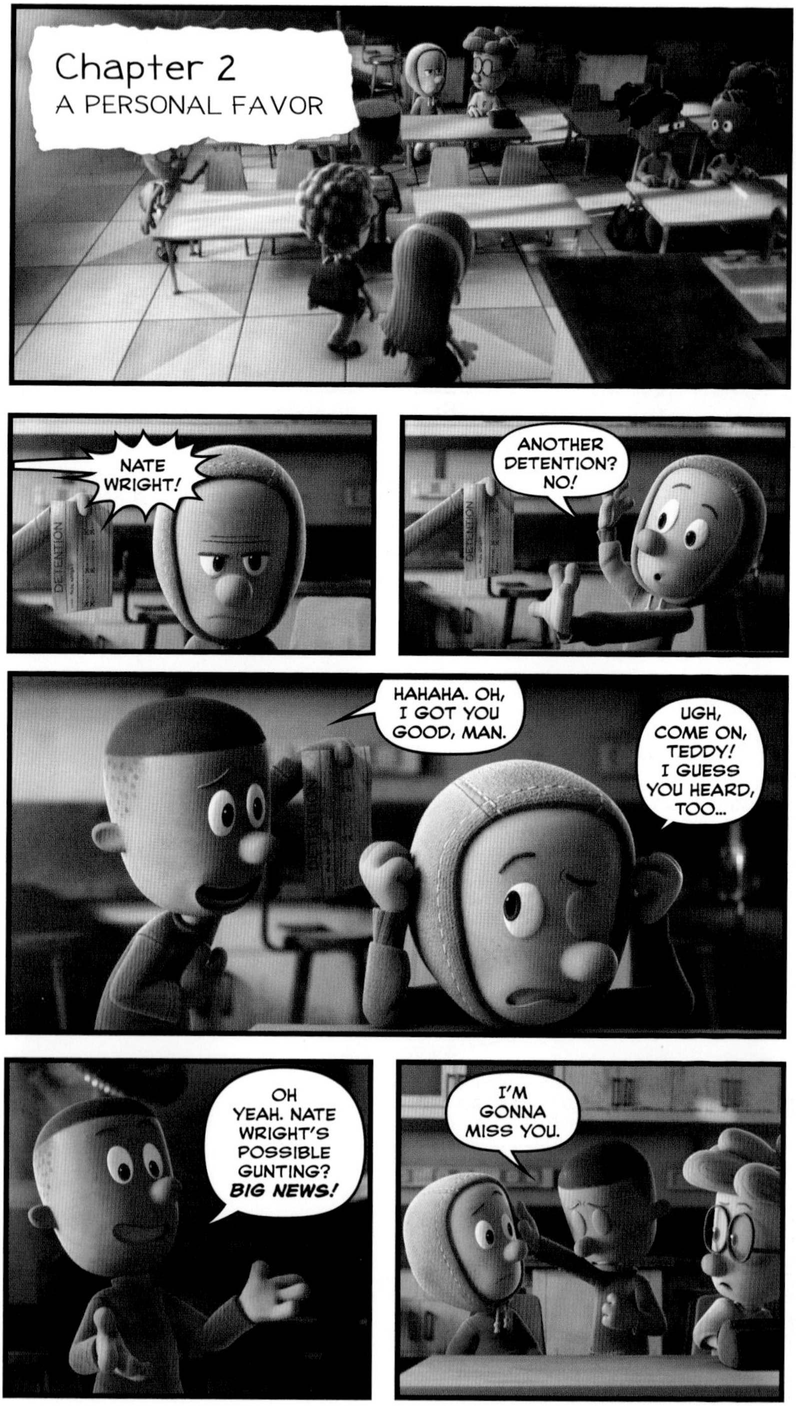
Chapter 2
A PERSONAL FAVOR
NATE WRIGHT!
ANOTHER DETENTION? NO!
HAHAHA. OH, I GOT YOU GOOD, MAN.
UGH, COME ON, TEDDY! I GUESS YOU HEARD, TOO...
OH YEAH. NATE WRIGHT'S POSSIBLE GUNTING? BIG NEWS!
I'M GONNA MISS YOU.

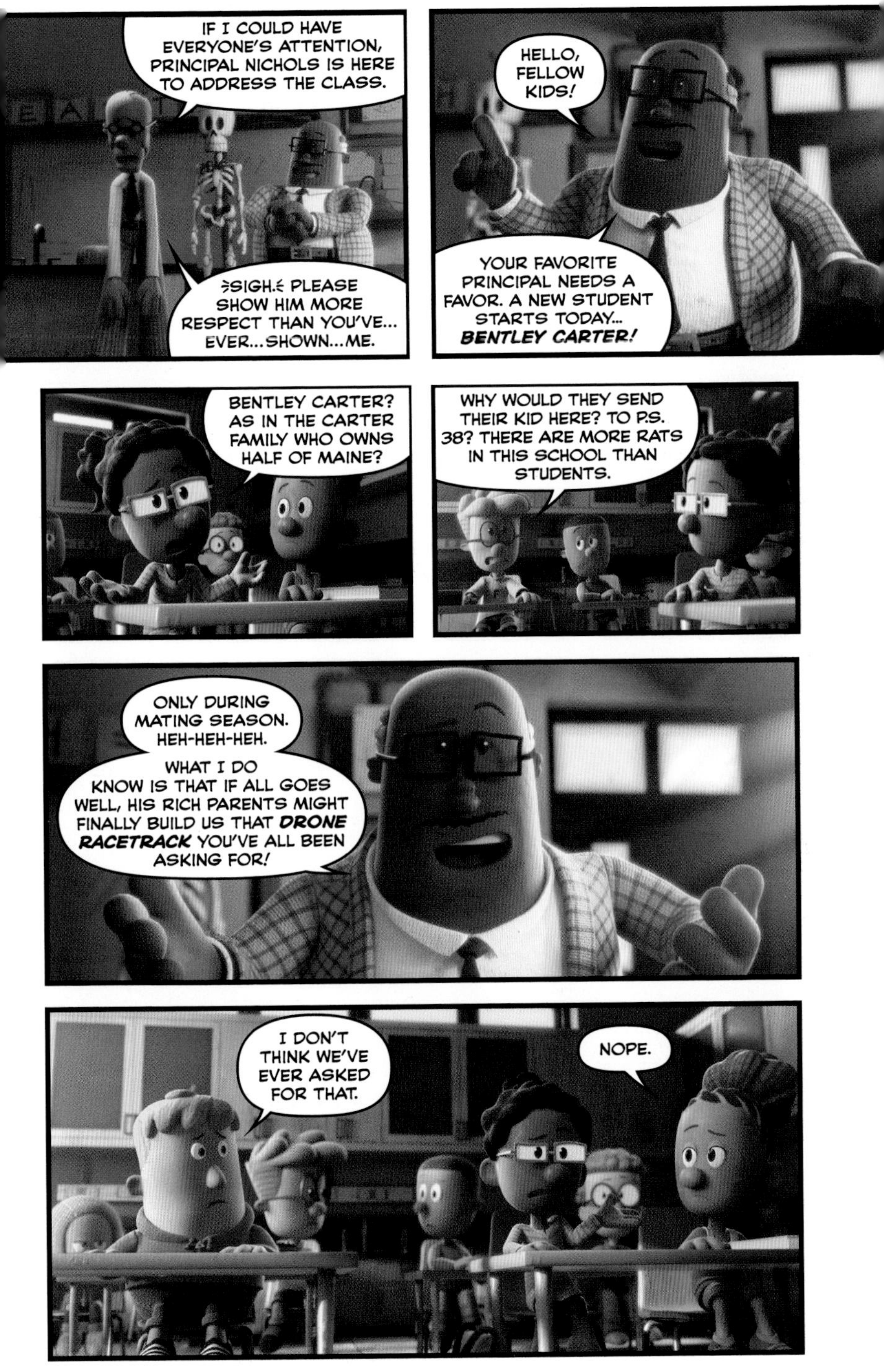
IF I COULD HAVE EVERYONE'S ATTENTION, PRINCIPAL NICHOLS IS HERE TO ADDRESS THE CLASS.
≥SIGH.≤ PLEASE SHOW HIM MORE RESPECT THAN YOU'VE... EVER...SHOWN...ME.
HELLO, FELLOW KIDS!
YOUR FAVORITE PRINCIPAL NEEDS A FAVOR. A NEW STUDENT STARTS TODAY... ***BENTLEY CARTER!***
BENTLEY CARTER? AS IN THE CARTER FAMILY WHO OWNS HALF OF MAINE?
WHY WOULD THEY SEND THEIR KID HERE? TO P.S. 38? THERE ARE MORE RATS IN THIS SCHOOL THAN STUDENTS.
ONLY DURING MATING SEASON. HEH-HEH-HEH.
WHAT I DO KNOW IS THAT IF ALL GOES WELL, HIS RICH PARENTS MIGHT FINALLY BUILD US THAT ***DRONE RACETRACK*** YOU'VE ALL BEEN ASKING FOR!
I DON'T THINK WE'VE EVER ASKED FOR THAT.
NOPE.

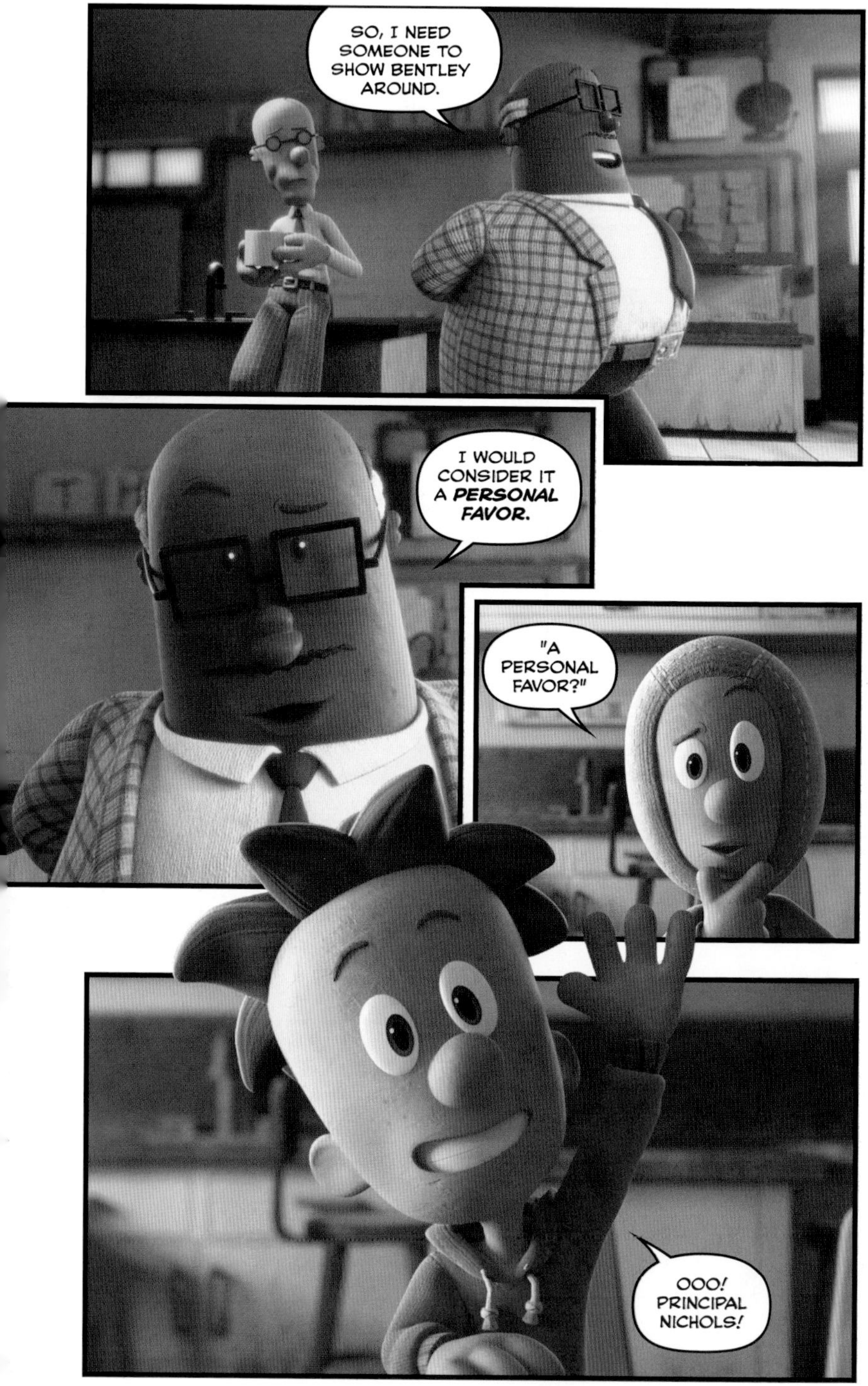
SO, I NEED SOMEONE TO SHOW BENTLEY AROUND.
I WOULD CONSIDER IT A **PERSONAL FAVOR.**
"A PERSONAL FAVOR?"
OOO! PRINCIPAL NICHOLS!

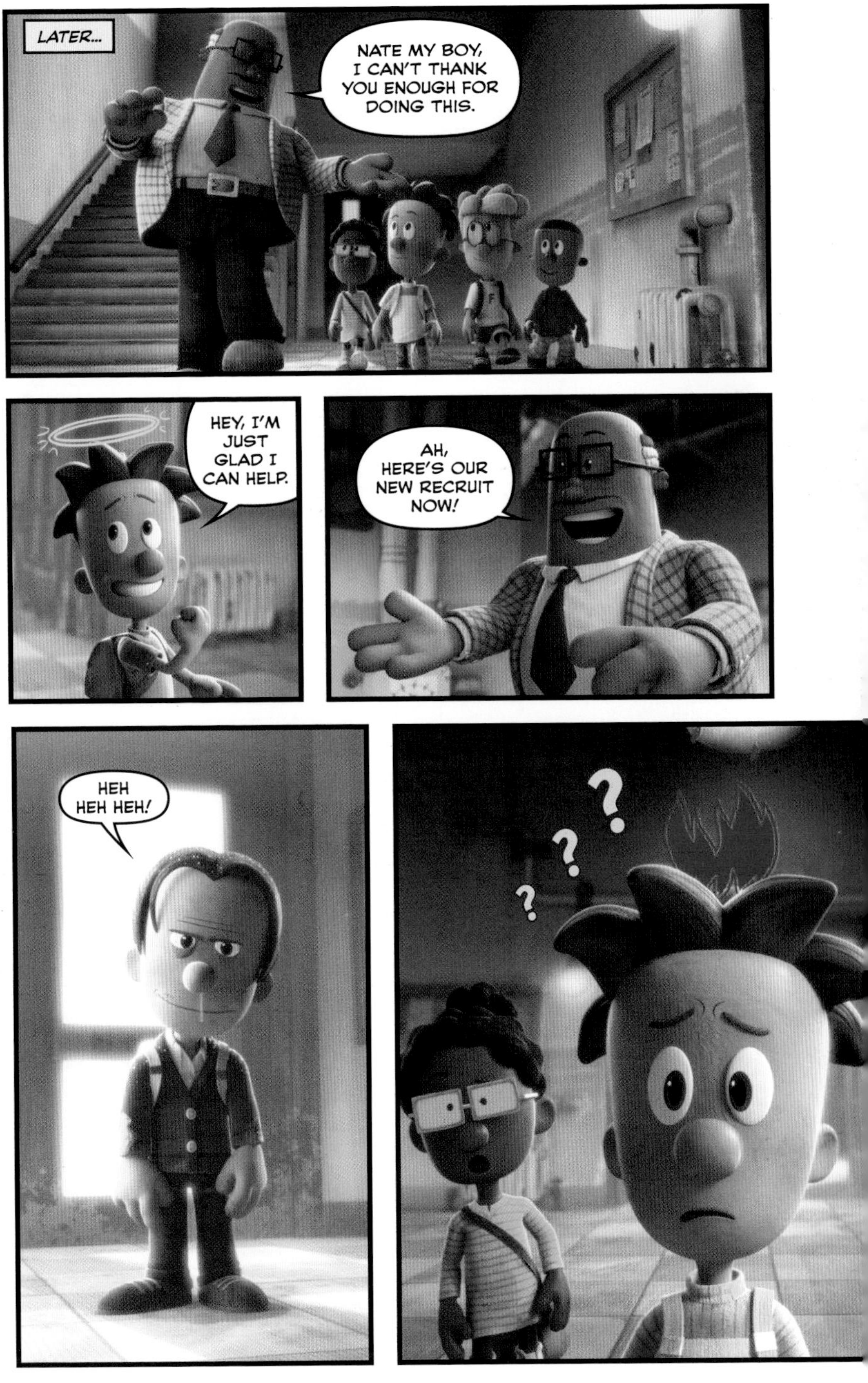
LATER...
NATE MY BOY, I CAN'T THANK YOU ENOUGH FOR DOING THIS.
HEY, I'M JUST GLAD I CAN HELP.
AH, HERE'S OUR NEW RECRUIT NOW!
HEH HEH HEH!
?
?
?

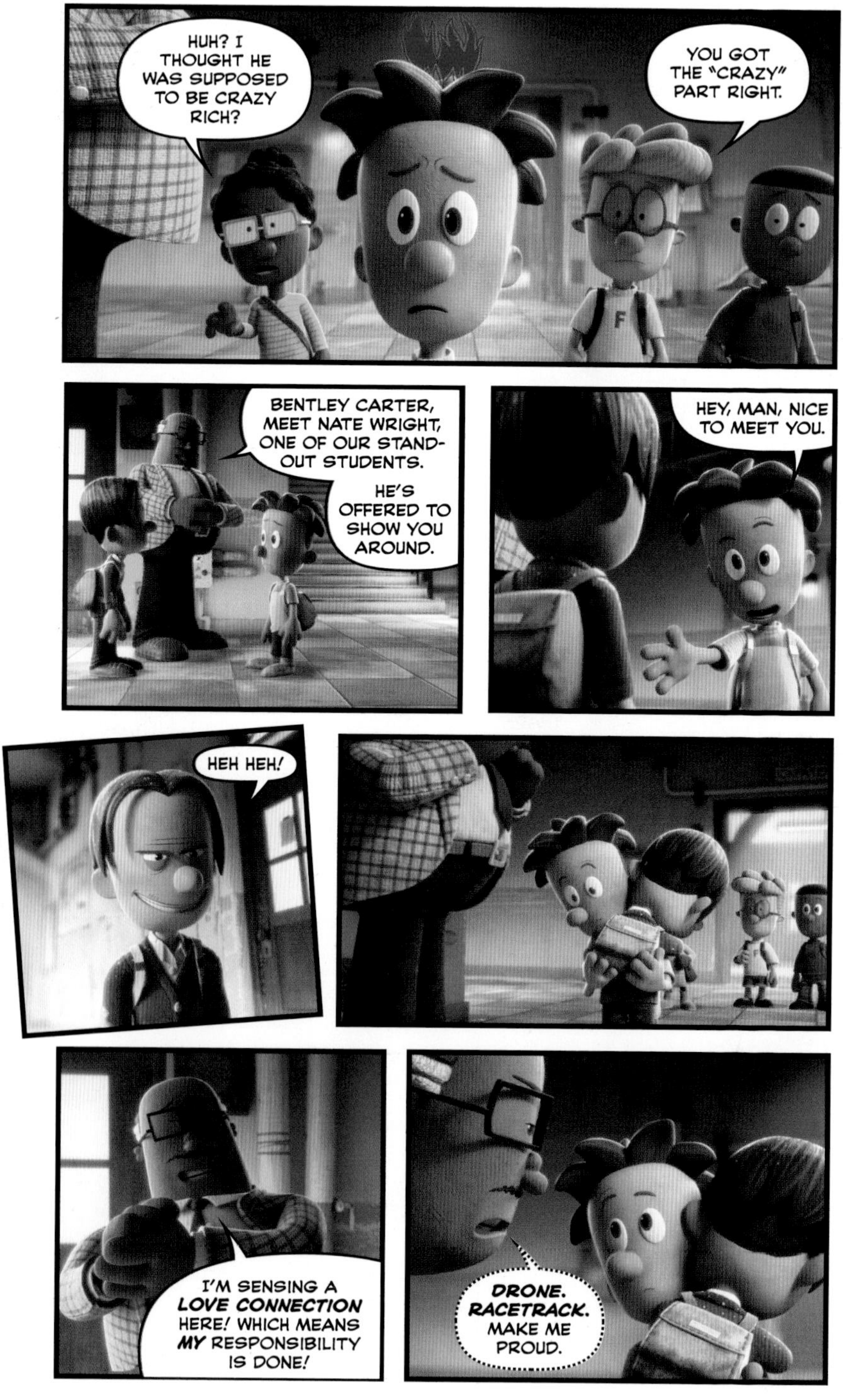
HUH? I THOUGHT HE WAS SUPPOSED TO BE CRAZY RICH?
YOU GOT THE "CRAZY" PART RIGHT.
BENTLEY CARTER, MEET NATE WRIGHT, ONE OF OUR STAND-OUT STUDENTS.
HE'S OFFERED TO SHOW YOU AROUND.
HEY, MAN, NICE TO MEET YOU.
HEH HEH!
I'M SENSING A LOVE CONNECTION HERE! WHICH MEANS MY RESPONSIBILITY IS DONE!
DRONE. RACETRACK. MAKE ME PROUD.

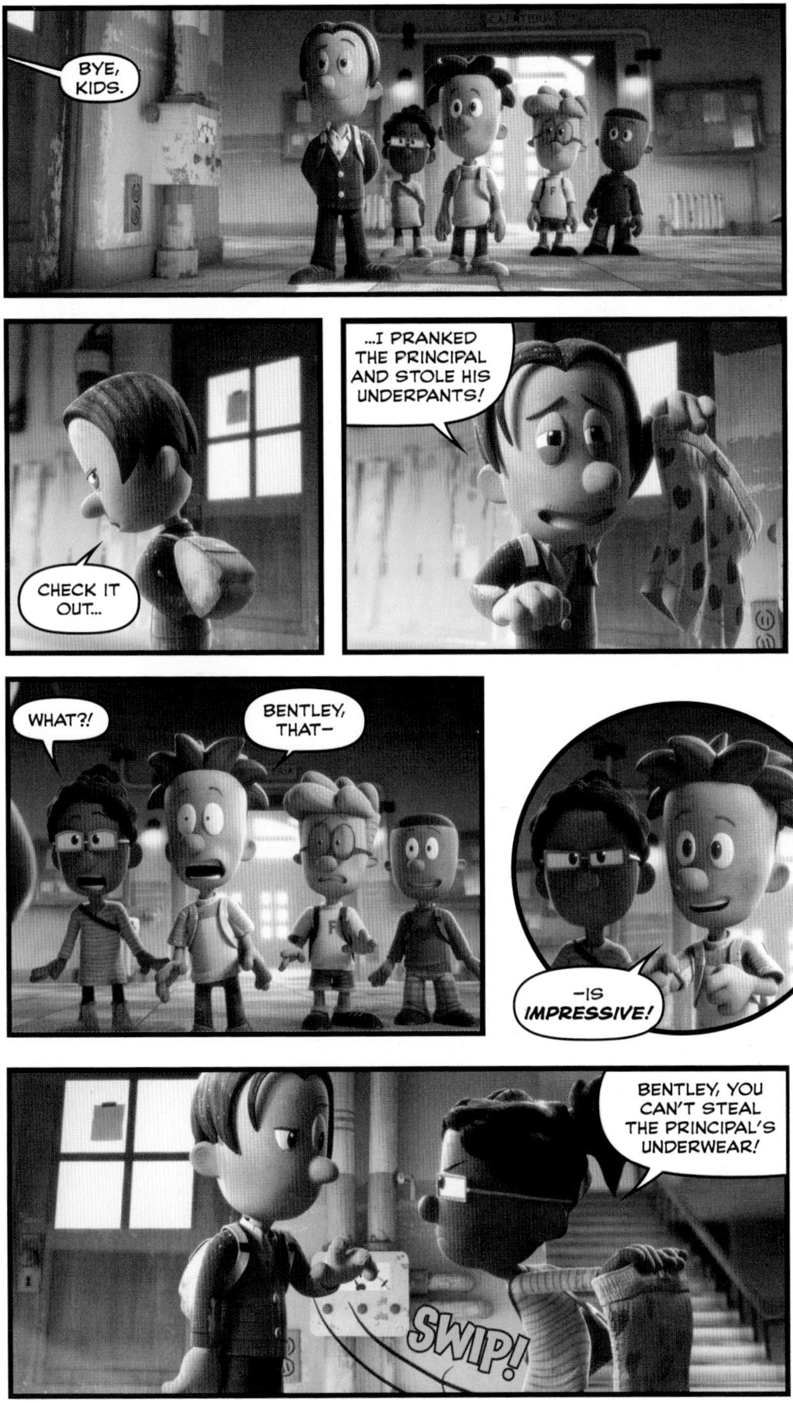
BYE, KIDS.
CHECK IT OUT...
...I PRANKED THE PRINCIPAL AND STOLE HIS UNDERPANTS!
WHAT?!
BENTLEY, THAT—
—IS *IMPRESSIVE!*
BENTLEY, YOU CAN'T STEAL THE PRINCIPAL'S UNDERWEAR!
SWIP!

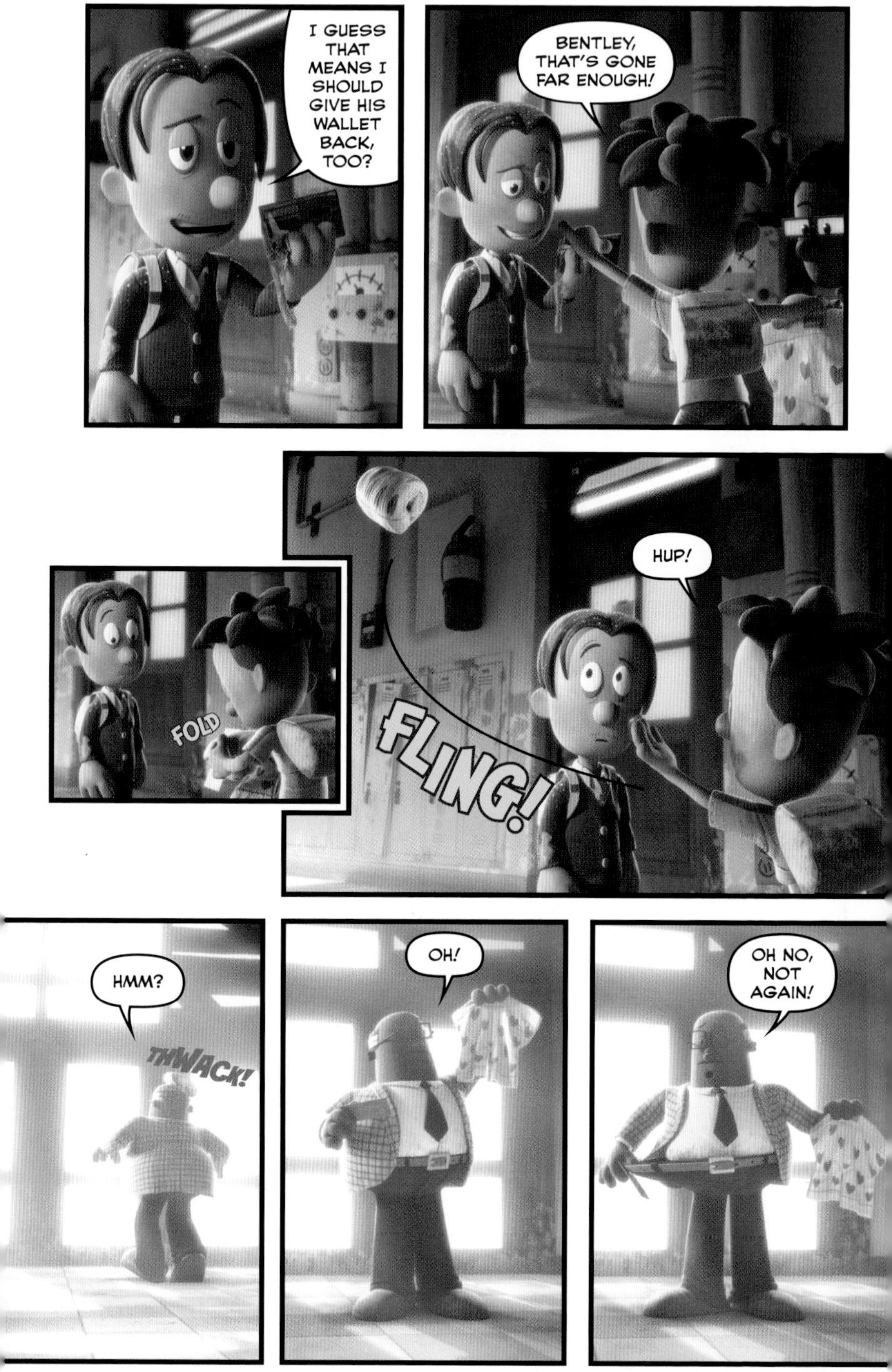
I GUESS THAT MEANS I SHOULD GIVE HIS WALLET BACK, TOO?
BENTLEY, THAT'S GONE FAR ENOUGH!
FOLD
HUP!
FLING!
HMM?
THWACK!
OH!
OH NO, NOT AGAIN!

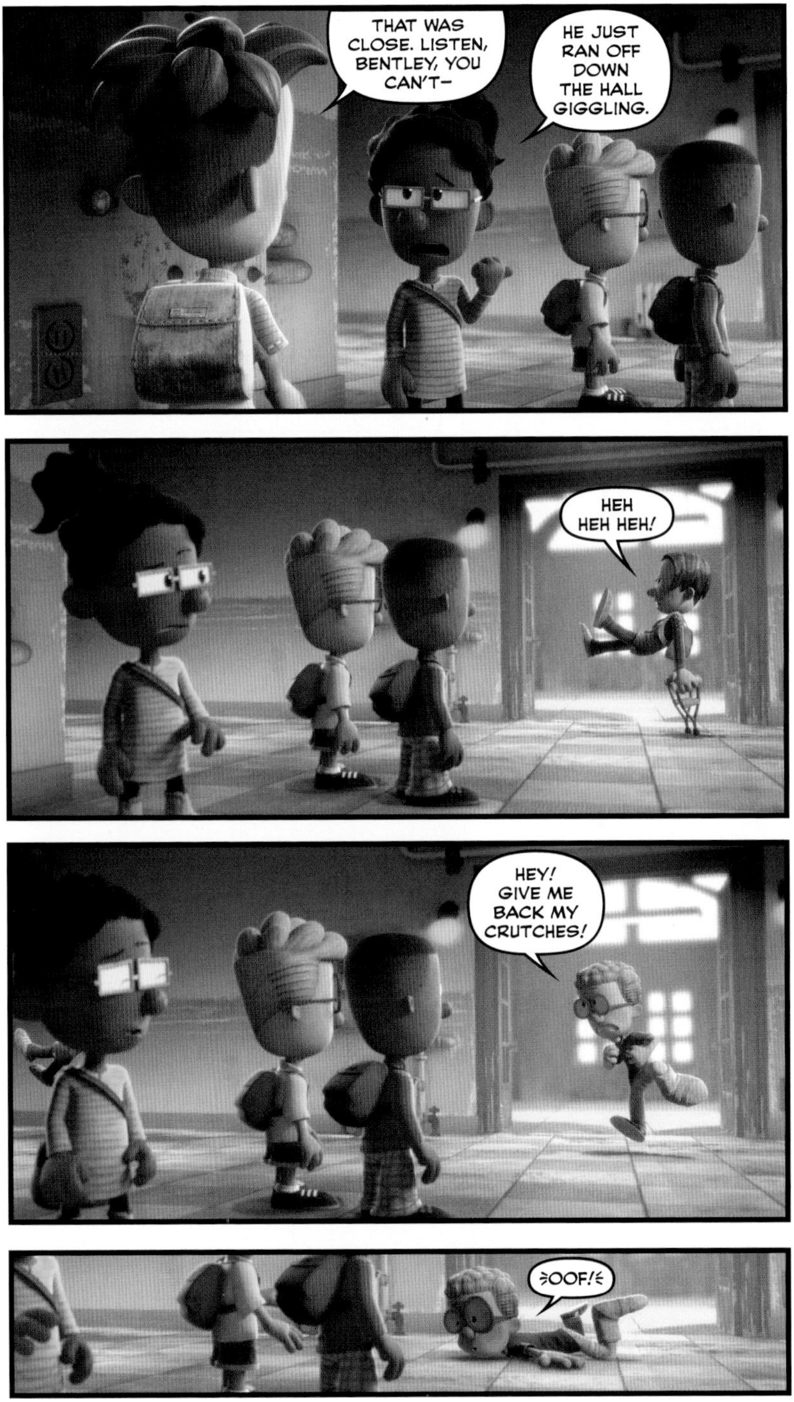
THAT WAS CLOSE. LISTEN, BENTLEY, YOU CAN'T–
HE JUST RAN OFF DOWN THE HALL GIGGLING.
HEH HEH HEH!
HEY! GIVE ME BACK MY CRUTCHES!
OOF!

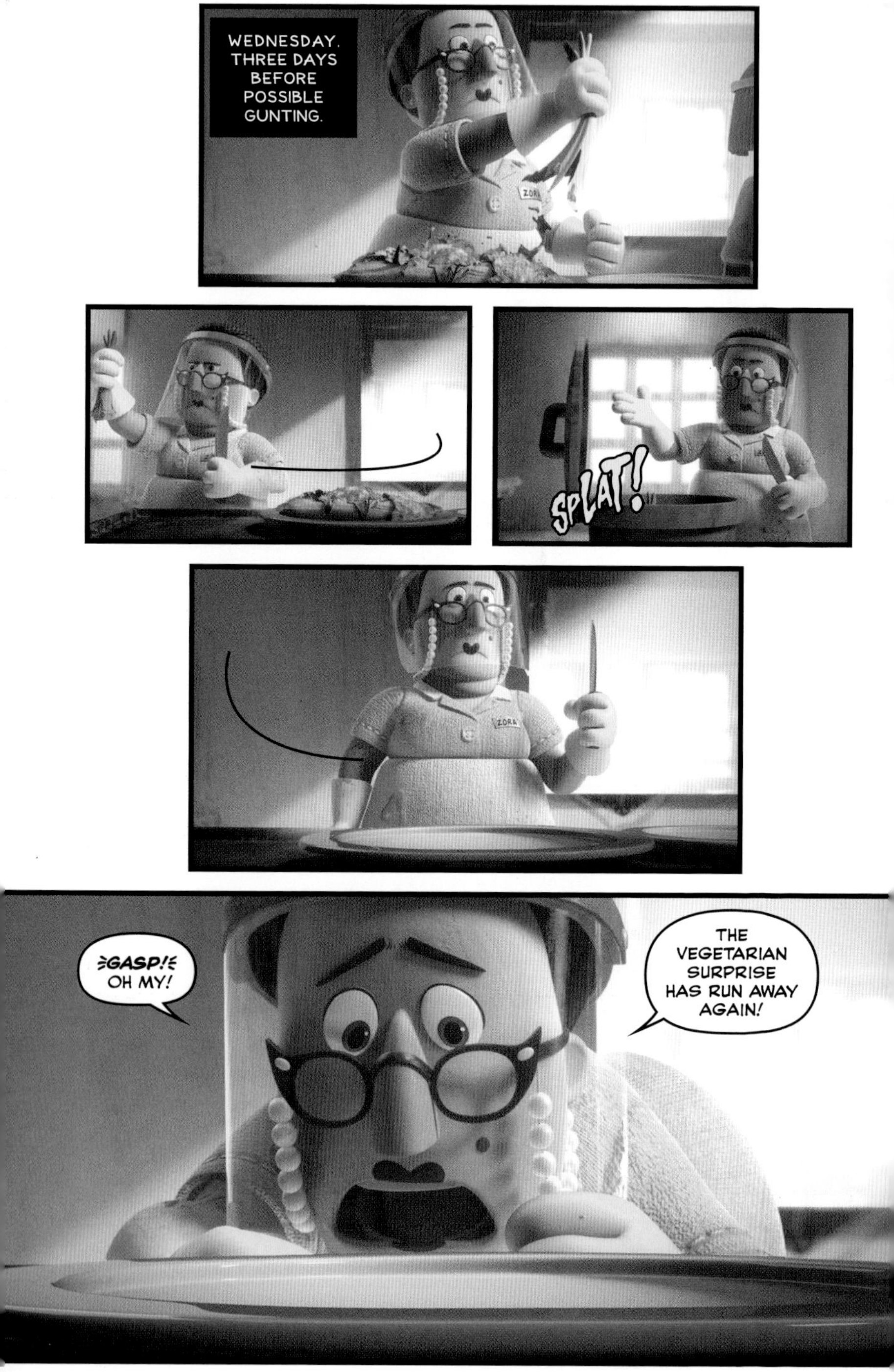
WEDNESDAY. THREE DAYS BEFORE POSSIBLE GUNTING.
ZORA
SPLAT!
ZORA
GASP! OH MY!
THE VEGETARIAN SURPRISE HAS RUN AWAY AGAIN!

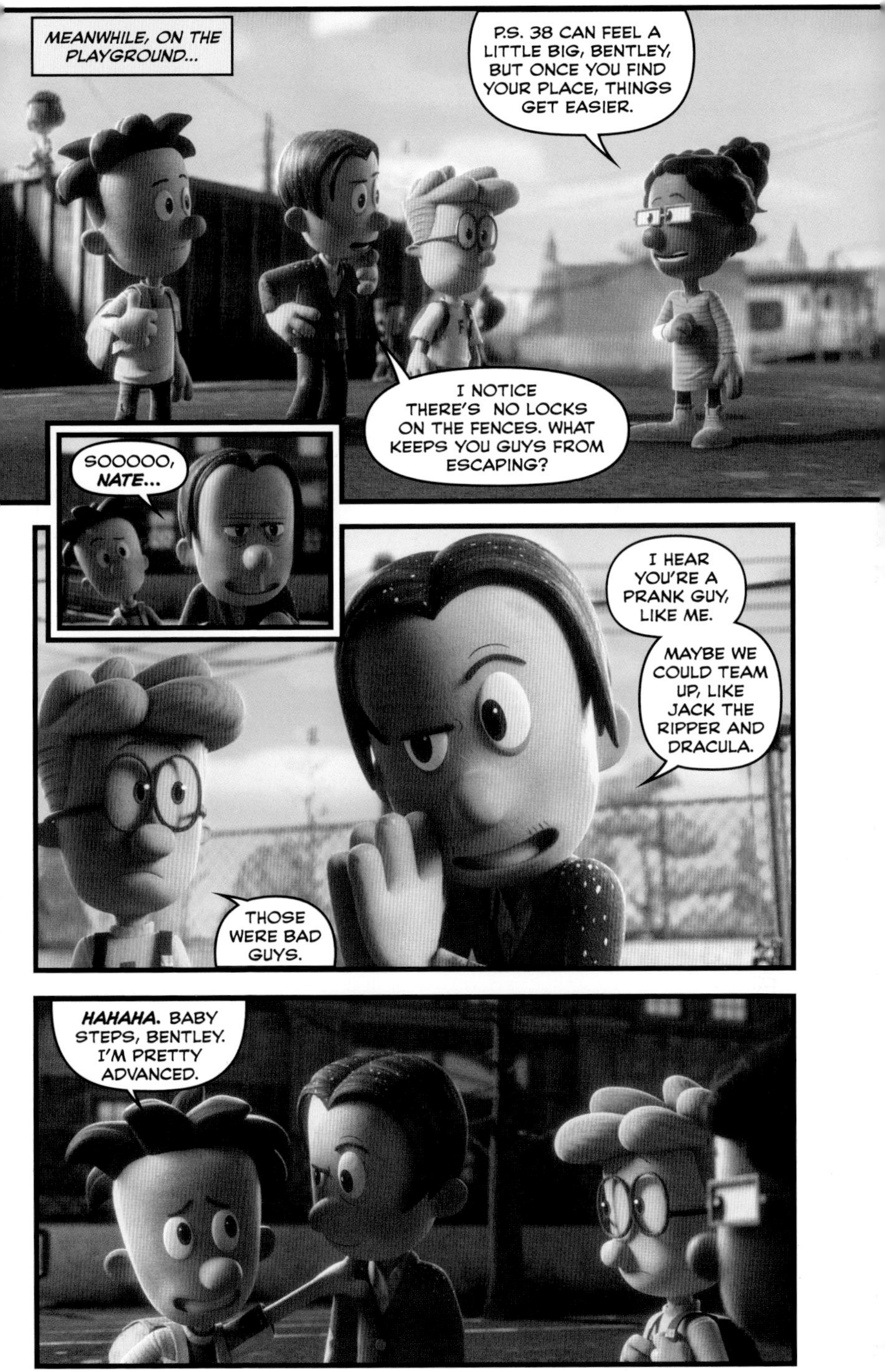
MEANWHILE, ON THE PLAYGROUND...
P.S. 38 CAN FEEL A LITTLE BIG, BENTLEY, BUT ONCE YOU FIND YOUR PLACE, THINGS GET EASIER.
I NOTICE THERE'S NO LOCKS ON THE FENCES. WHAT KEEPS YOU GUYS FROM ESCAPING?
SOOOOO, *NATE...*
I HEAR YOU'RE A PRANK GUY, LIKE ME.
MAYBE WE COULD TEAM UP, LIKE JACK THE RIPPER AND DRACULA.
THOSE WERE BAD GUYS.
HAHAHA. BABY STEPS, BENTLEY. I'M PRETTY ADVANCED.

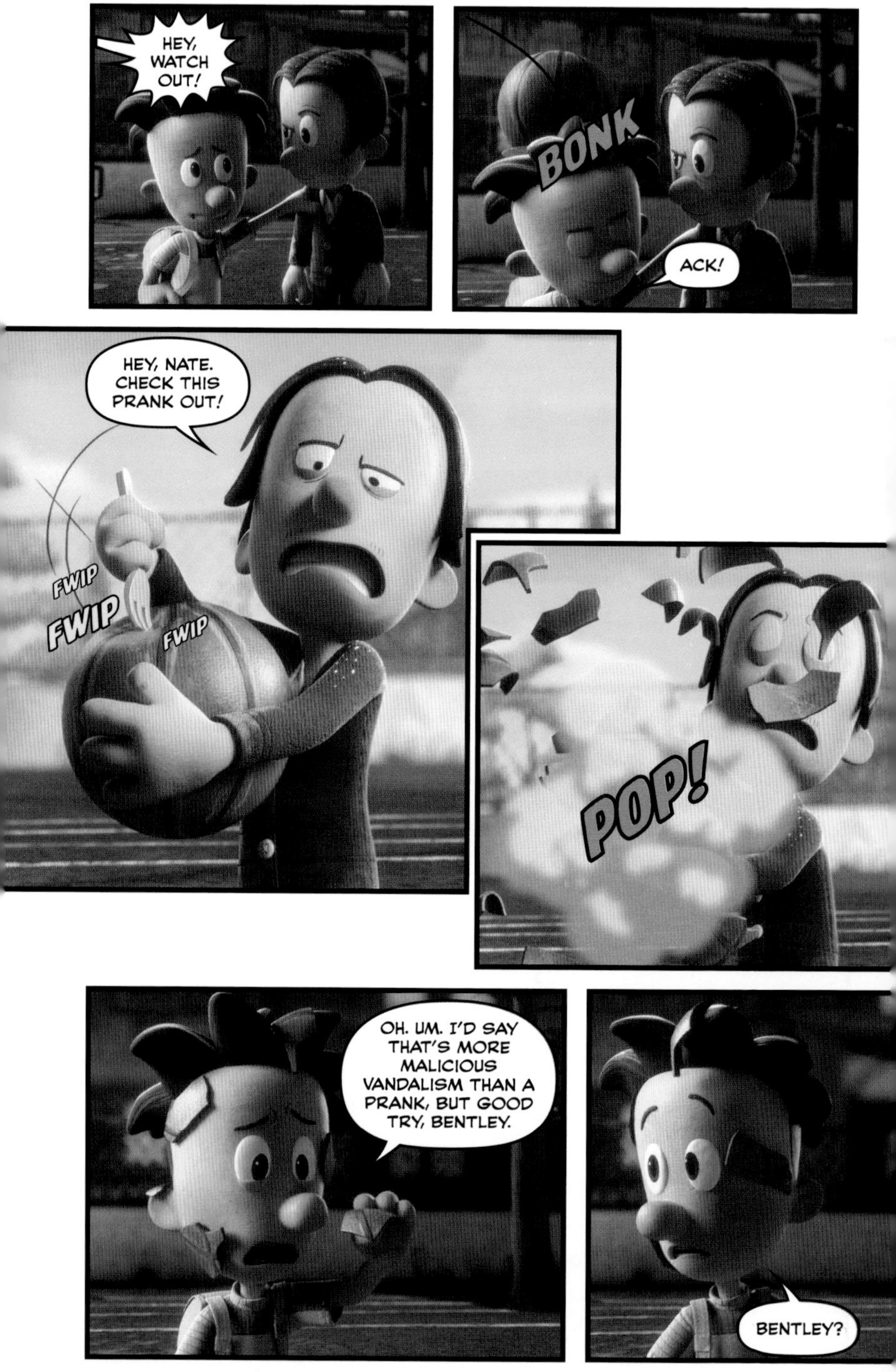
HEY, WATCH OUT!
BONK
ACK!
HEY, NATE. CHECK THIS PRANK OUT!
FWIP
FWIP
FWIP
POP!
OH. UM. I'D SAY THAT'S MORE MALICIOUS VANDALISM THAN A PRANK, BUT GOOD TRY, BENTLEY.
BENTLEY?

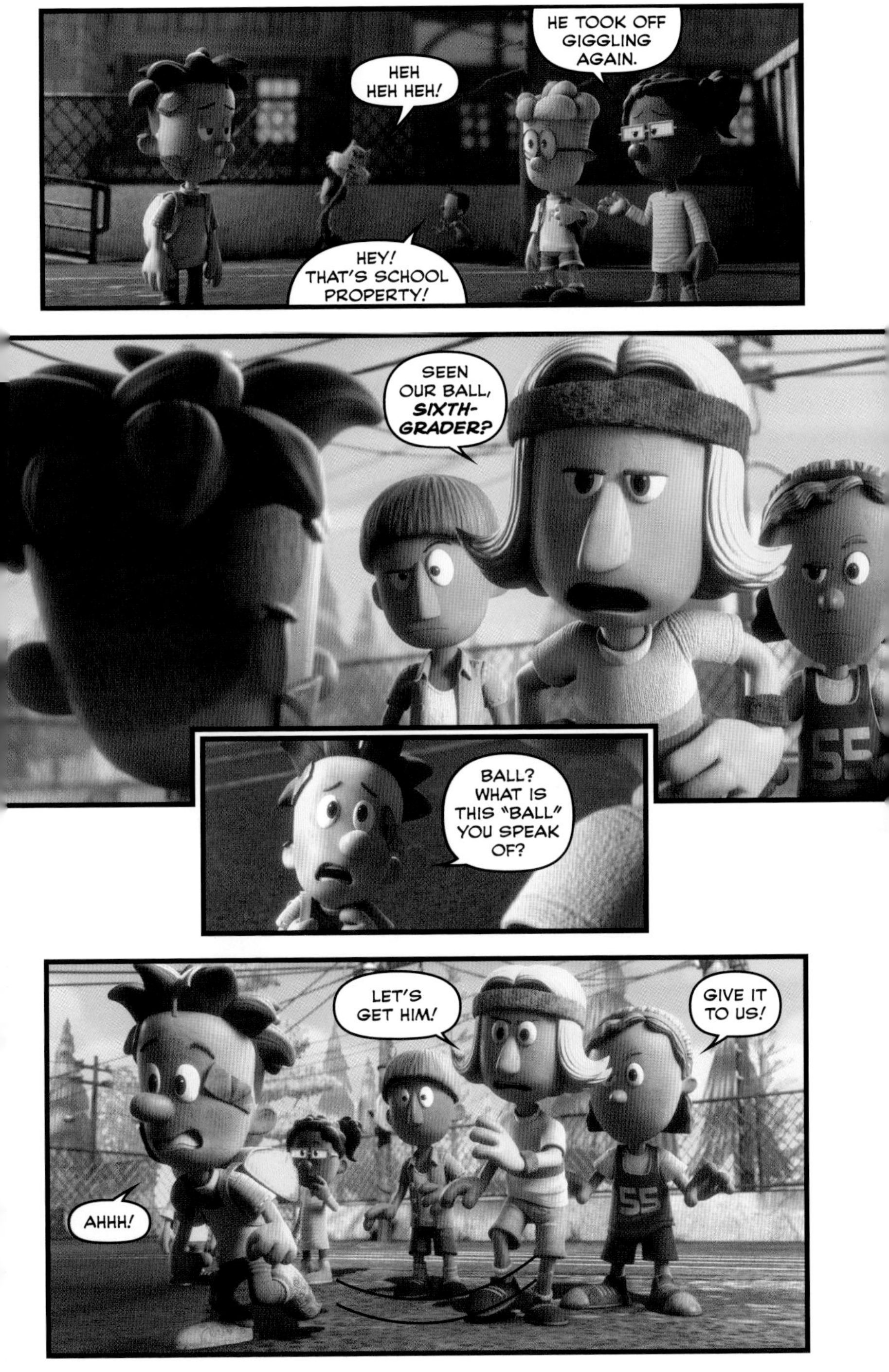
HEH HEH HEH!
HE TOOK OFF GIGGLING AGAIN.
HEY! THAT'S SCHOOL PROPERTY!
SEEN OUR BALL, SIXTH-GRADER?
BALL? WHAT IS THIS "BALL" YOU SPEAK OF?
LET'S GET HIM!
GIVE IT TO US!
AHHH!

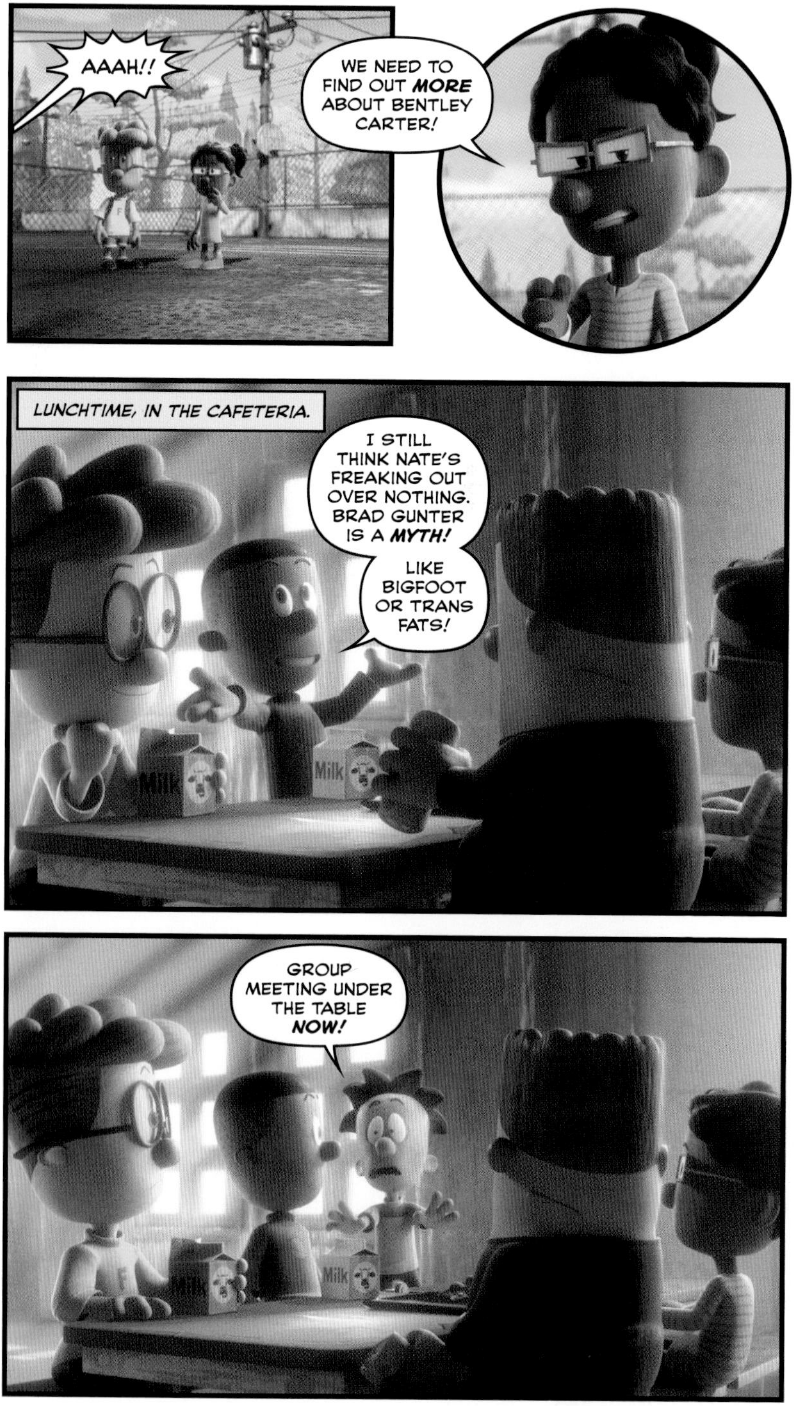
AAAH!!
WE NEED TO FIND OUT MORE ABOUT BENTLEY CARTER!
LUNCHTIME, IN THE CAFETERIA.
I STILL THINK NATE'S FREAKING OUT OVER NOTHING. BRAD GUNTER IS A MYTH!
LIKE BIGFOOT OR TRANS FATS!
GROUP MEETING UNDER THE TABLE NOW!

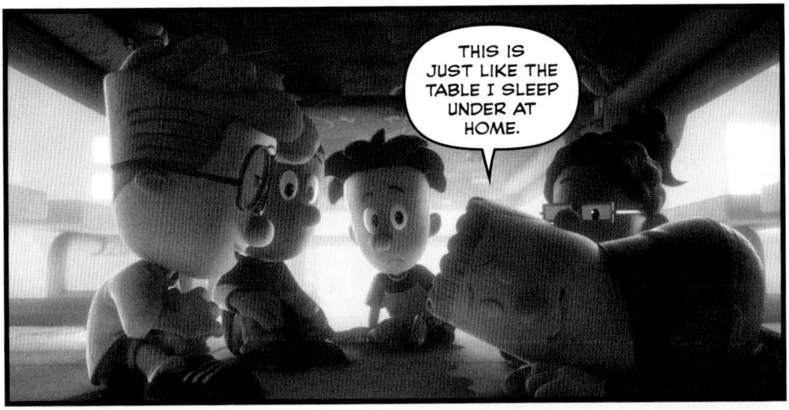
THIS IS JUST LIKE THE TABLE I SLEEP UNDER AT HOME.

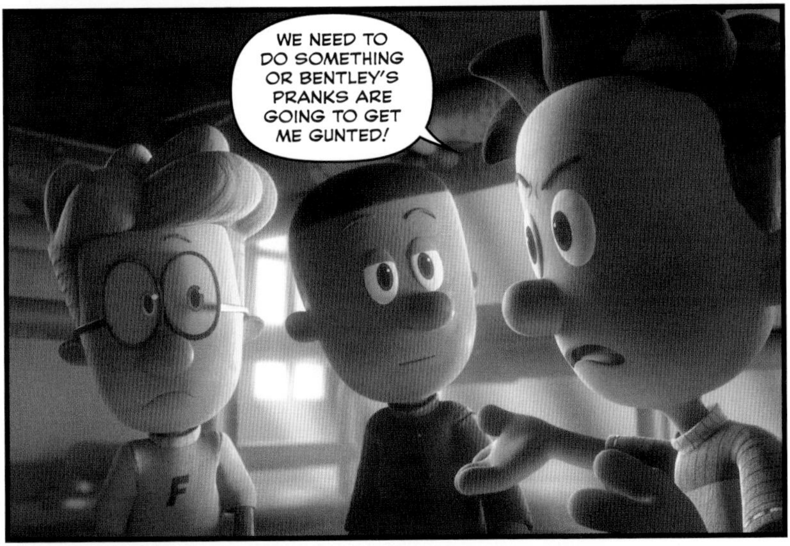
WE NEED TO DO SOMETHING OR BENTLEY'S PRANKS ARE GOING TO GET ME GUNTED!

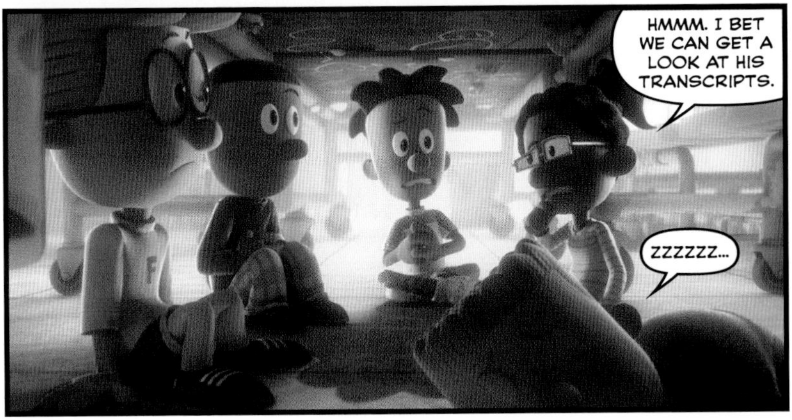
HMMM. I BET WE CAN GET A LOOK AT HIS TRANSCRIPTS.
ZZZZZZ...

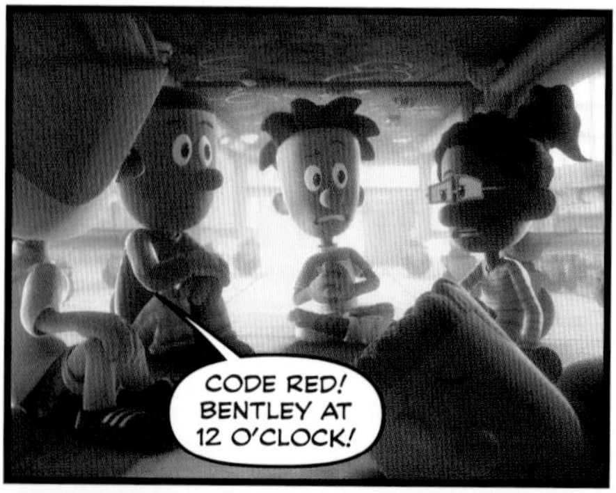
CODE RED! BENTLEY AT 12 O'CLOCK!

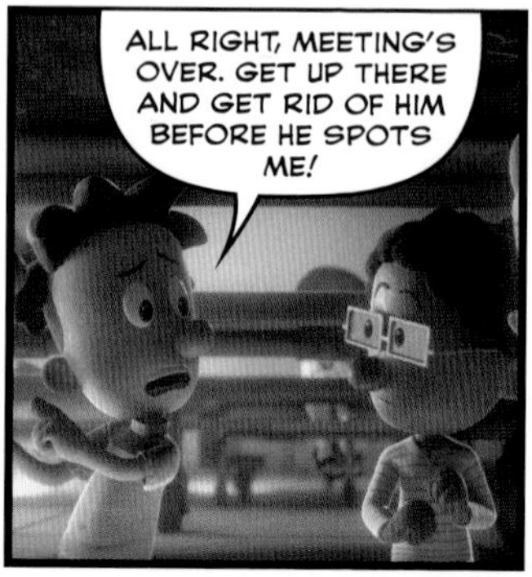
ALL RIGHT, MEETING'S OVER. GET UP THERE AND GET RID OF HIM BEFORE HE SPOTS ME!

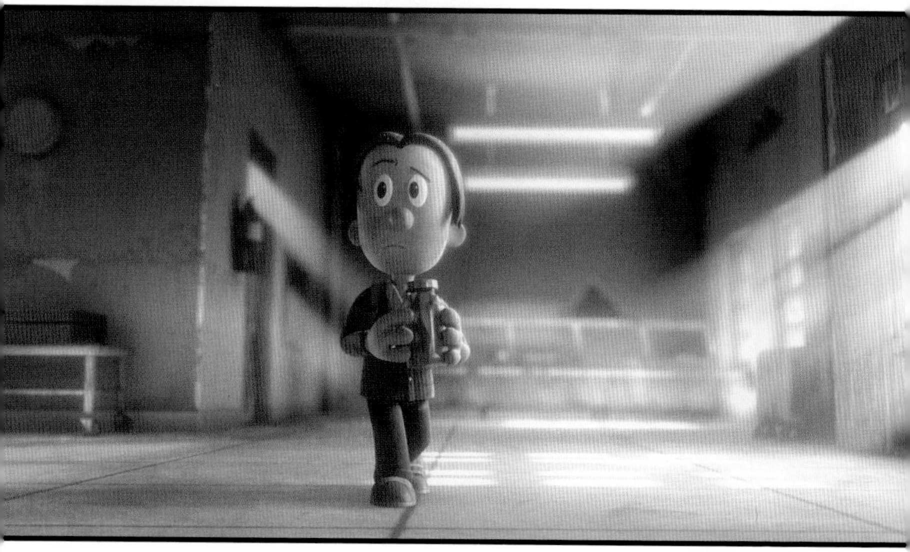

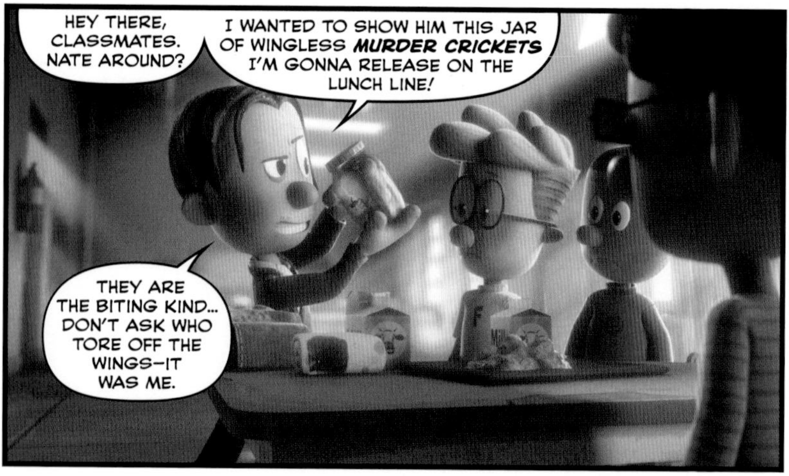
HEY THERE, CLASSMATES. NATE AROUND?
I WANTED TO SHOW HIM THIS JAR OF WINGLESS ***MURDER CRICKETS*** I'M GONNA RELEASE ON THE LUNCH LINE!
THEY ARE THE BITING KIND... DON'T ASK WHO TORE OFF THE WINGS—IT WAS ME.

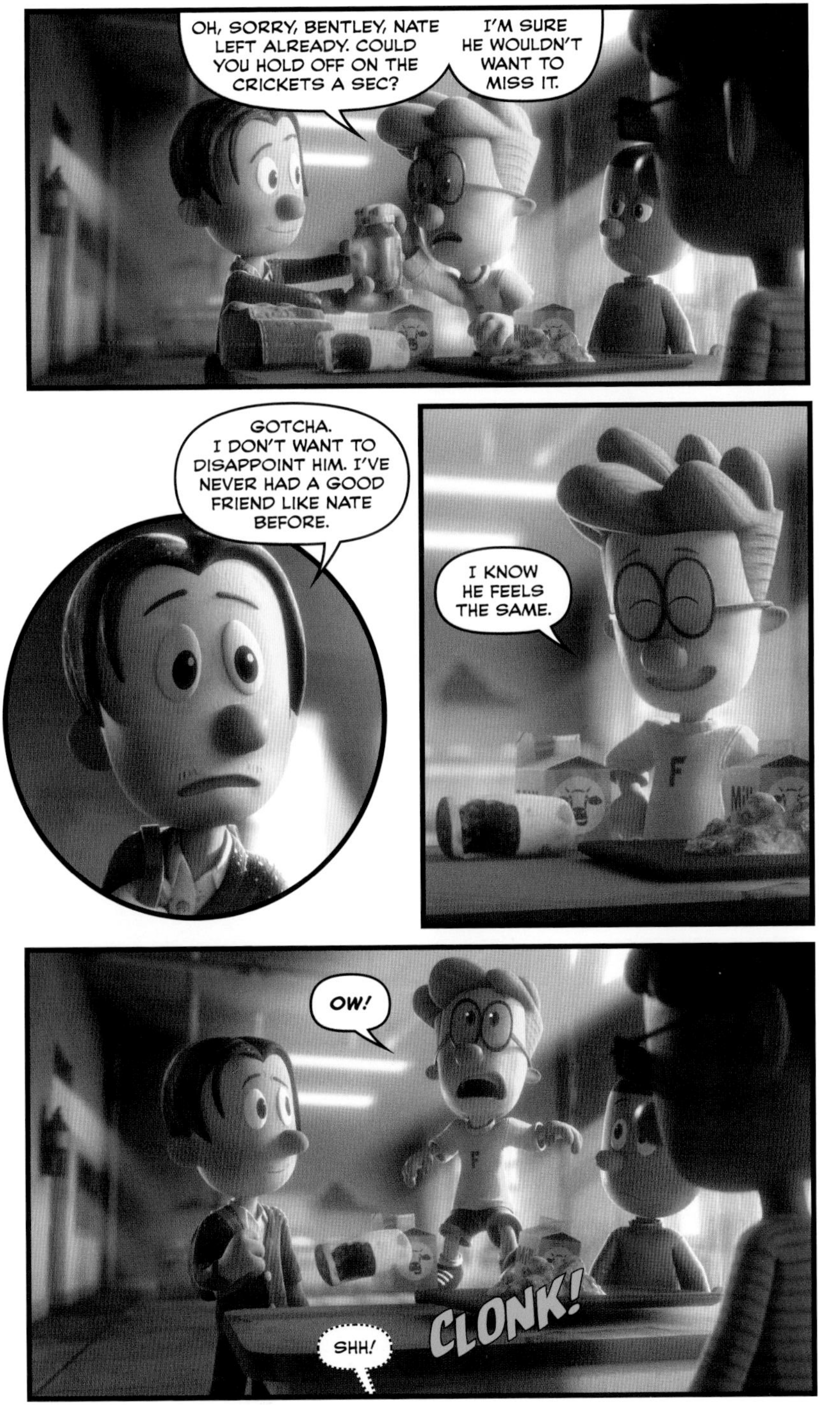
OH, SORRY, BENTLEY, NATE LEFT ALREADY. COULD YOU HOLD OFF ON THE CRICKETS A SEC?
I'M SURE HE WOULDN'T WANT TO MISS IT.
GOTCHA. I DON'T WANT TO DISAPPOINT HIM. I'VE NEVER HAD A GOOD FRIEND LIKE NATE BEFORE.
I KNOW HE FEELS THE SAME.
OW!
CLONK!
SHH!

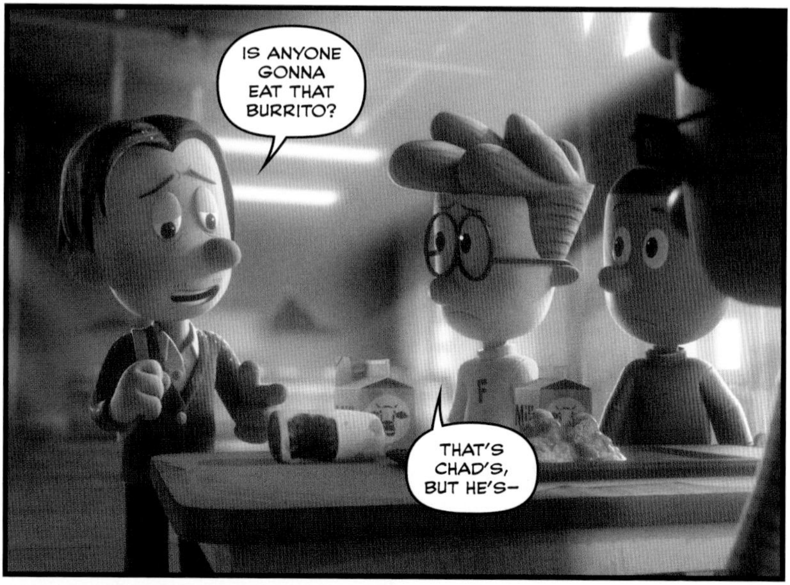
IS ANYONE GONNA EAT THAT BURRITO?
THAT'S CHAD'S, BUT HE'S—

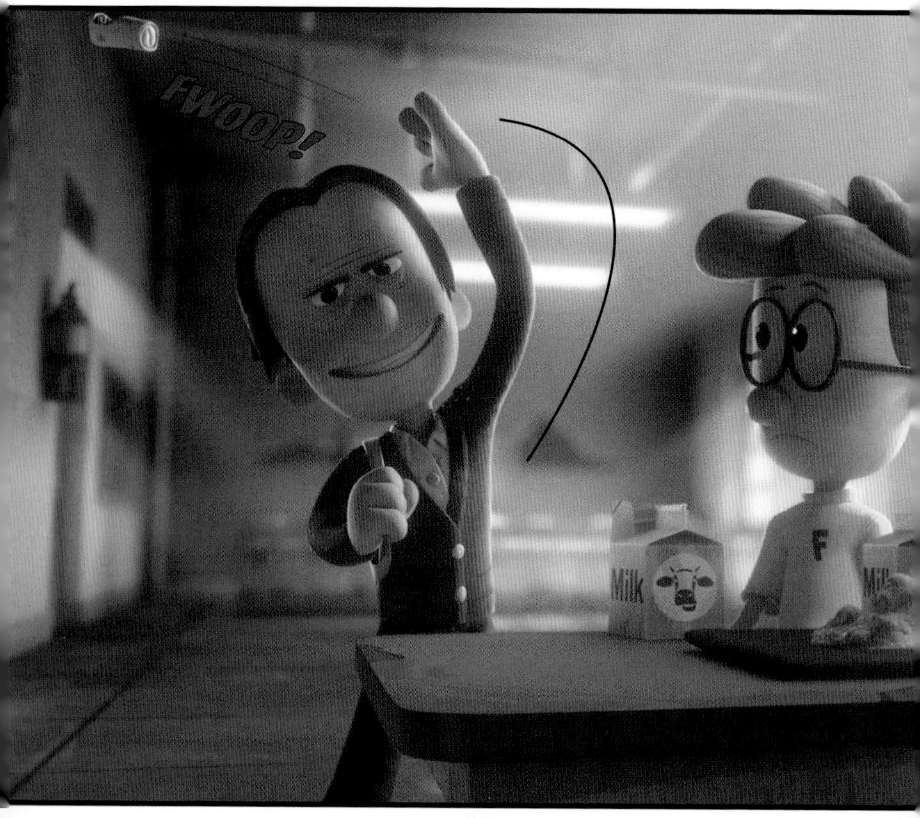
FWOOP!

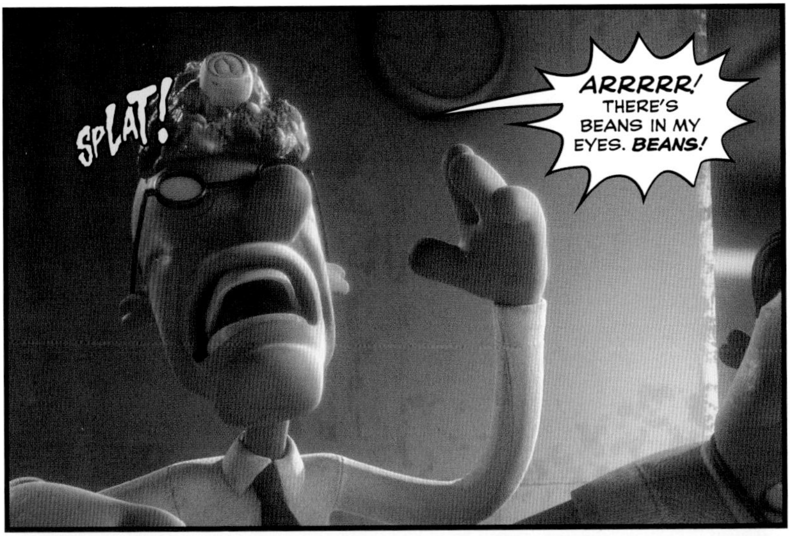
SPLAT!
ARRRRR! THERE'S BEANS IN MY EYES. BEANS!

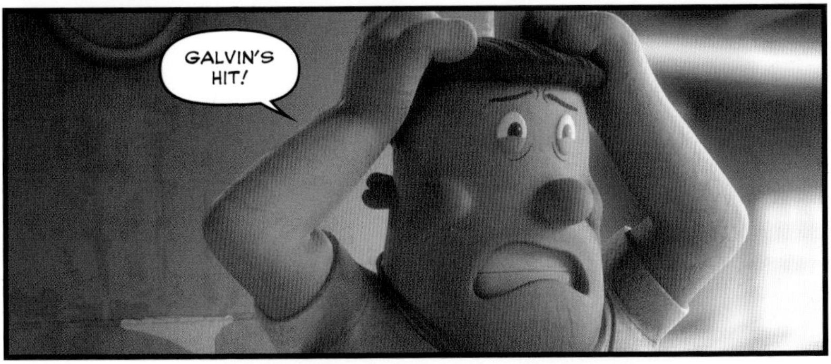
GALVIN'S HIT!

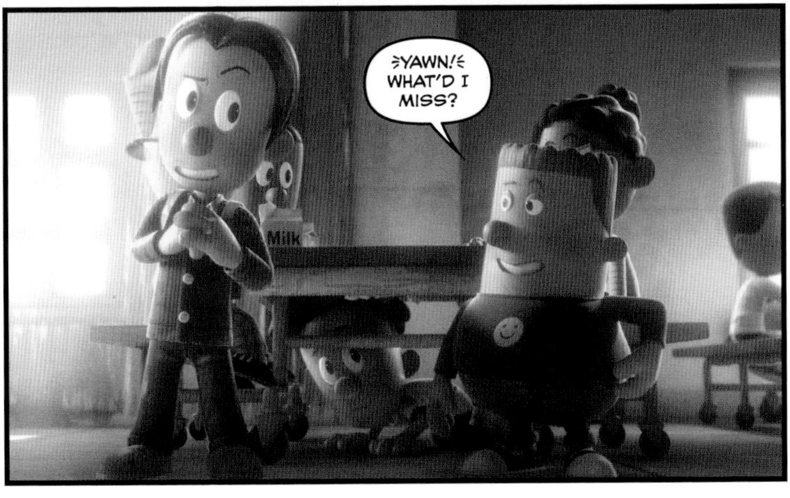
YAWN! WHAT'D I MISS?
Milk

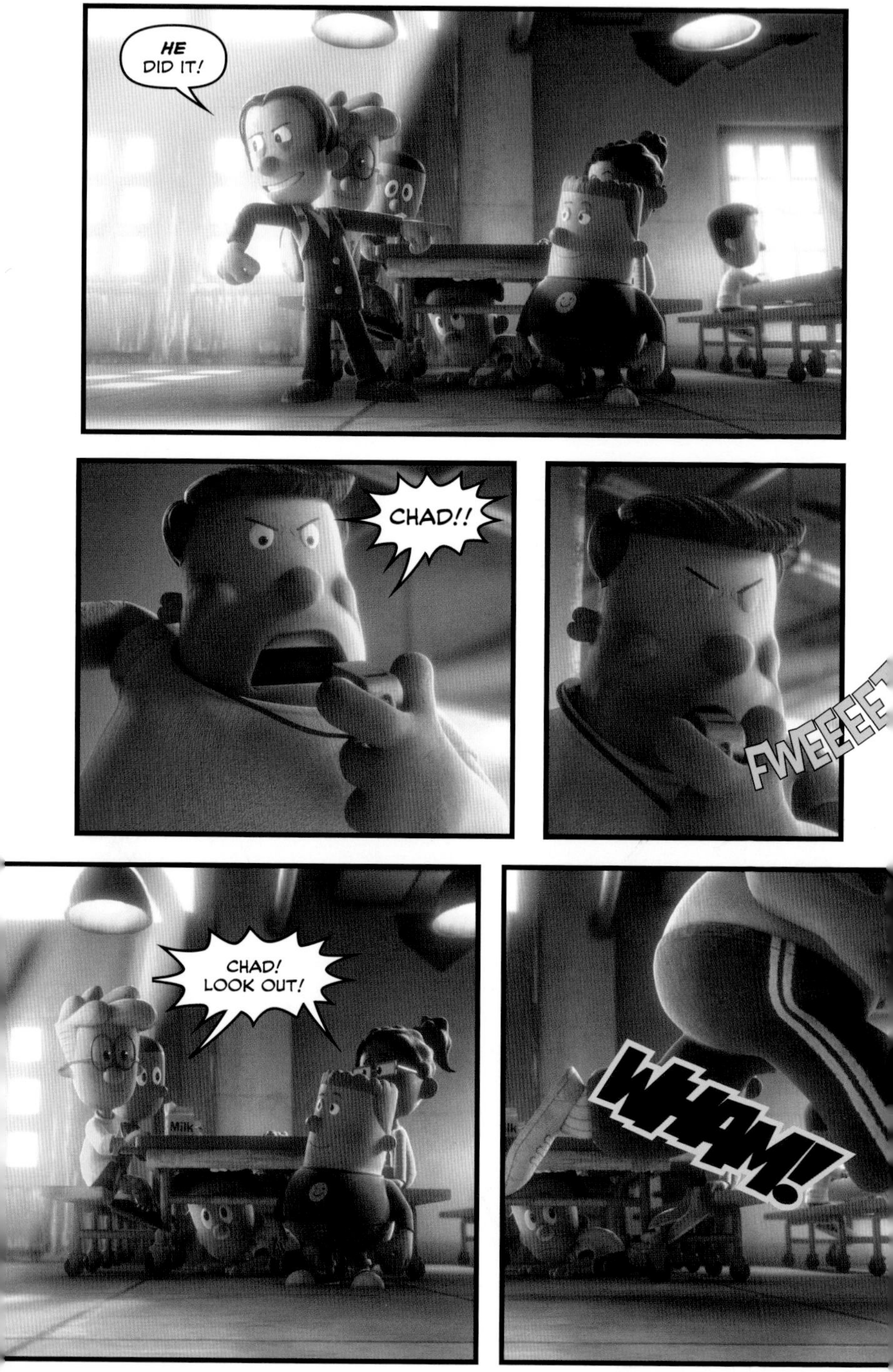
HE DID IT!
CHAD!!
FWEEEET
CHAD! LOOK OUT!
WHAM!!

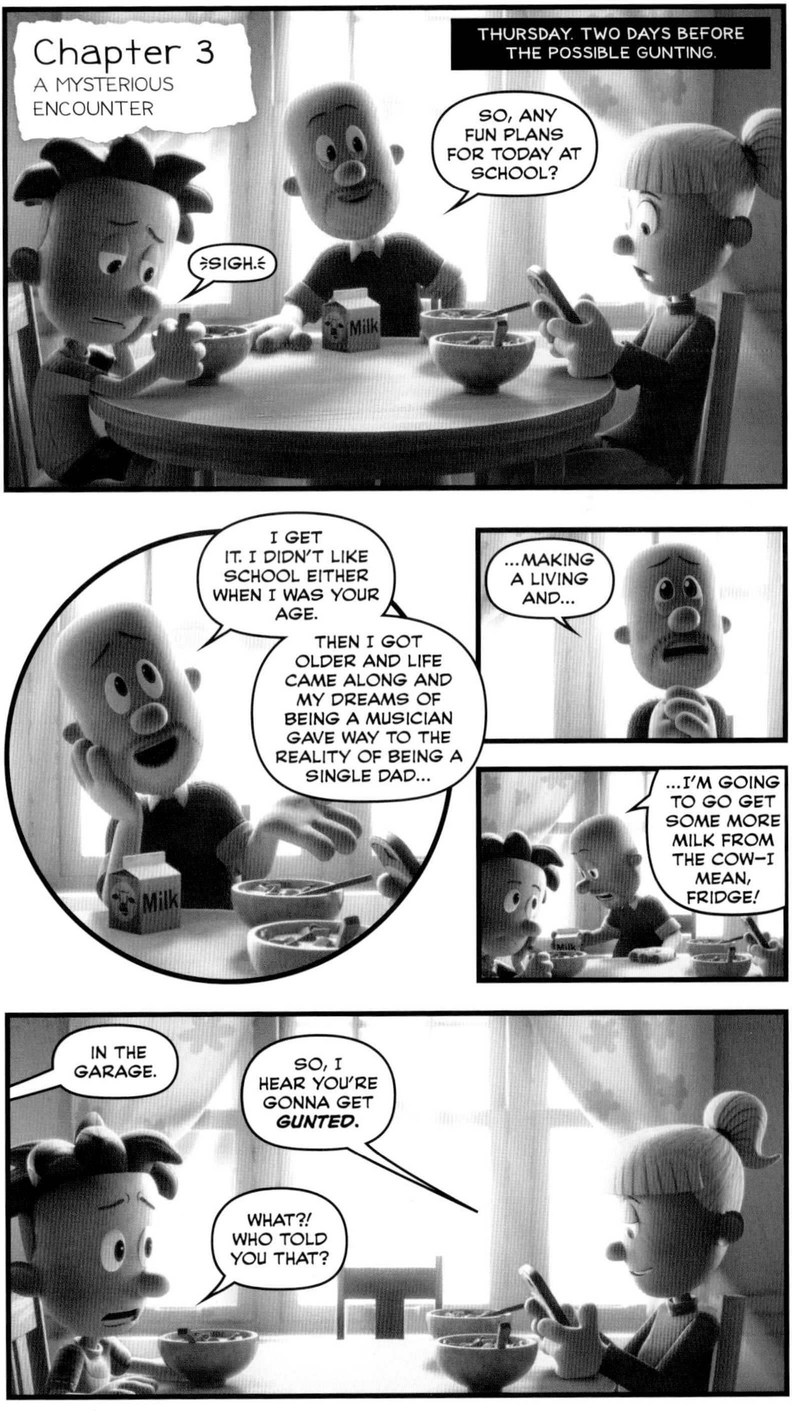
Chapter 3
A MYSTERIOUS ENCOUNTER
THURSDAY. TWO DAYS BEFORE THE POSSIBLE GUNTING.
SO, ANY FUN PLANS FOR TODAY AT SCHOOL?
SIGH.
Milk
I GET IT. I DIDN'T LIKE SCHOOL EITHER WHEN I WAS YOUR AGE.
THEN I GOT OLDER AND LIFE CAME ALONG AND MY DREAMS OF BEING A MUSICIAN GAVE WAY TO THE REALITY OF BEING A SINGLE DAD...
Milk
...MAKING A LIVING AND...
...I'M GOING TO GO GET SOME MORE MILK FROM THE COW—I MEAN, FRIDGE!
IN THE GARAGE.
SO, I HEAR YOU'RE GONNA GET ***GUNTED.***
WHAT?! WHO TOLD YOU THAT?

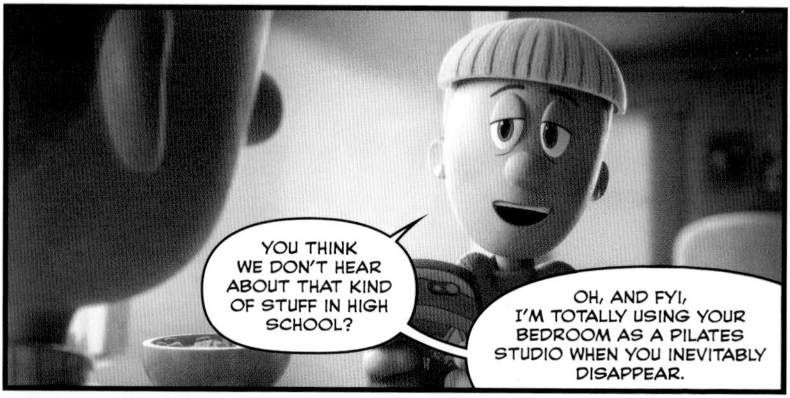
YOU THINK WE DON'T HEAR ABOUT THAT KIND OF STUFF IN HIGH SCHOOL?
OH, AND FYI, I'M TOTALLY USING YOUR BEDROOM AS A PILATES STUDIO WHEN YOU INEVITABLY DISAPPEAR.

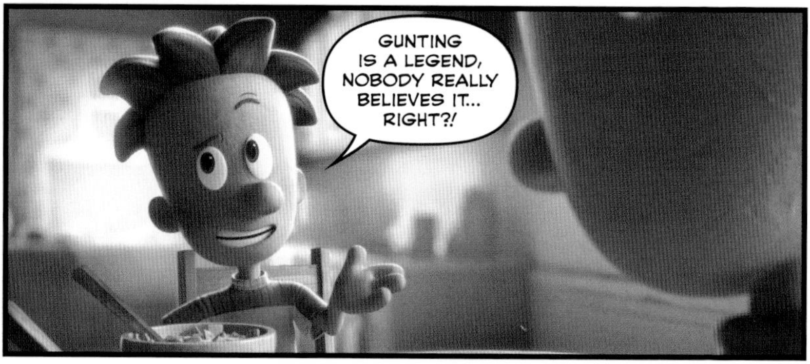
GUNTING IS A LEGEND, NOBODY REALLY BELIEVES IT... RIGHT?!

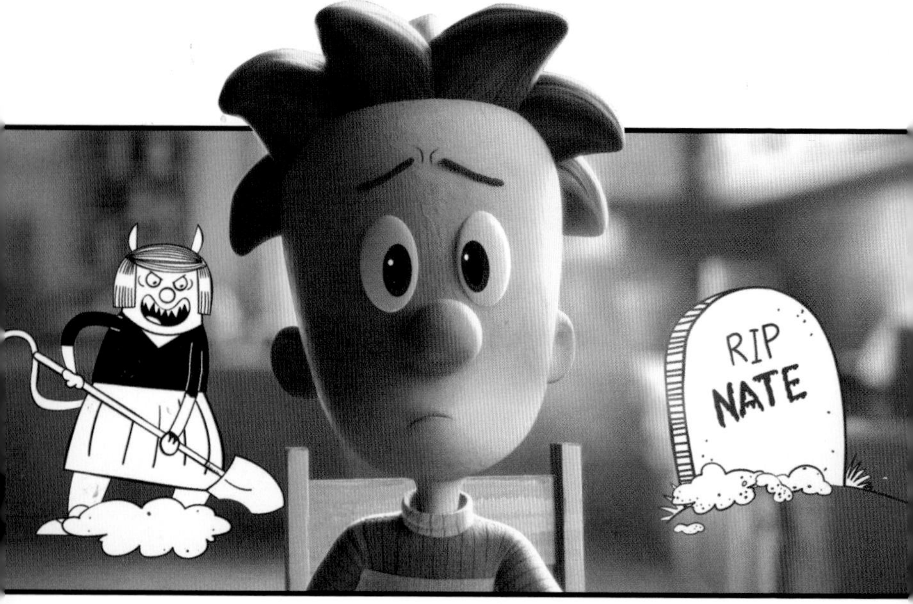
RIP
NATE

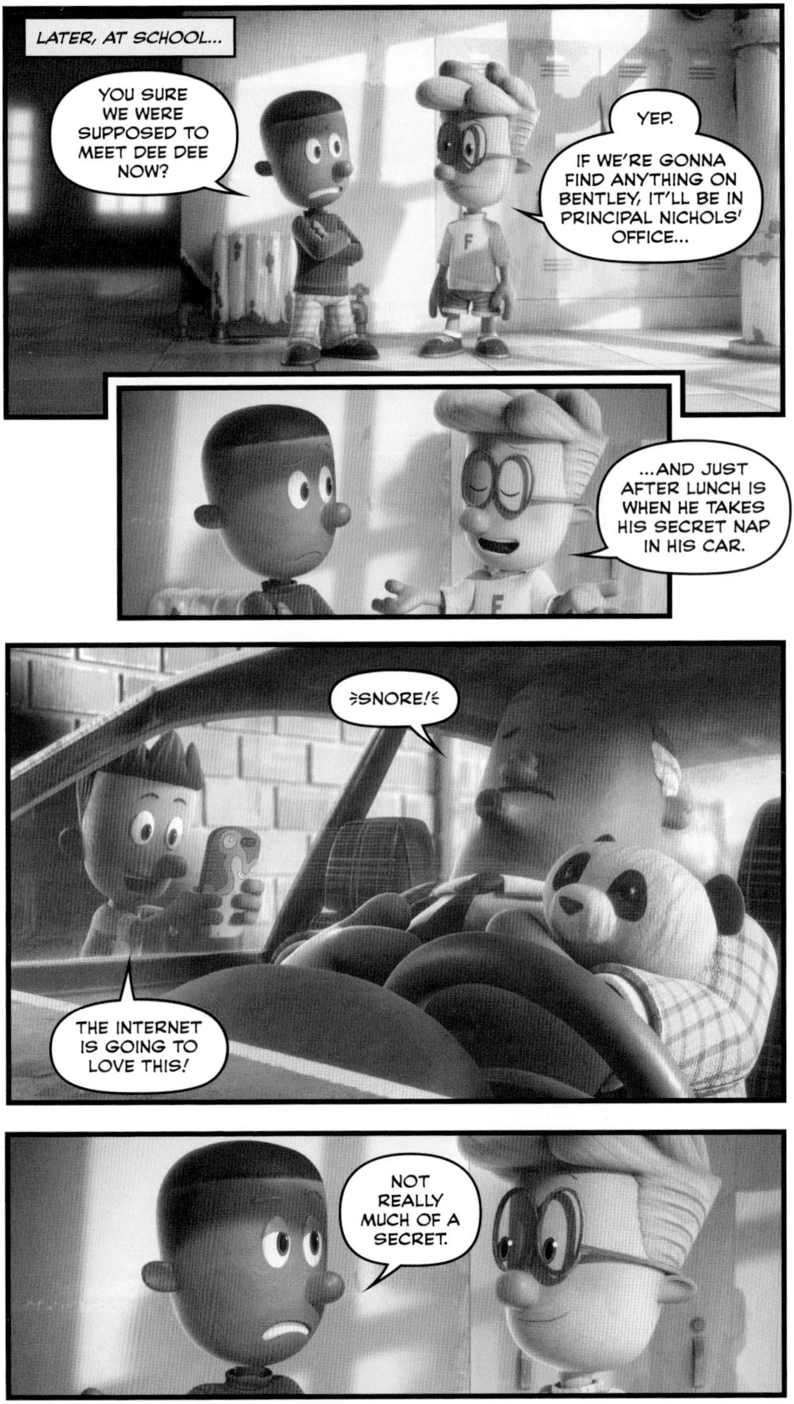
LATER, AT SCHOOL...
YOU SURE WE WERE SUPPOSED TO MEET DEE DEE NOW?
YEP.
IF WE'RE GONNA FIND ANYTHING ON BENTLEY, IT'LL BE IN PRINCIPAL NICHOLS' OFFICE...
...AND JUST AFTER LUNCH IS WHEN HE TAKES HIS SECRET NAP IN HIS CAR.
SNORE!
THE INTERNET IS GOING TO LOVE THIS!
NOT REALLY MUCH OF A SECRET.

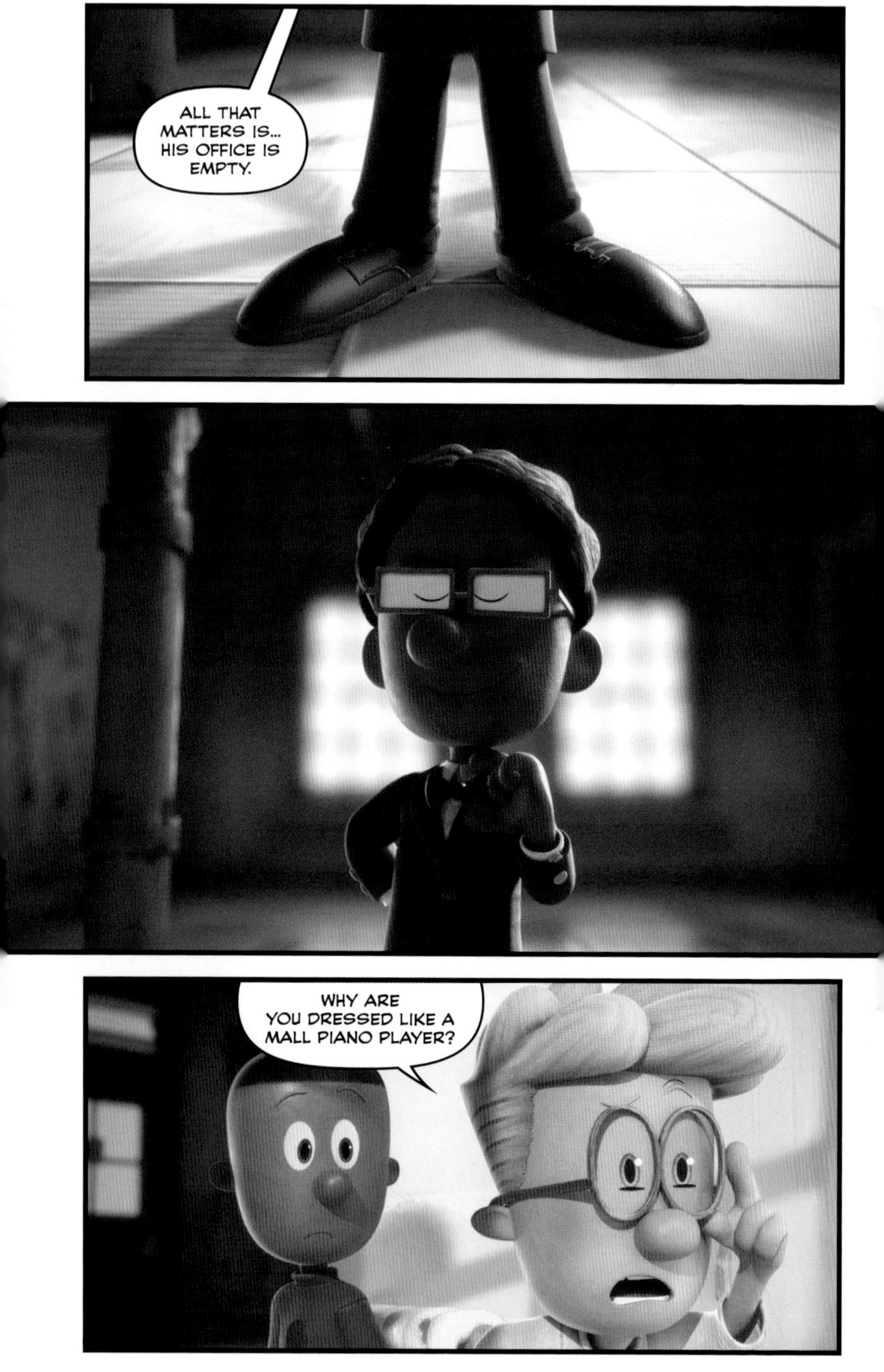
ALL THAT MATTERS IS... HIS OFFICE IS EMPTY.
WHY ARE YOU DRESSED LIKE A MALL PIANO PLAYER?

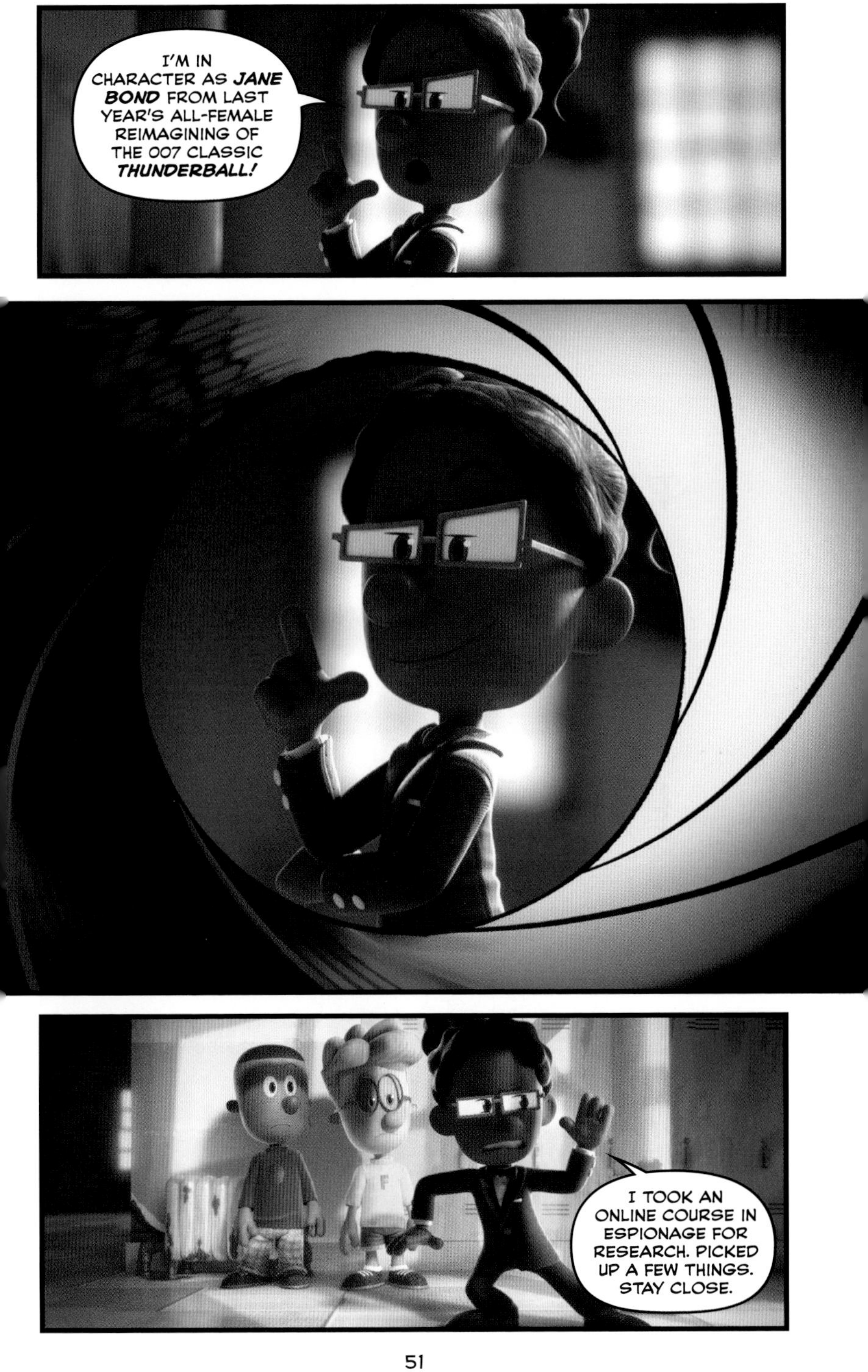
I'M IN CHARACTER AS JANE BOND FROM LAST YEAR'S ALL-FEMALE REIMAGINING OF THE 007 CLASSIC THUNDERBALL!
I TOOK AN ONLINE COURSE IN ESPIONAGE FOR RESEARCH. PICKED UP A FEW THINGS. STAY CLOSE.

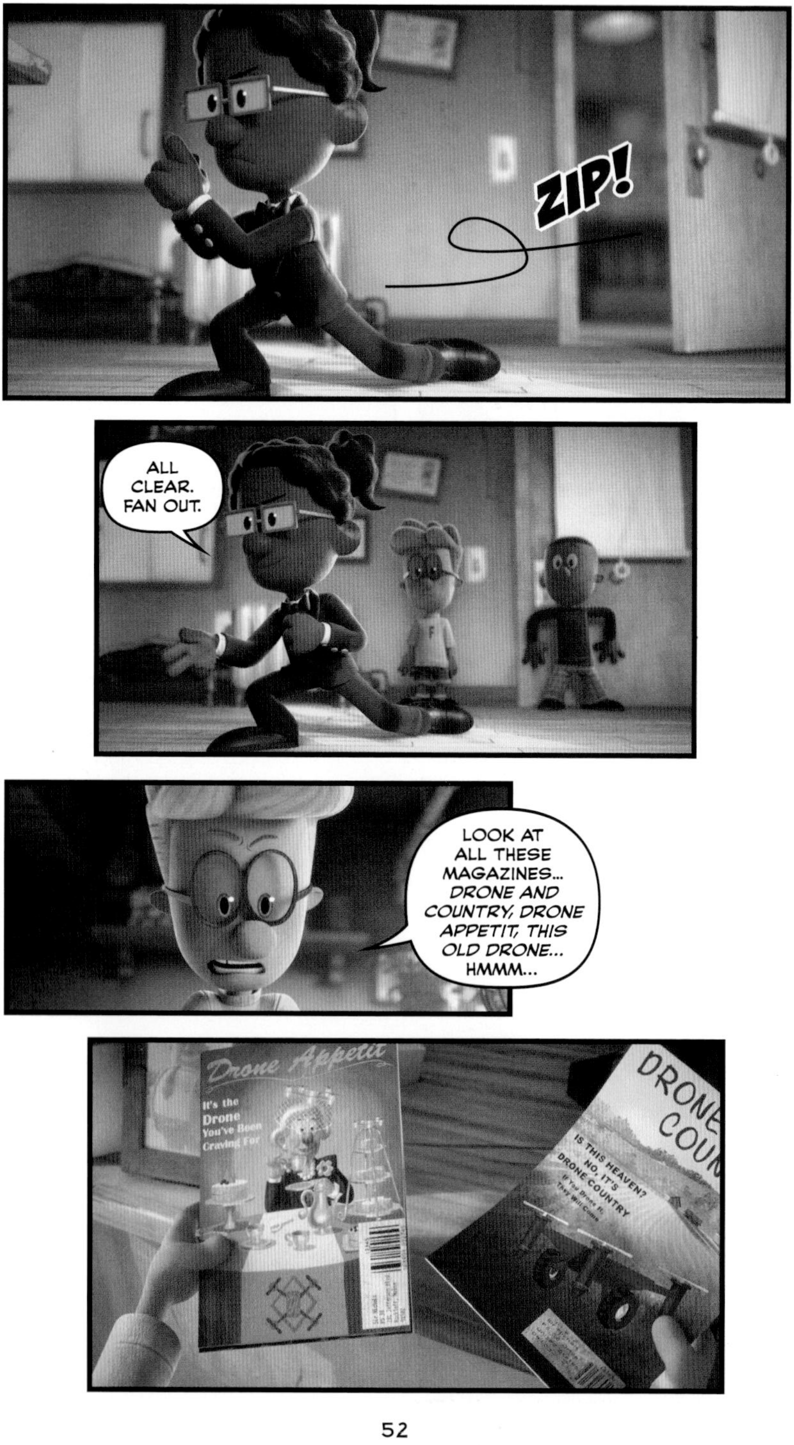
ZIP!
ALL CLEAR. FAN OUT.
LOOK AT ALL THESE MAGAZINES... *DRONE AND COUNTRY, DRONE APPETIT, THIS OLD DRONE...* HMMM...
Drone Appetit
It's the Drone You've Been Craving For
DRONE
IS THIS HEAVEN? NO, IT'S DRONE COUNTRY

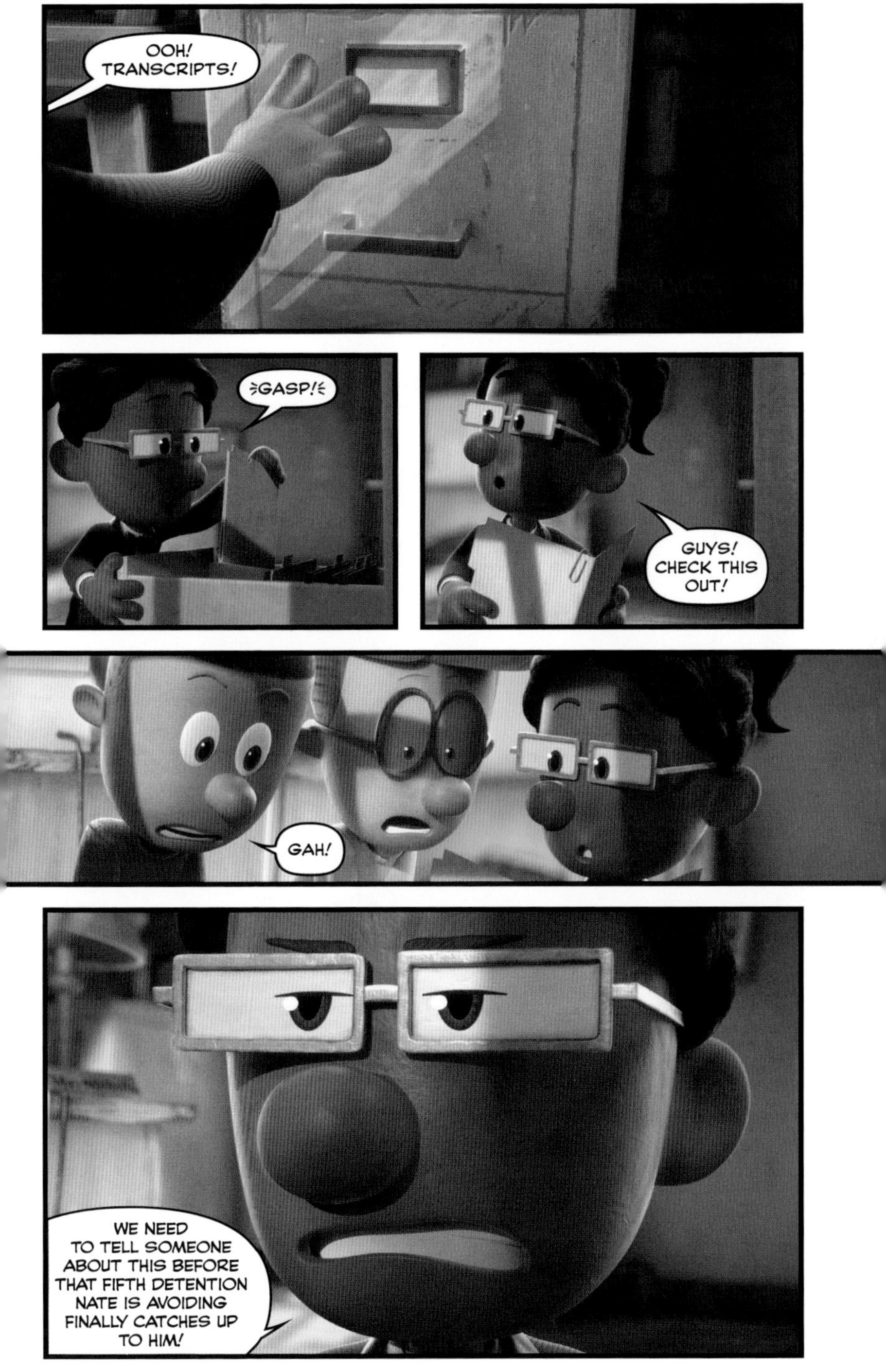
OOH! TRANSCRIPTS!
GASP!
GUYS! CHECK THIS OUT!
GAH!
WE NEED TO TELL SOMEONE ABOUT THIS BEFORE THAT FIFTH DETENTION NATE IS AVOIDING FINALLY CATCHES UP TO HIM!

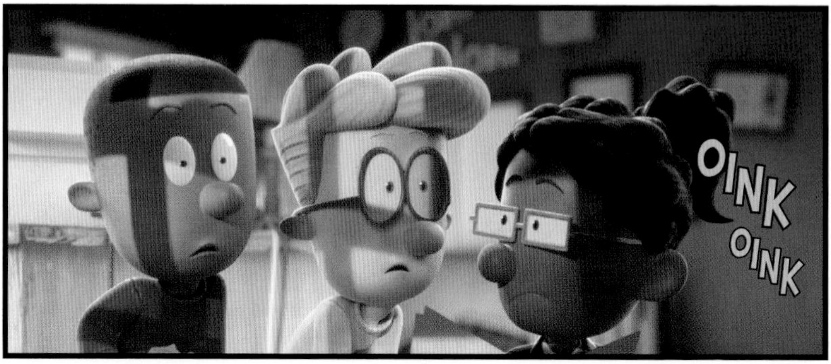
OINK
OINK

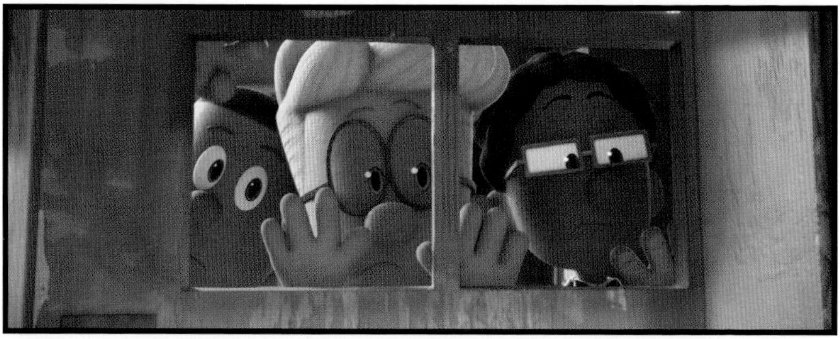

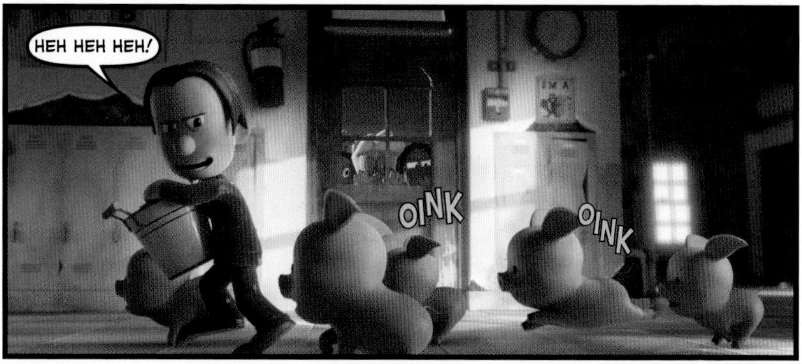
HEH HEH HEH!
OINK
OINK

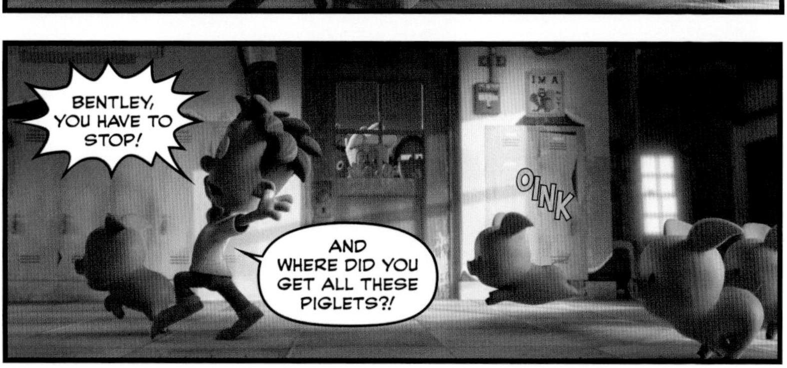
BENTLEY, YOU HAVE TO STOP!
OINK
AND WHERE DID YOU GET ALL THESE PIGLETS?!

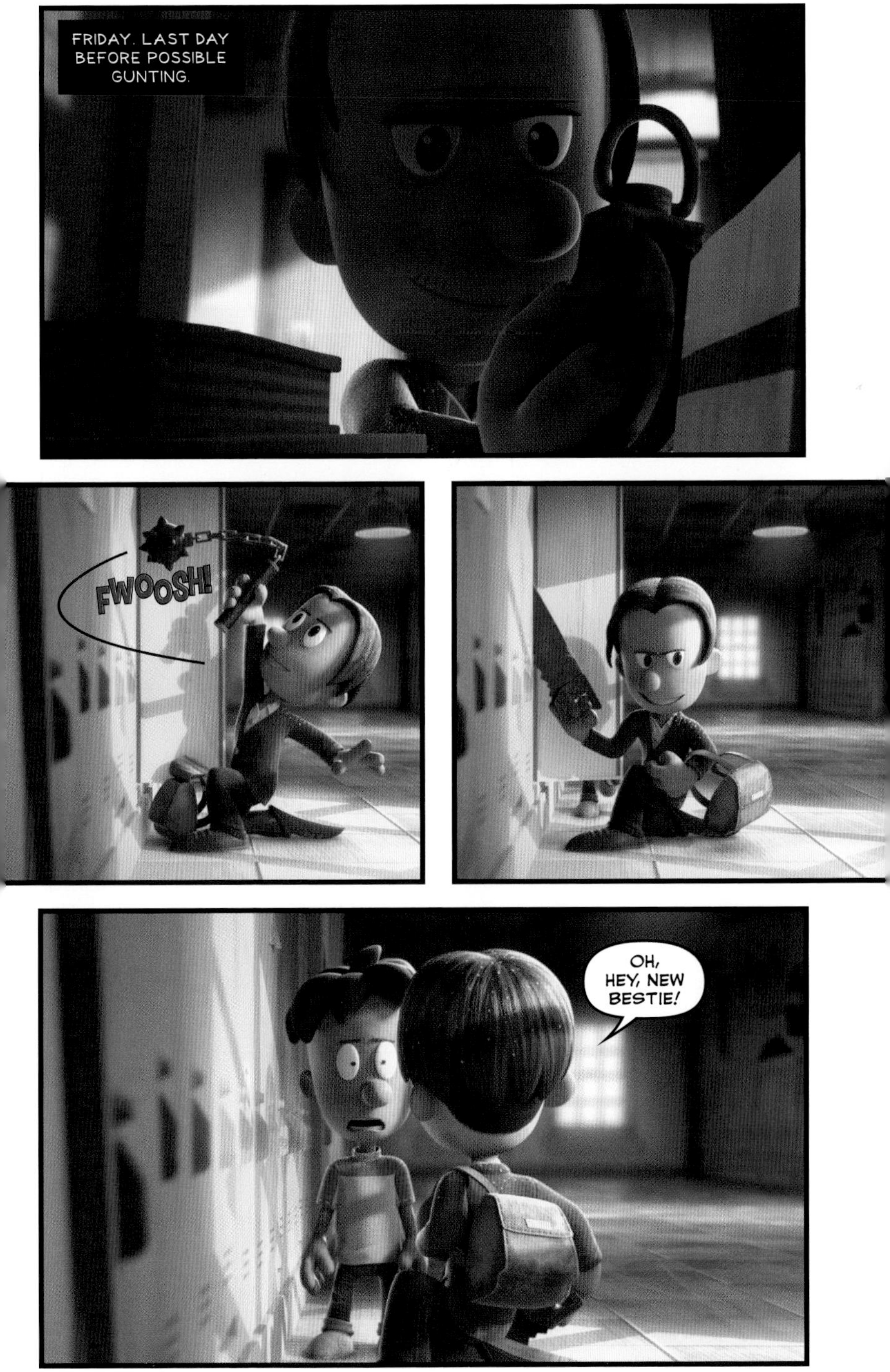
FRIDAY. LAST DAY BEFORE POSSIBLE GUNTING.
FWOOSH!
OH, HEY, NEW BESTIE!

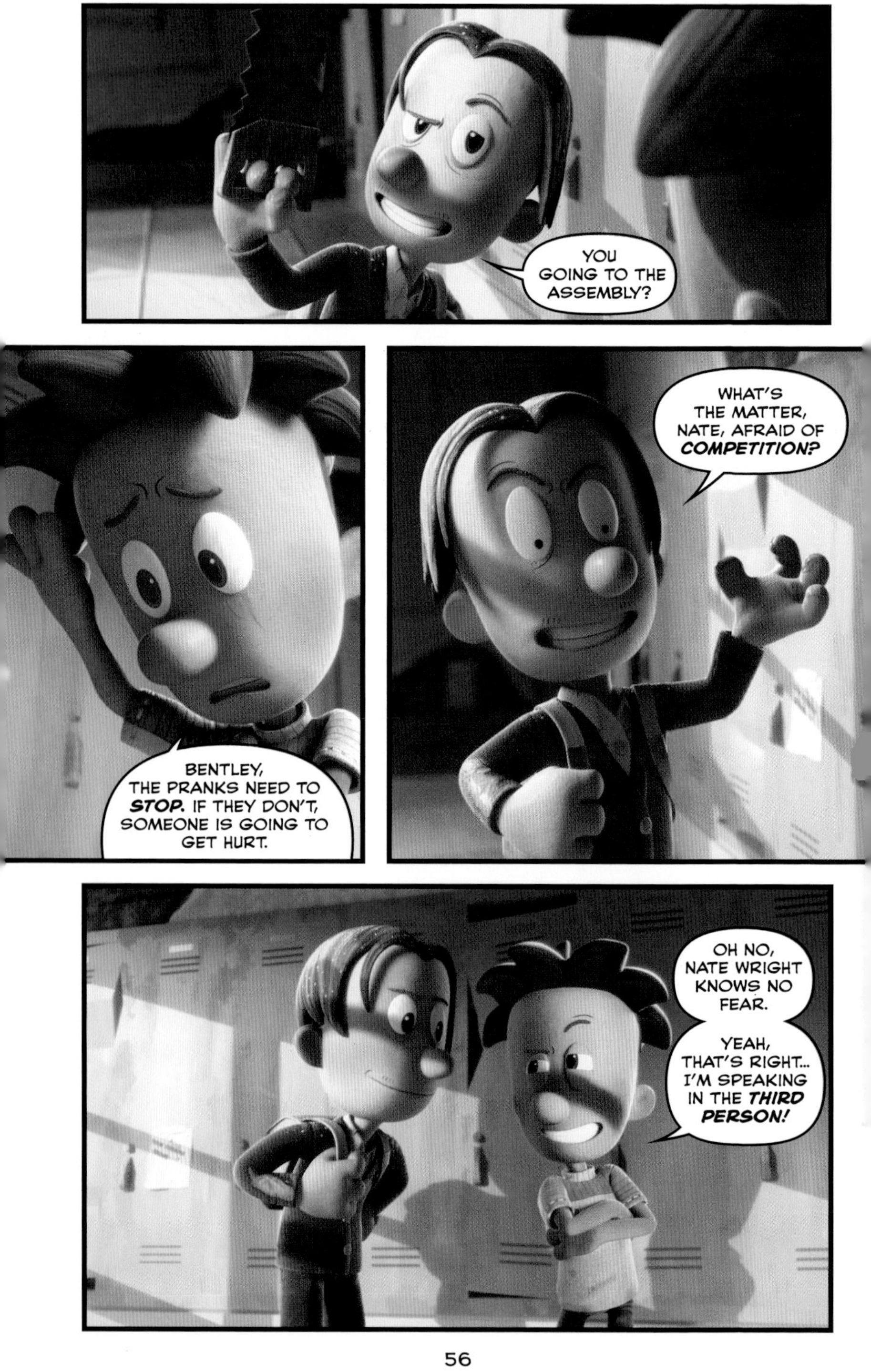
YOU GOING TO THE ASSEMBLY?
BENTLEY, THE PRANKS NEED TO ***STOP.*** IF THEY DON'T, SOMEONE IS GOING TO GET HURT.
WHAT'S THE MATTER, NATE, AFRAID OF ***COMPETITION?***
OH NO, NATE WRIGHT KNOWS NO FEAR.
YEAH, THAT'S RIGHT... I'M SPEAKING IN THE ***THIRD PERSON!***

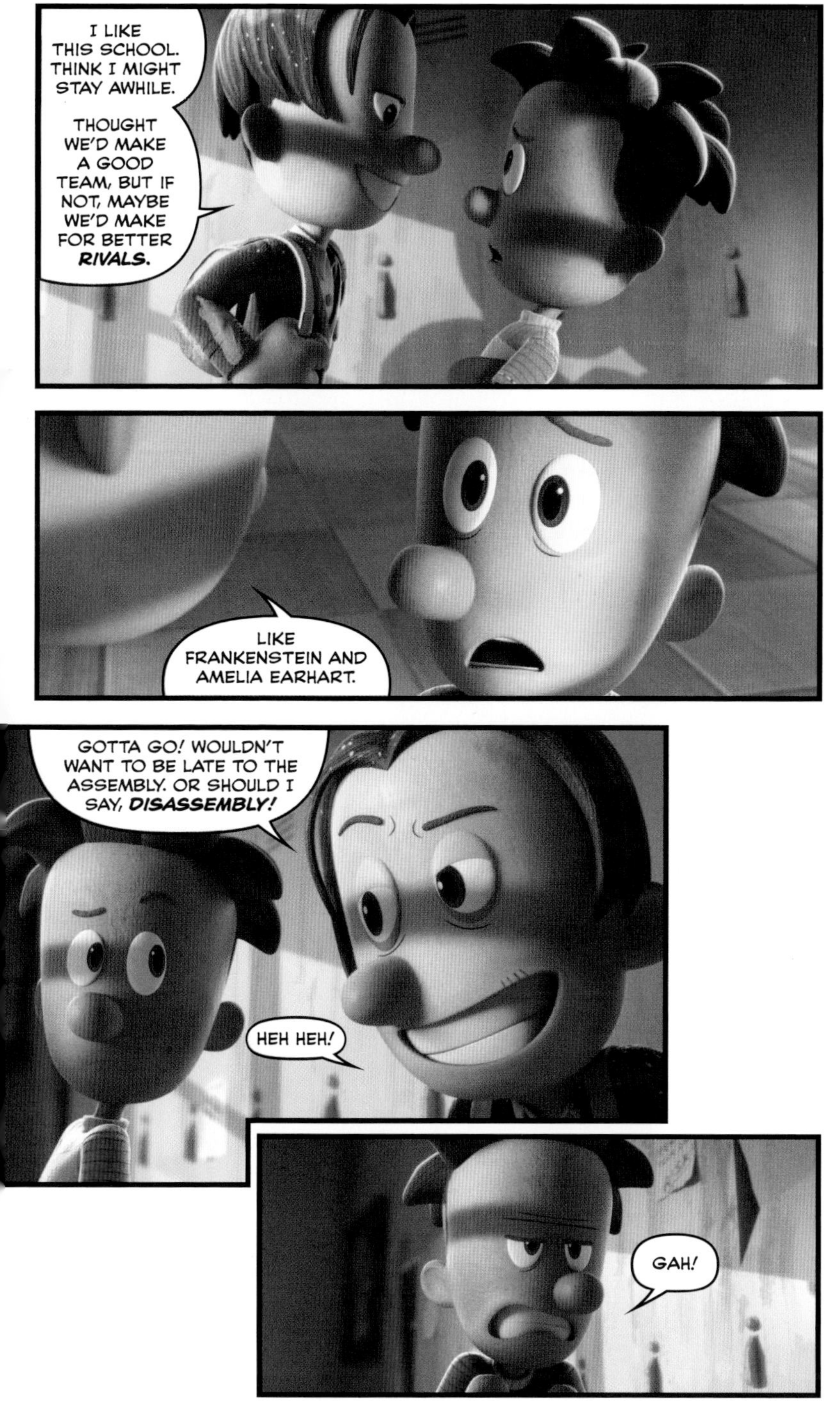
I LIKE THIS SCHOOL. THINK I MIGHT STAY AWHILE.
THOUGHT WE'D MAKE A GOOD TEAM, BUT IF NOT, MAYBE WE'D MAKE FOR BETTER *RIVALS.*
LIKE FRANKENSTEIN AND AMELIA EARHART.
GOTTA GO! WOULDN'T WANT TO BE LATE TO THE ASSEMBLY. OR SHOULD I SAY, *DISASSEMBLY!*
HEH HEH!
GAH!

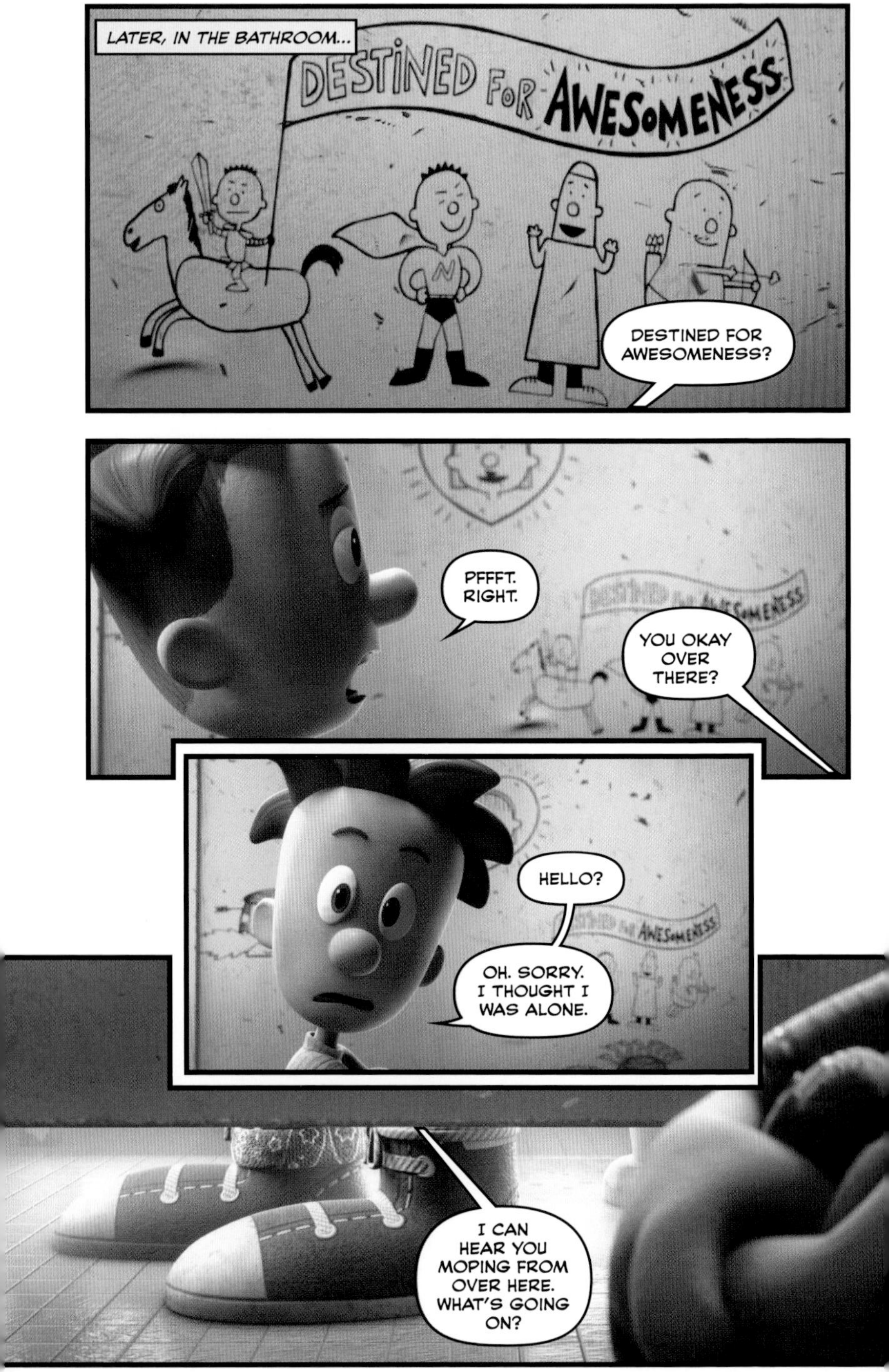
LATER, IN THE BATHROOM...
DESTINED FOR AWESOMENESS
DESTINED FOR AWESOMENESS?
PFFFT. RIGHT.
YOU OKAY OVER THERE?
HELLO?
OH. SORRY. I THOUGHT I WAS ALONE.
I CAN HEAR YOU MOPING FROM OVER HERE. WHAT'S GOING ON?

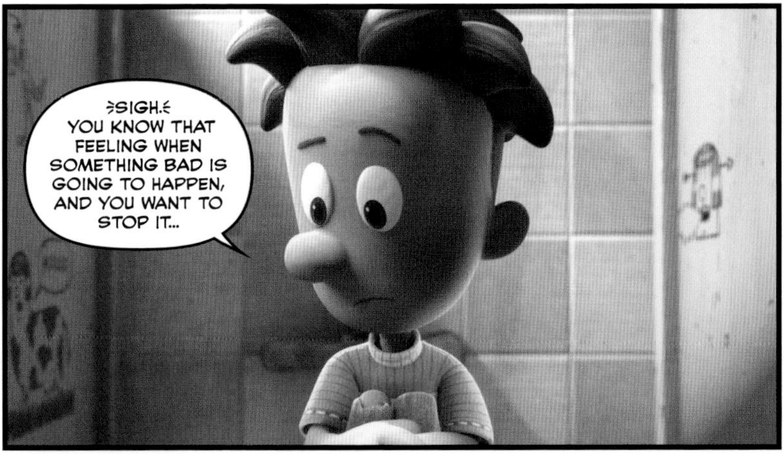
⋺SIGH.⋲ YOU KNOW THAT FEELING WHEN SOMETHING BAD IS GOING TO HAPPEN, AND YOU WANT TO STOP IT...

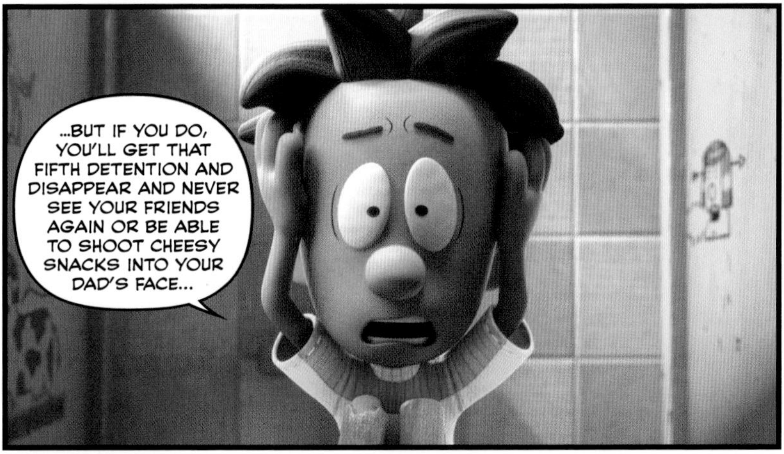
...BUT IF YOU DO, YOU'LL GET THAT FIFTH DETENTION AND DISAPPEAR AND NEVER SEE YOUR FRIENDS AGAIN OR BE ABLE TO SHOOT CHEESY SNACKS INTO YOUR DAD'S FACE...

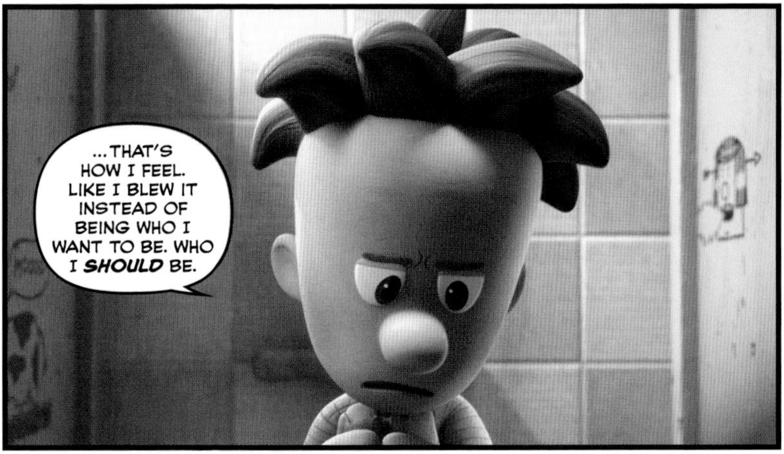
...THAT'S HOW I FEEL. LIKE I BLEW IT INSTEAD OF BEING WHO I WANT TO BE. WHO I ***SHOULD*** BE.

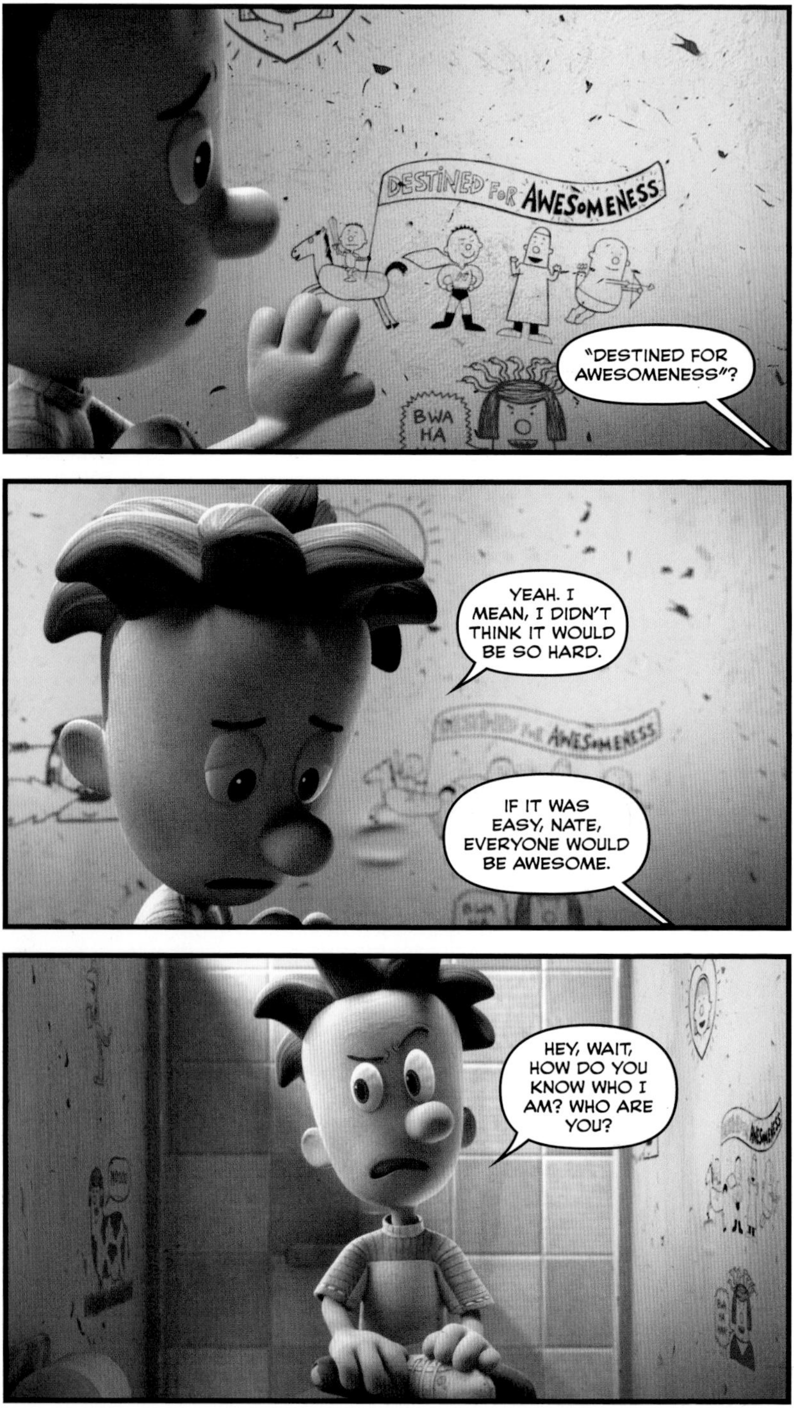
DESTINED FOR AWESOMENESS
BWA HA
"DESTINED FOR AWESOMENESS"?
YEAH. I MEAN, I DIDN'T THINK IT WOULD BE SO HARD.
IF IT WAS EASY, NATE, EVERYONE WOULD BE AWESOME.
HEY, WAIT, HOW DO YOU KNOW WHO I AM? WHO ARE YOU?

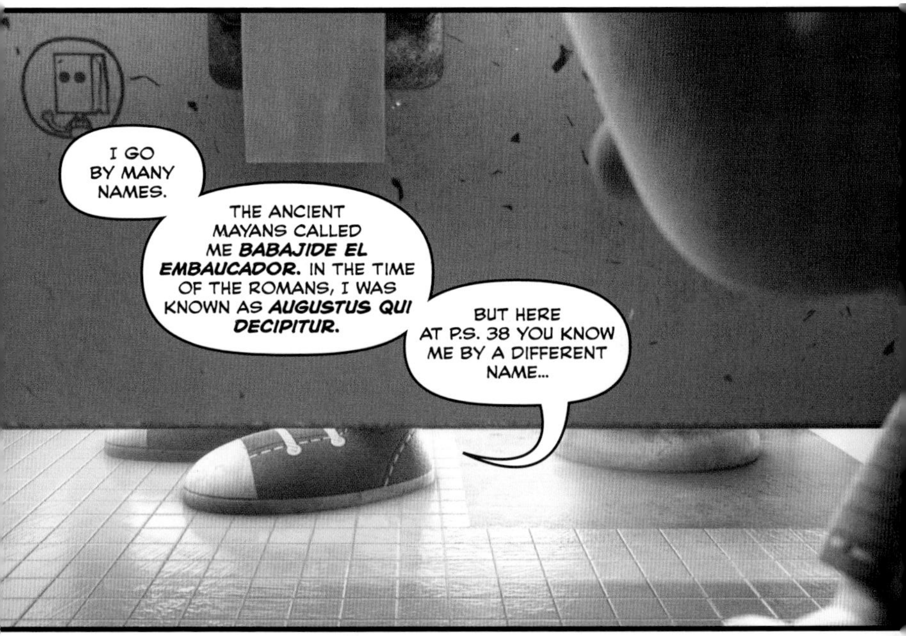
I GO BY MANY NAMES.
THE ANCIENT MAYANS CALLED ME **BABAJIDE EL EMBAUCADOR.** IN THE TIME OF THE ROMANS, I WAS KNOWN AS **AUGUSTUS QUI DECIPITUR.**
BUT HERE AT P.S. 38 YOU KNOW ME BY A DIFFERENT NAME...

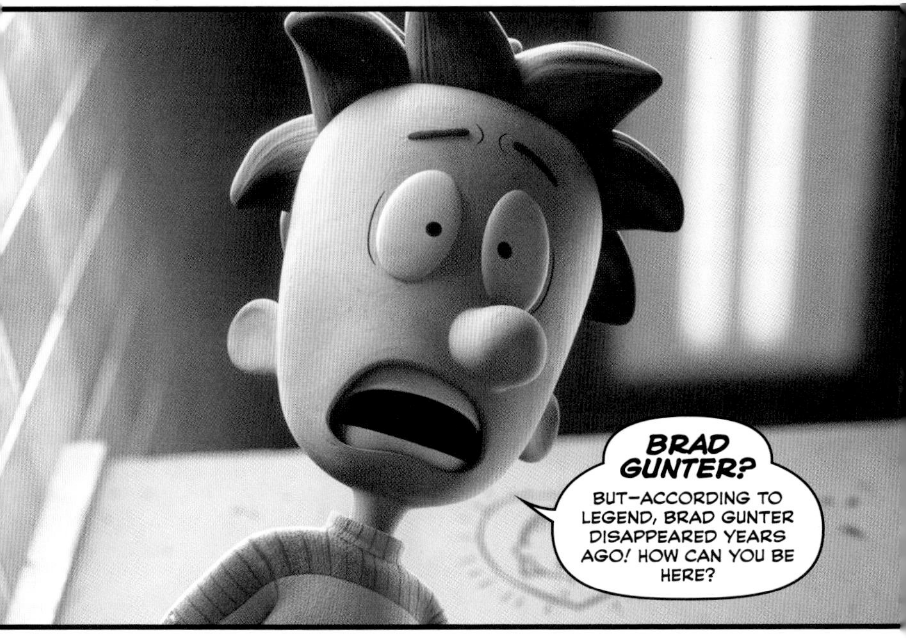
BRAD GUNTER?
BUT–ACCORDING TO LEGEND, BRAD GUNTER DISAPPEARED YEARS AGO! HOW CAN YOU BE HERE?

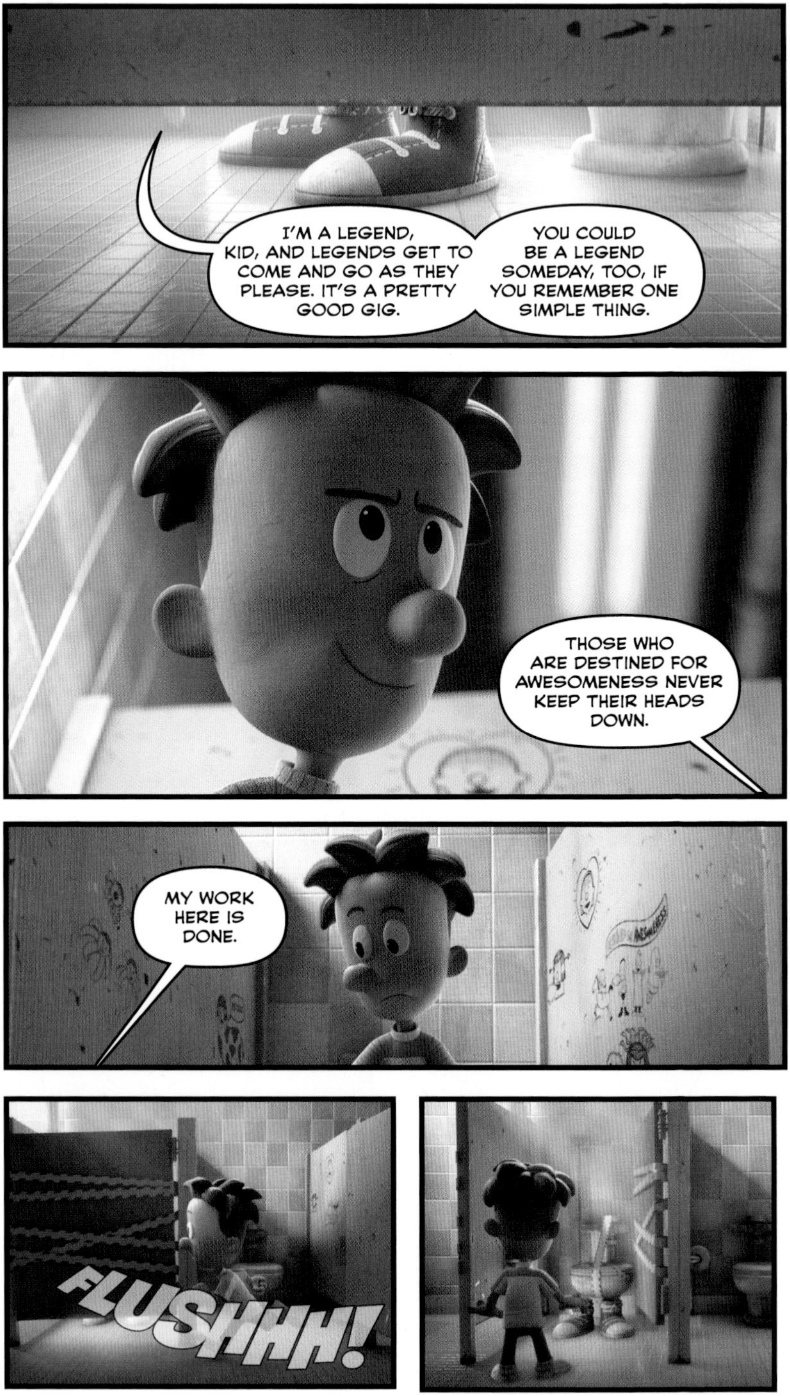
I'M A LEGEND, KID, AND LEGENDS GET TO COME AND GO AS THEY PLEASE. IT'S A PRETTY GOOD GIG.
YOU COULD BE A LEGEND SOMEDAY, TOO, IF YOU REMEMBER ONE SIMPLE THING.
THOSE WHO ARE DESTINED FOR AWESOMENESS NEVER KEEP THEIR HEADS DOWN.
MY WORK HERE IS DONE.
FLUSHHH!

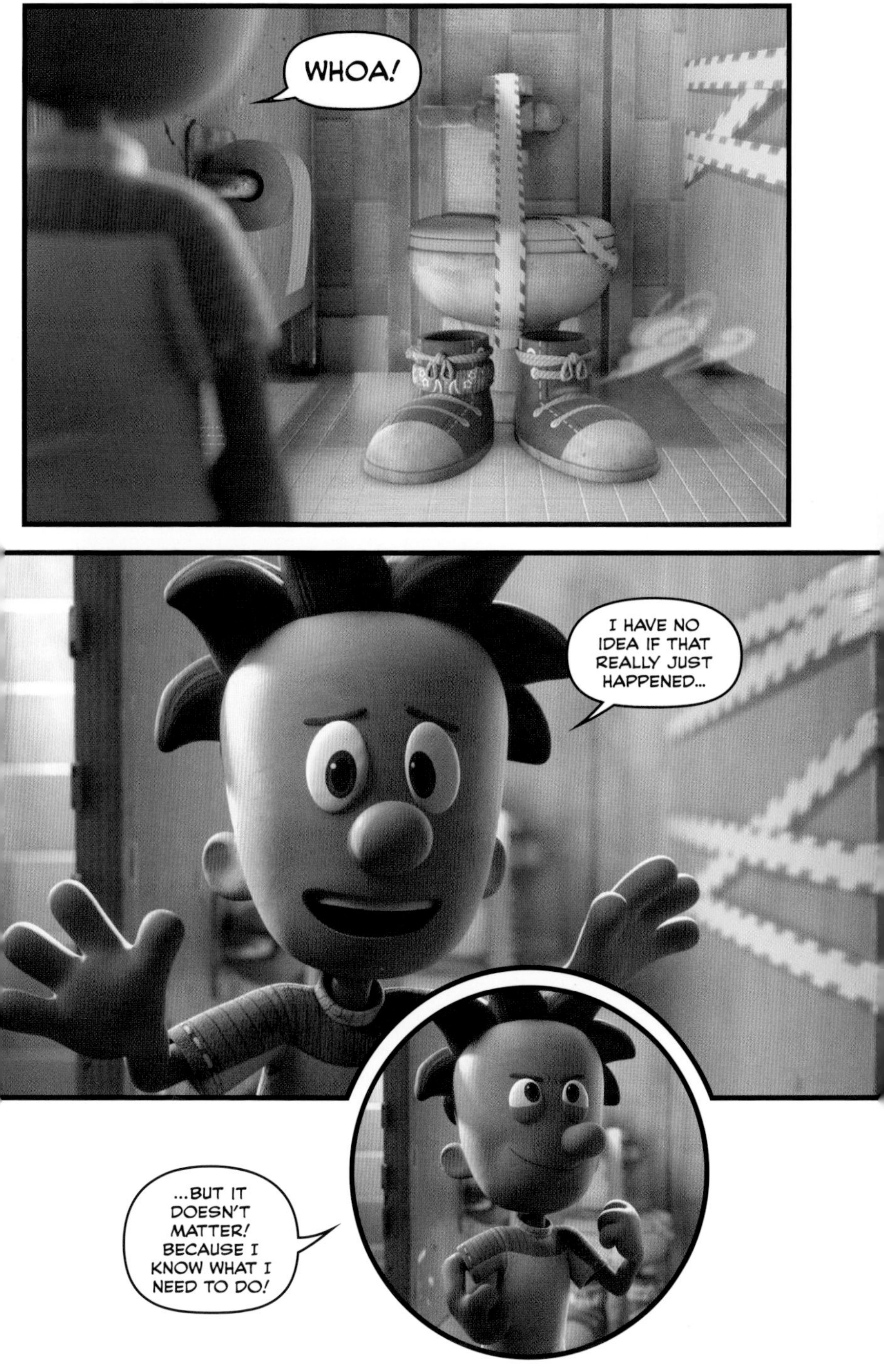
WHOA!
I HAVE NO IDEA IF THAT REALLY JUST HAPPENED...
...BUT IT DOESN'T MATTER! BECAUSE I KNOW WHAT I NEED TO DO!

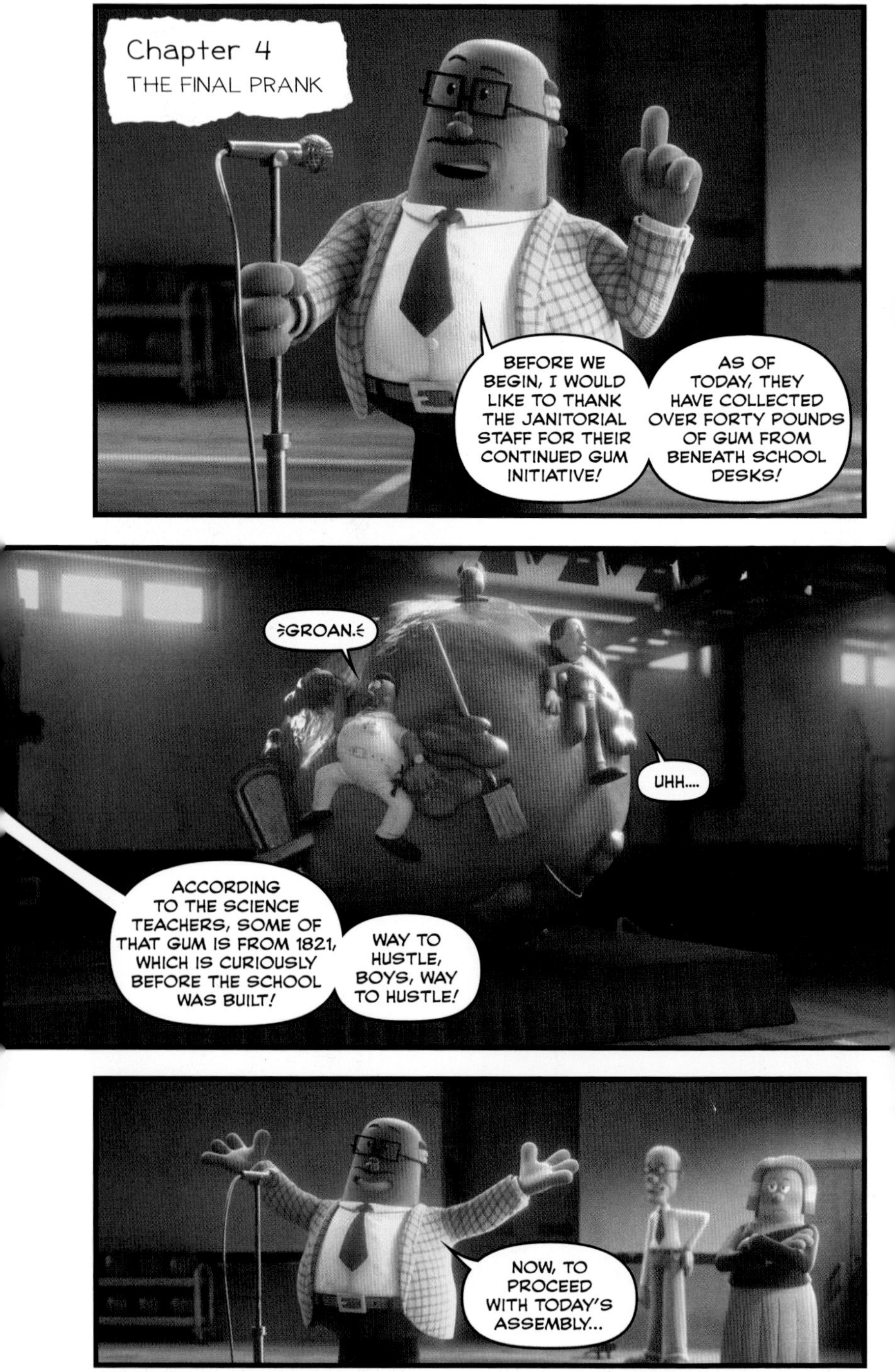
Chapter 4
THE FINAL PRANK
BEFORE WE BEGIN, I WOULD LIKE TO THANK THE JANITORIAL STAFF FOR THEIR CONTINUED GUM INITIATIVE!
AS OF TODAY, THEY HAVE COLLECTED OVER FORTY POUNDS OF GUM FROM BENEATH SCHOOL DESKS!
GROAN.
UHH....
ACCORDING TO THE SCIENCE TEACHERS, SOME OF THAT GUM IS FROM 1821, WHICH IS CURIOUSLY BEFORE THE SCHOOL WAS BUILT!
WAY TO HUSTLE, BOYS, WAY TO HUSTLE!
NOW, TO PROCEED WITH TODAY'S ASSEMBLY...

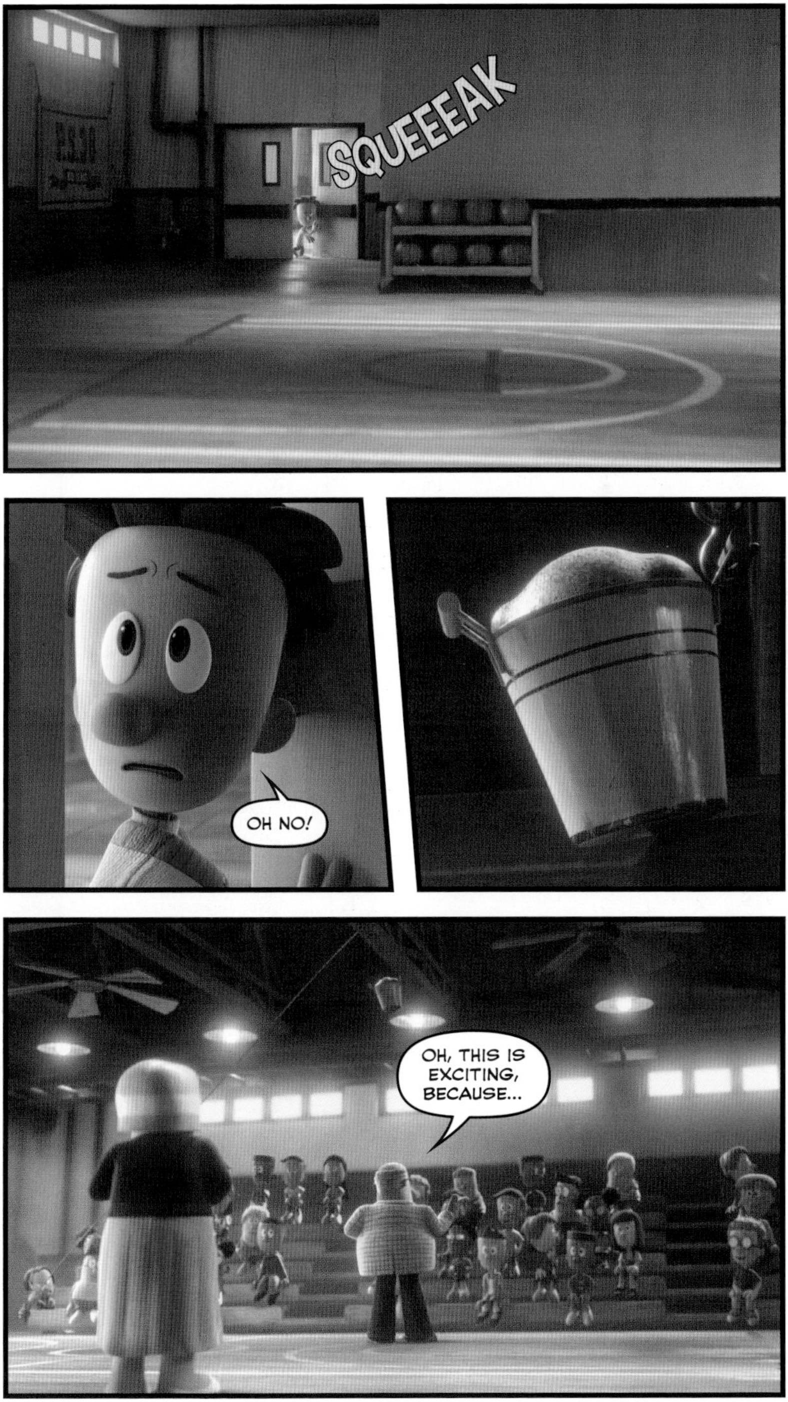
SQUEEEAK
OH NO!
OH, THIS IS EXCITING, BECAUSE...

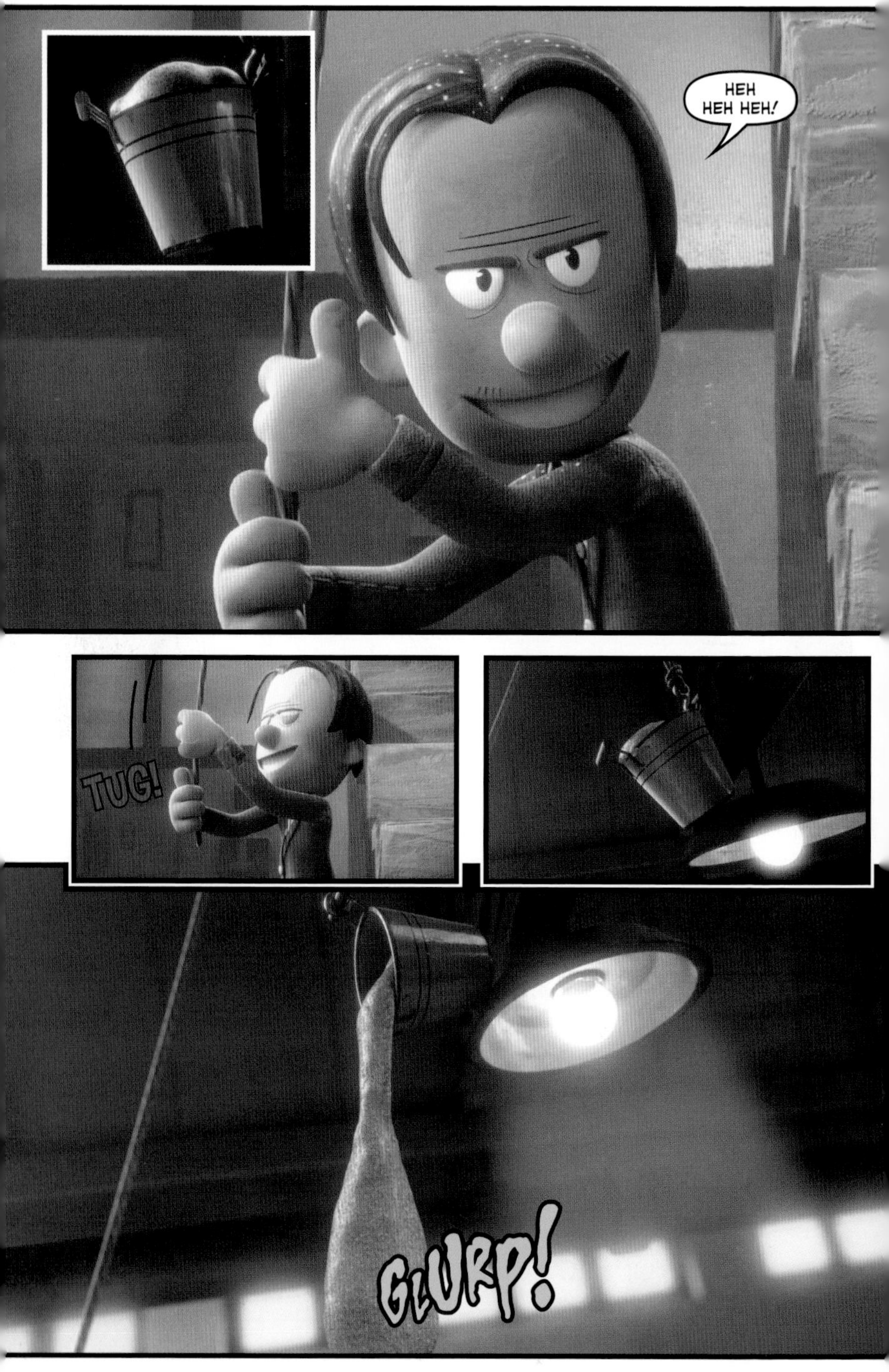
HEH
HEH HEH!
TUG!
GLURP!

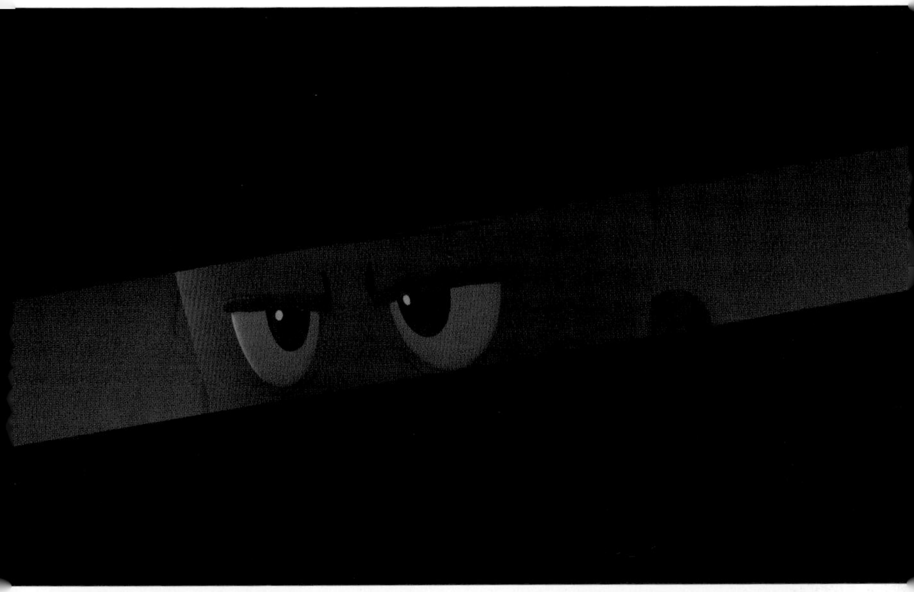

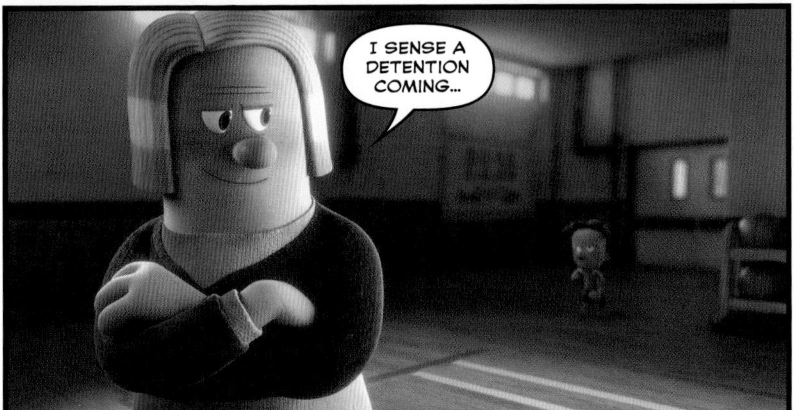
I SENSE A DETENTION COMING...

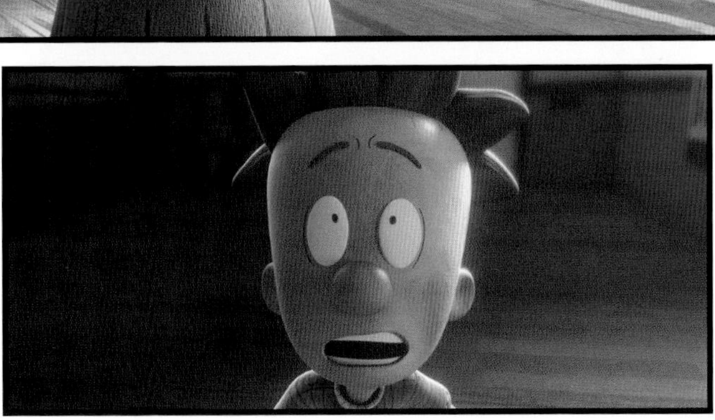

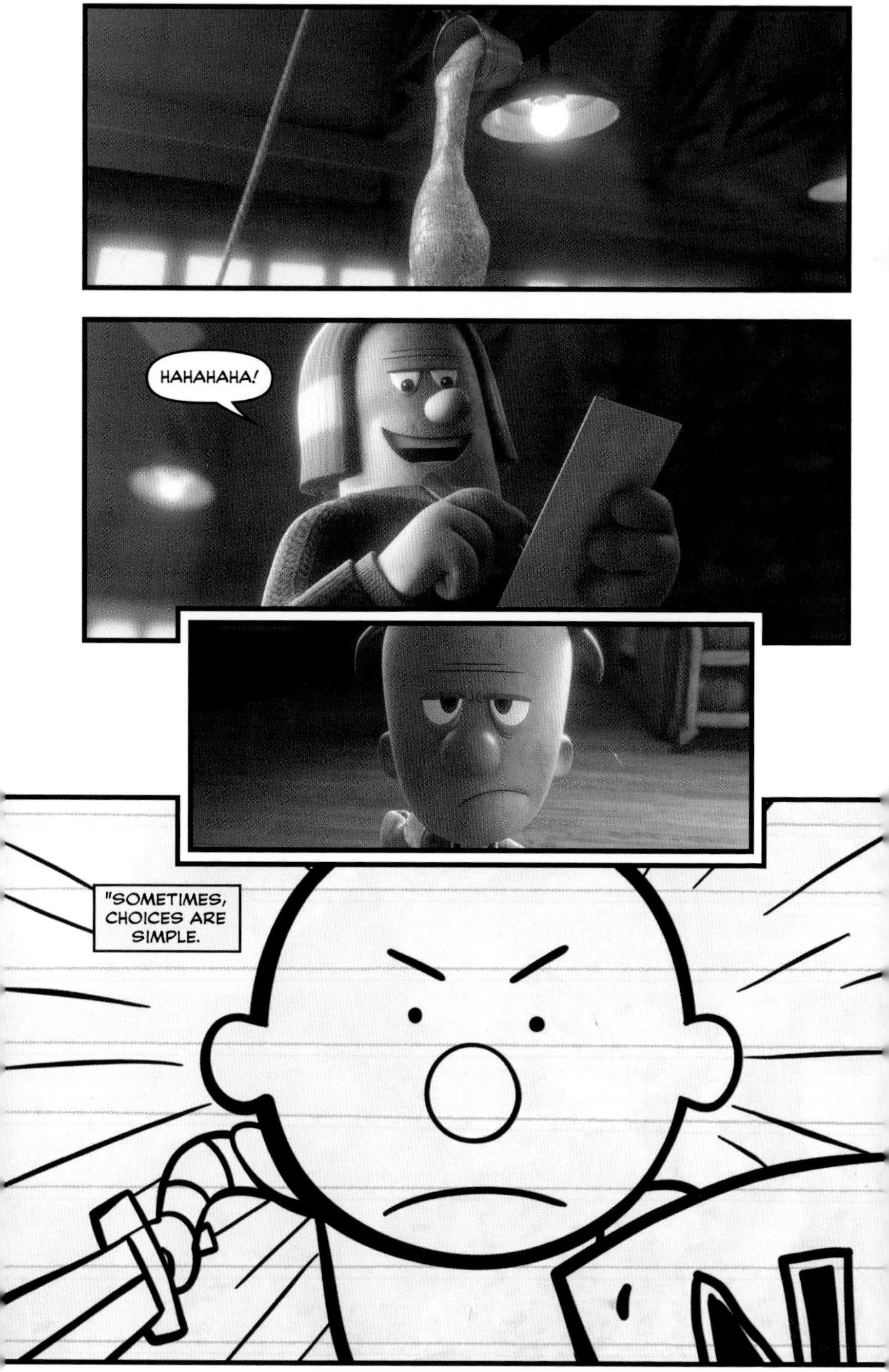

HAHAHAHA!
"SOMETIMES, CHOICES ARE SIMPLE.

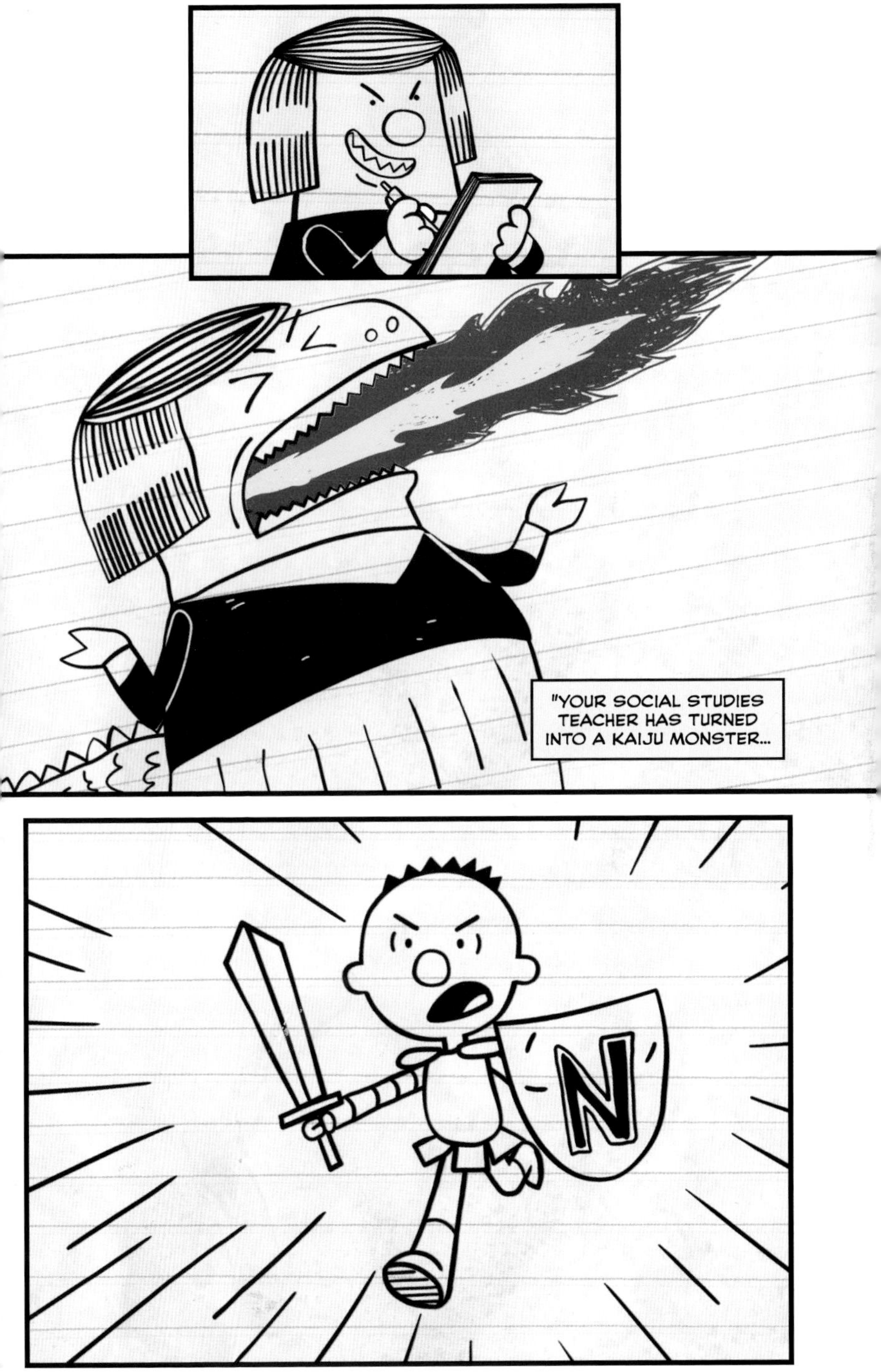
"YOUR SOCIAL STUDIES TEACHER HAS TURNED INTO A KAIJU MONSTER...
N

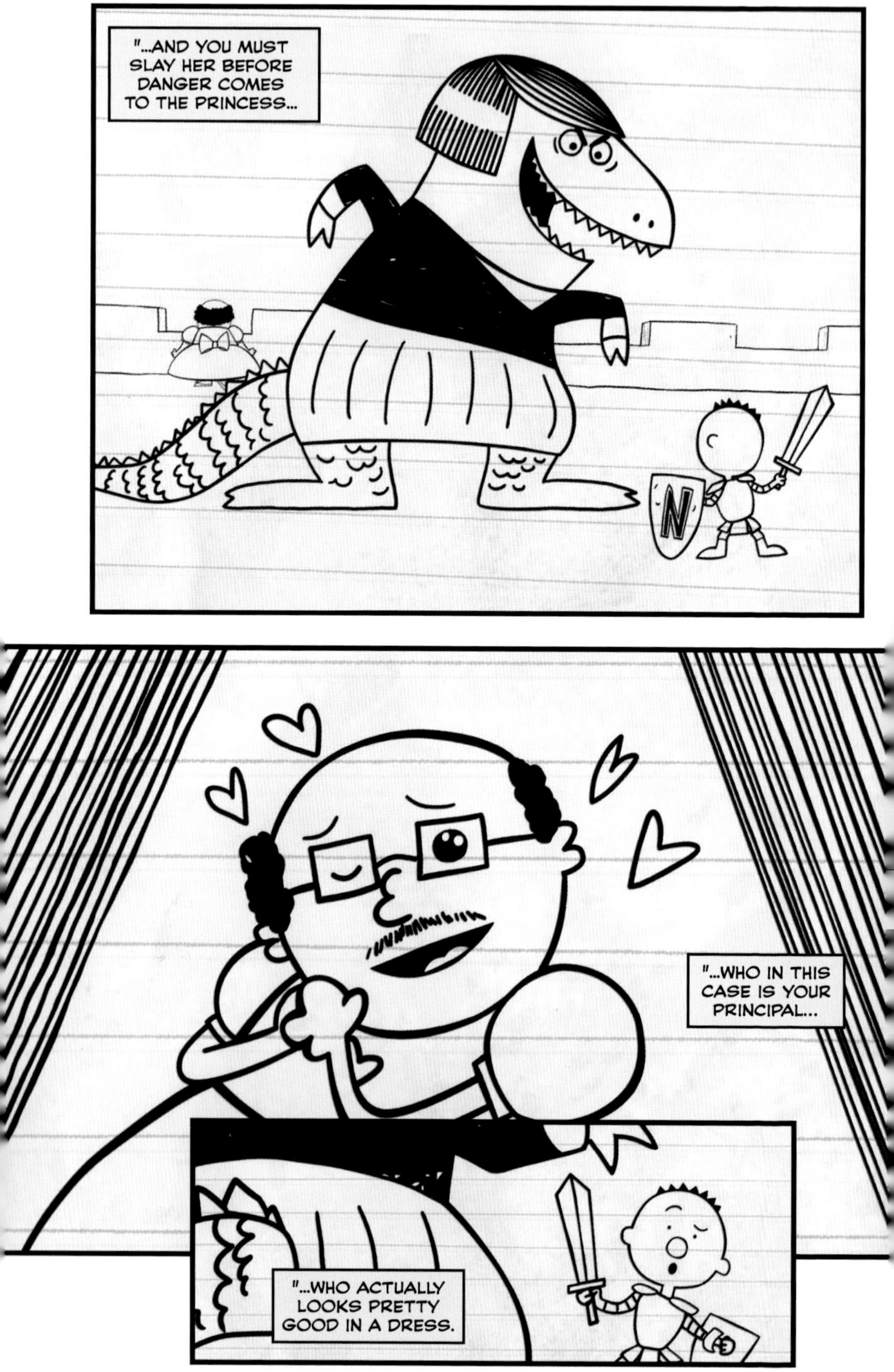
"...AND YOU MUST SLAY HER BEFORE DANGER COMES TO THE PRINCESS...
N
"...WHO IN THIS CASE IS YOUR PRINCIPAL...
"...WHO ACTUALLY LOOKS PRETTY GOOD IN A DRESS.

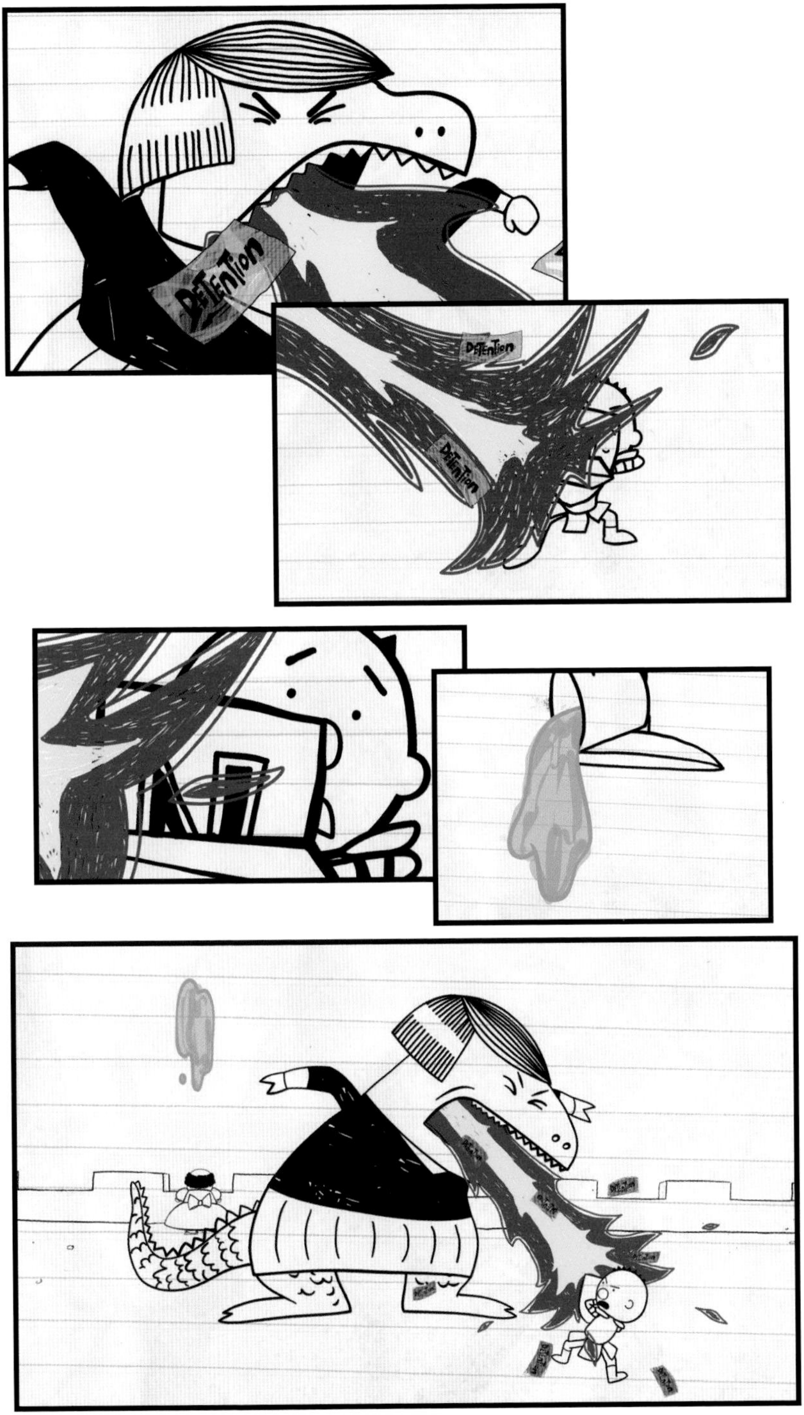
DETENTION
DETENTION
DETENTION

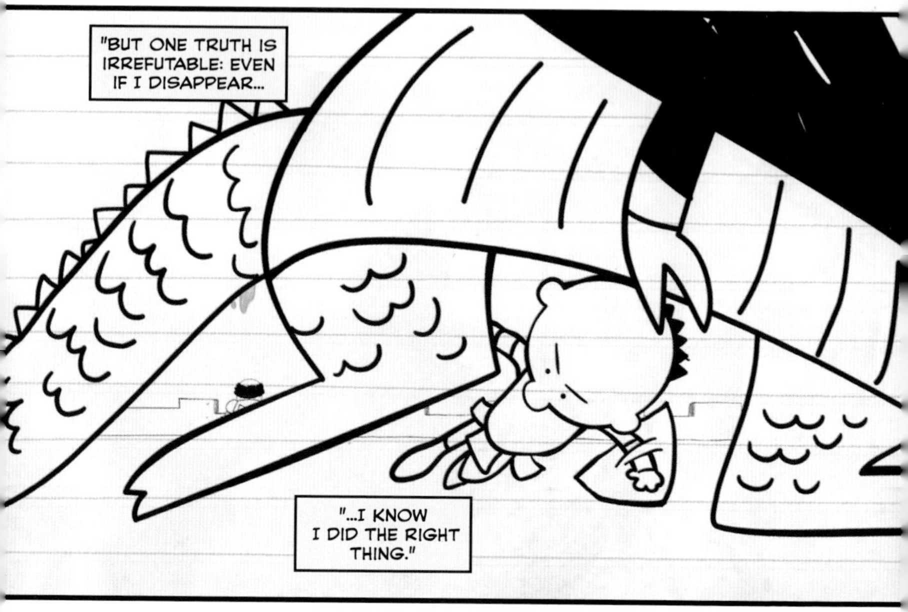
"BUT ONE TRUTH IS IRREFUTABLE: EVEN IF I DISAPPEAR...
"...I KNOW I DID THE RIGHT THING."

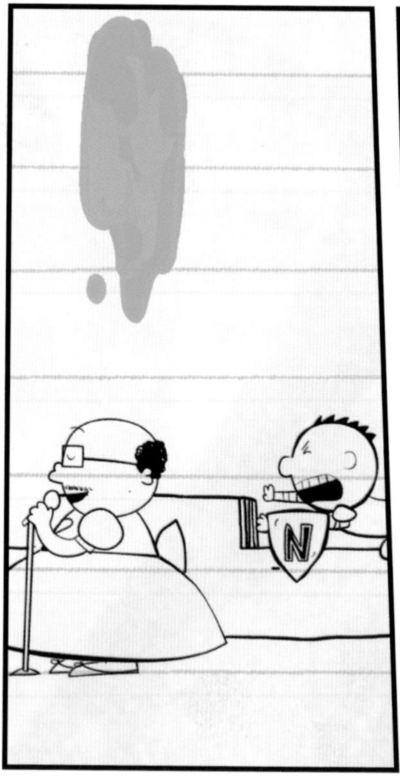

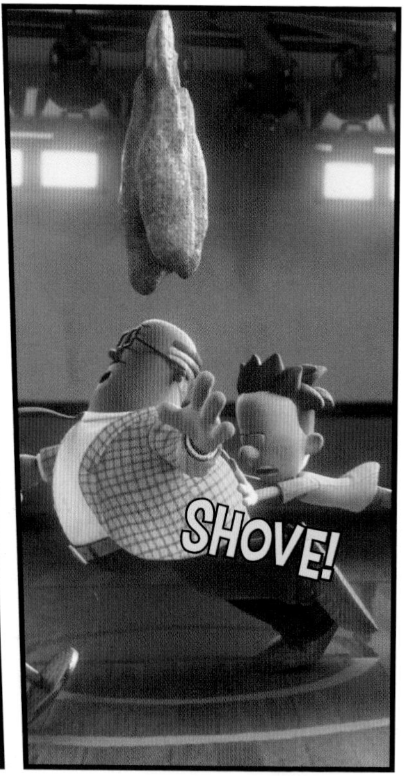
SHOVE!

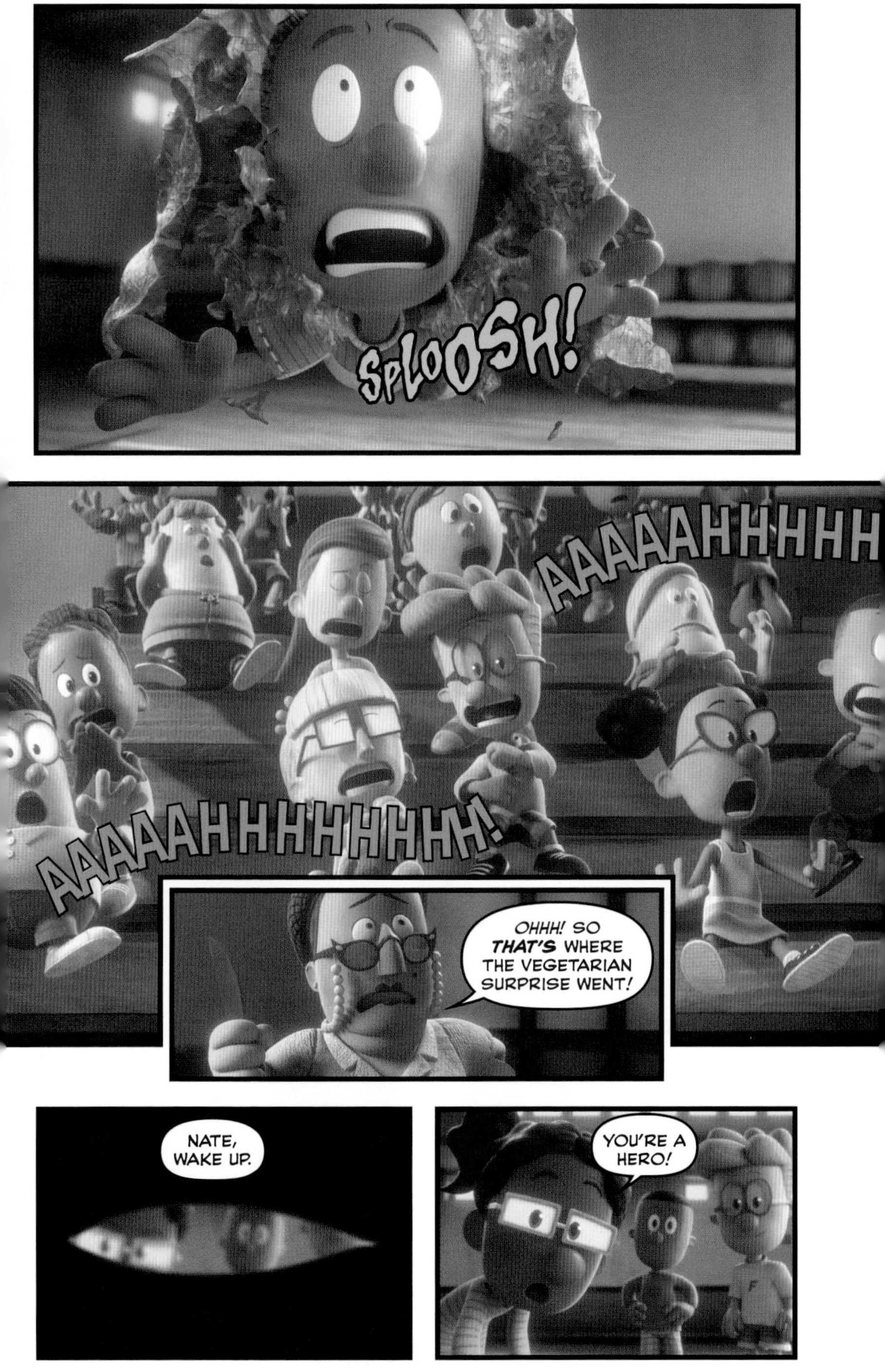
SPLOOSH!
AAAAAHHHHH
AAAAAHHHHHHHH!
OHHH! SO ***THAT'S*** WHERE THE VEGETARIAN SURPRISE WENT!
NATE, WAKE UP.
YOU'RE A HERO!

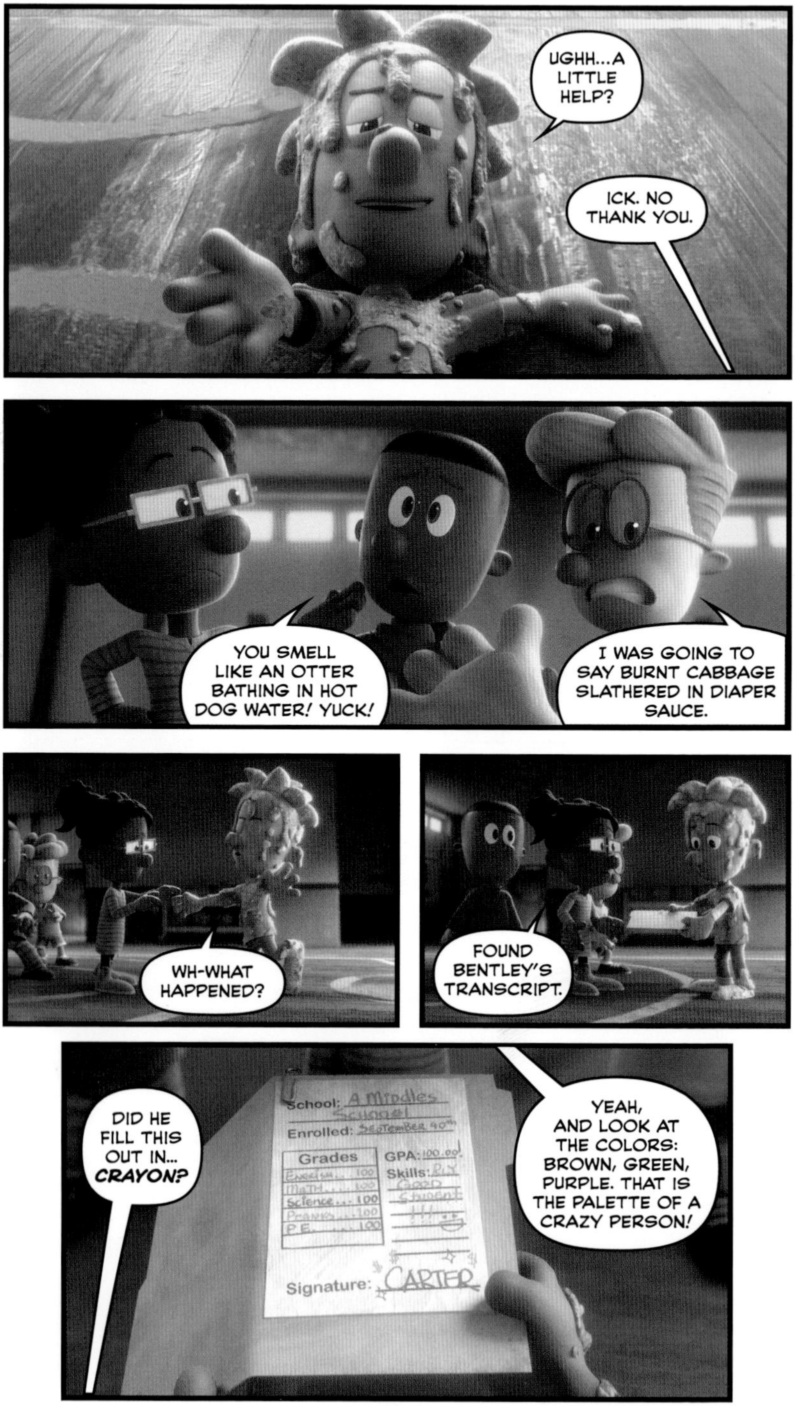
UGHH...A LITTLE HELP?
ICK. NO THANK YOU.
YOU SMELL LIKE AN OTTER BATHING IN HOT DOG WATER! YUCK!
I WAS GOING TO SAY BURNT CABBAGE SLATHERED IN DIAPER SAUCE.
WH-WHAT HAPPENED?
FOUND BENTLEY'S TRANSCRIPT.
School:
Enrolled:
Grades
GPA:
Skills:
Signature: CARTER
DID HE FILL THIS OUT IN... ***CRAYON?***
YEAH, AND LOOK AT THE COLORS: BROWN, GREEN, PURPLE. THAT IS THE PALETTE OF A CRAZY PERSON!

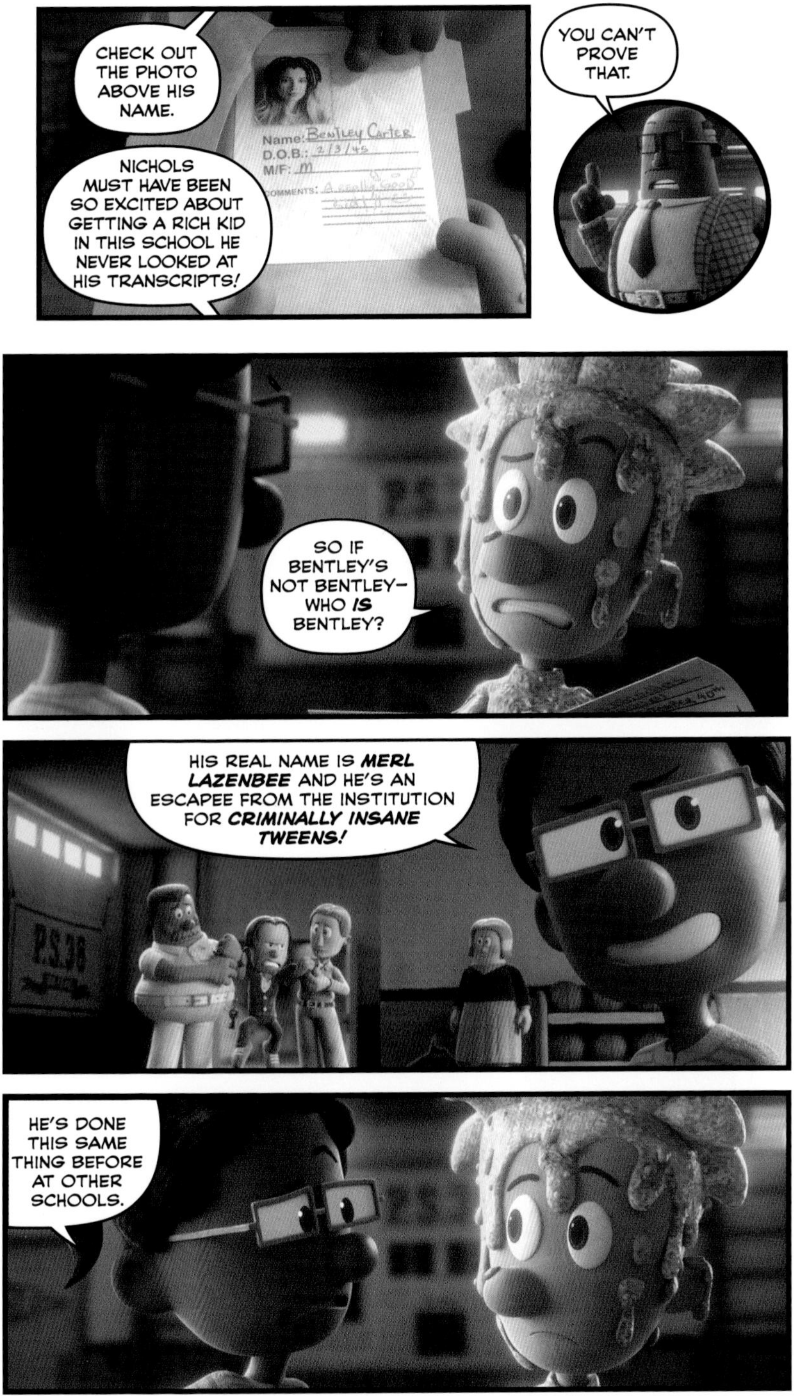
CHECK OUT THE PHOTO ABOVE HIS NAME.
NICHOLS MUST HAVE BEEN SO EXCITED ABOUT GETTING A RICH KID IN THIS SCHOOL HE NEVER LOOKED AT HIS TRANSCRIPTS!
Name: Bentley Carter
D.O.B.: 2/3/45
M/F: m
COMMENTS:
YOU CAN'T PROVE THAT.
SO IF BENTLEY'S NOT BENTLEY— WHO *IS* BENTLEY?
HIS REAL NAME IS ***MERL LAZENBEE*** AND HE'S AN ESCAPEE FROM THE INSTITUTION FOR ***CRIMINALLY INSANE TWEENS!***
HE'S DONE THIS SAME THING BEFORE AT OTHER SCHOOLS.

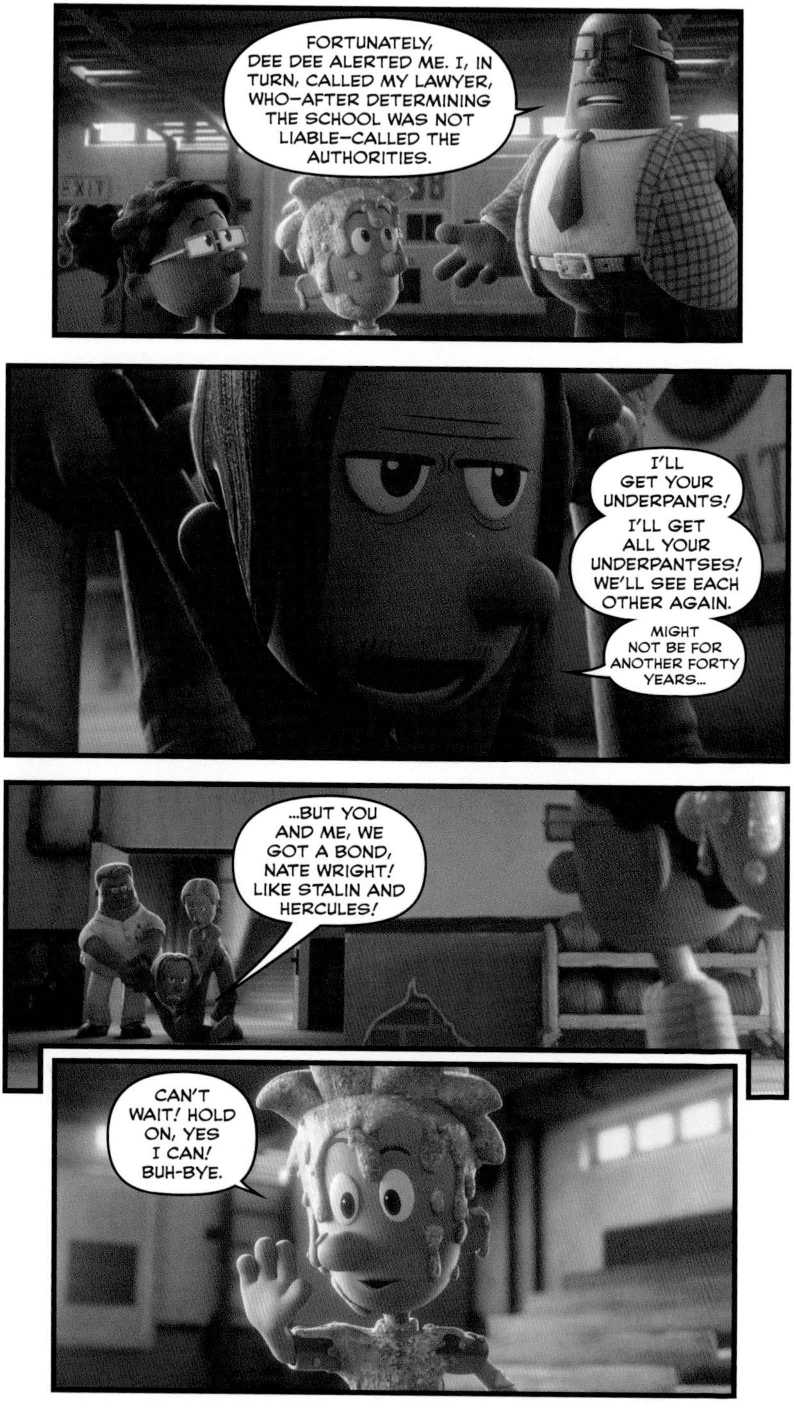
FORTUNATELY, DEE DEE ALERTED ME. I, IN TURN, CALLED MY LAWYER, WHO—AFTER DETERMINING THE SCHOOL WAS NOT LIABLE—CALLED THE AUTHORITIES.
I'LL GET YOUR UNDERPANTS!
I'LL GET ALL YOUR UNDERPANTSES! WE'LL SEE EACH OTHER AGAIN.
MIGHT NOT BE FOR ANOTHER FORTY YEARS...
...BUT YOU AND ME, WE GOT A BOND, NATE WRIGHT! LIKE STALIN AND HERCULES!
CAN'T WAIT! HOLD ON, YES I CAN! BUH-BYE.

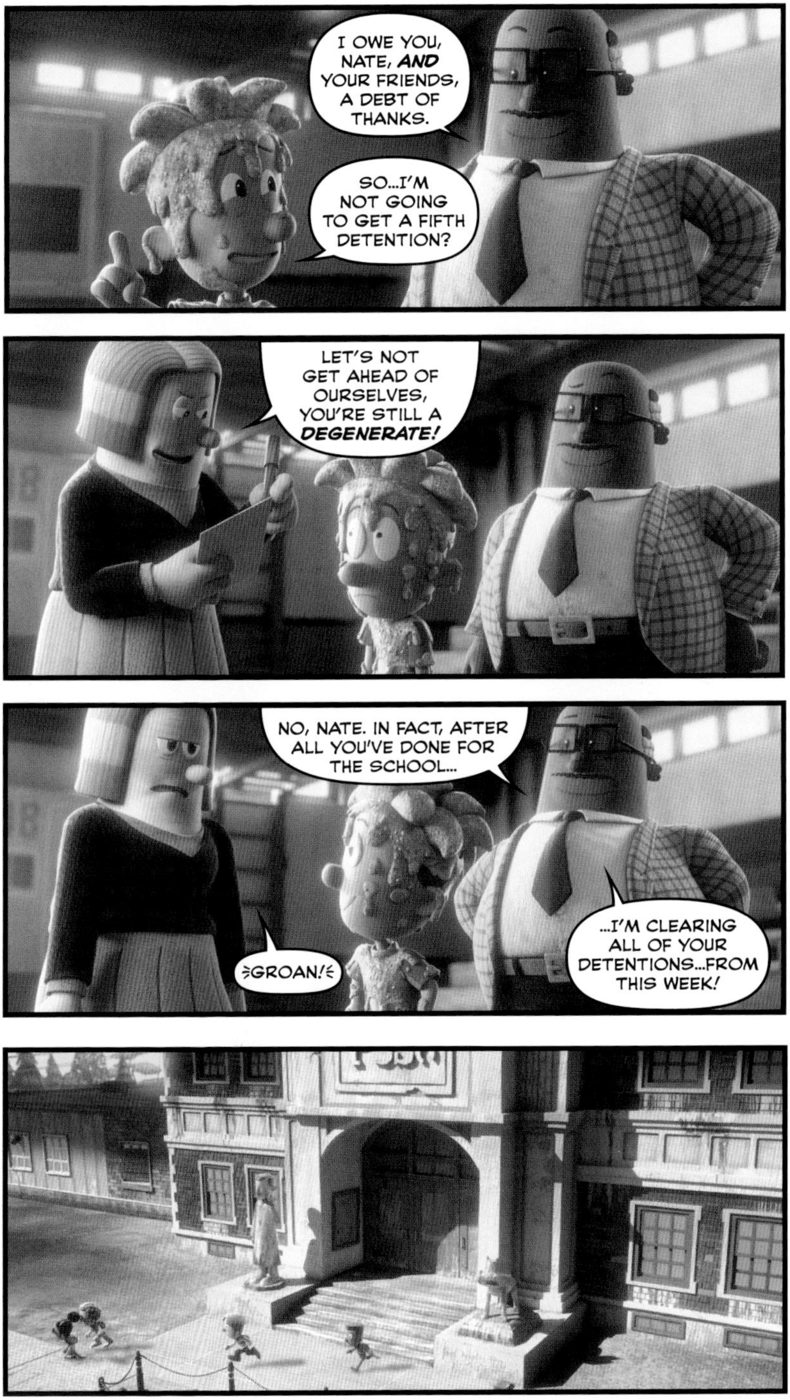

I OWE YOU, NATE, **AND** YOUR FRIENDS, A DEBT OF THANKS.
SO...I'M NOT GOING TO GET A FIFTH DETENTION?
LET'S NOT GET AHEAD OF OURSELVES, YOU'RE STILL A **DEGENERATE!**
NO, NATE. IN FACT, AFTER ALL YOU'VE DONE FOR THE SCHOOL...
...I'M CLEARING ALL OF YOUR DETENTIONS...FROM THIS WEEK!
GROAN!

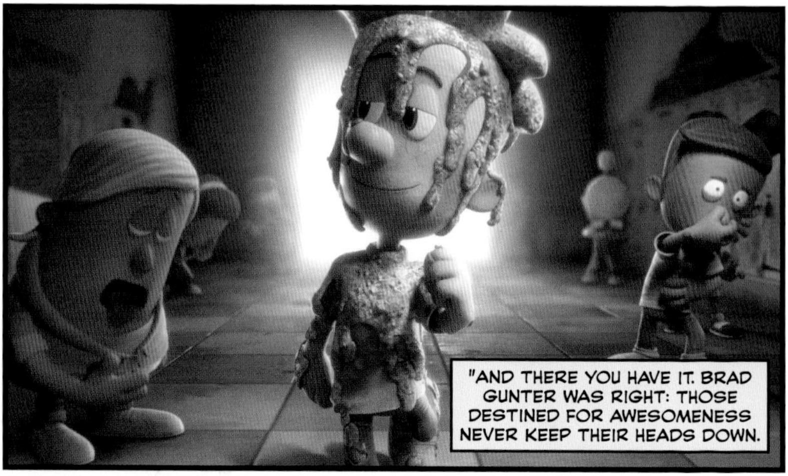
"AND THERE YOU HAVE IT. BRAD GUNTER WAS RIGHT: THOSE DESTINED FOR AWESOMENESS NEVER KEEP THEIR HEADS DOWN.

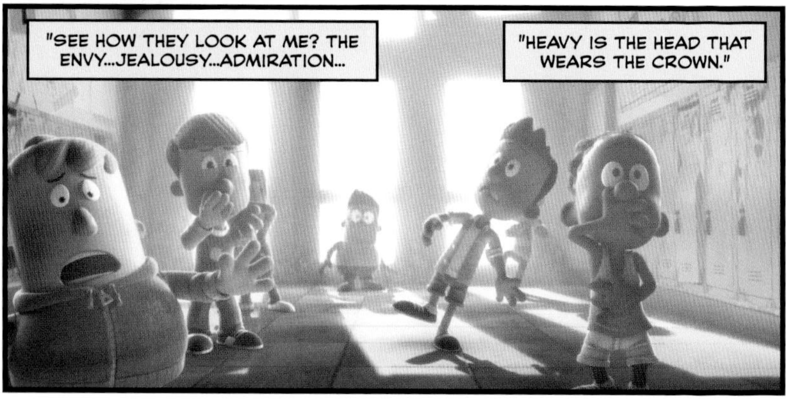
"SEE HOW THEY LOOK AT ME? THE ENVY...JEALOUSY...ADMIRATION...
"HEAVY IS THE HEAD THAT WEARS THE CROWN."

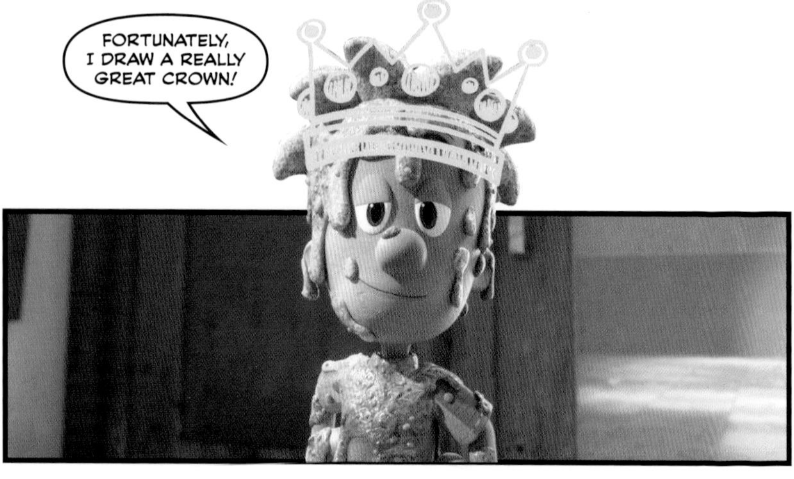
FORTUNATELY, I DRAW A REALLY GREAT CROWN!

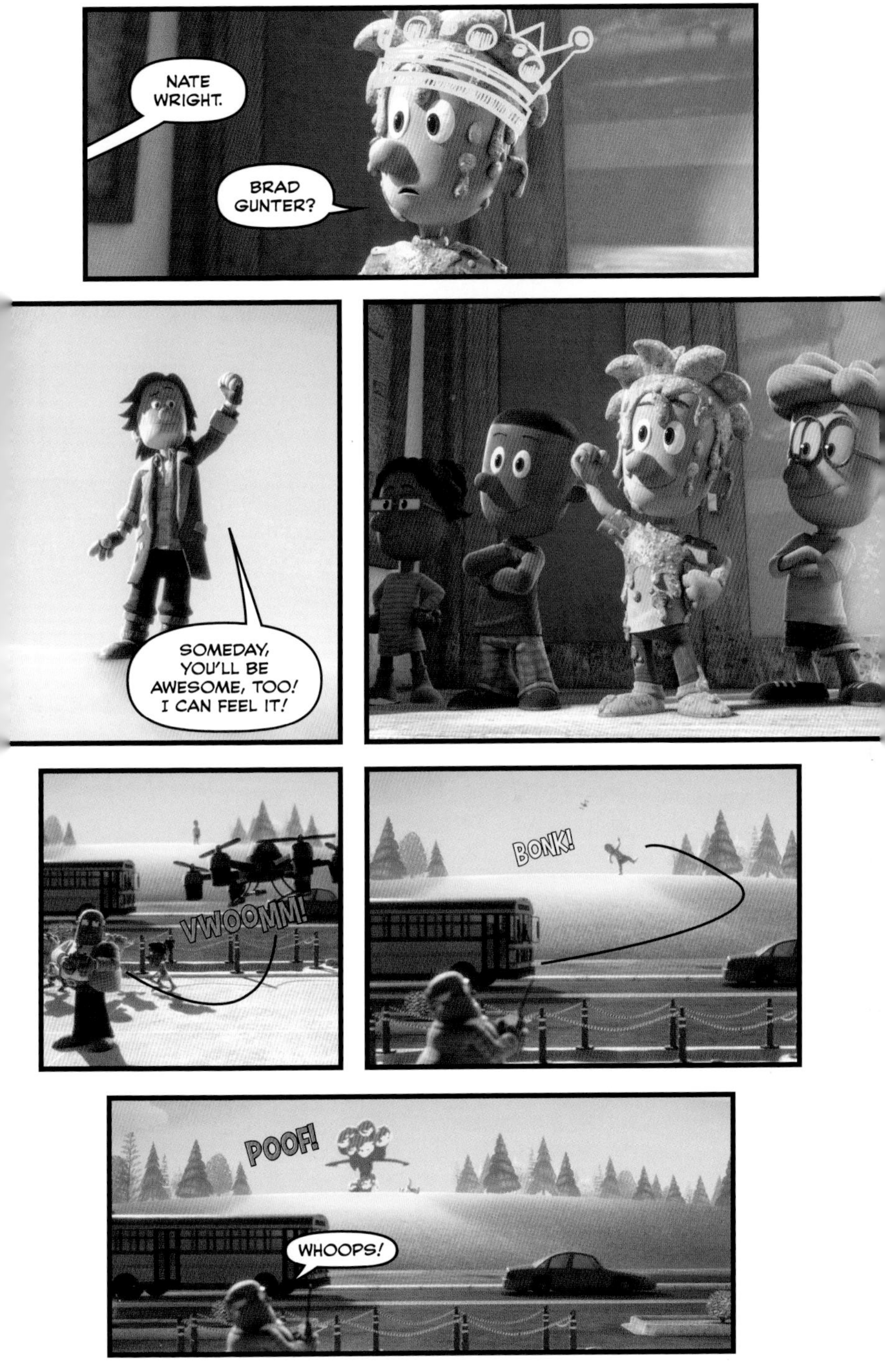
NATE WRIGHT.
BRAD GUNTER?
SOMEDAY, YOU'LL BE AWESOME, TOO! I CAN FEEL IT!
VWOOMM!
BONK!
POOF!
WHOOPS!

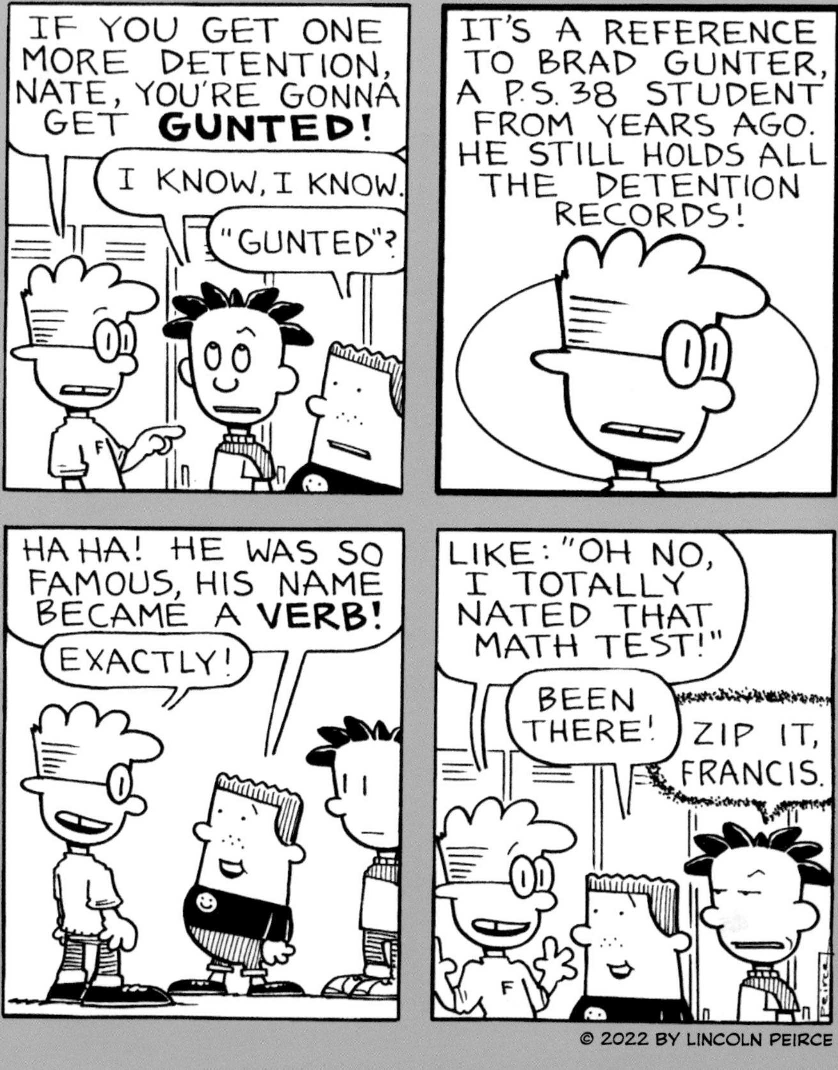
IF YOU GET ONE MORE DETENTION, NATE, YOU'RE GONNA GET **GUNTED!**
I KNOW, I KNOW.
"GUNTED"?
IT'S A REFERENCE TO BRAD GUNTER, A P.S. 38 STUDENT FROM YEARS AGO. HE STILL HOLDS ALL THE DETENTION RECORDS!
HA HA! HE WAS SO FAMOUS, HIS NAME BECAME A **VERB!**
EXACTLY!
LIKE: "OH NO, I TOTALLY NATED THAT MATH TEST!"
BEEN THERE!
ZIP IT, FRANCIS.
PEIRCE

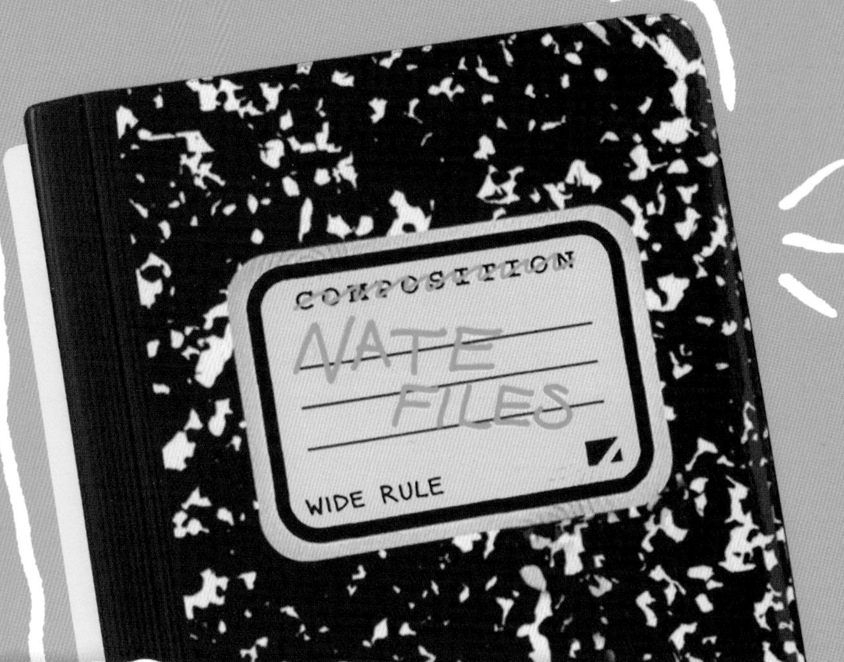
COMPOSITION
NATE FILES
WIDE RULE

Go Nate!
It's Your Birthday

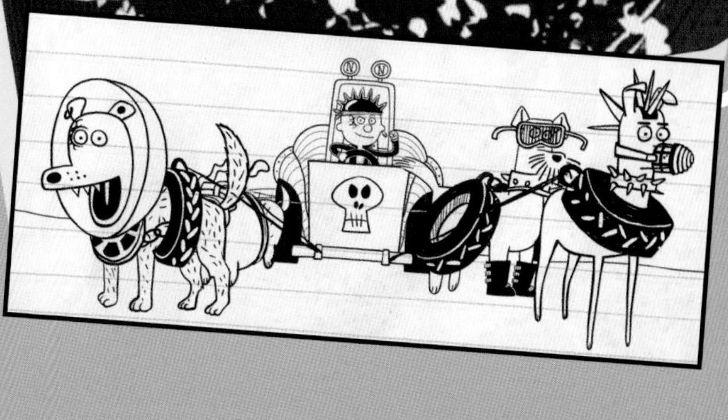

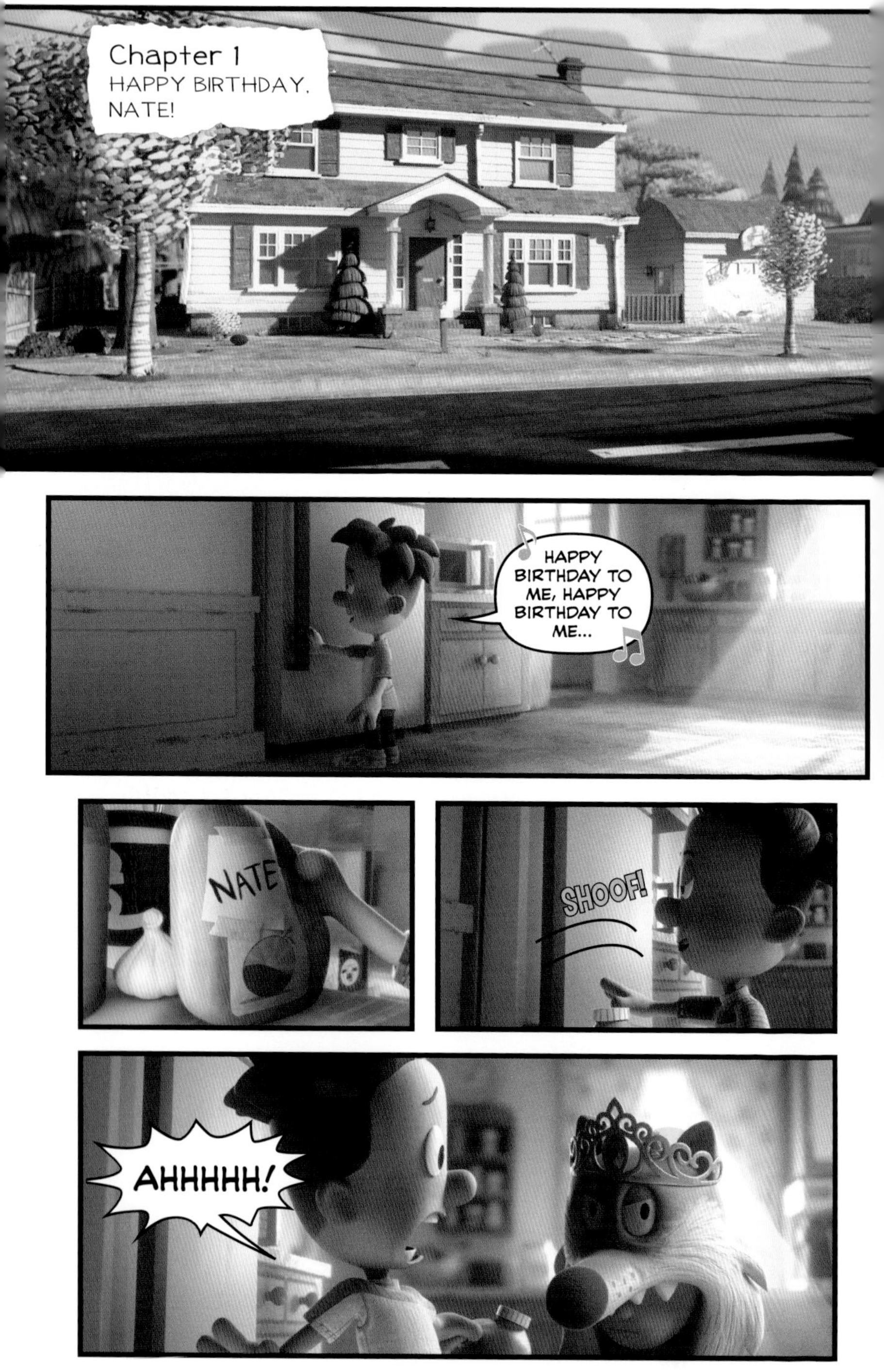
Chapter 1
HAPPY BIRTHDAY, NATE!
HAPPY BIRTHDAY TO ME, HAPPY BIRTHDAY TO ME...
NATE
SHOOF!
AHHHHH!

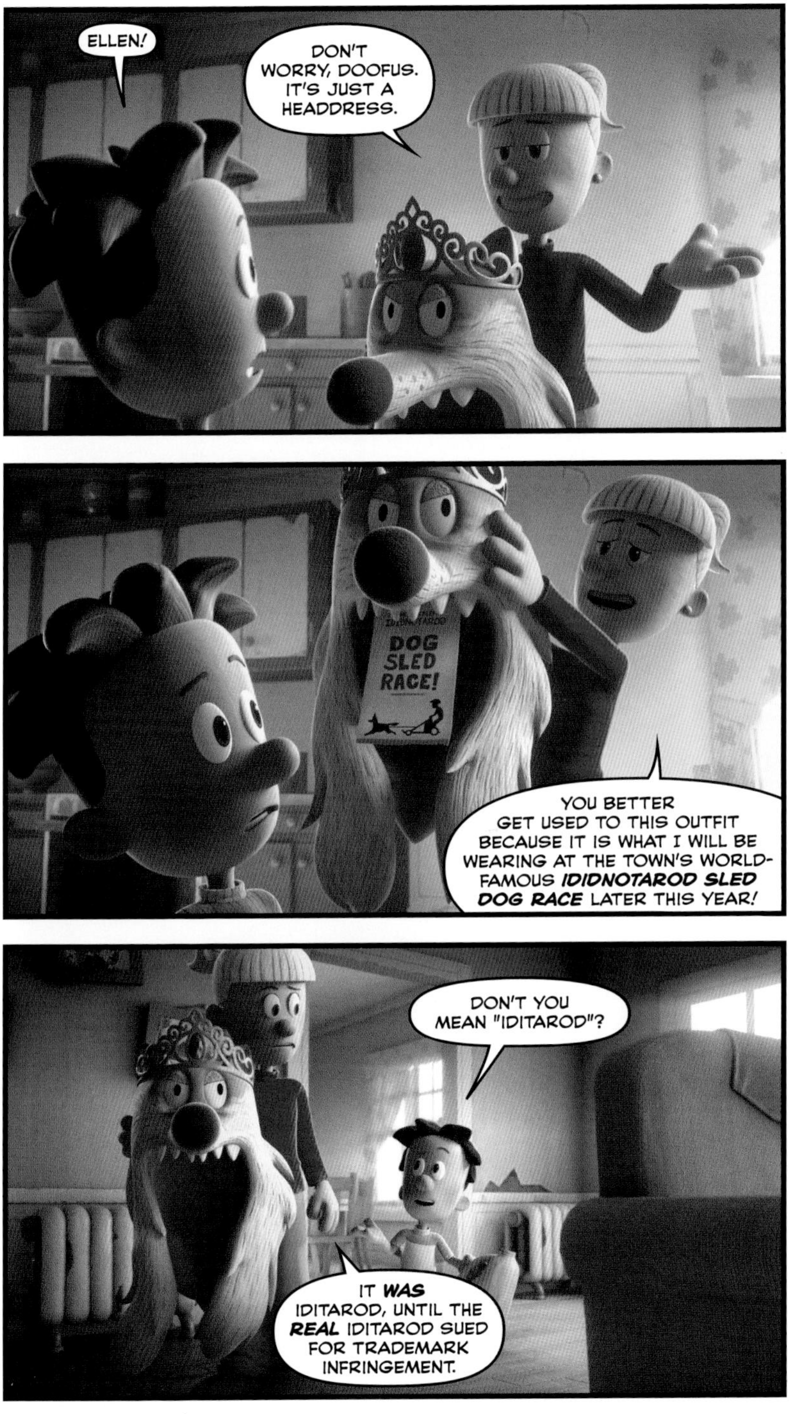
ELLEN!
DON'T WORRY, DOOFUS. IT'S JUST A HEADDRESS.
DOG SLED RACE!
YOU BETTER GET USED TO THIS OUTFIT BECAUSE IT IS WHAT I WILL BE WEARING AT THE TOWN'S WORLD-FAMOUS ***IDIDNOTAROD SLED DOG RACE*** LATER THIS YEAR!
DON'T YOU MEAN "IDITAROD"?
IT ***WAS*** IDITAROD, UNTIL THE ***REAL*** IDITAROD SUED FOR TRADEMARK INFRINGEMENT.

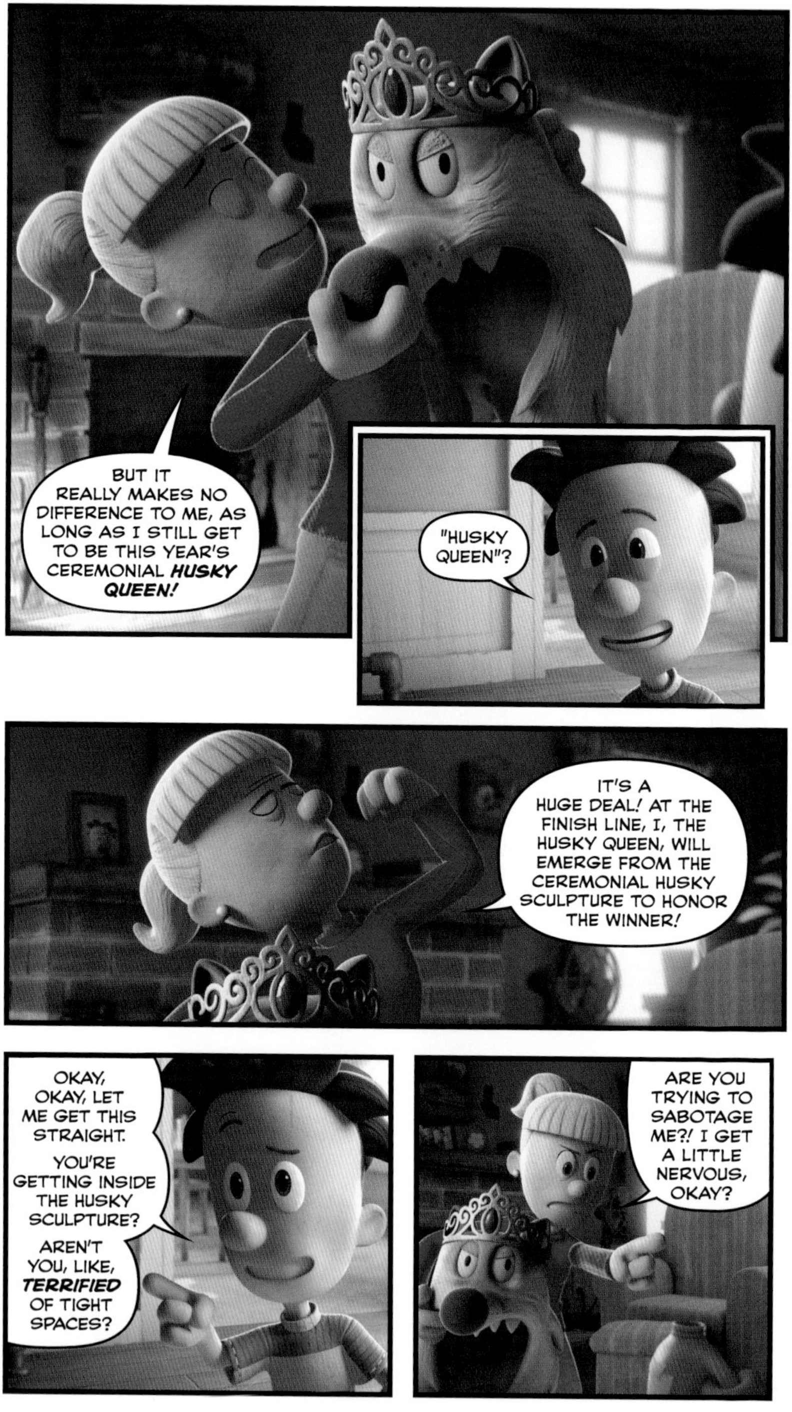
BUT IT REALLY MAKES NO DIFFERENCE TO ME, AS LONG AS I STILL GET TO BE THIS YEAR'S CEREMONIAL ***HUSKY QUEEN!***
"HUSKY QUEEN"?
IT'S A HUGE DEAL! AT THE FINISH LINE, I, THE HUSKY QUEEN, WILL EMERGE FROM THE CEREMONIAL HUSKY SCULPTURE TO HONOR THE WINNER!
OKAY, OKAY, LET ME GET THIS STRAIGHT.
YOU'RE GETTING INSIDE THE HUSKY SCULPTURE?
AREN'T YOU, LIKE, ***TERRIFIED*** OF TIGHT SPACES?
ARE YOU TRYING TO SABOTAGE ME?! I GET A LITTLE NERVOUS, OKAY?

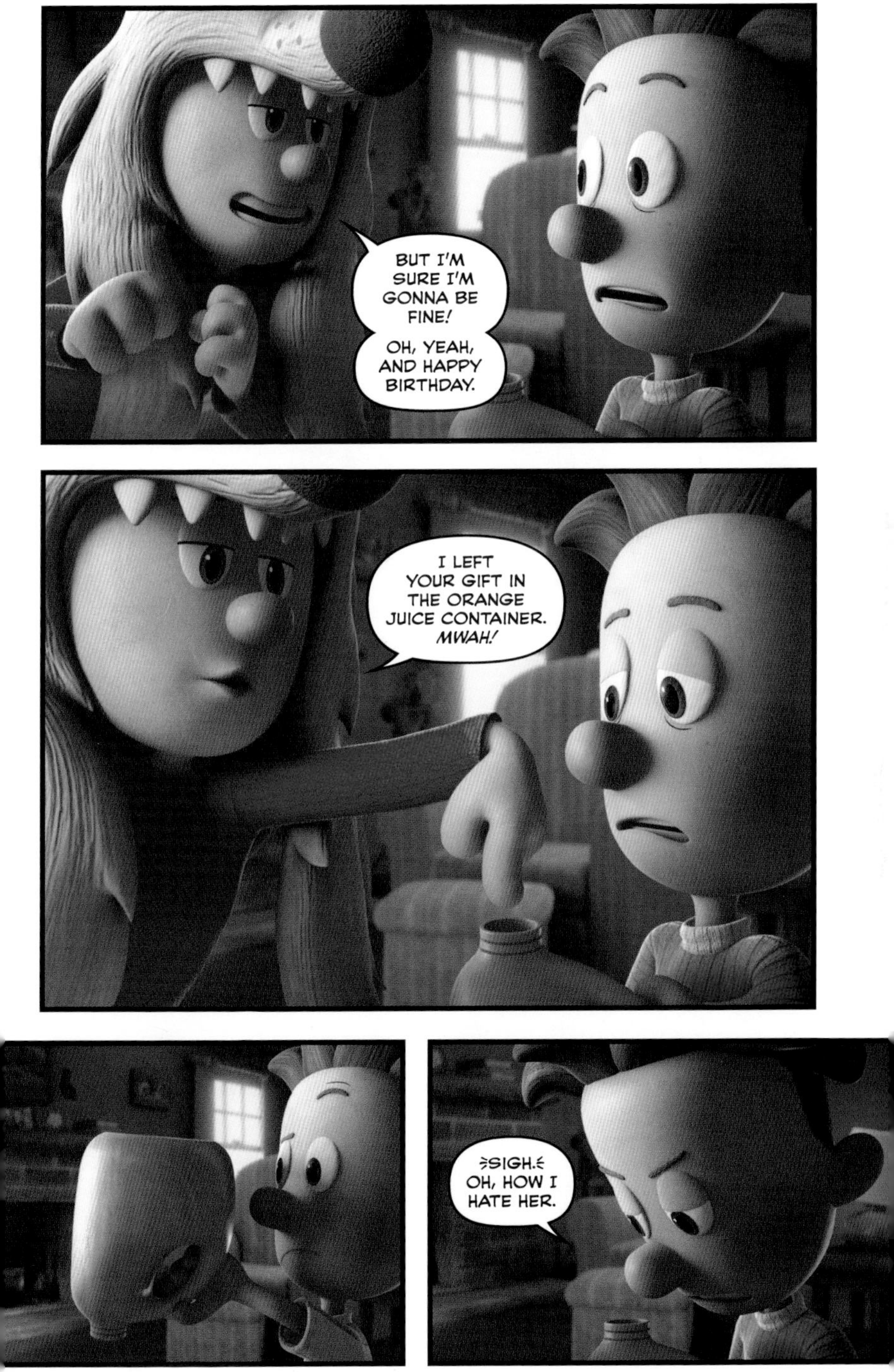
BUT I'M SURE I'M GONNA BE FINE!
OH, YEAH, AND HAPPY BIRTHDAY.
I LEFT YOUR GIFT IN THE ORANGE JUICE CONTAINER. *MWAH!*
≶SIGH.≶ OH, HOW I HATE HER.

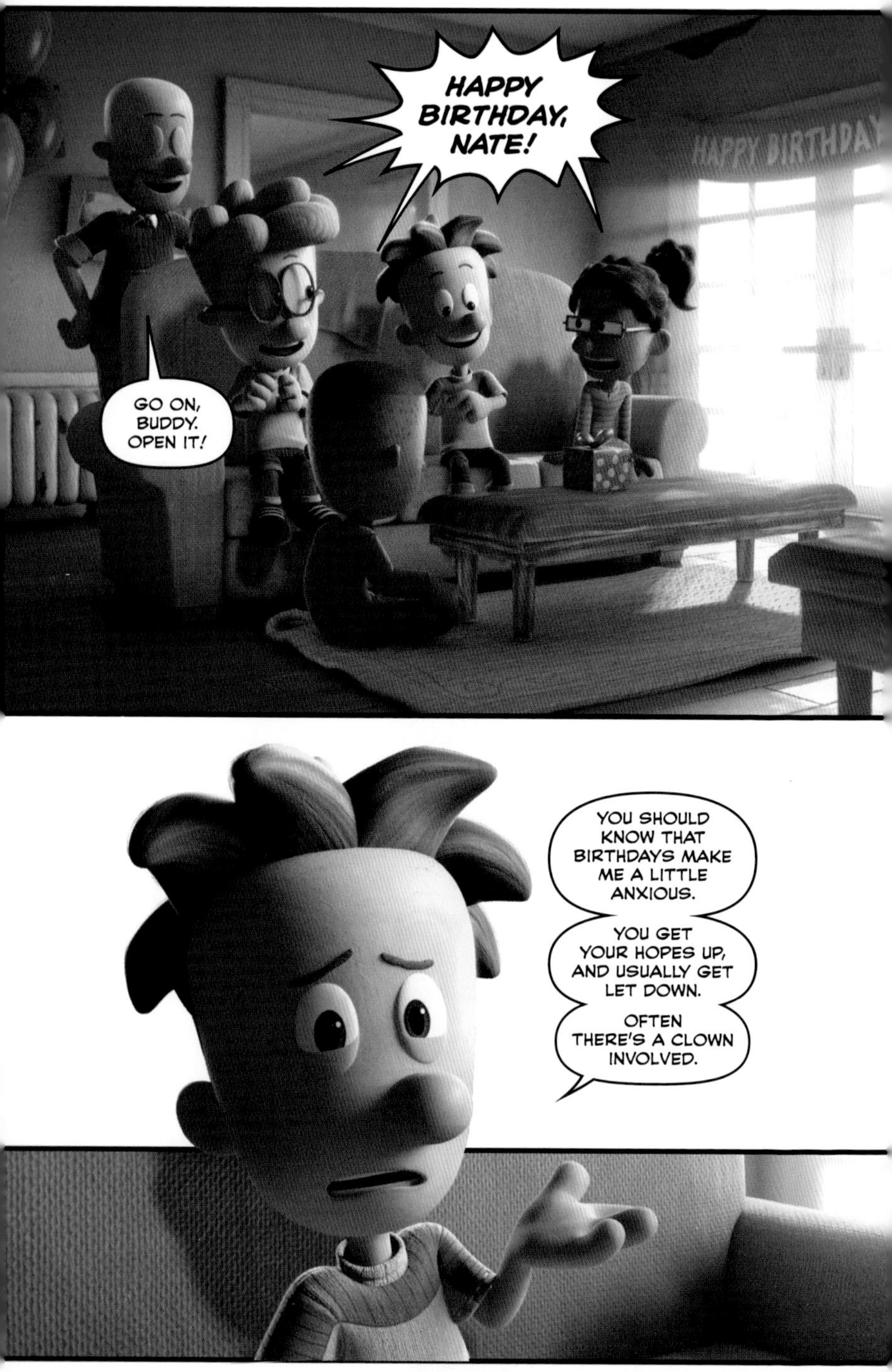
HAPPY BIRTHDAY, NATE!
GO ON, BUDDY. OPEN IT!
HAPPY BIRTHDAY
YOU SHOULD KNOW THAT BIRTHDAYS MAKE ME A LITTLE ANXIOUS.
YOU GET YOUR HOPES UP, AND USUALLY GET LET DOWN.
OFTEN THERE'S A CLOWN INVOLVED.

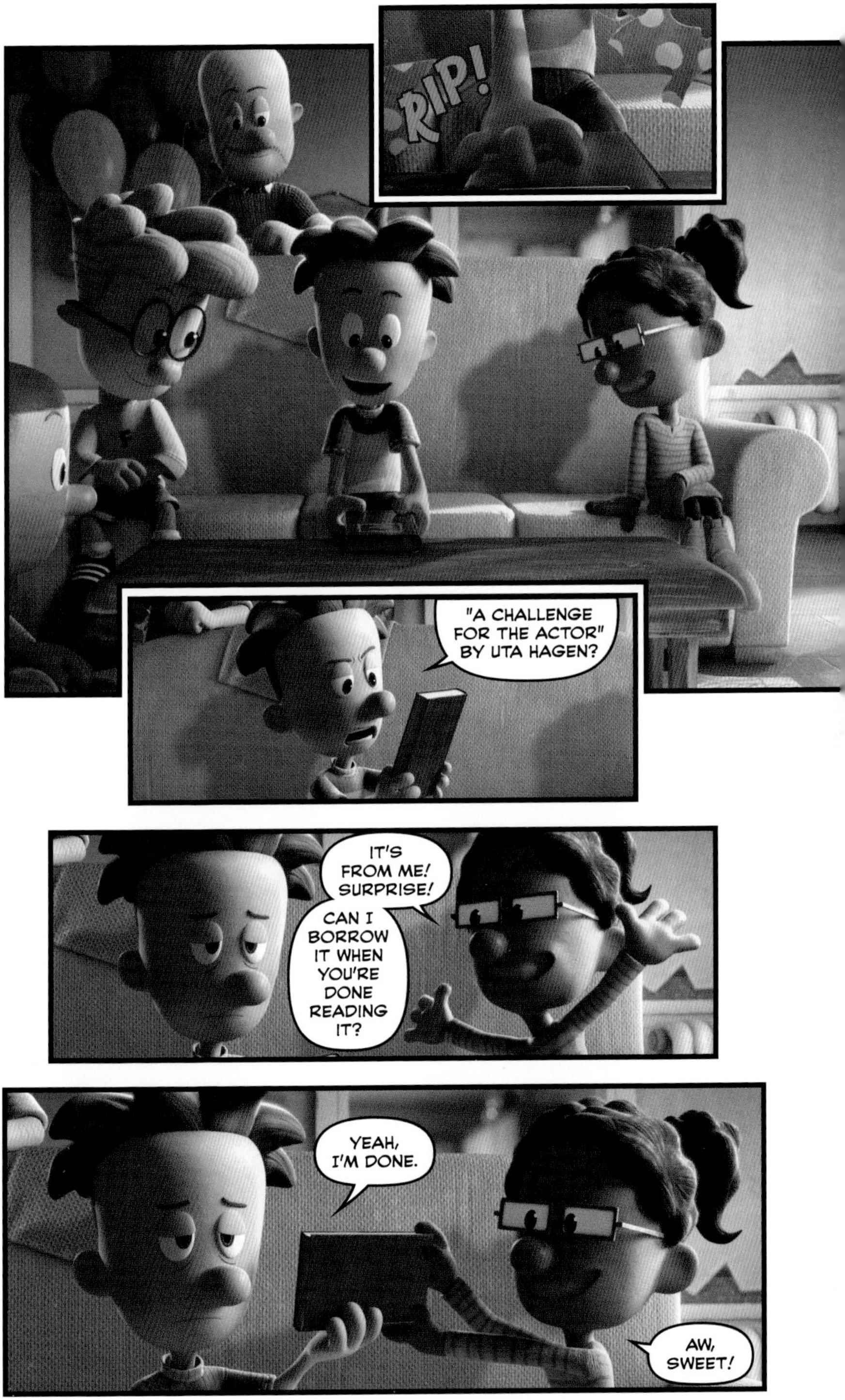
RIP!
"A CHALLENGE FOR THE ACTOR" BY UTA HAGEN?
IT'S FROM ME! SURPRISE!
CAN I BORROW IT WHEN YOU'RE DONE READING IT?
YEAH, I'M DONE.
AW, SWEET!

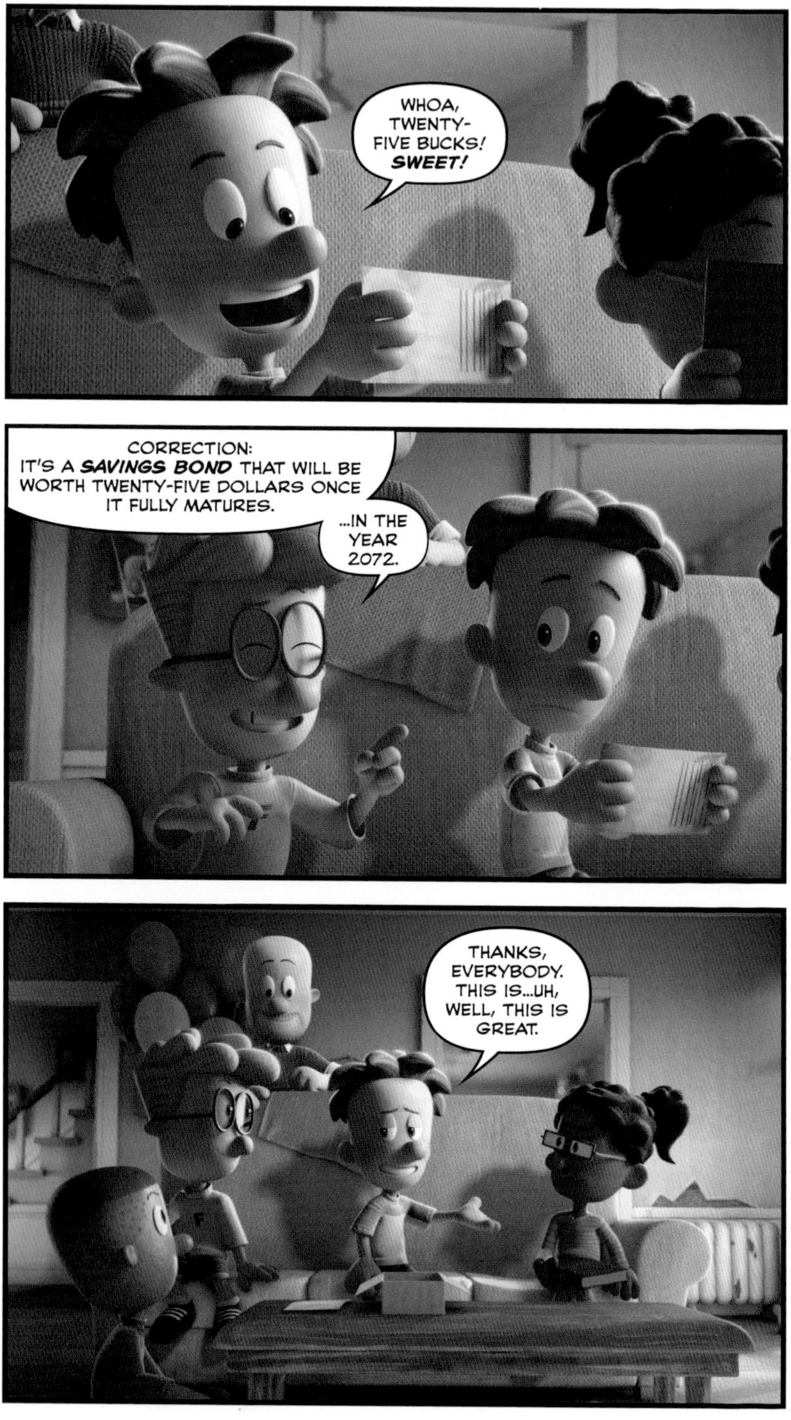
WHOA, TWENTY-FIVE BUCKS! ***SWEET!***
CORRECTION: IT'S A ***SAVINGS BOND*** THAT WILL BE WORTH TWENTY-FIVE DOLLARS ONCE IT FULLY MATURES.
...IN THE YEAR 2072.
THANKS, EVERYBODY. THIS IS...UH, WELL, THIS IS GREAT.

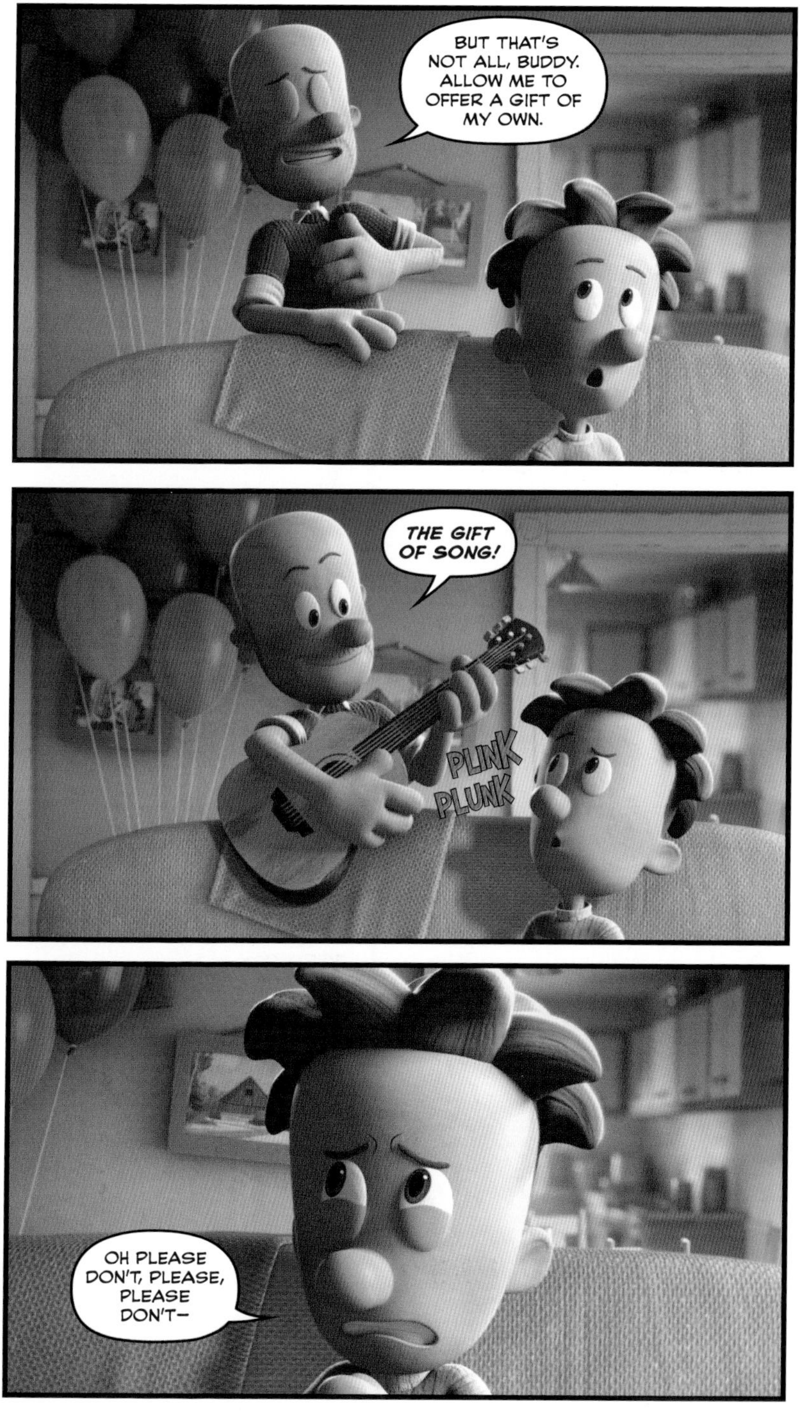
BUT THAT'S NOT ALL, BUDDY. ALLOW ME TO OFFER A GIFT OF MY OWN.
THE GIFT OF SONG!
PLINK
PLUNK
OH PLEASE DON'T, PLEASE, PLEASE DON'T–

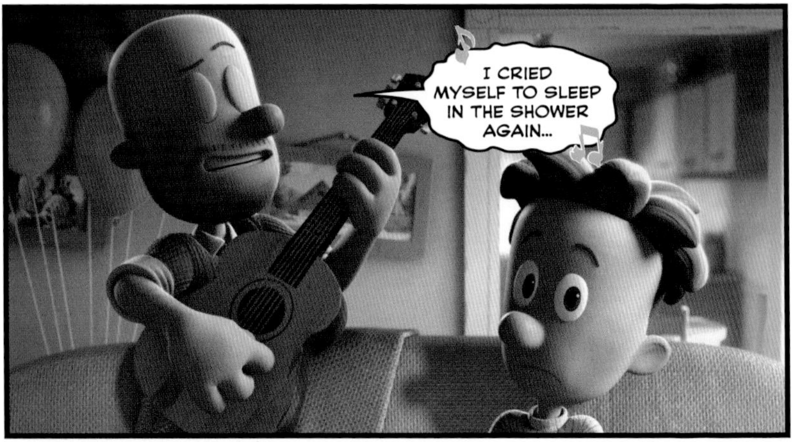
I CRIED MYSELF TO SLEEP IN THE SHOWER AGAIN...

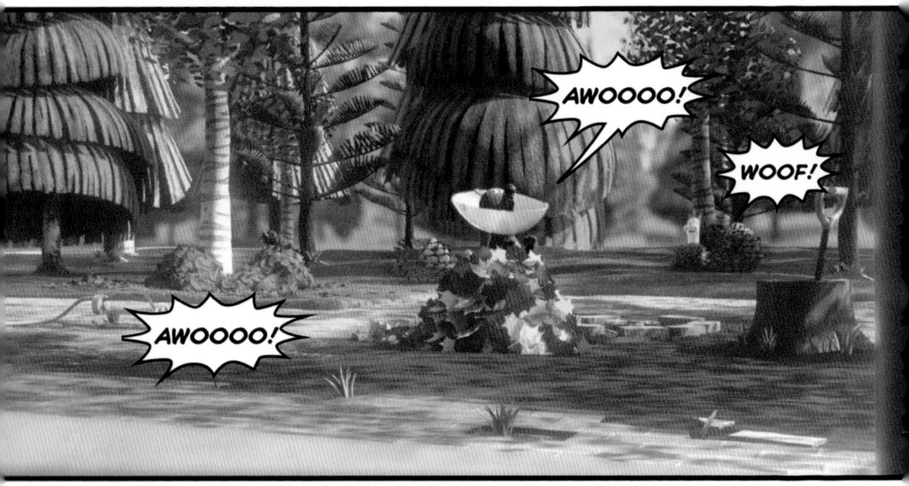
AWOOOO!
WOOF!
AWOOOO!

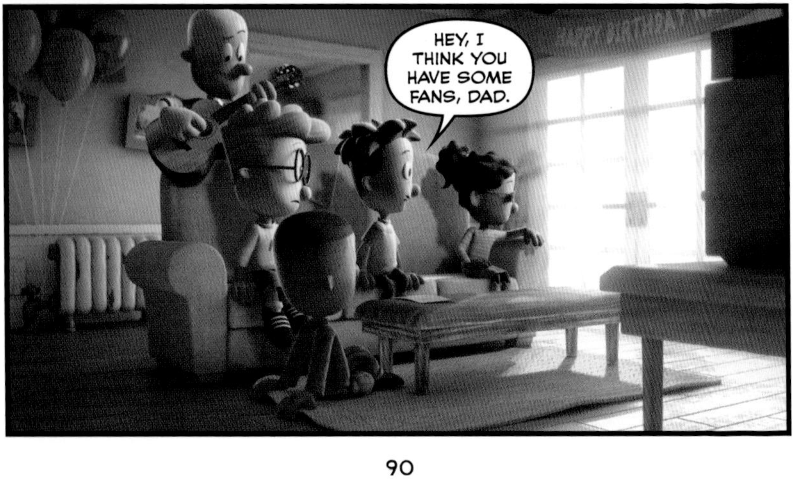
HEY, I THINK YOU HAVE SOME FANS, DAD.

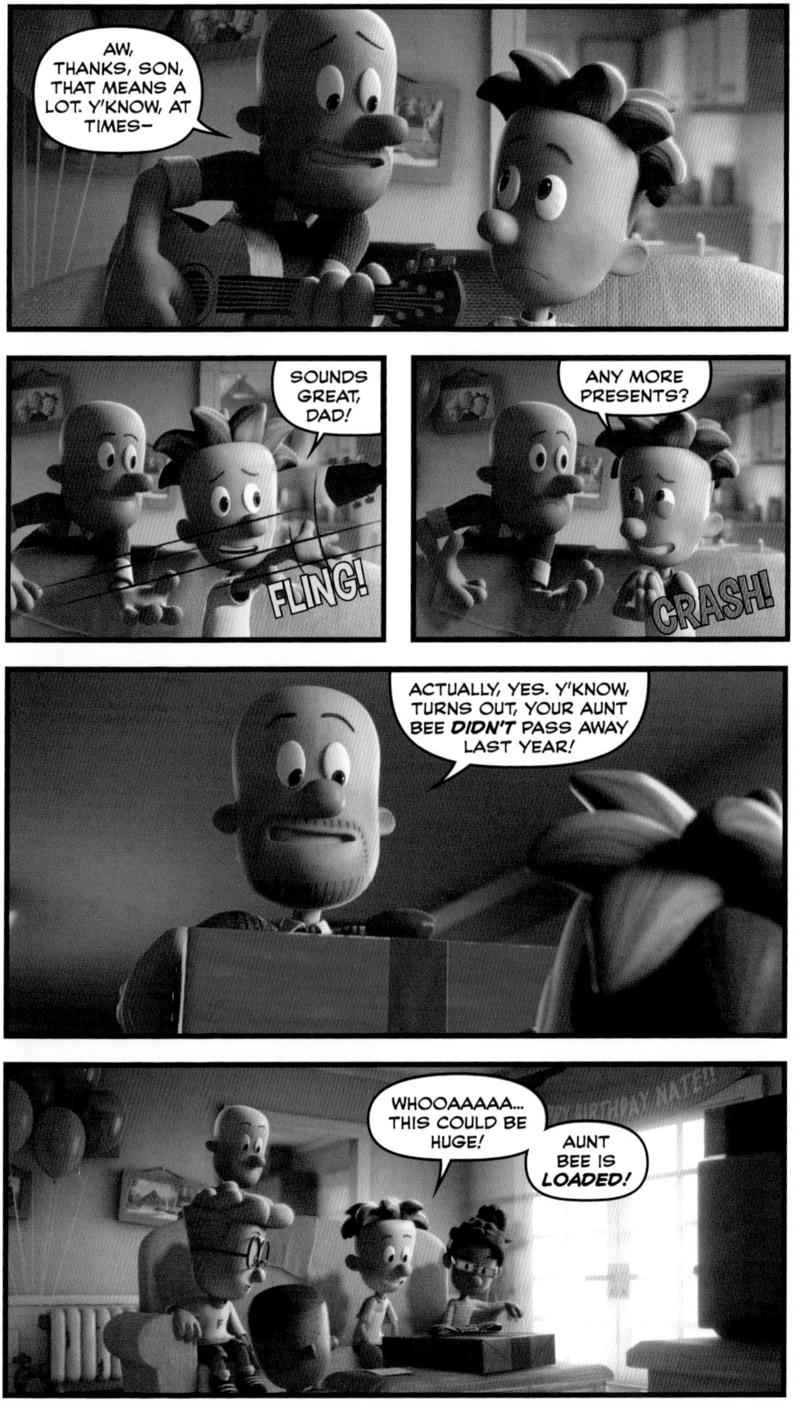
AW, THANKS, SON, THAT MEANS A LOT. Y'KNOW, AT TIMES—
SOUNDS GREAT, DAD!
FLING!
ANY MORE PRESENTS?
CRASH!
ACTUALLY, YES. Y'KNOW, TURNS OUT, YOUR AUNT BEE ***DIDN'T*** PASS AWAY LAST YEAR!
WHOOAAAAA... THIS COULD BE HUGE!
AUNT BEE IS ***LOADED!***

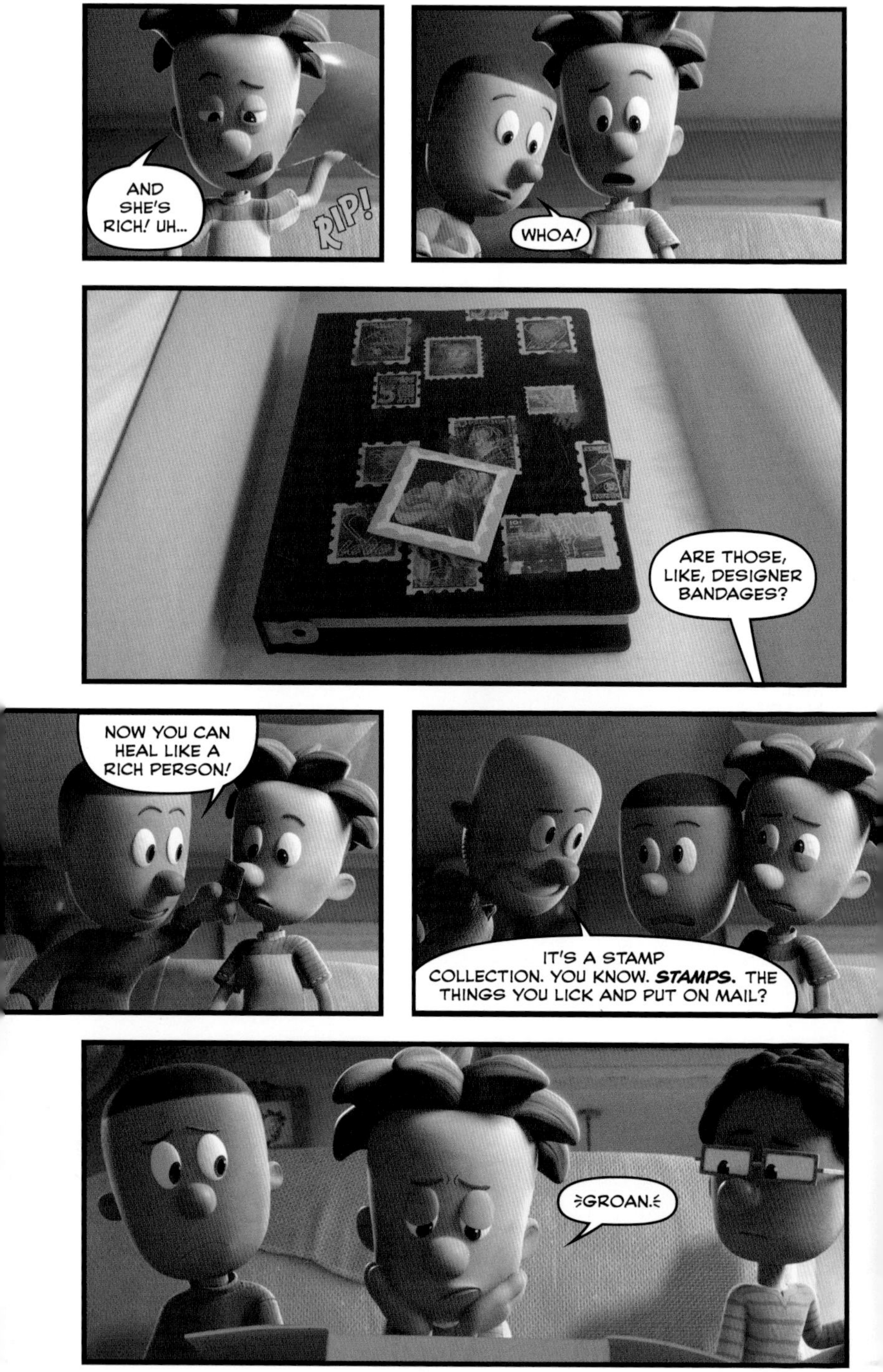
AND SHE'S RICH! UH...
RIP!
WHOA!
ARE THOSE, LIKE, DESIGNER BANDAGES?
NOW YOU CAN HEAL LIKE A RICH PERSON!
IT'S A STAMP COLLECTION. YOU KNOW. ***STAMPS.*** THE THINGS YOU LICK AND PUT ON MAIL?
GROAN.

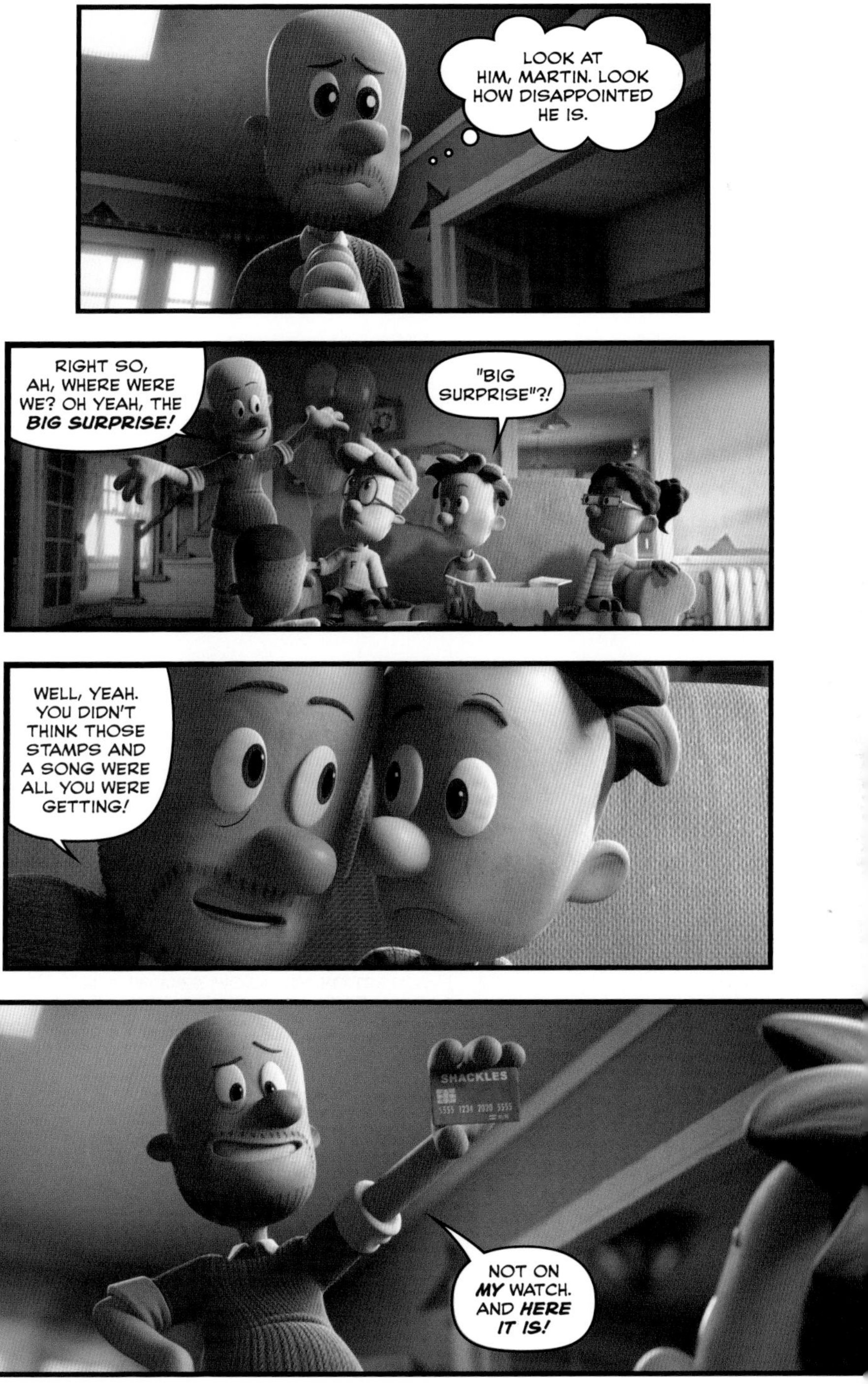
LOOK AT HIM, MARTIN. LOOK HOW DISAPPOINTED HE IS.
RIGHT SO, AH, WHERE WERE WE? OH YEAH, THE ***BIG SURPRISE!***
"BIG SURPRISE"?!
WELL, YEAH. YOU DIDN'T THINK THOSE STAMPS AND A SONG WERE ALL YOU WERE GETTING!
SHACKLES
NOT ON ***MY*** WATCH. AND ***HERE IT IS!***

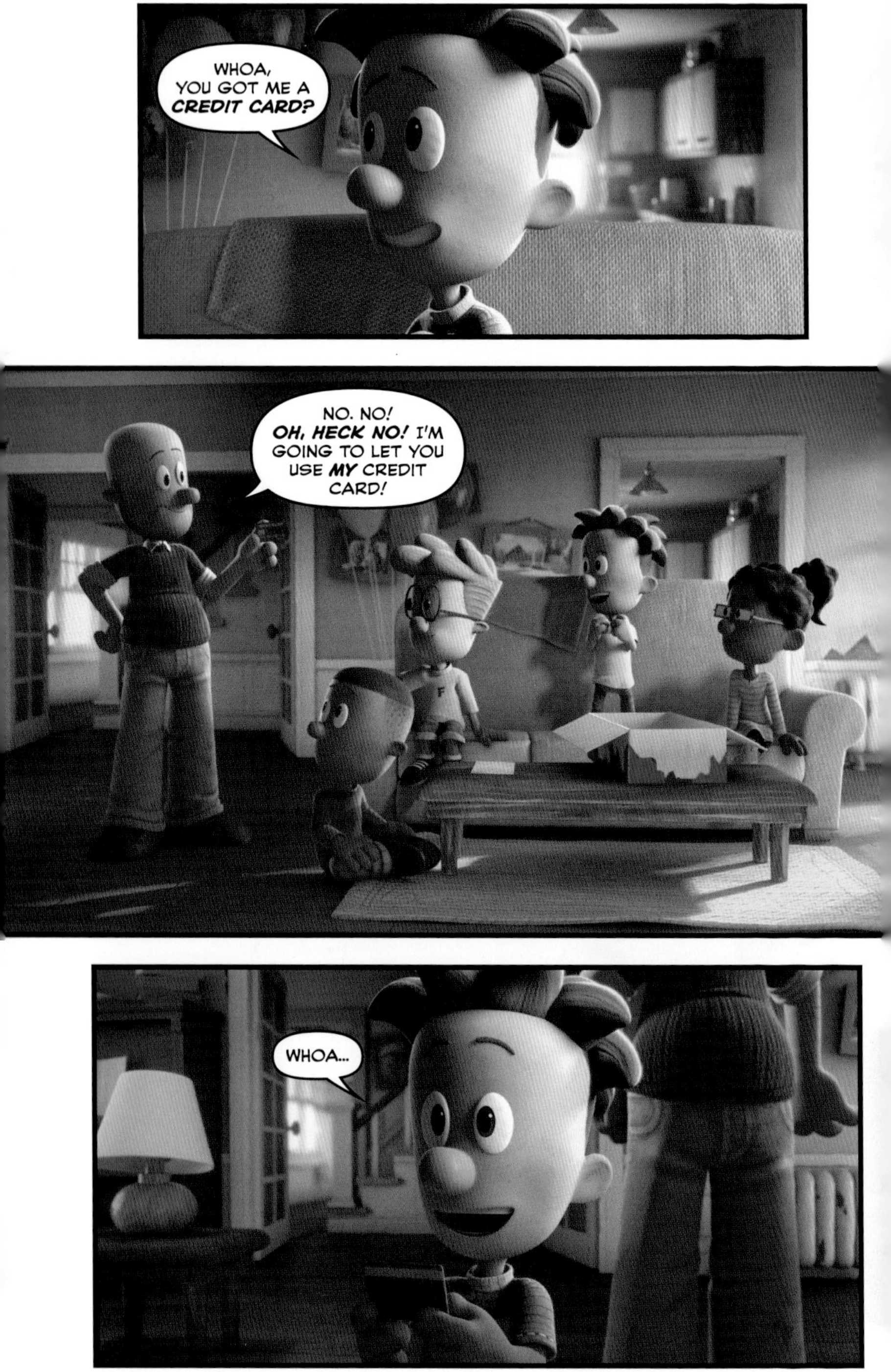
WHOA, YOU GOT ME A ***CREDIT CARD?***
NO. NO! ***OH, HECK NO!*** I'M GOING TO LET YOU USE ***MY*** CREDIT CARD!
WHOA...

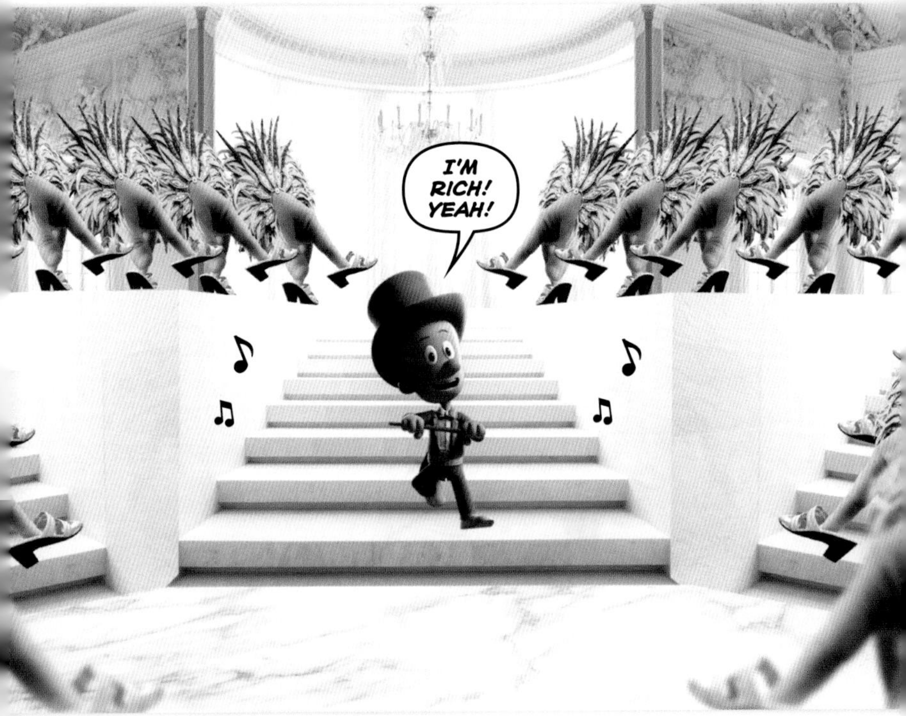
I'M RICH! YEAH!

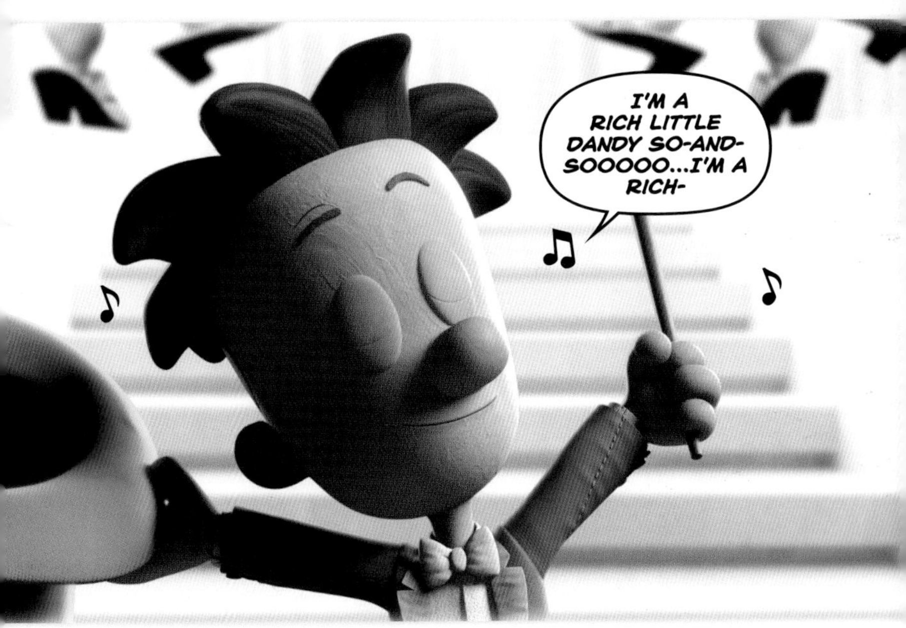
I'M A RICH LITTLE DANDY SO-AND-SOOOOO...I'M A RICH-

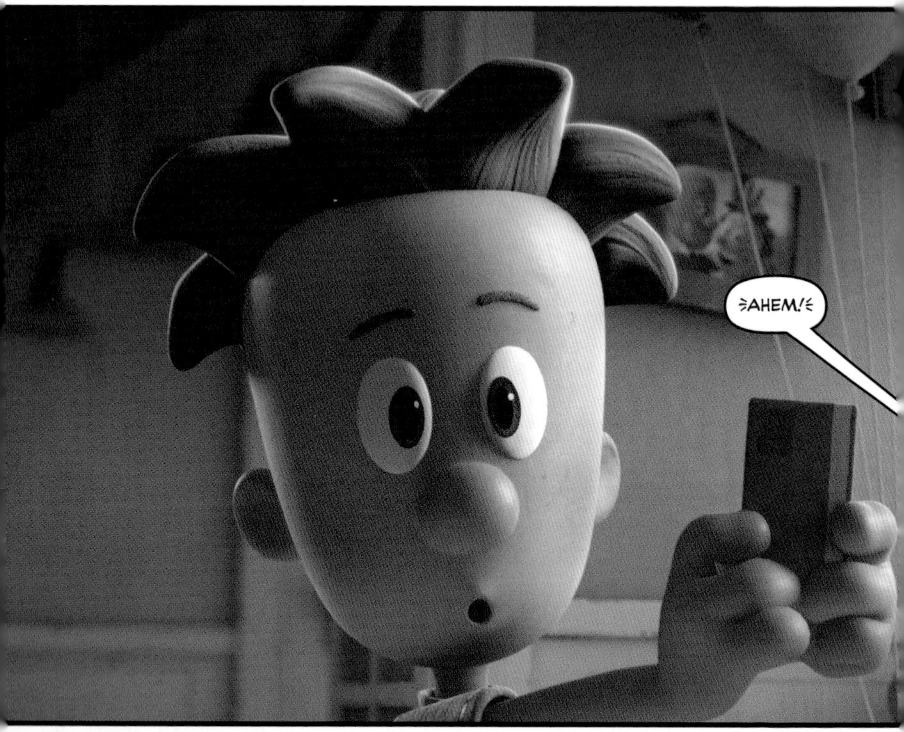
AHEM!

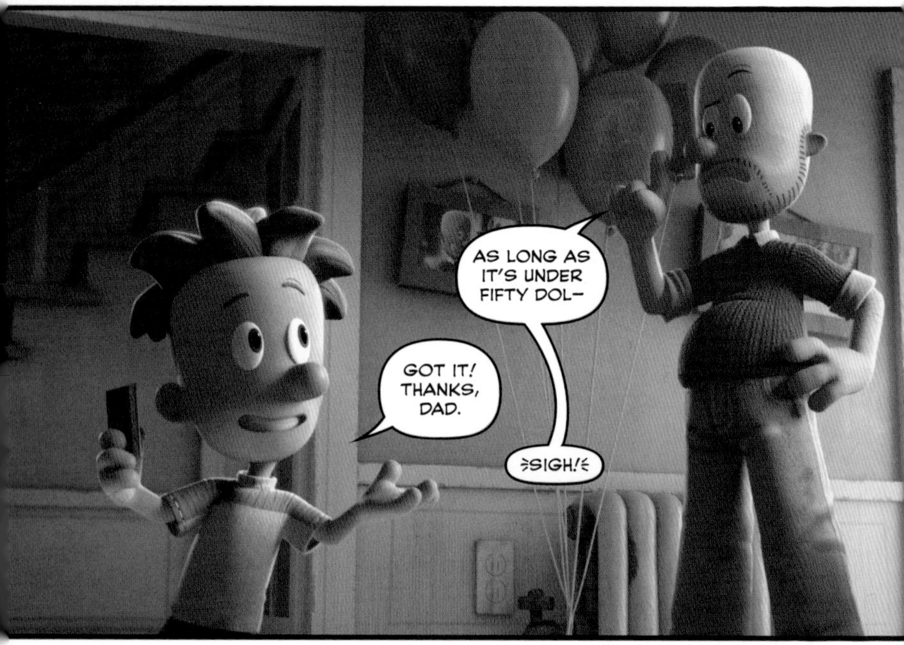
AS LONG AS IT'S UNDER FIFTY DOL–
GOT IT! THANKS, DAD.
SIGH!

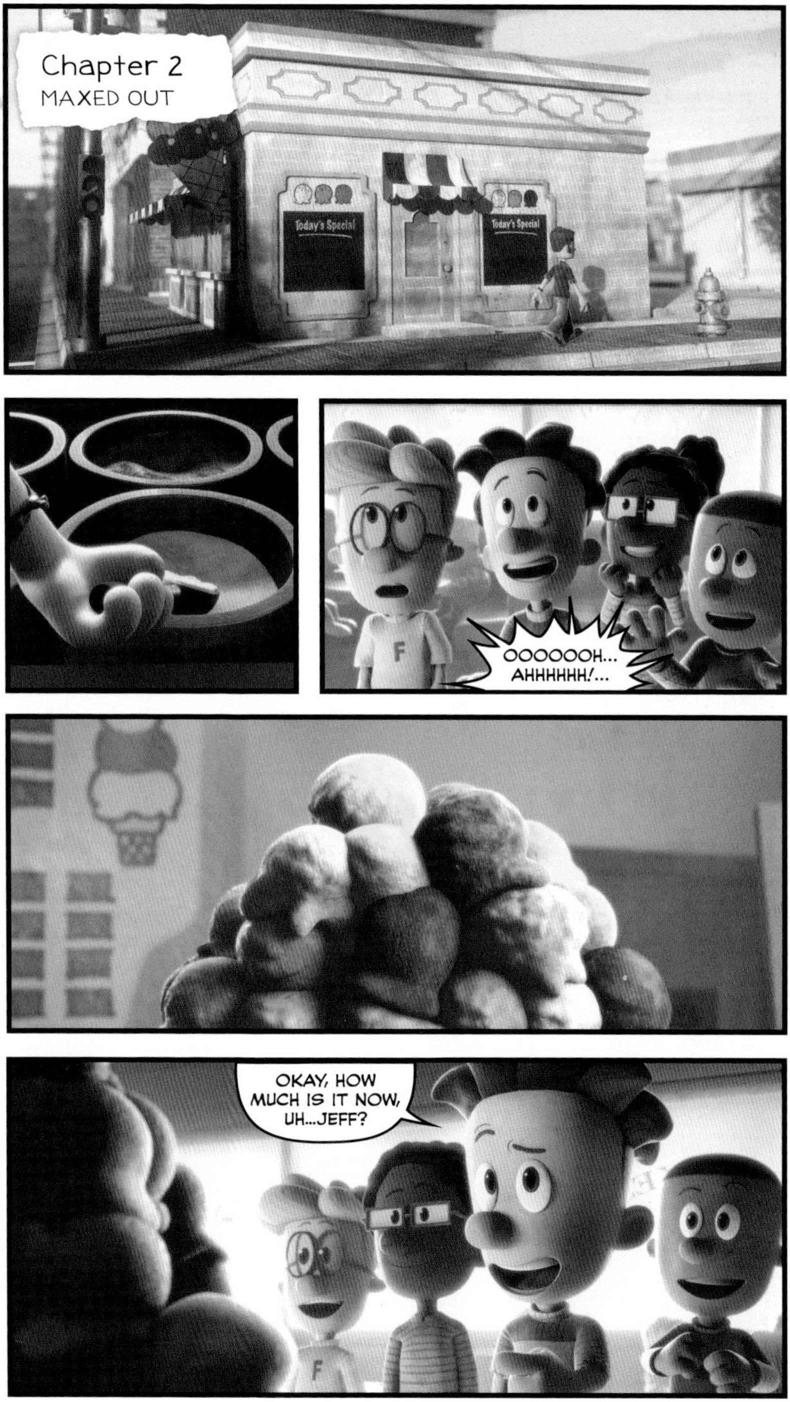
Chapter 2
MAXED OUT
Today's Special
Today's Special
OOOOOOH... AHHHHHH!...
OKAY, HOW MUCH IS IT NOW, UH...JEFF?

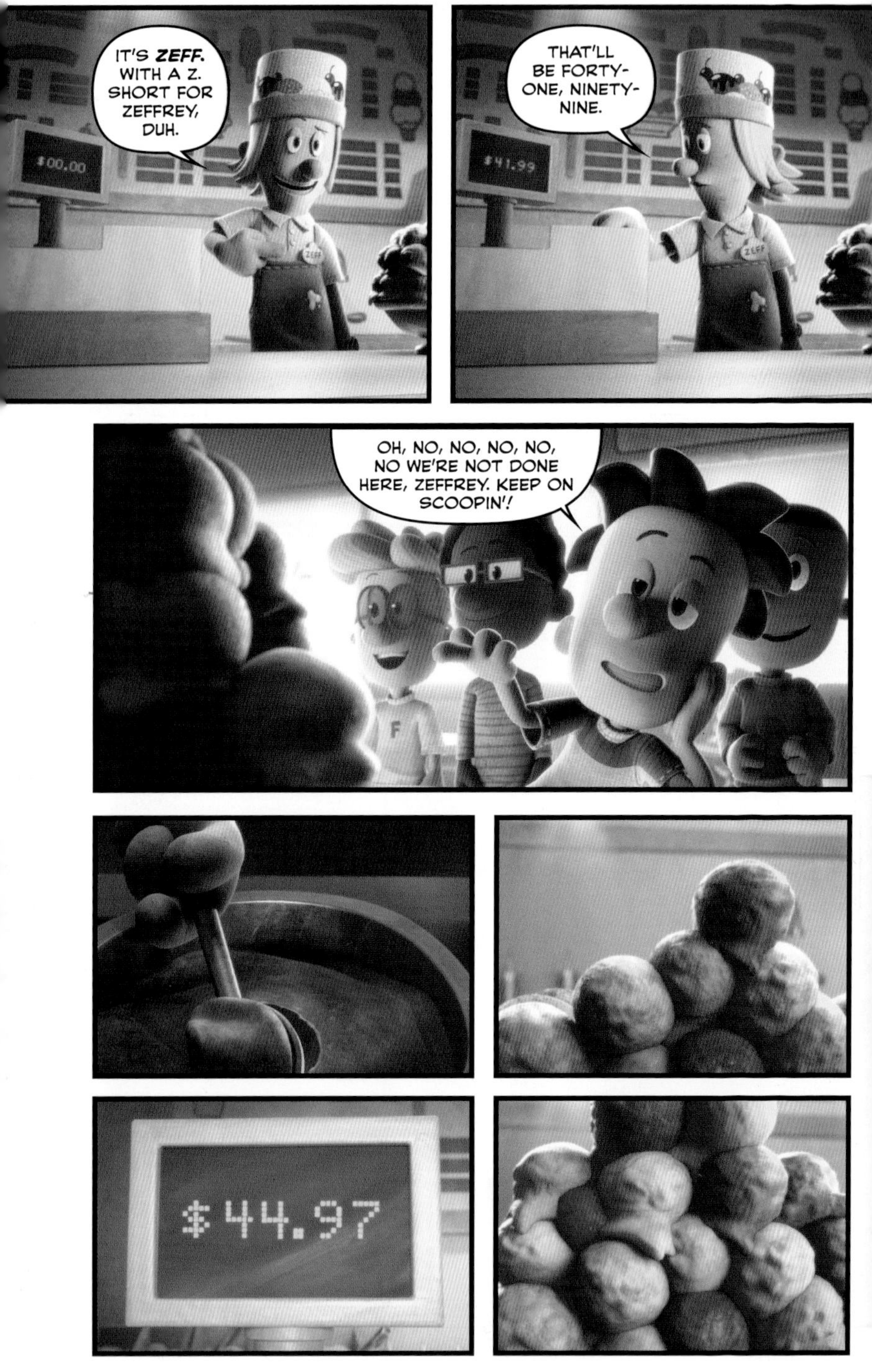
IT'S ZEFF. WITH A Z. SHORT FOR ZEFFREY, DUH.
$00.00
THAT'LL BE FORTY-ONE, NINETY-NINE.
$41.99
OH, NO, NO, NO, NO, NO WE'RE NOT DONE HERE, ZEFFREY. KEEP ON SCOOPIN'!
$44.97

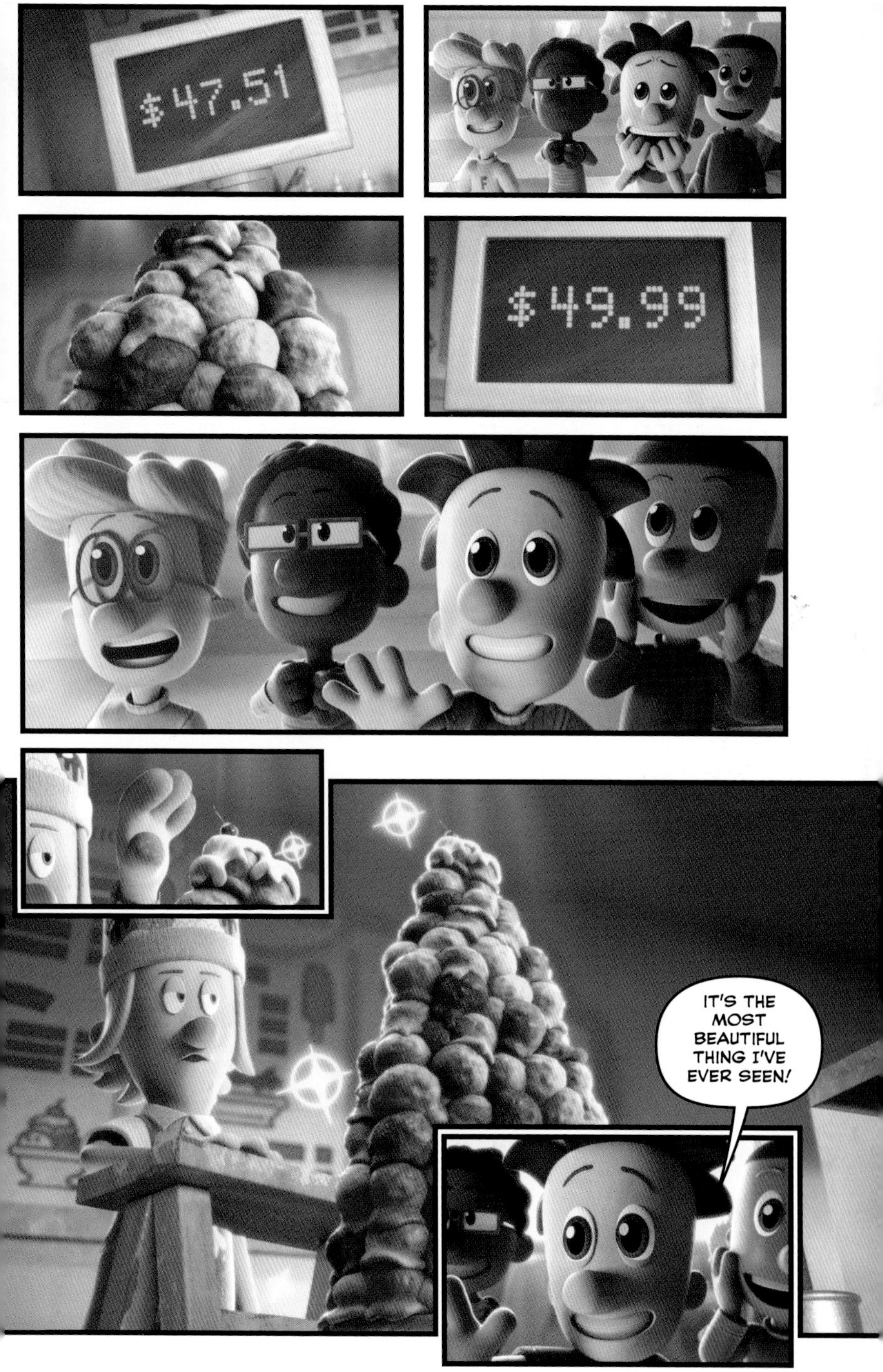
$47.51
$49.99
IT'S THE MOST BEAUTIFUL THING I'VE EVER SEEN!

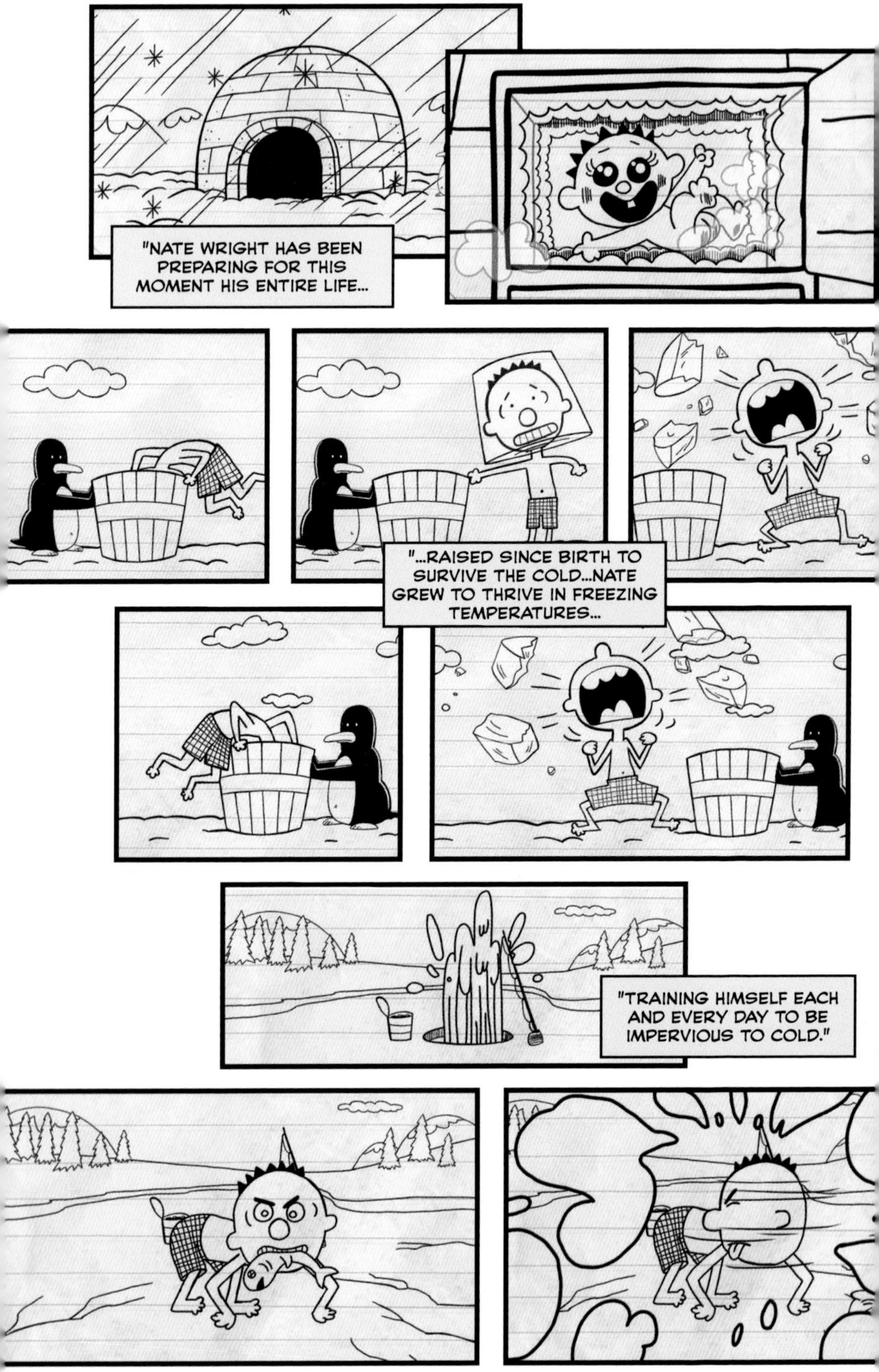
"NATE WRIGHT HAS BEEN PREPARING FOR THIS MOMENT HIS ENTIRE LIFE...
"...RAISED SINCE BIRTH TO SURVIVE THE COLD...NATE GREW TO THRIVE IN FREEZING TEMPERATURES...
"TRAINING HIMSELF EACH AND EVERY DAY TO BE IMPERVIOUS TO COLD."

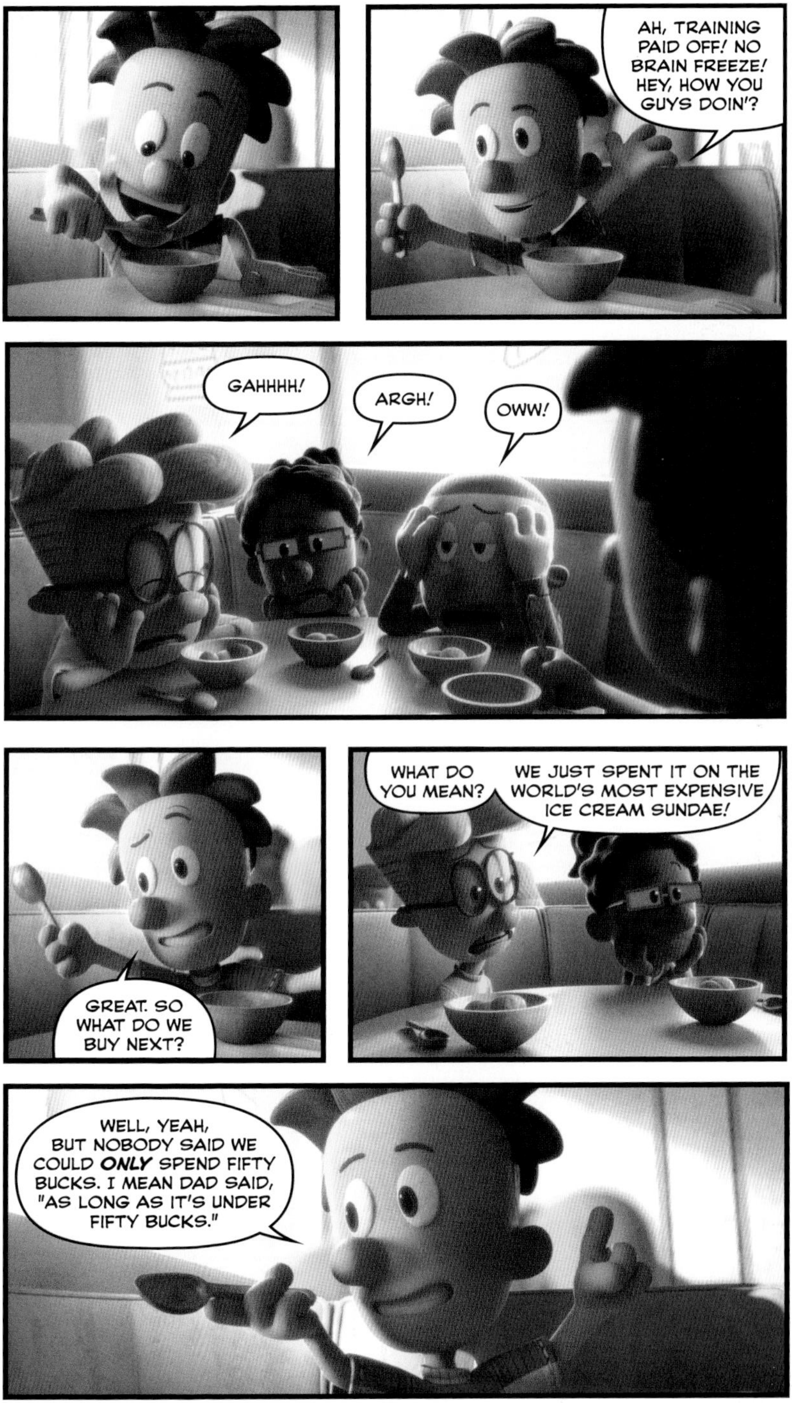
AH, TRAINING PAID OFF! NO BRAIN FREEZE! HEY, HOW YOU GUYS DOIN'?
GAHHHH!
ARGH!
OWW!
GREAT. SO WHAT DO WE BUY NEXT?
WHAT DO YOU MEAN?
WE JUST SPENT IT ON THE WORLD'S MOST EXPENSIVE ICE CREAM SUNDAE!
WELL, YEAH, BUT NOBODY SAID WE COULD **ONLY** SPEND FIFTY BUCKS. I MEAN DAD SAID, "AS LONG AS IT'S UNDER FIFTY BUCKS."

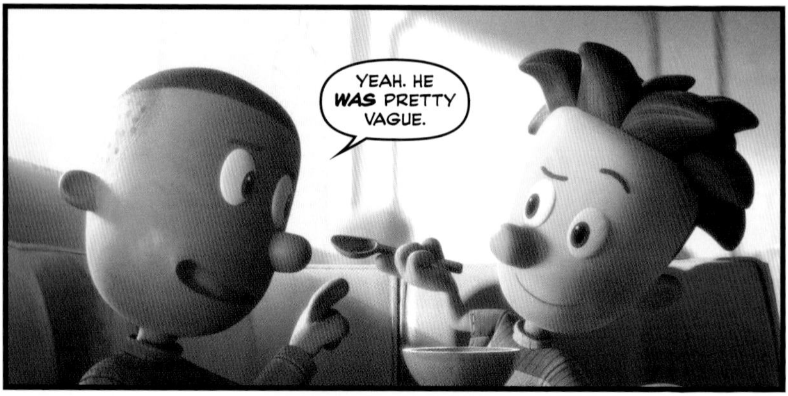
YEAH. HE *WAS* PRETTY VAGUE.

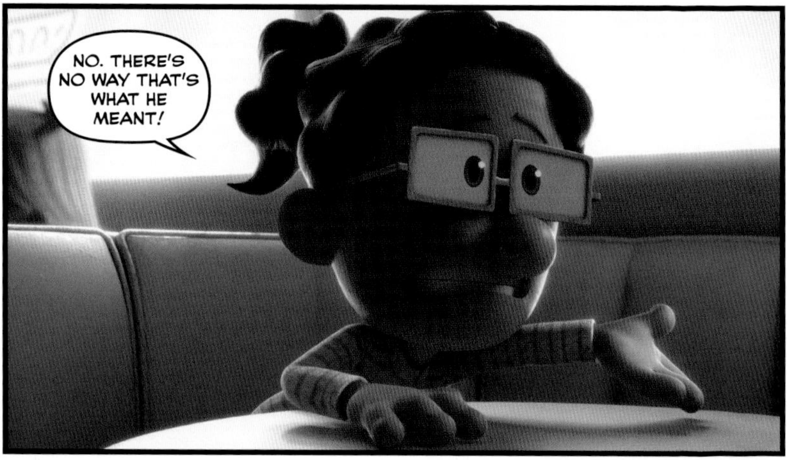
NO. THERE'S NO WAY THAT'S WHAT HE MEANT!

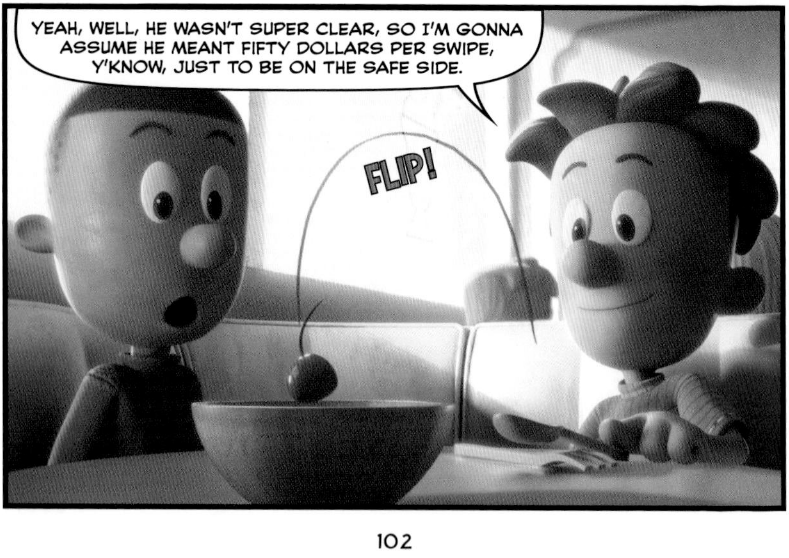
YEAH, WELL, HE WASN'T SUPER CLEAR, SO I'M GONNA ASSUME HE MEANT FIFTY DOLLARS PER SWIPE, Y'KNOW, JUST TO BE ON THE SAFE SIDE.
FLIP!

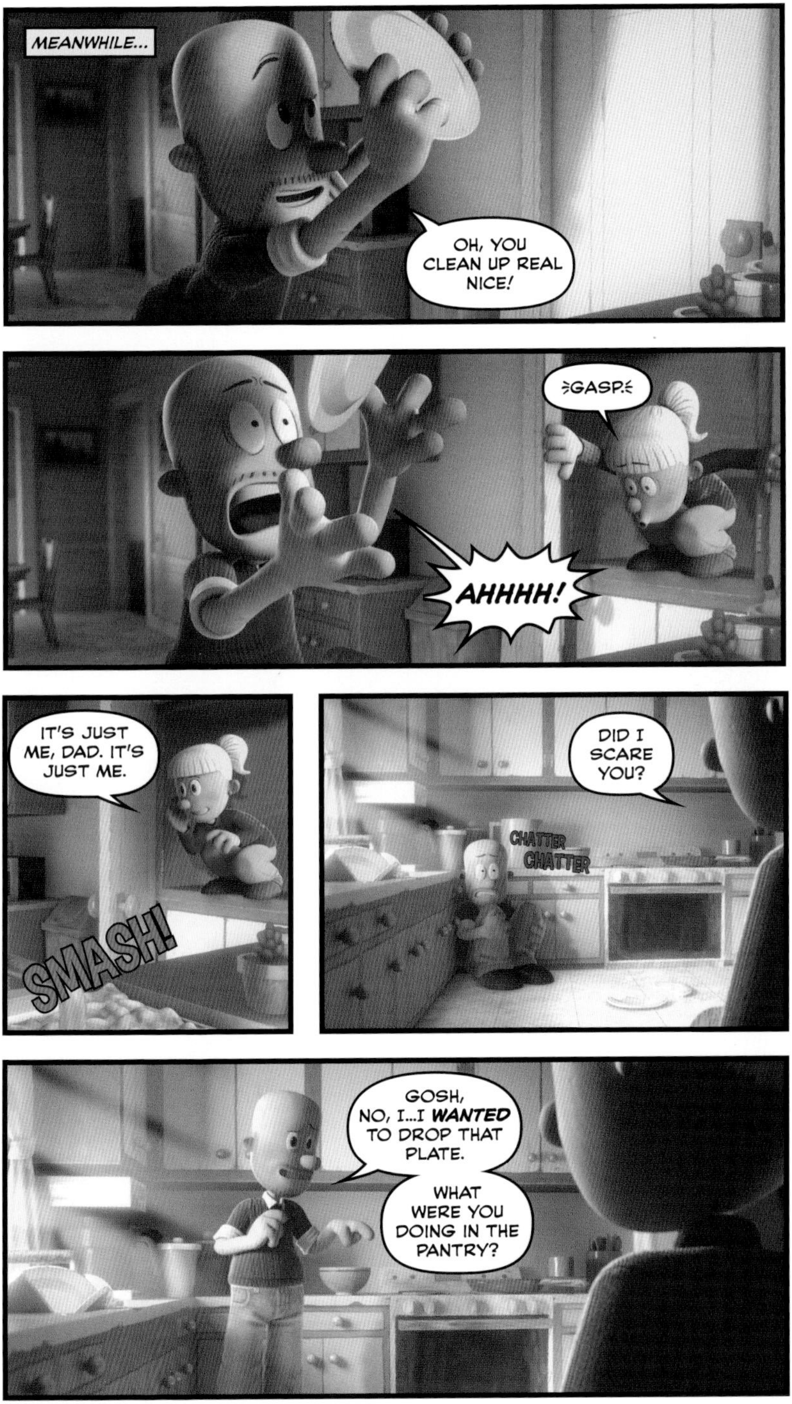
MEANWHILE...
OH, YOU CLEAN UP REAL NICE!
GASP.
AHHHH!
IT'S JUST ME, DAD. IT'S JUST ME.
SMASH!
DID I SCARE YOU?
CHATTER
CHATTER
GOSH, NO, I...I **WANTED** TO DROP THAT PLATE.
WHAT WERE YOU DOING IN THE PANTRY?

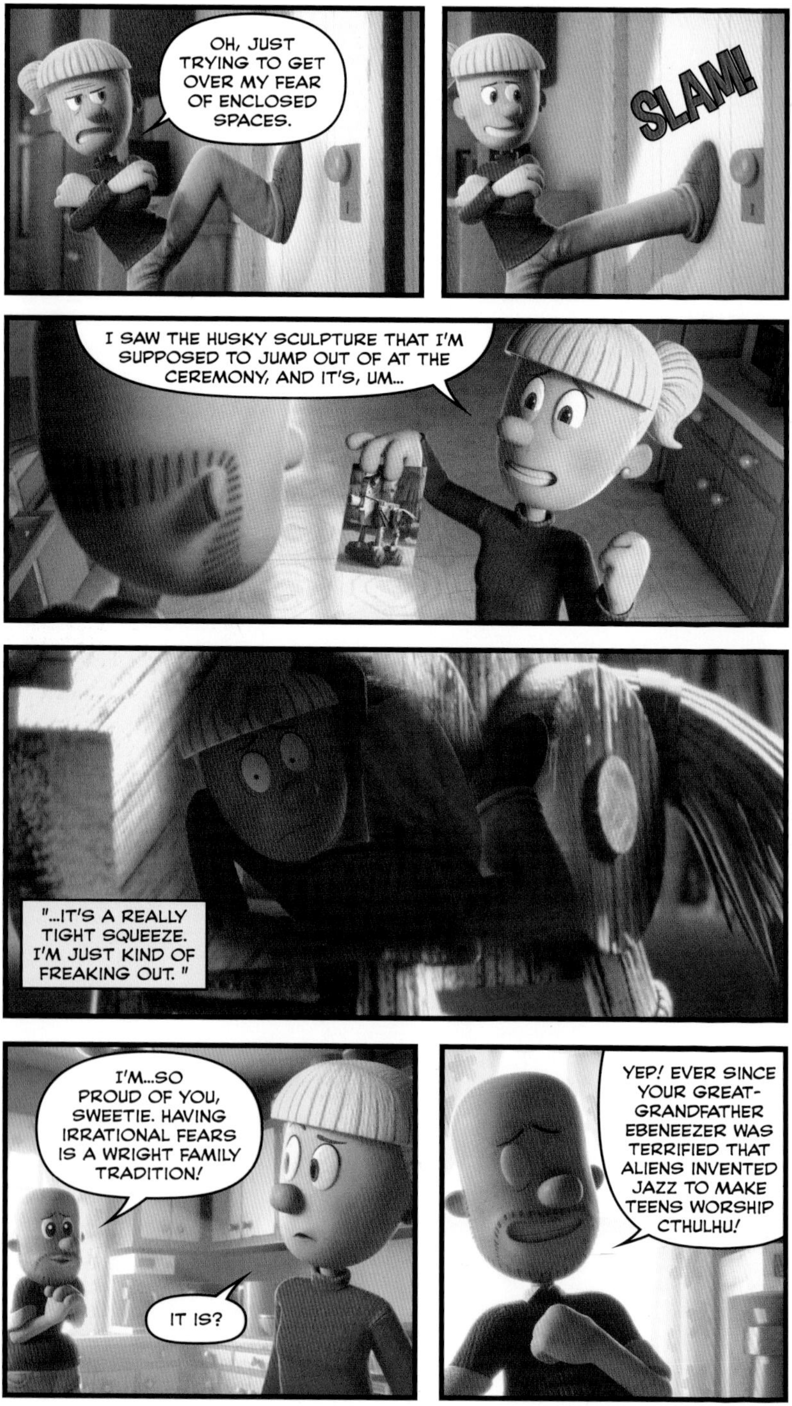
OH, JUST TRYING TO GET OVER MY FEAR OF ENCLOSED SPACES.
SLAM!
I SAW THE HUSKY SCULPTURE THAT I'M SUPPOSED TO JUMP OUT OF AT THE CEREMONY, AND IT'S, UM...
"...IT'S A REALLY TIGHT SQUEEZE. I'M JUST KIND OF FREAKING OUT."
I'M...SO PROUD OF YOU, SWEETIE. HAVING IRRATIONAL FEARS IS A WRIGHT FAMILY TRADITION!
IT IS?
YEP! EVER SINCE YOUR GREAT-GRANDFATHER EBENEEZER WAS TERRIFIED THAT ALIENS INVENTED JAZZ TO MAKE TEENS WORSHIP CTHULHU!

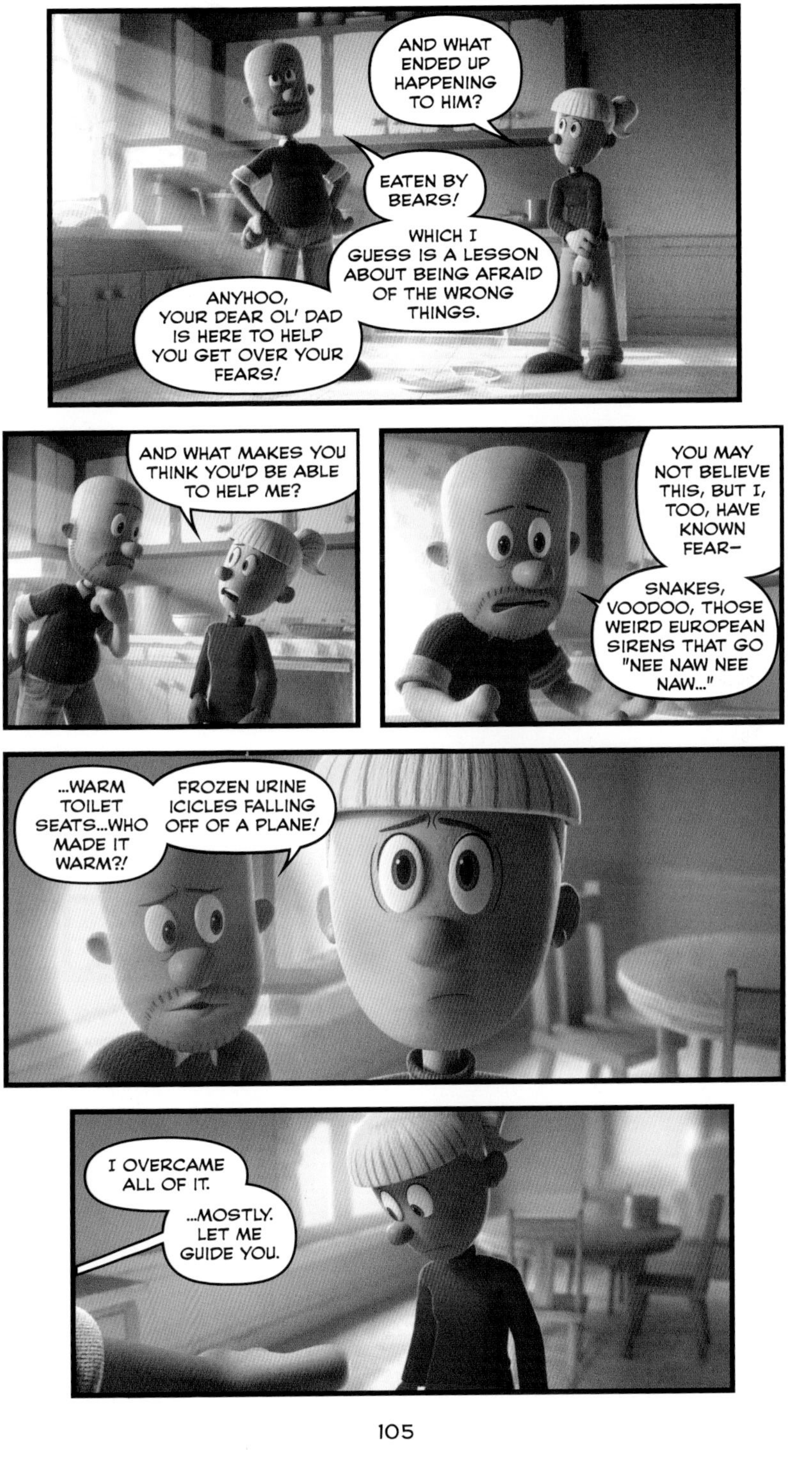
AND WHAT ENDED UP HAPPENING TO HIM?
EATEN BY BEARS!
WHICH I GUESS IS A LESSON ABOUT BEING AFRAID OF THE WRONG THINGS.
ANYHOO, YOUR DEAR OL' DAD IS HERE TO HELP YOU GET OVER YOUR FEARS!
AND WHAT MAKES YOU THINK YOU'D BE ABLE TO HELP ME?
YOU MAY NOT BELIEVE THIS, BUT I, TOO, HAVE KNOWN FEAR–
SNAKES, VOODOO, THOSE WEIRD EUROPEAN SIRENS THAT GO "NEE NAW NEE NAW..."
FROZEN URINE ICICLES FALLING OFF OF A PLANE!
...WARM TOILET SEATS...WHO MADE IT WARM?!
I OVERCAME ALL OF IT.
...MOSTLY. LET ME GUIDE YOU.

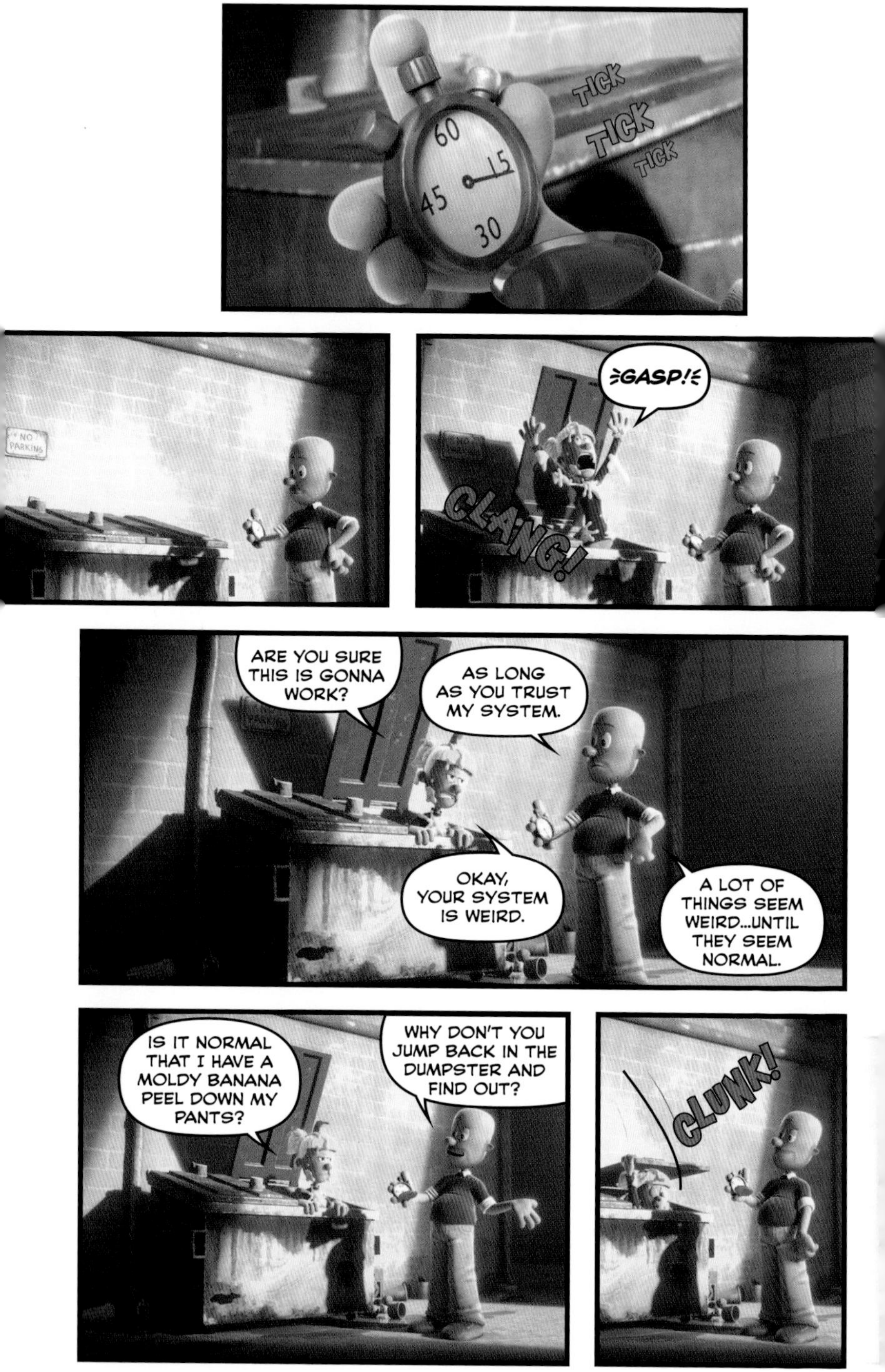
60
15
45
30
TICK
TICK
TICK
NO PARKING
GASP!
CLANG!
ARE YOU SURE THIS IS GONNA WORK?
AS LONG AS YOU TRUST MY SYSTEM.
OKAY, YOUR SYSTEM IS WEIRD.
A LOT OF THINGS SEEM WEIRD...UNTIL THEY SEEM NORMAL.
IS IT NORMAL THAT I HAVE A MOLDY BANANA PEEL DOWN MY PANTS?
WHY DON'T YOU JUMP BACK IN THE DUMPSTER AND FIND OUT?
CLUNK!

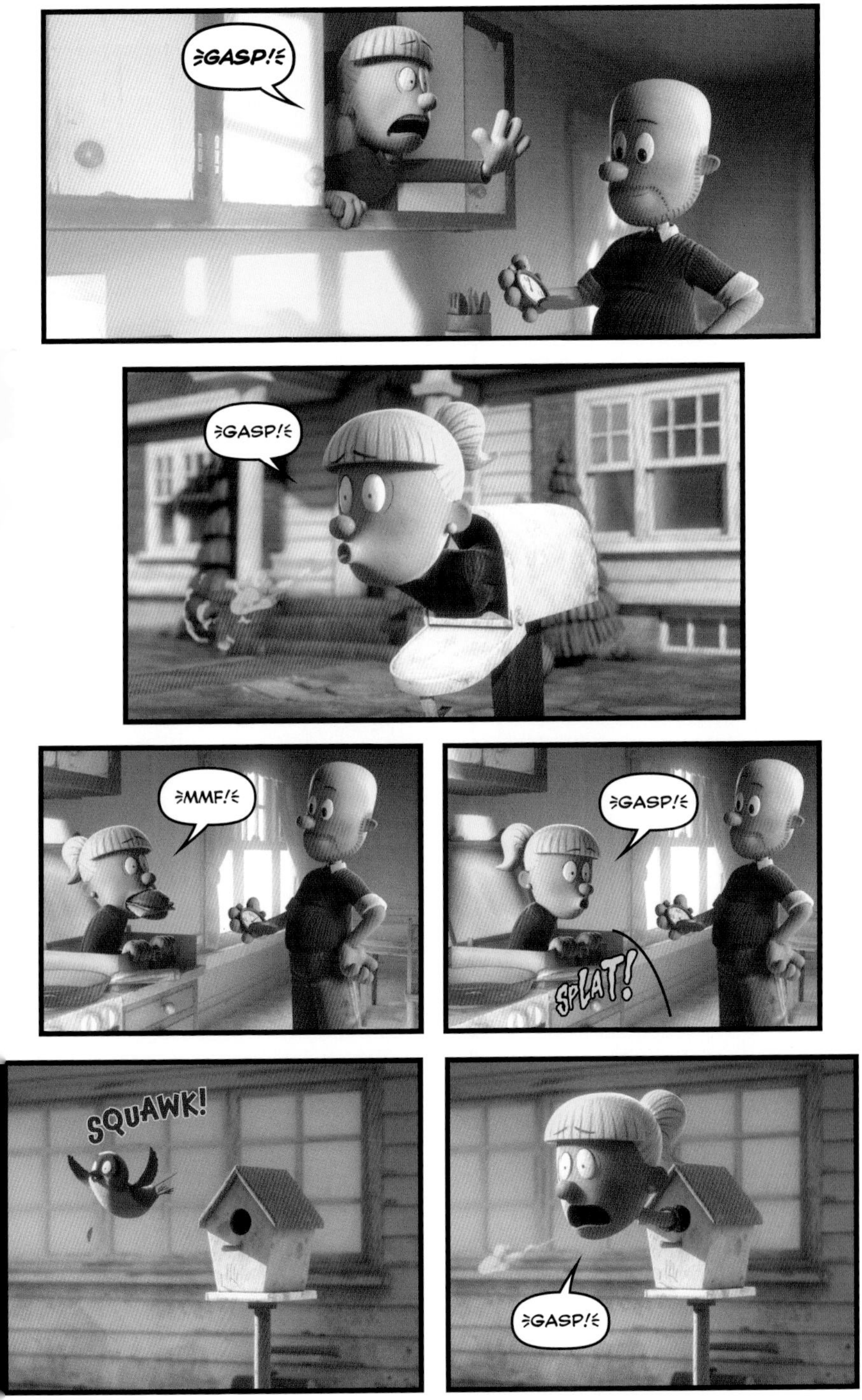
GASP!
GASP!
MMF!
GASP!
SPLAT!
SQUAWK!
GASP!

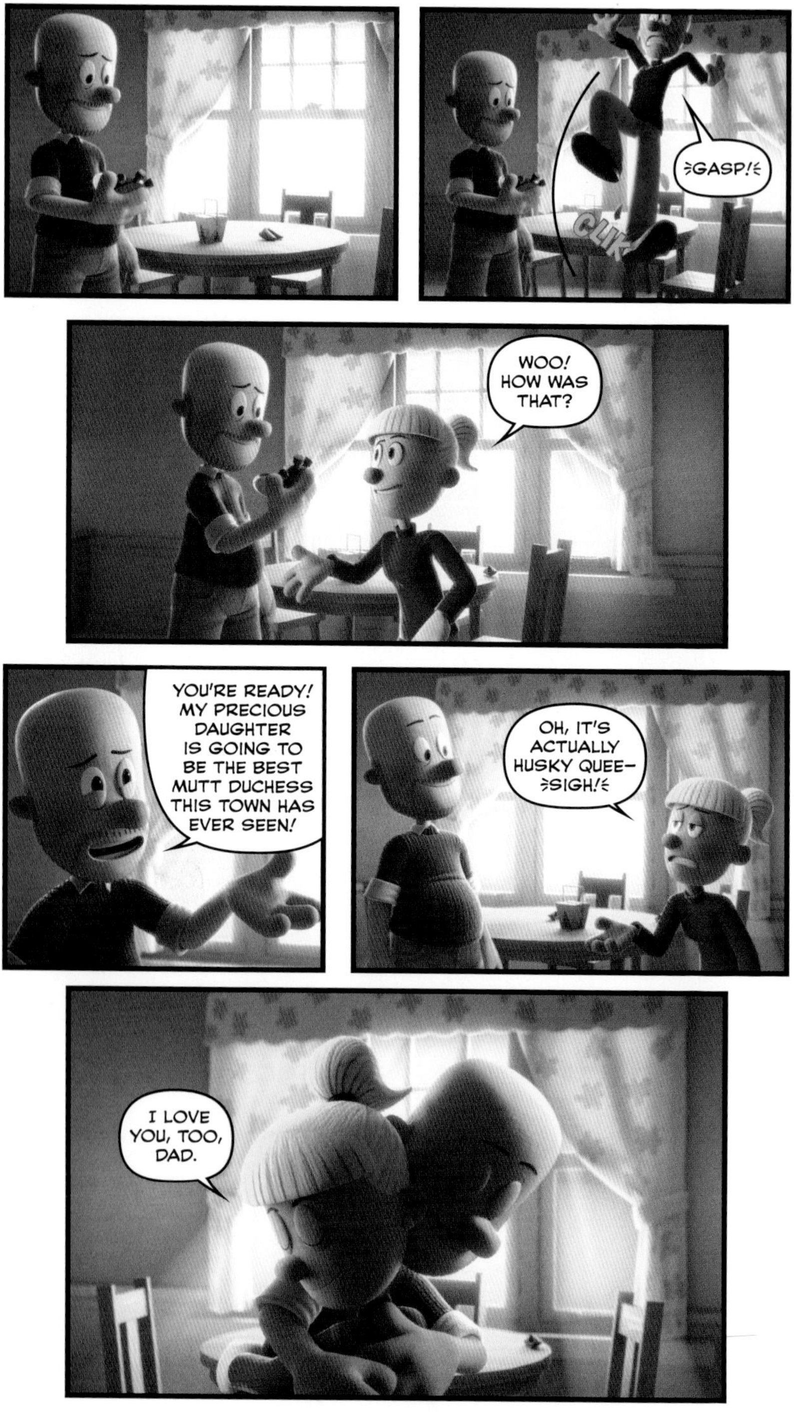
GASP!
CLIK
WOO! HOW WAS THAT?
YOU'RE READY! MY PRECIOUS DAUGHTER IS GOING TO BE THE BEST MUTT DUCHESS THIS TOWN HAS EVER SEEN!
OH, IT'S ACTUALLY HUSKY QUEE— SIGH!
I LOVE YOU, TOO, DAD.

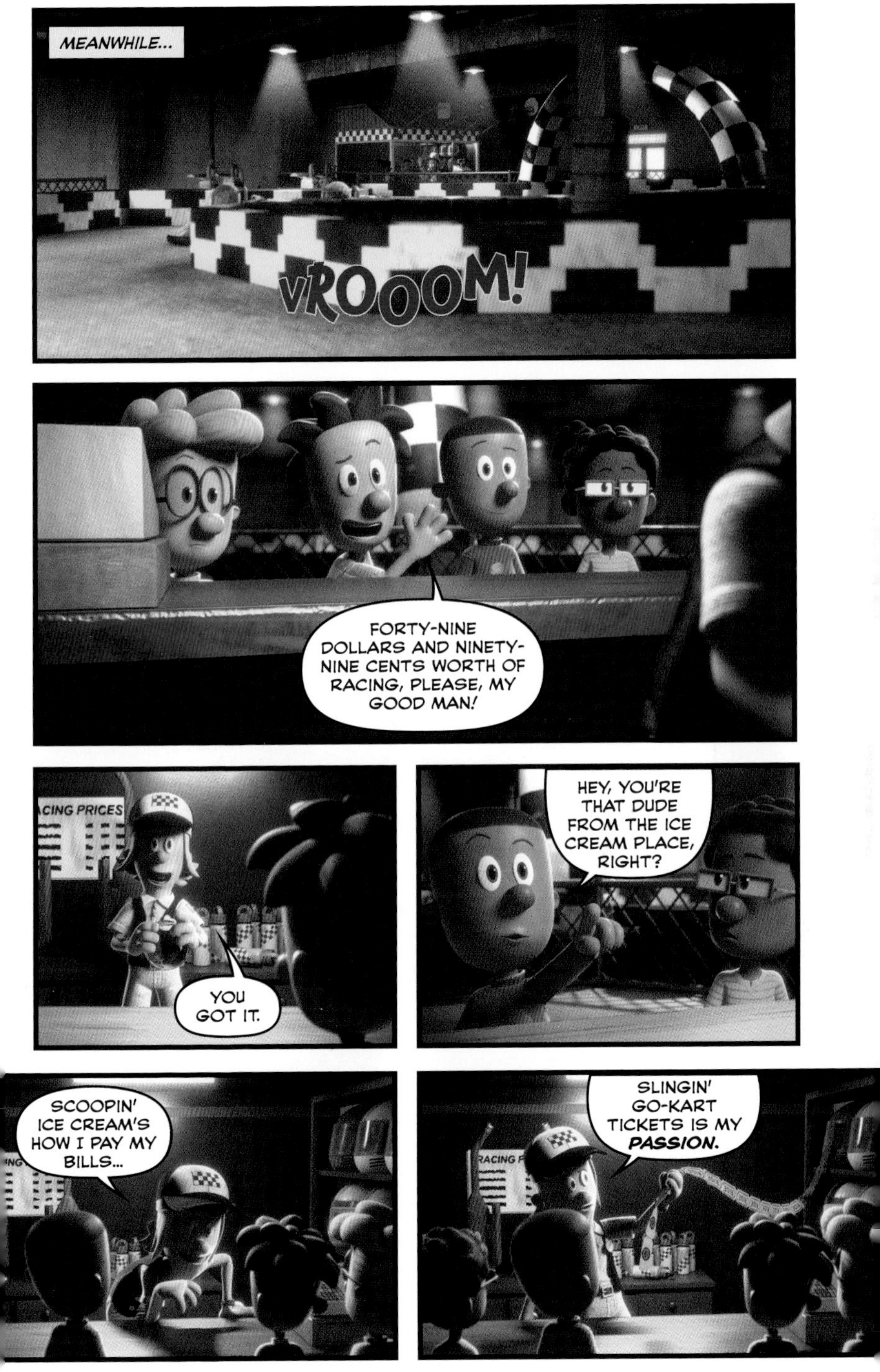
MEANWHILE...
VROOOM!
FORTY-NINE DOLLARS AND NINETY-NINE CENTS WORTH OF RACING, PLEASE, MY GOOD MAN!
CING PRICES
YOU GOT IT.
HEY, YOU'RE THAT DUDE FROM THE ICE CREAM PLACE, RIGHT?
SCOOPIN' ICE CREAM'S HOW I PAY MY BILLS...
SLINGIN' GO-KART TICKETS IS MY ***PASSION.***

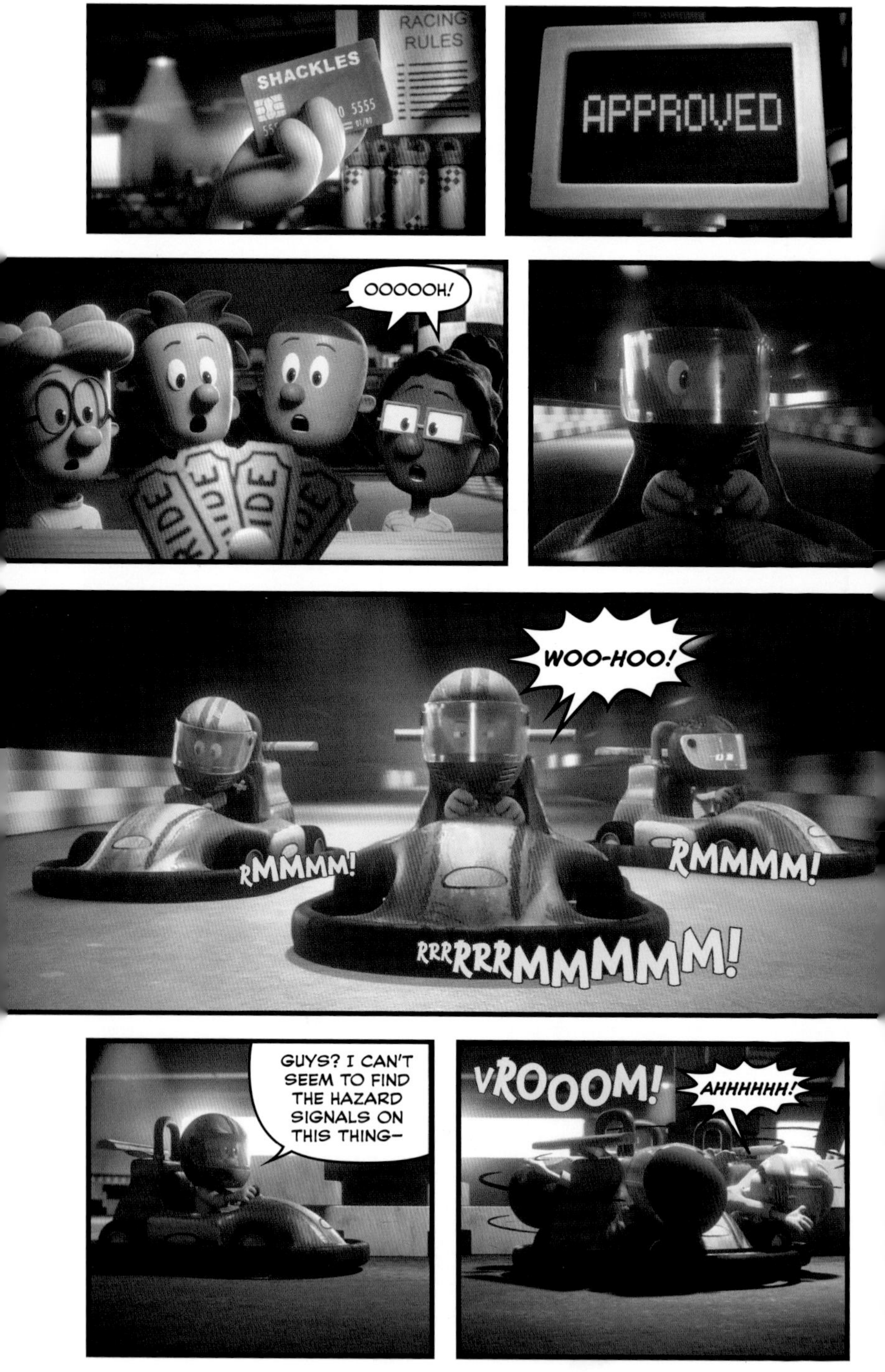
RACING RULES
SHACKLES
APPROVED
OOOOOH!
RIDE
WOO-HOO!
RMMMM!
RMMMM!
RRRRRRMMMMMM!
GUYS? I CAN'T SEEM TO FIND THE HAZARD SIGNALS ON THIS THING–
VROOOM!
AHHHHHH!

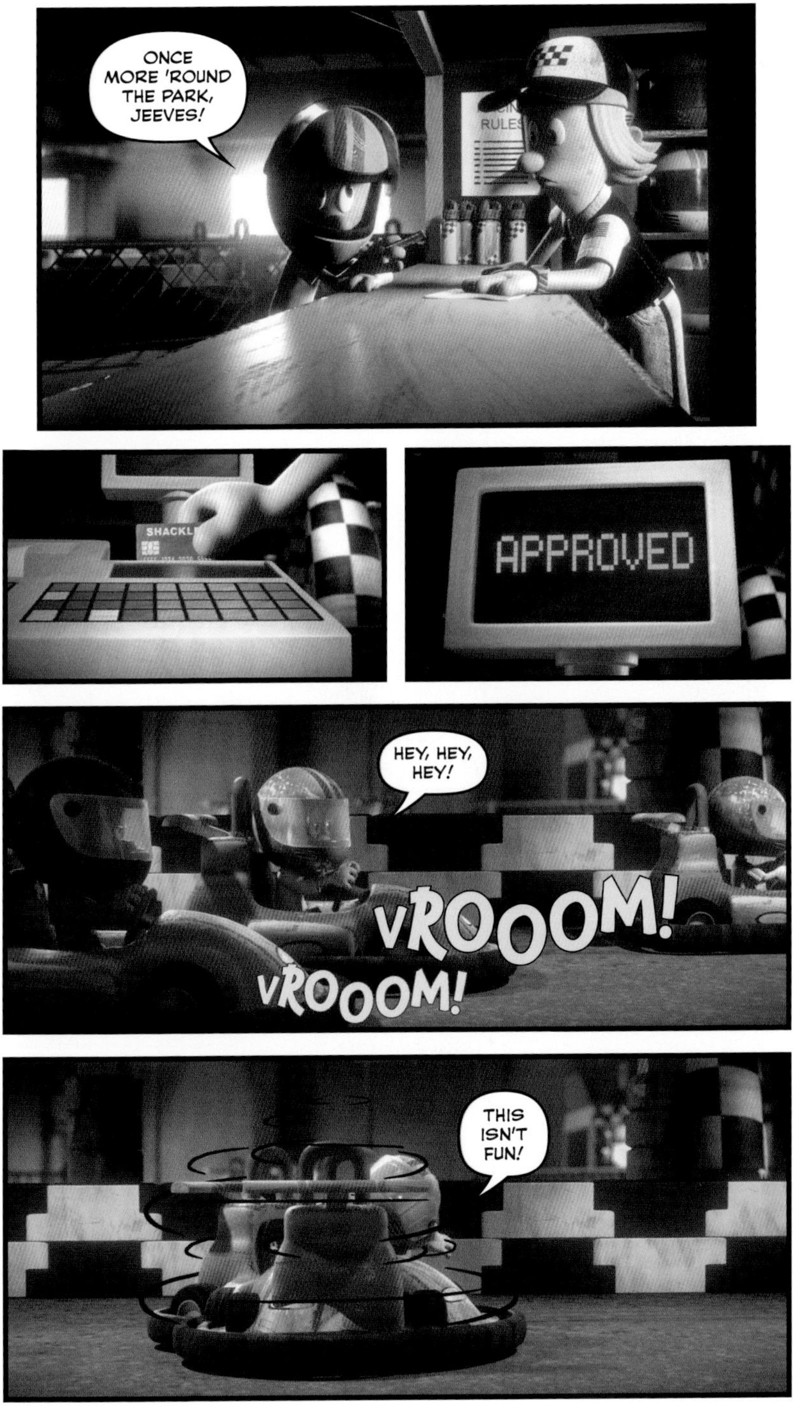
ONCE MORE 'ROUND THE PARK, JEEVES!
RULES
APPROVED
HEY, HEY, HEY!
VROOOM!
VROOOM!
THIS ISN'T FUN!

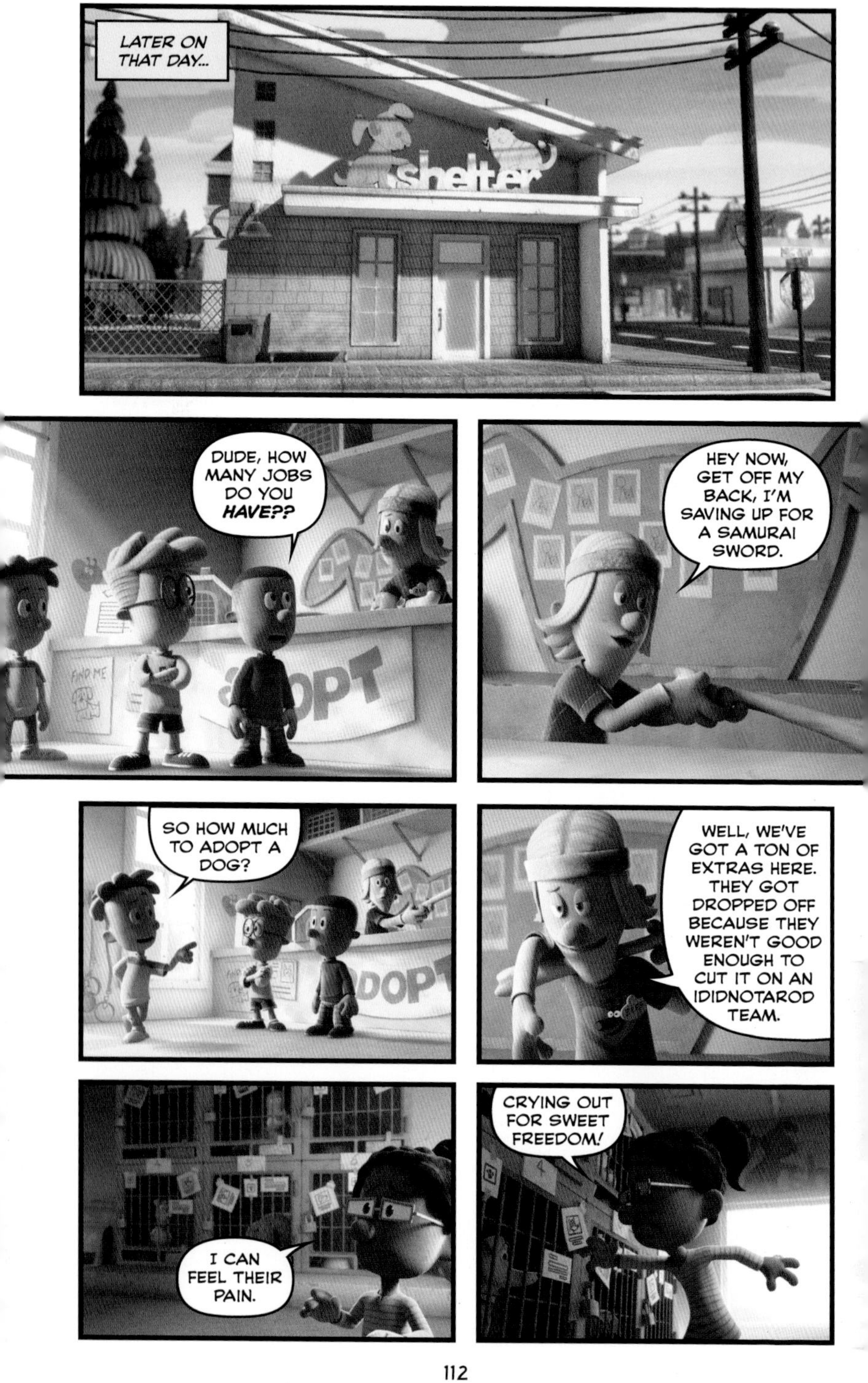
LATER ON THAT DAY...
shelter
DUDE, HOW MANY JOBS DO YOU *HAVE??*
ADOPT
FIND ME
HEY NOW, GET OFF MY BACK, I'M SAVING UP FOR A SAMURAI SWORD.
SO HOW MUCH TO ADOPT A DOG?
ADOPT
WELL, WE'VE GOT A TON OF EXTRAS HERE. THEY GOT DROPPED OFF BECAUSE THEY WEREN'T GOOD ENOUGH TO CUT IT ON AN IDIDNOTAROD TEAM.
I CAN FEEL THEIR PAIN.
CRYING OUT FOR SWEET FREEDOM!

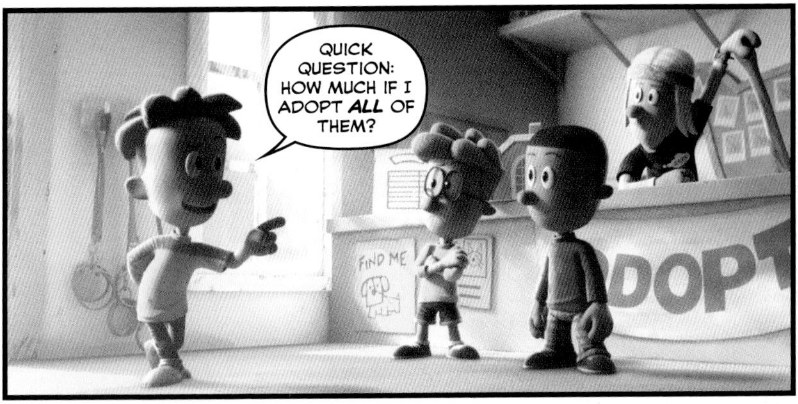
QUICK QUESTION: HOW MUCH IF I ADOPT ALL OF THEM?
FIND ME
DOPT

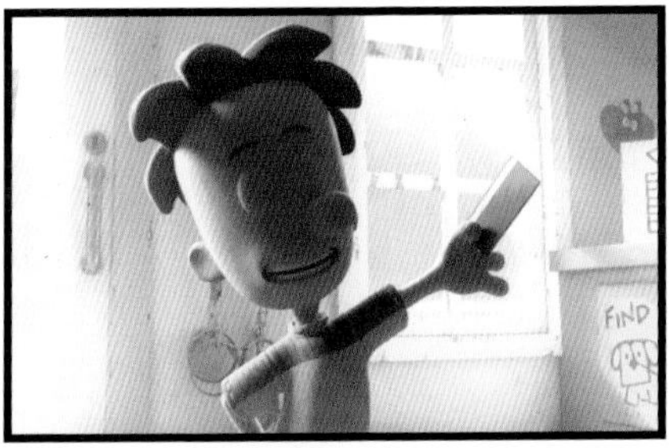
FIND

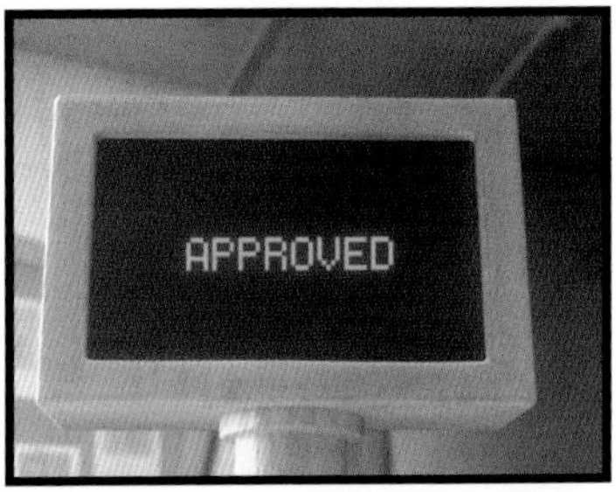
APPROVED

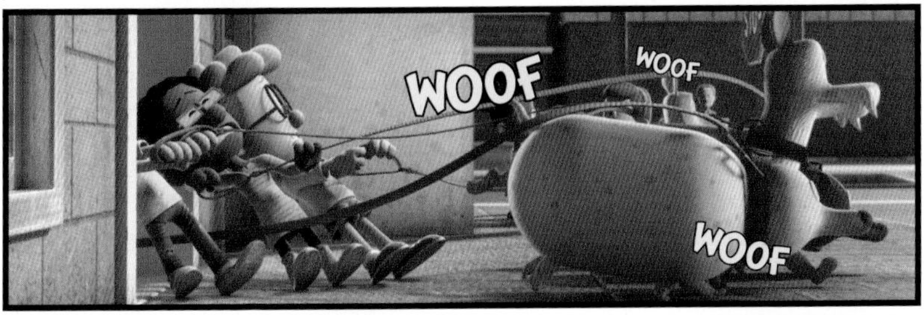
WOOF
WOOF
WOOF

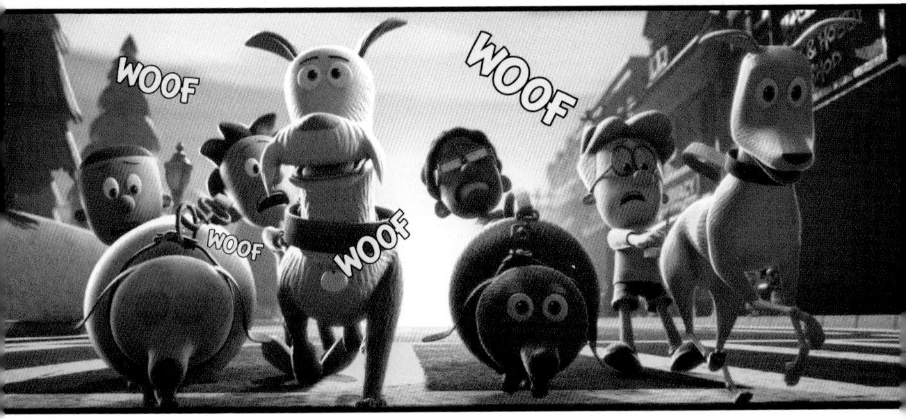
WOOF
WOOF
WOOF
WOOF

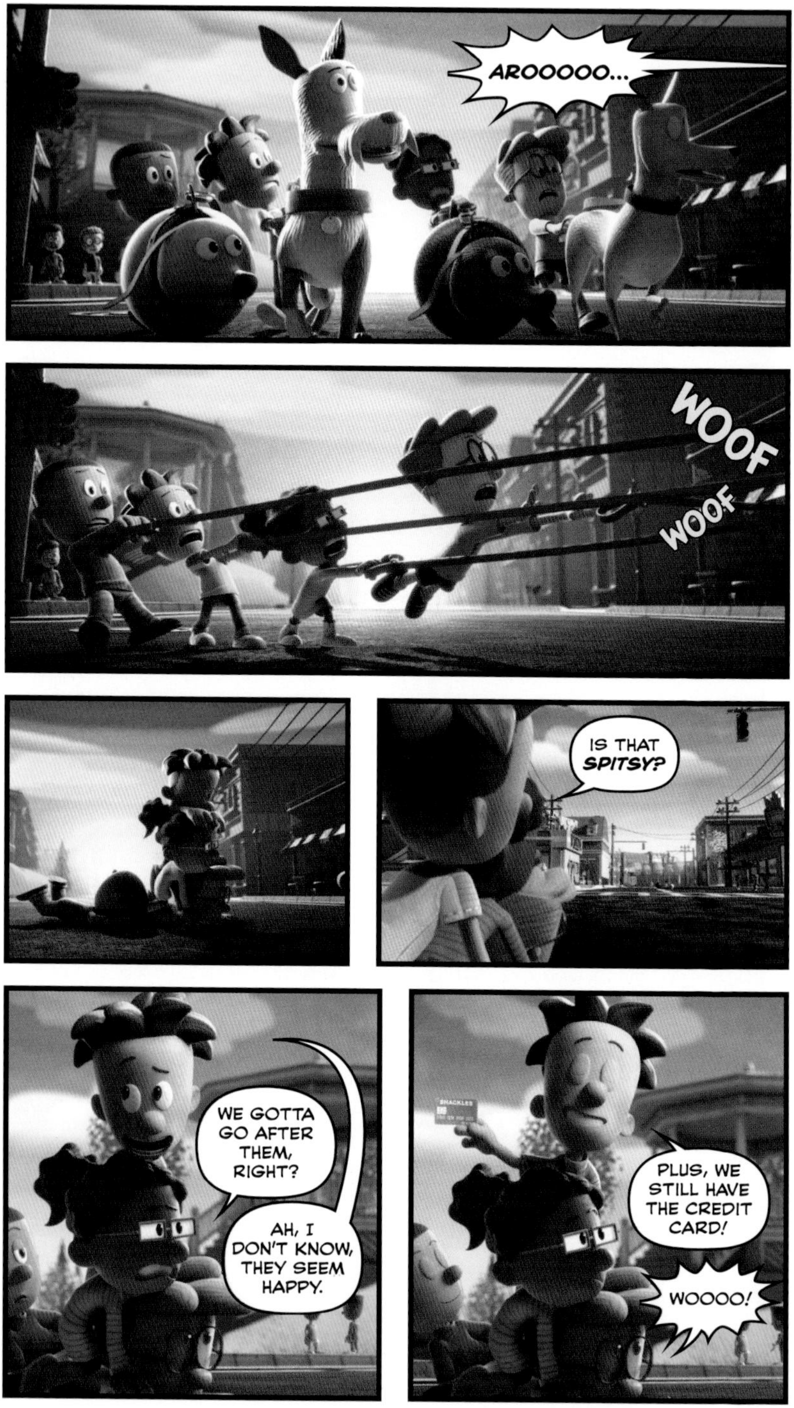
AROOOOO...
WOOF
WOOF
IS THAT SPITSY?
WE GOTTA GO AFTER THEM, RIGHT?
AH, I DON'T KNOW, THEY SEEM HAPPY.
PLUS, WE STILL HAVE THE CREDIT CARD!
WOOOO!

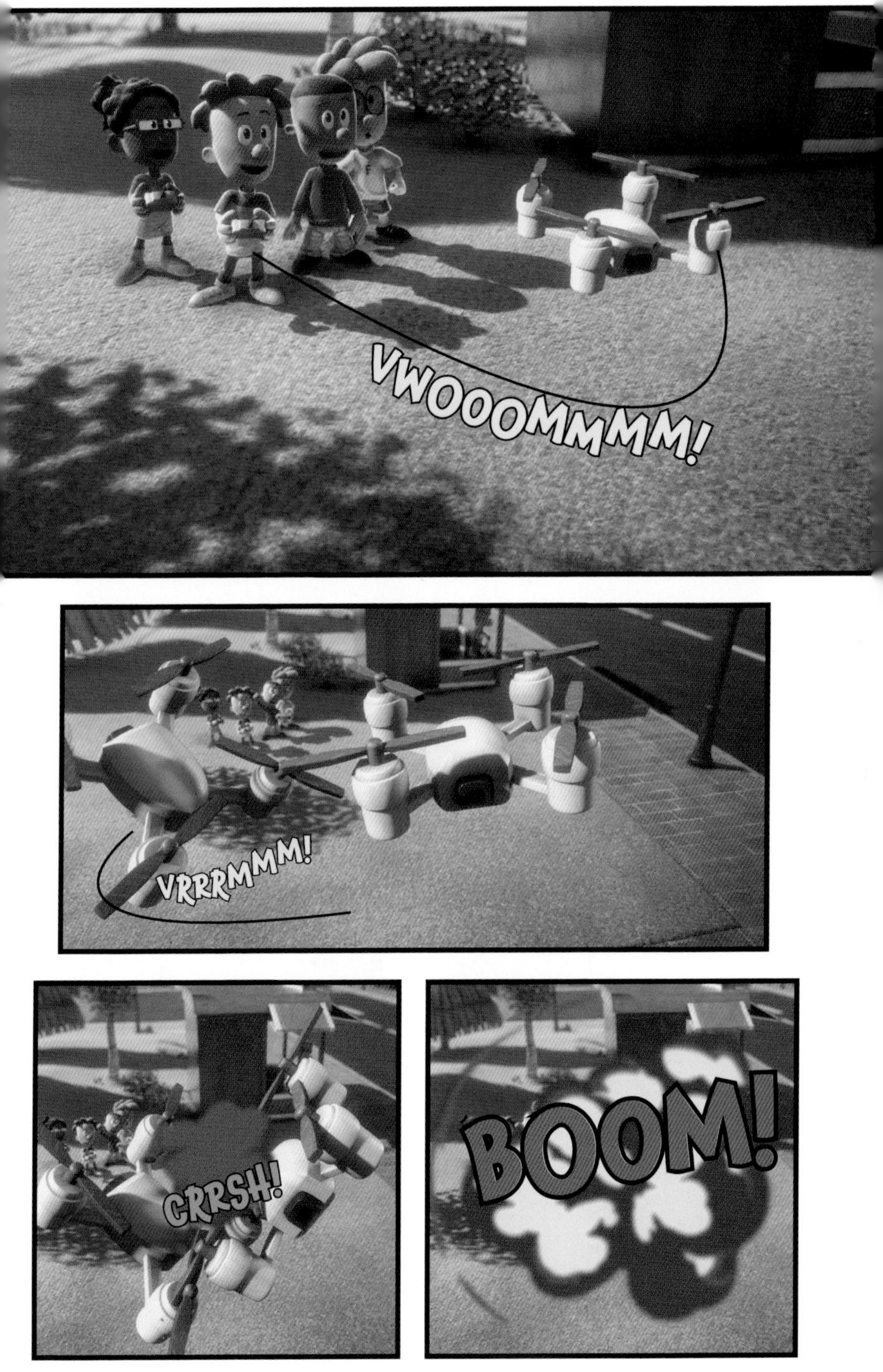
VWOOOMMMMM!
VRRRMMM!
CRRSH!
BOOM!

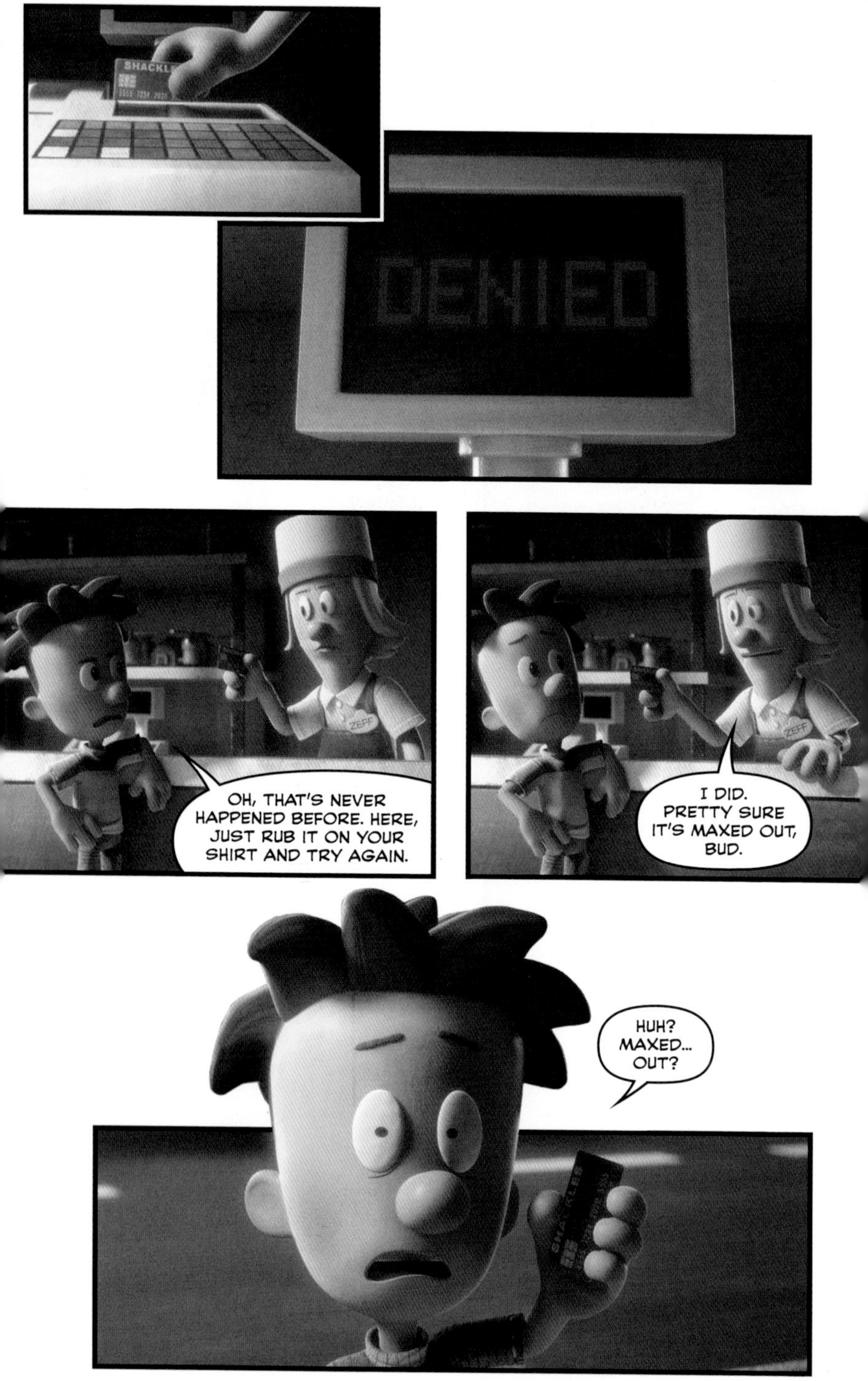
DENIED
OH, THAT'S NEVER HAPPENED BEFORE. HERE, JUST RUB IT ON YOUR SHIRT AND TRY AGAIN.
I DID. PRETTY SURE IT'S MAXED OUT, BUD.
HUH? MAXED... OUT?

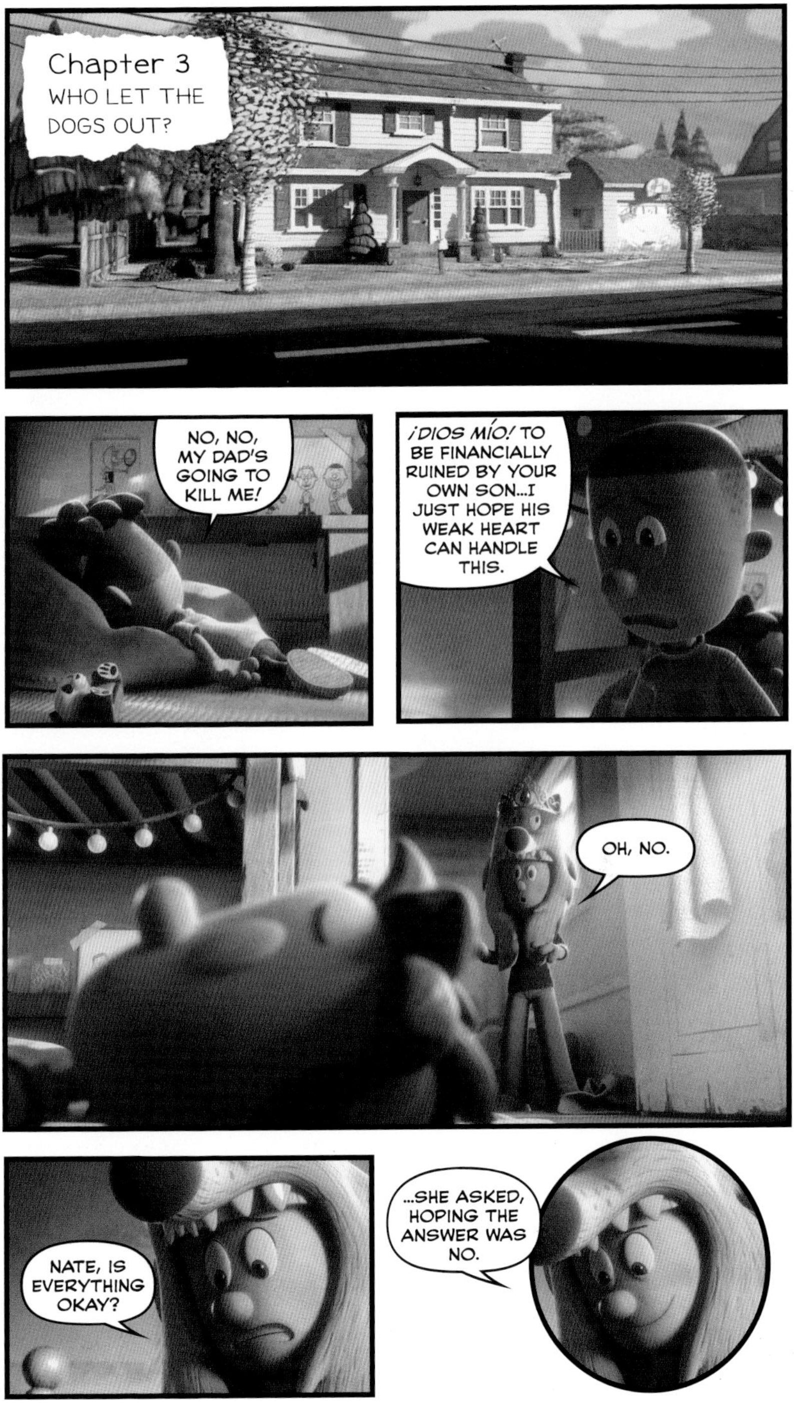
Chapter 3
WHO LET THE DOGS OUT?
NO, NO, MY DAD'S GOING TO KILL ME!
¡DIOS MÍO! TO BE FINANCIALLY RUINED BY YOUR OWN SON...I JUST HOPE HIS WEAK HEART CAN HANDLE THIS.
OH, NO.
NATE, IS EVERYTHING OKAY?
...SHE ASKED, HOPING THE ANSWER WAS NO.

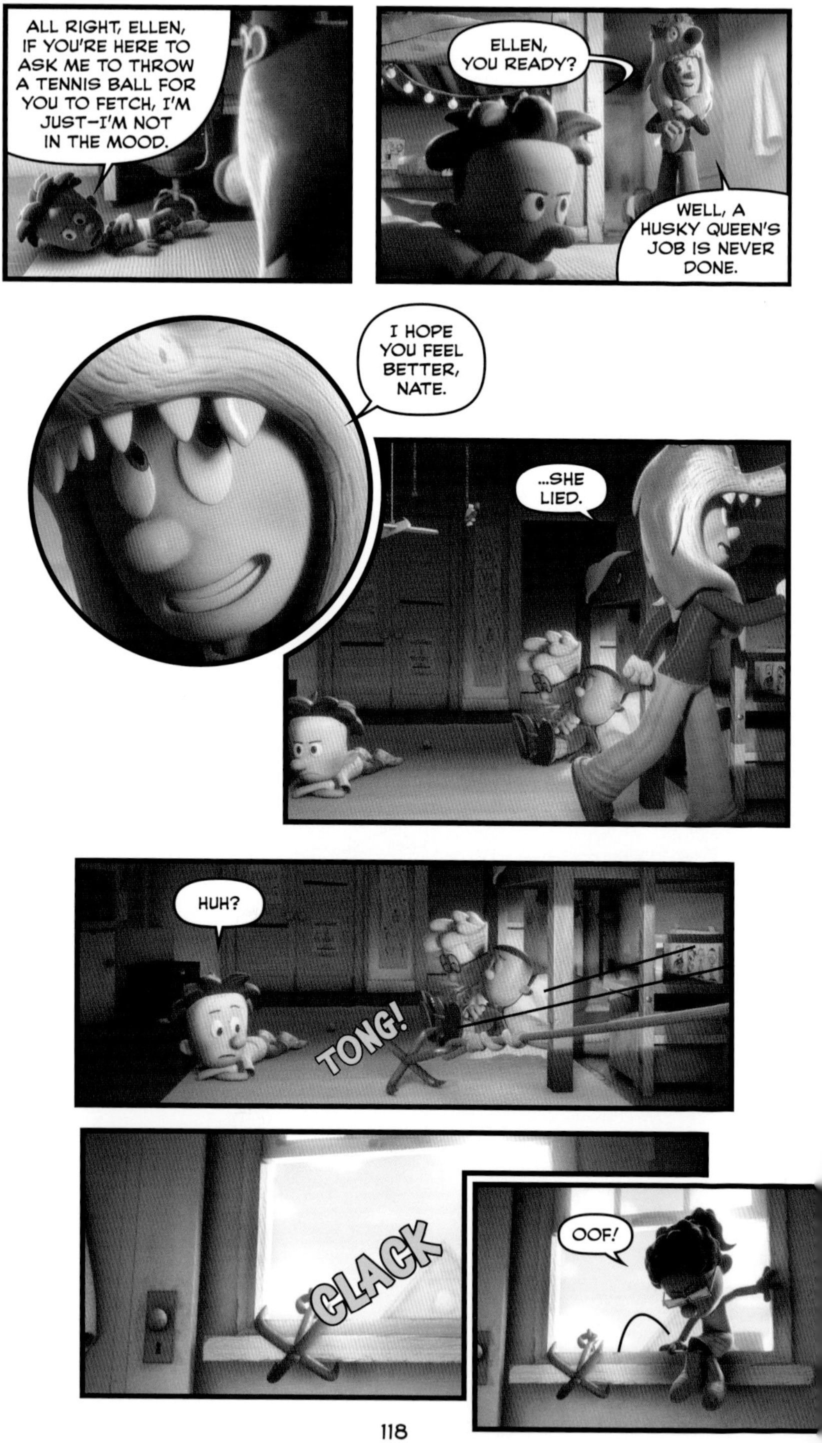
ALL RIGHT, ELLEN, IF YOU'RE HERE TO ASK ME TO THROW A TENNIS BALL FOR YOU TO FETCH, I'M JUST—I'M NOT IN THE MOOD.
ELLEN, YOU READY?
WELL, A HUSKY QUEEN'S JOB IS NEVER DONE.
I HOPE YOU FEEL BETTER, NATE.
...SHE LIED.
HUH?
TONG!
CLACK
OOF!

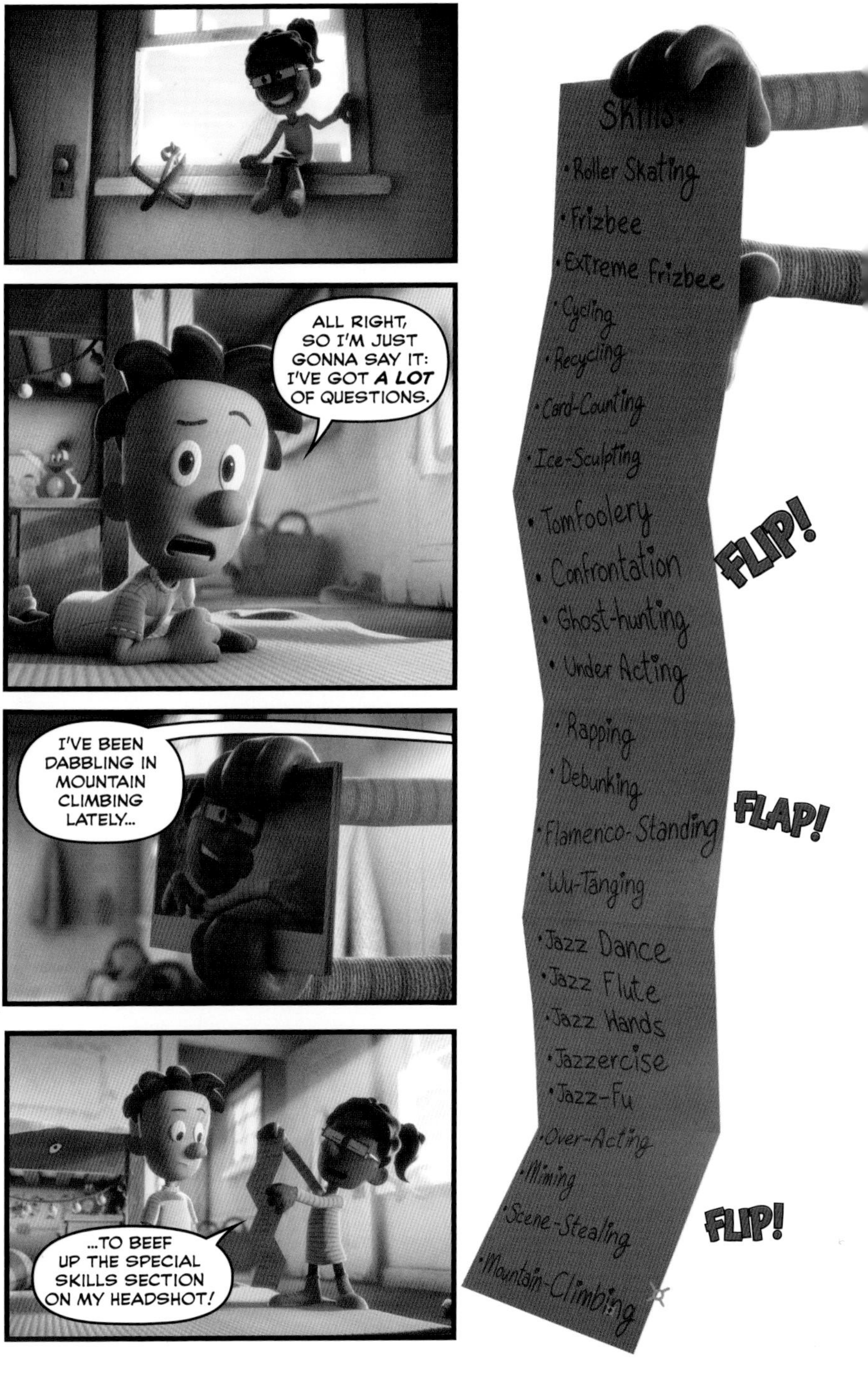
ALL RIGHT, SO I'M JUST GONNA SAY IT: I'VE GOT **A LOT** OF QUESTIONS.
I'VE BEEN DABBLING IN MOUNTAIN CLIMBING LATELY...
...TO BEEF UP THE SPECIAL SKILLS SECTION ON MY HEADSHOT!
Skills:
•Roller Skating
•Frizbee
•Extreme Frizbee
•Cycling
•Recycling
•Card-Counting
•Ice-Sculpting
•Tomfoolery
•Confrontation
•Ghost-hunting
•Under Acting
•Rapping
•Debunking
•Flamenco-Standing
•Wu-Tanging
•Jazz Dance
•Jazz Flute
•Jazz Hands
•Jazzercise
•Jazz-Fu
•Over-Acting
•Miming
•Scene-Stealing
•Mountain-Climbing
FLIP!
FLAP!
FLIP!

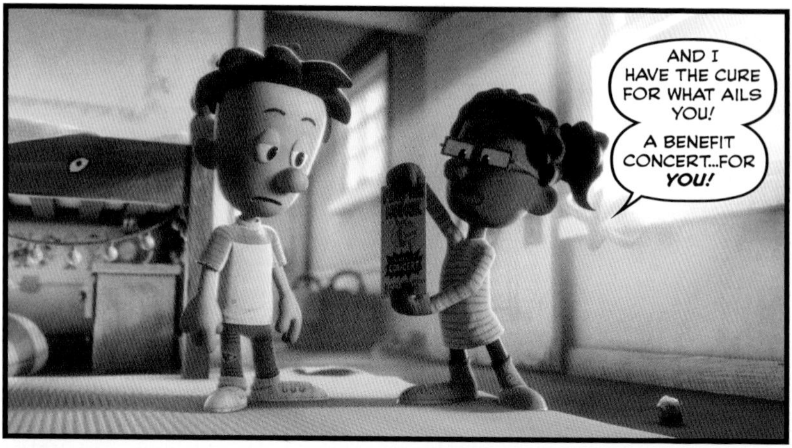
AND I HAVE THE CURE FOR WHAT AILS YOU!
A BENEFIT CONCERT...FOR *YOU!*

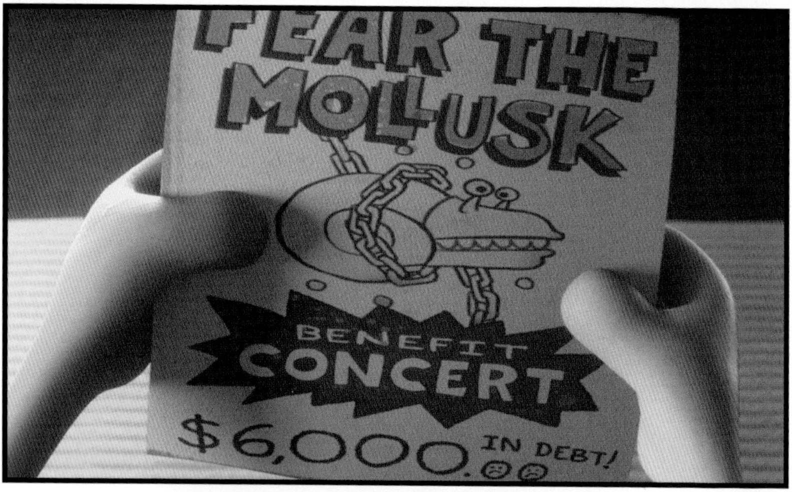
FEAR THE MOLLUSK
BENEFIT CONCERT
$6,000.
IN DEBT!

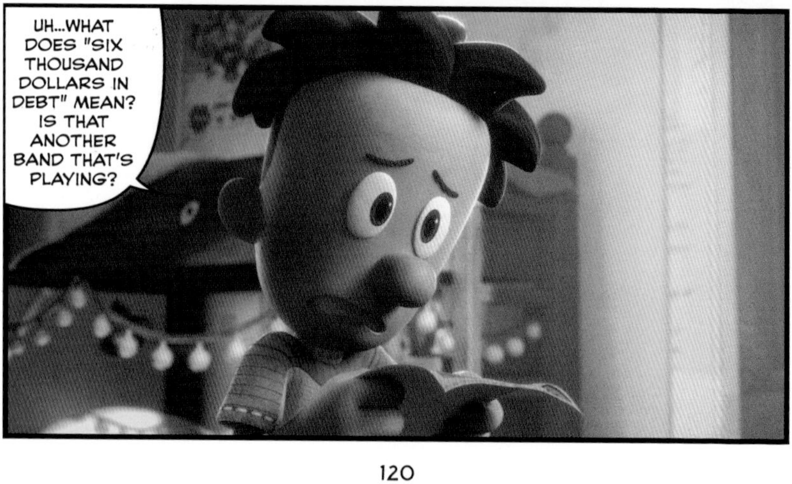
UH...WHAT DOES "SIX THOUSAND DOLLARS IN DEBT" MEAN? IS THAT ANOTHER BAND THAT'S PLAYING?

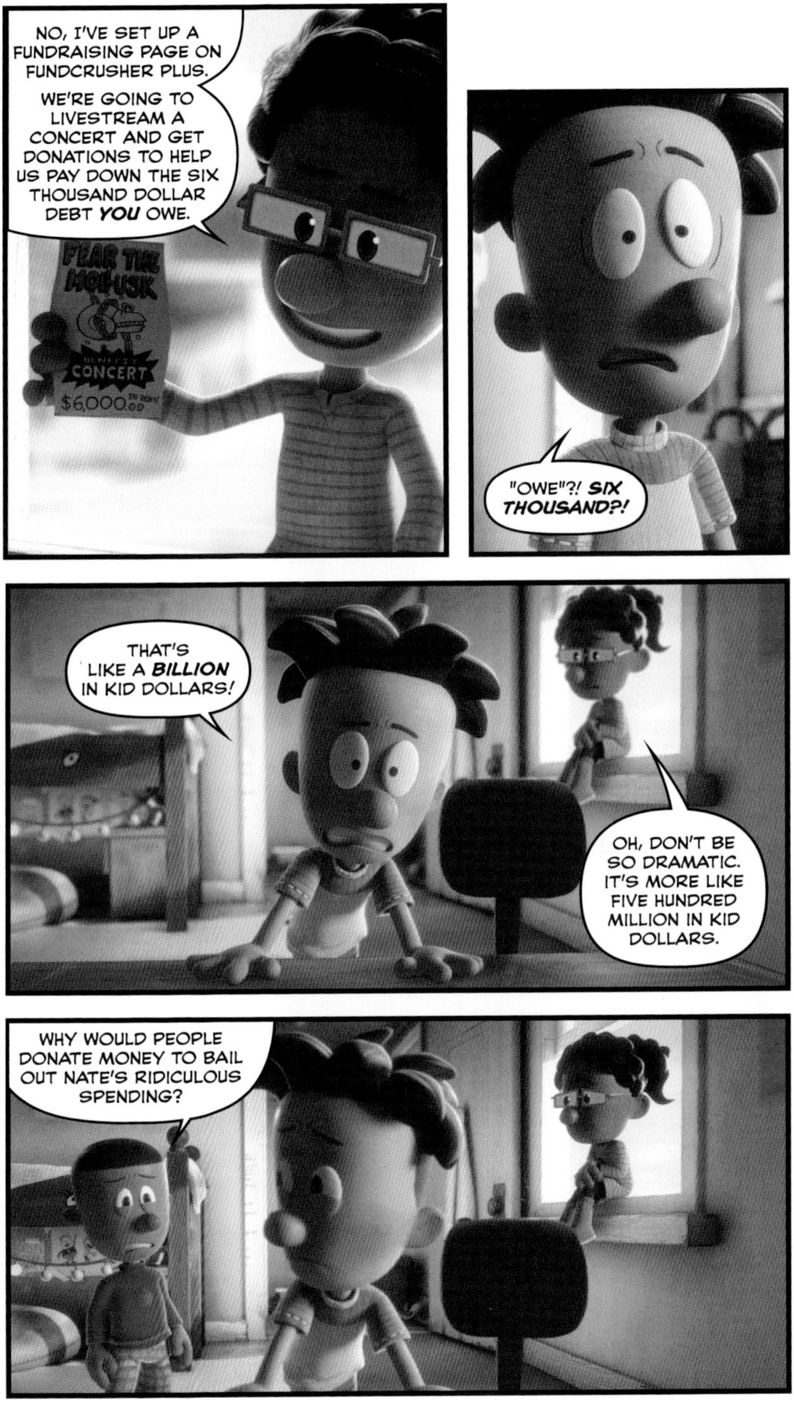
NO, I'VE SET UP A FUNDRAISING PAGE ON FUNDCRUSHER PLUS.
WE'RE GOING TO LIVESTREAM A CONCERT AND GET DONATIONS TO HELP US PAY DOWN THE SIX THOUSAND DOLLAR DEBT ***YOU*** OWE.
CONCERT
$6,000.00
"OWE"?! ***SIX THOUSAND?!***
THAT'S LIKE A ***BILLION*** IN KID DOLLARS!
OH, DON'T BE SO DRAMATIC. IT'S MORE LIKE FIVE HUNDRED MILLION IN KID DOLLARS.
WHY WOULD PEOPLE DONATE MONEY TO BAIL OUT NATE'S RIDICULOUS SPENDING?

WELL, I MAY HAVE HINTED THAT NATE HAS A RARE DISEASE: RASHISNIFFACHONDRIA. SYMPTOMS INCLUDE DRY, ITCHY RASH—

W-WAIT, WAIT, I REALLY *AM* KIND OF ITCHY.

SCRATCH SCRATCH

LOSS OF SENSE OF SMELL—

≷SNIFF≷ HANG ON, DO YOU GUYS SMELL THAT? ME NEITHER!

DRY MOUTH.

MOUTH... SO DRY! PLEASE...TELL ME...THERE'S... A CURE!

OH, NATE, THERE IS NO CURE BECAUSE I'M MAKING UP THE SYMPTOMS AS I GO!

OH. THAT'S PERFECT! HEY, DEE DEE, YOUR IDEA SOUNDS TOTALLY INSANE. LET'S DO IT!

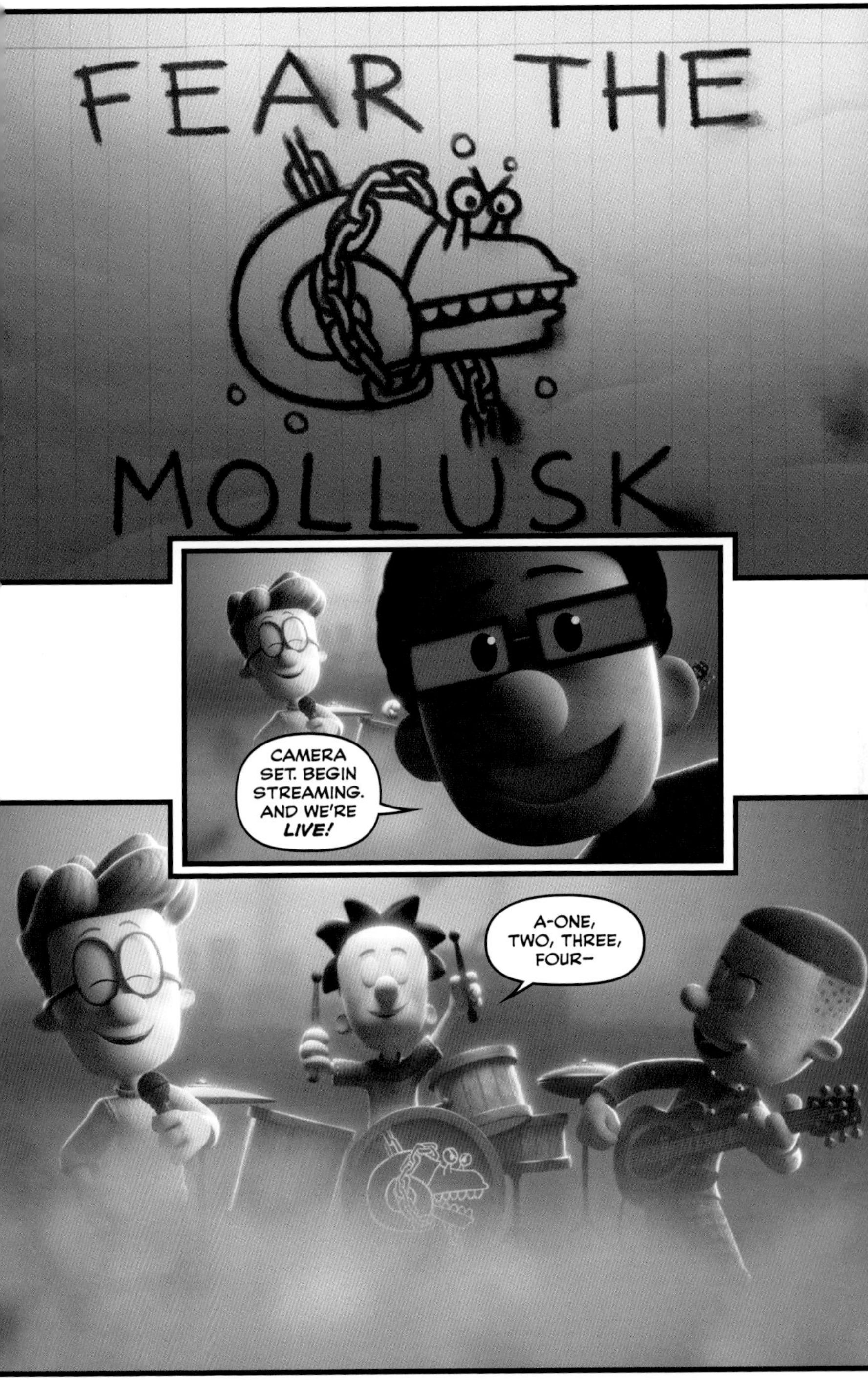
FEAR THE
MOLLUSK
CAMERA SET. BEGIN STREAMING. AND WE'RE LIVE!
A-ONE, TWO, THREE, FOUR—

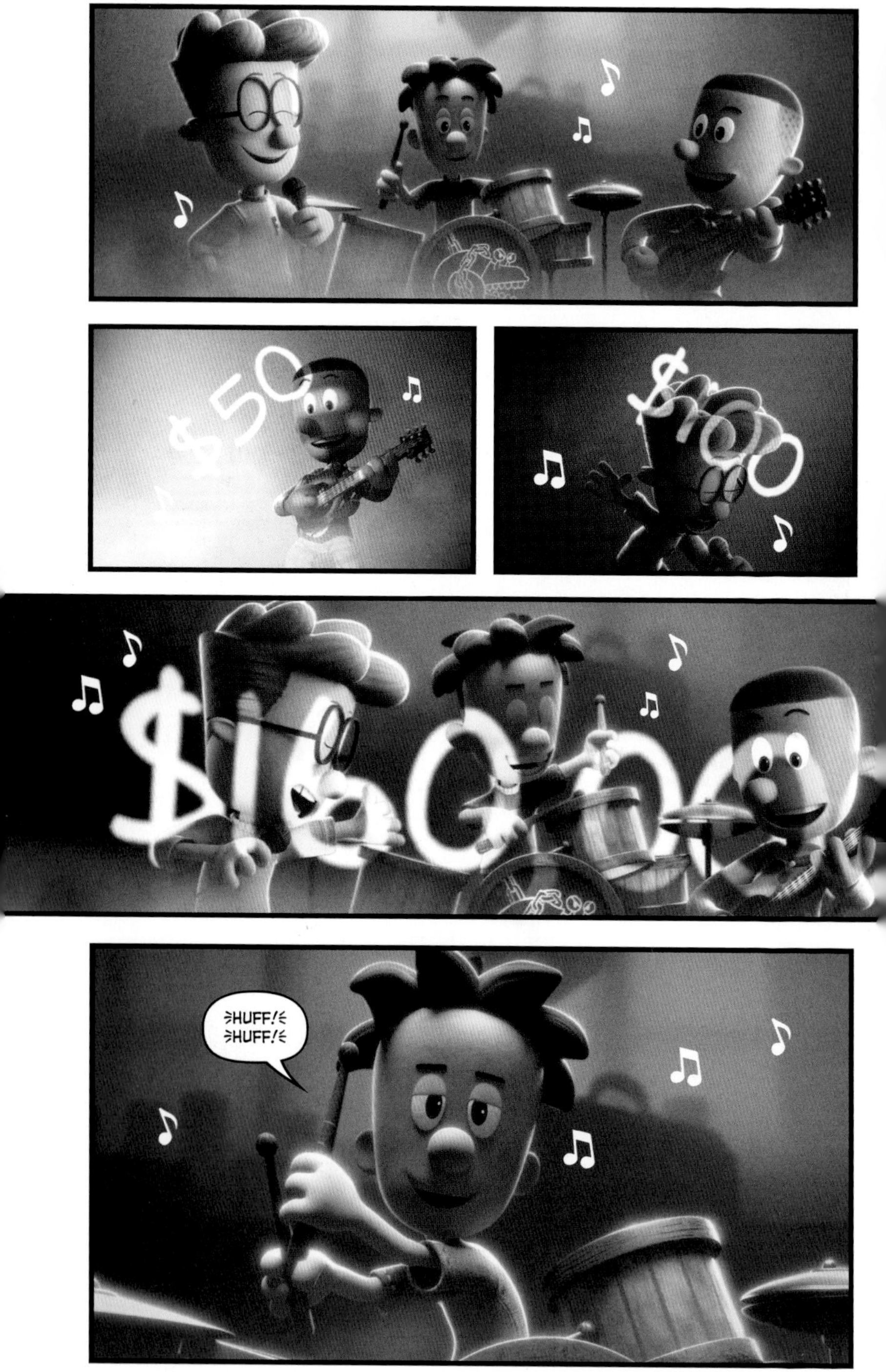
$50
$100
HUFF!
HUFF!

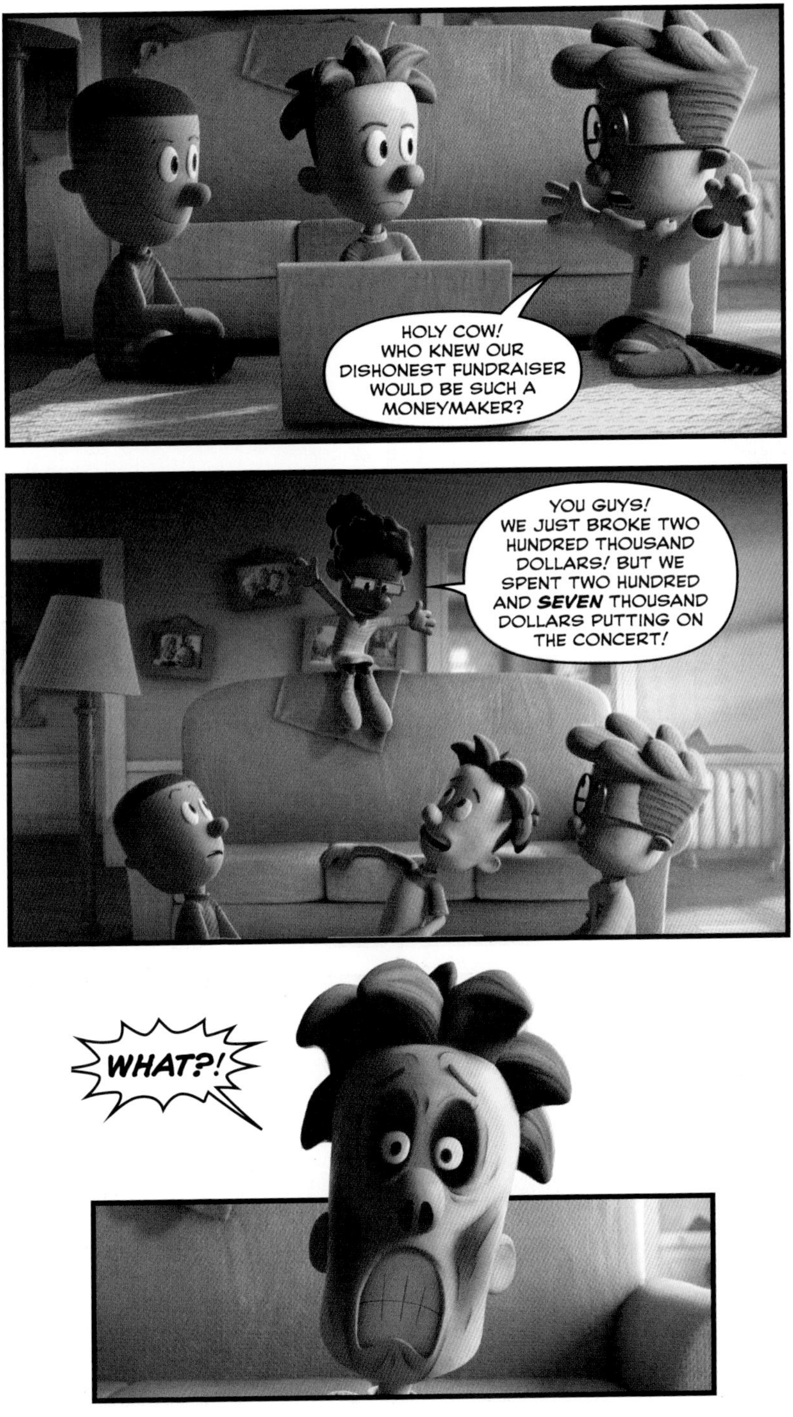
HOLY COW! WHO KNEW OUR DISHONEST FUNDRAISER WOULD BE SUCH A MONEYMAKER?
YOU GUYS! WE JUST BROKE TWO HUNDRED THOUSAND DOLLARS! BUT WE SPENT TWO HUNDRED AND **SEVEN** THOUSAND DOLLARS PUTTING ON THE CONCERT!
WHAT?!

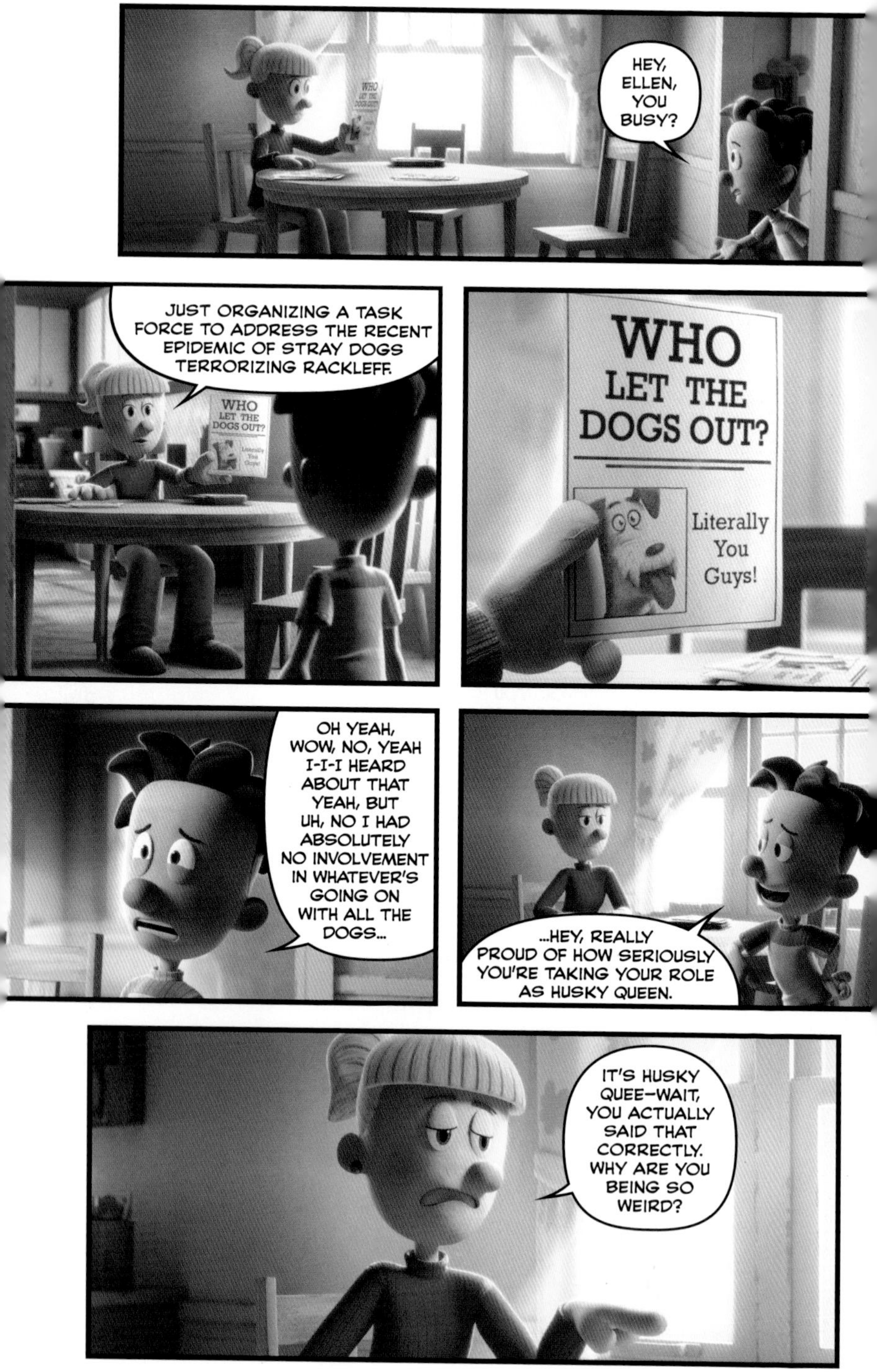
HEY, ELLEN, YOU BUSY?
WHO LET THE DOGS OUT?
JUST ORGANIZING A TASK FORCE TO ADDRESS THE RECENT EPIDEMIC OF STRAY DOGS TERRORIZING RACKLEFF.
WHO LET THE DOGS OUT?
Literally You Guys!
OH YEAH, WOW, NO, YEAH I-I-I HEARD ABOUT THAT YEAH, BUT UH, NO I HAD ABSOLUTELY NO INVOLVEMENT IN WHATEVER'S GOING ON WITH ALL THE DOGS...
...HEY, REALLY PROUD OF HOW SERIOUSLY YOU'RE TAKING YOUR ROLE AS HUSKY QUEEN.
IT'S HUSKY QUEE—WAIT, YOU ACTUALLY SAID THAT CORRECTLY. WHY ARE YOU BEING SO WEIRD?

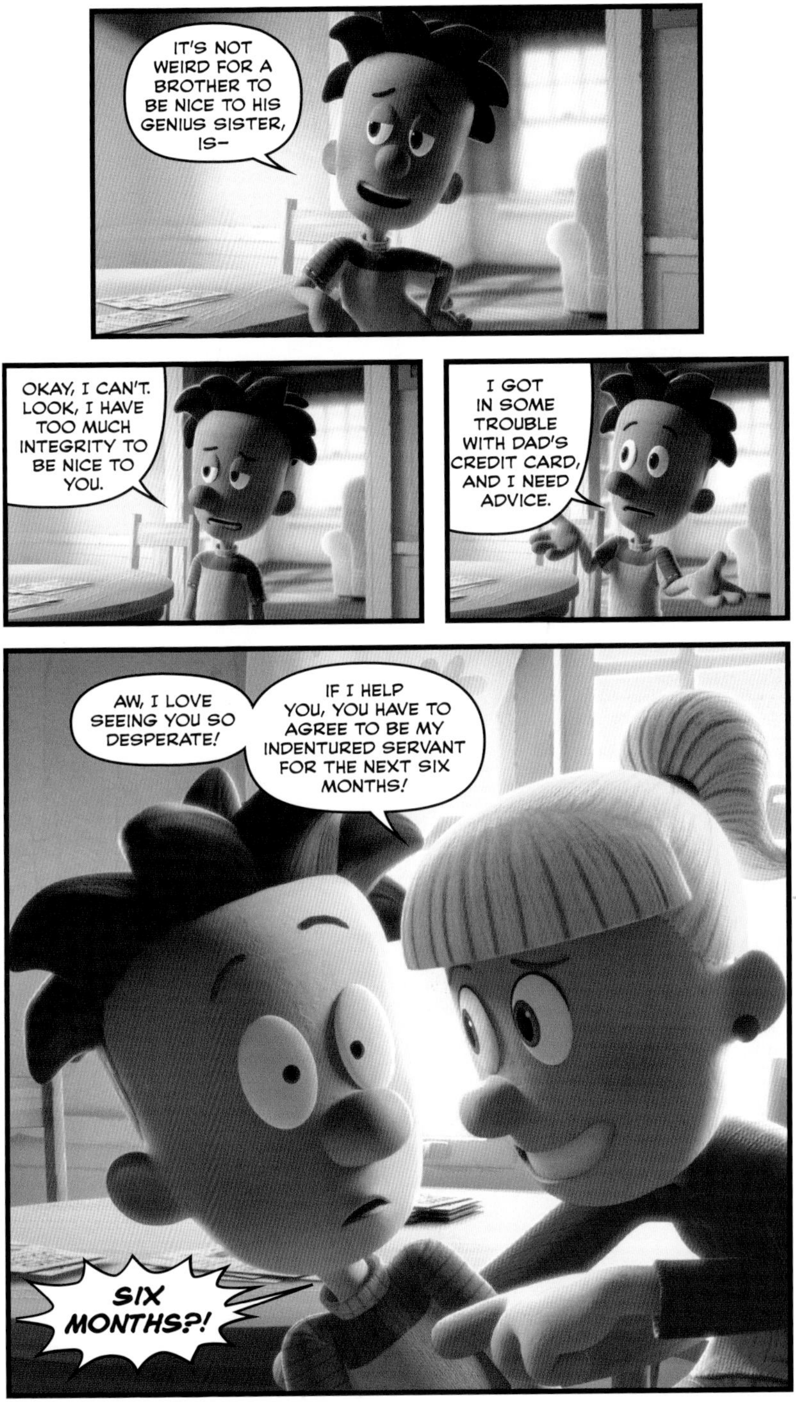
IT'S NOT WEIRD FOR A BROTHER TO BE NICE TO HIS GENIUS SISTER, IS–
OKAY, I CAN'T. LOOK, I HAVE TOO MUCH INTEGRITY TO BE NICE TO YOU.
I GOT IN SOME TROUBLE WITH DAD'S CREDIT CARD, AND I NEED ADVICE.
AW, I LOVE SEEING YOU SO DESPERATE!
IF I HELP YOU, YOU HAVE TO AGREE TO BE MY INDENTURED SERVANT FOR THE NEXT SIX MONTHS!
SIX MONTHS?!

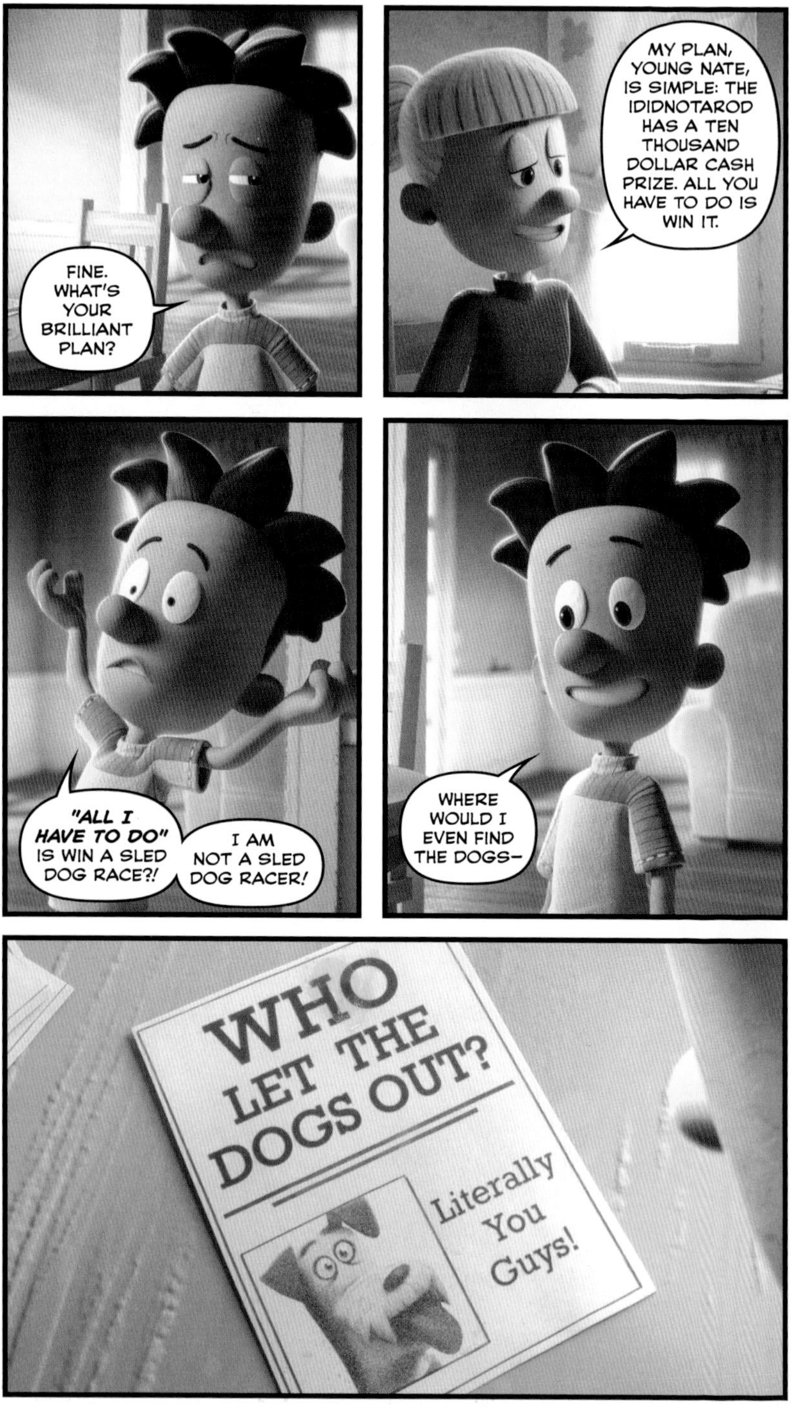
FINE. WHAT'S YOUR BRILLIANT PLAN?
MY PLAN, YOUNG NATE, IS SIMPLE: THE IDIDNOTAROD HAS A TEN THOUSAND DOLLAR CASH PRIZE. ALL YOU HAVE TO DO IS WIN IT.
"ALL I HAVE TO DO" IS WIN A SLED DOG RACE?!
I AM NOT A SLED DOG RACER!
WHERE WOULD I EVEN FIND THE DOGS–
WHO LET THE DOGS OUT?
Literally You Guys!

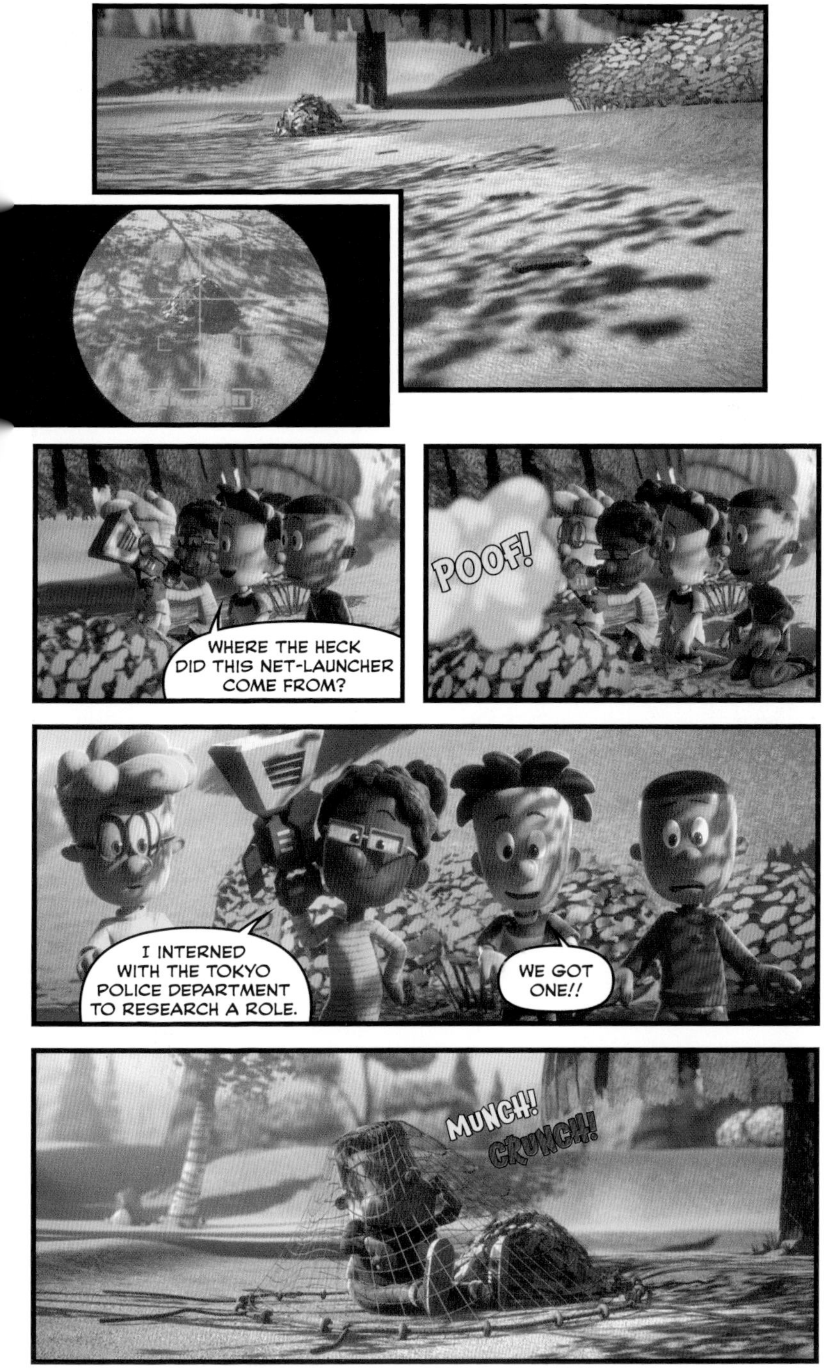
WHERE THE HECK DID THIS NET-LAUNCHER COME FROM?
POOF!
I INTERNED WITH THE TOKYO POLICE DEPARTMENT TO RESEARCH A ROLE.
WE GOT ONE!!
MUNCH!
CRUNCH!

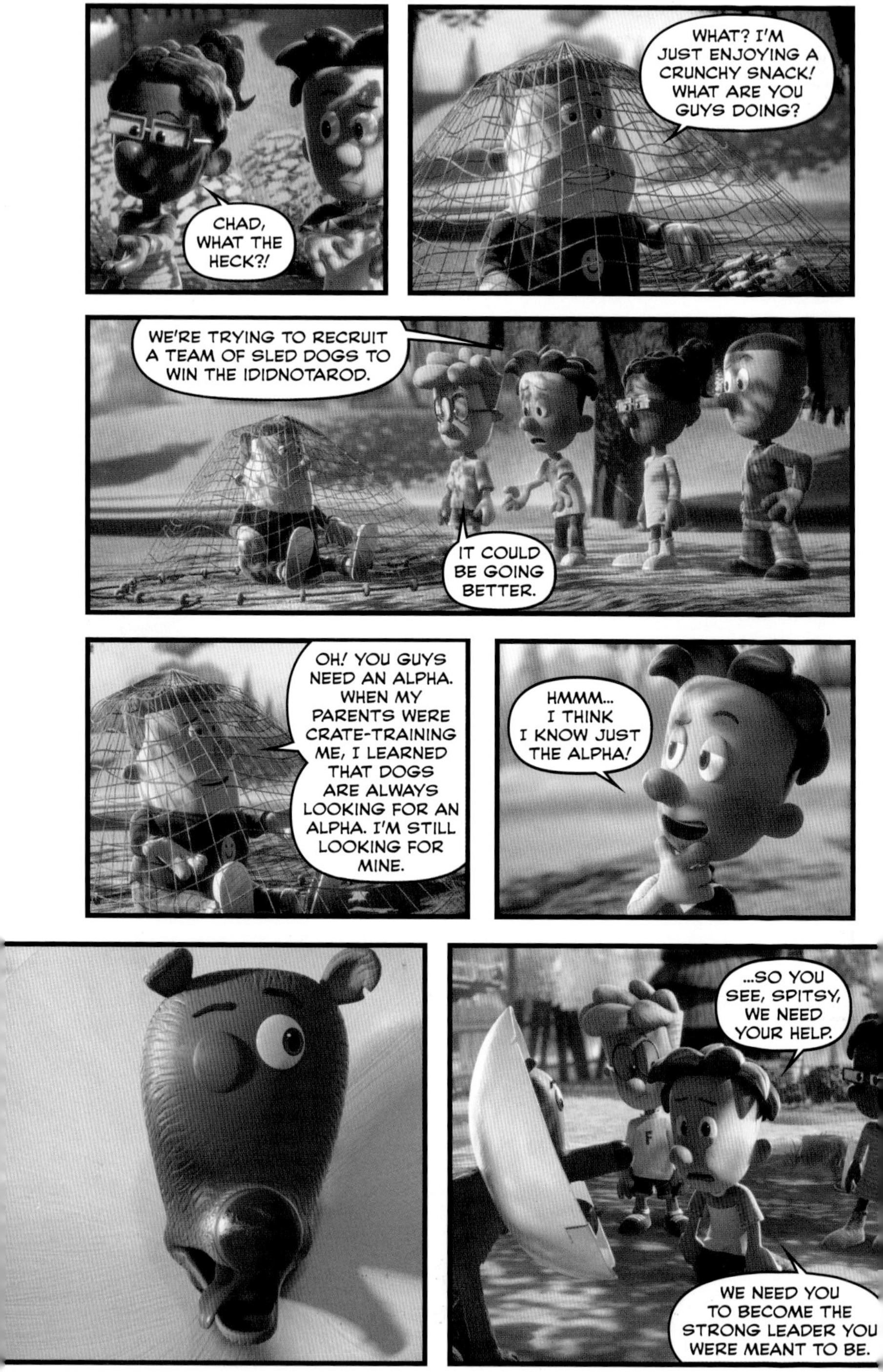
CHAD, WHAT THE HECK?!
WHAT? I'M JUST ENJOYING A CRUNCHY SNACK! WHAT ARE YOU GUYS DOING?
WE'RE TRYING TO RECRUIT A TEAM OF SLED DOGS TO WIN THE IDIDNOTAROD.
IT COULD BE GOING BETTER.
OH! YOU GUYS NEED AN ALPHA. WHEN MY PARENTS WERE CRATE-TRAINING ME, I LEARNED THAT DOGS ARE ALWAYS LOOKING FOR AN ALPHA. I'M STILL LOOKING FOR MINE.
HMMM... I THINK I KNOW JUST THE ALPHA!
...SO YOU SEE, SPITSY, WE NEED YOUR HELP.
WE NEED YOU TO BECOME THE STRONG LEADER YOU WERE MEANT TO BE.

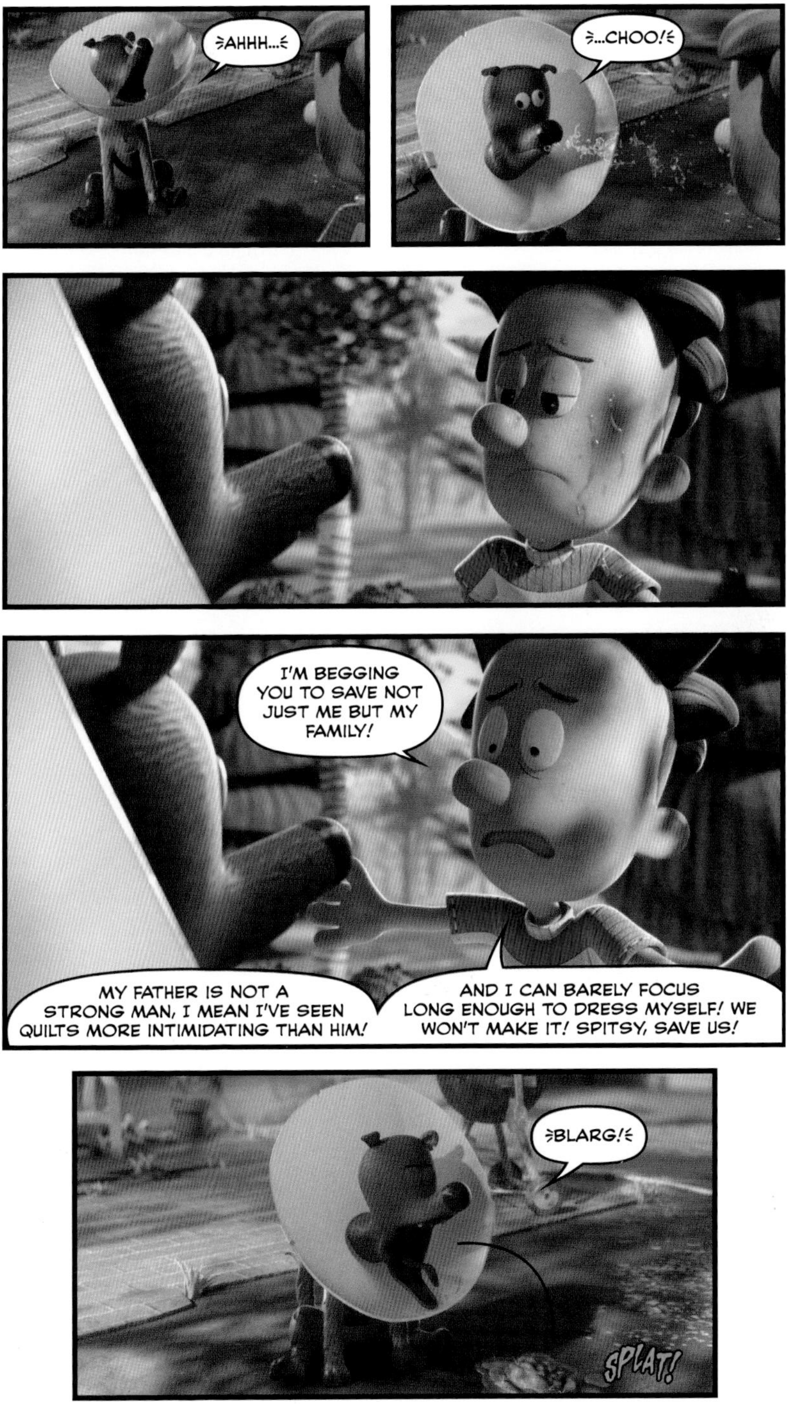

AHHH...
...CHOO!
I'M BEGGING YOU TO SAVE NOT JUST ME BUT MY FAMILY!
MY FATHER IS NOT A STRONG MAN, I MEAN I'VE SEEN QUILTS MORE INTIMIDATING THAN HIM!
AND I CAN BARELY FOCUS LONG ENOUGH TO DRESS MYSELF! WE WON'T MAKE IT! SPITSY, SAVE US!
BLARG!
SPLAT!

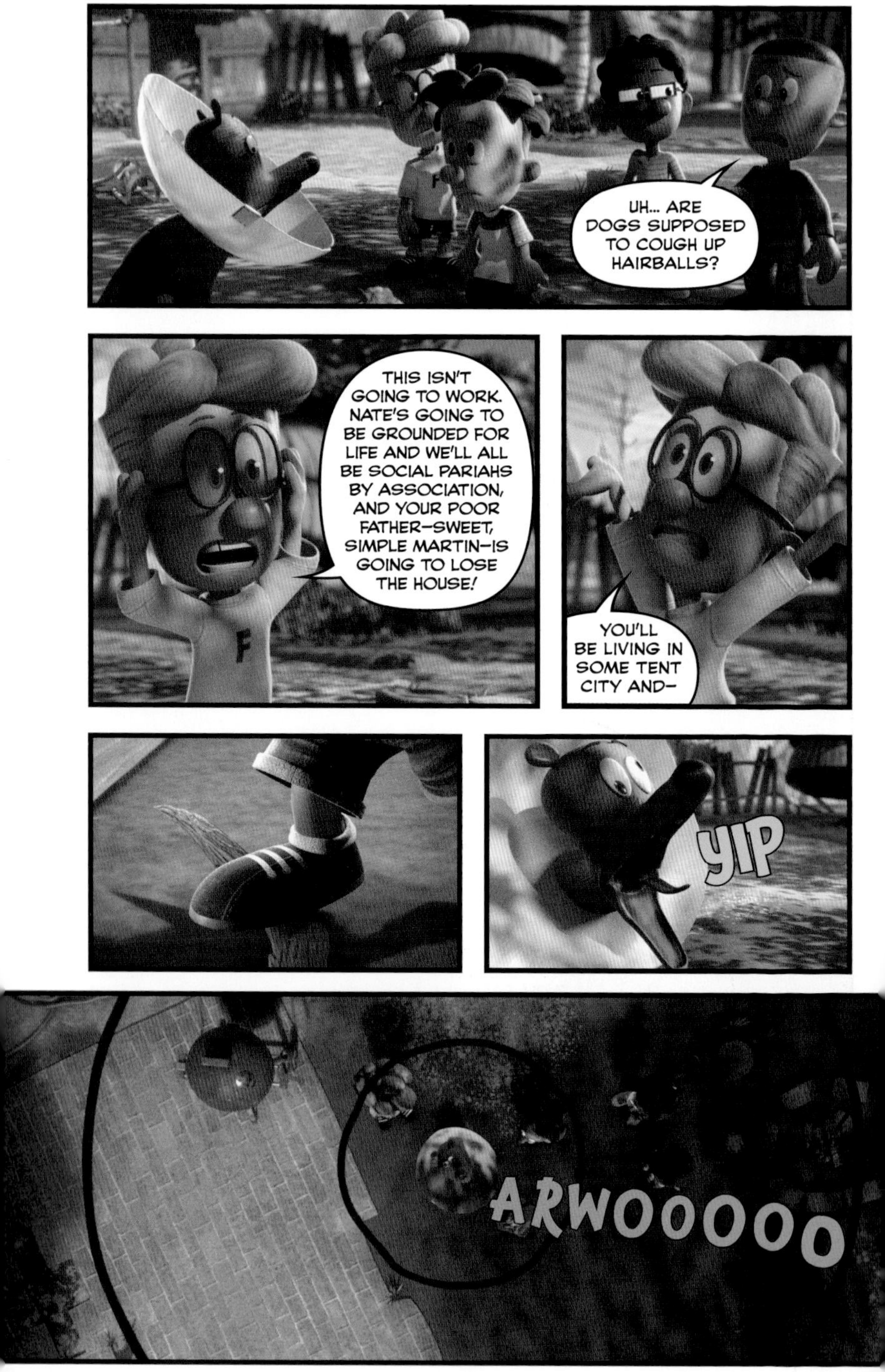
UH... ARE DOGS SUPPOSED TO COUGH UP HAIRBALLS?
THIS ISN'T GOING TO WORK. NATE'S GOING TO BE GROUNDED FOR LIFE AND WE'LL ALL BE SOCIAL PARIAHS BY ASSOCIATION, AND YOUR POOR FATHER—SWEET, SIMPLE MARTIN—IS GOING TO LOSE THE HOUSE!
YOU'LL BE LIVING IN SOME TENT CITY AND—
YIP
ARWOOOOO

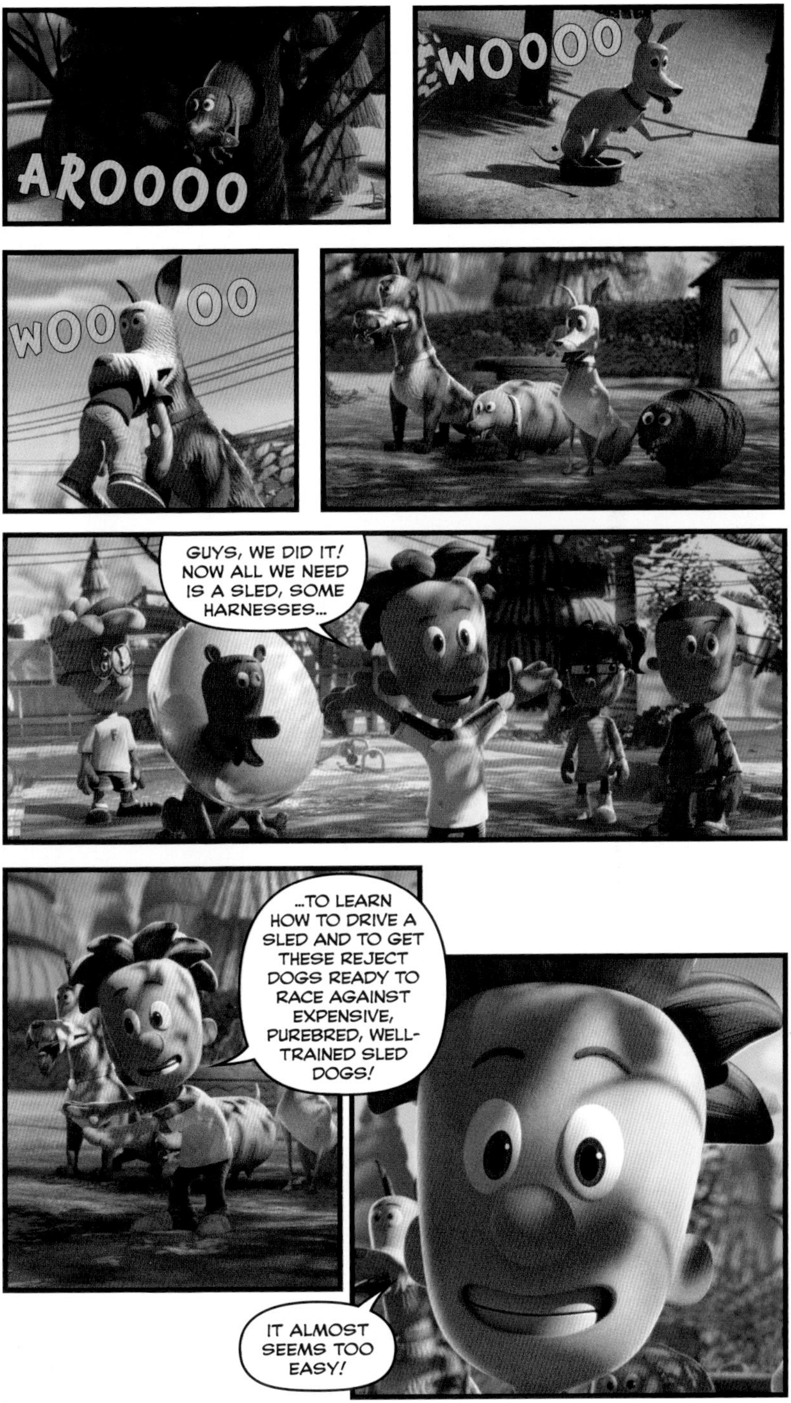
AROOOO
WOOOO
WOO OO
GUYS, WE DID IT! NOW ALL WE NEED IS A SLED, SOME HARNESSES...
...TO LEARN HOW TO DRIVE A SLED AND TO GET THESE REJECT DOGS READY TO RACE AGAINST EXPENSIVE, PUREBRED, WELL-TRAINED SLED DOGS!
IT ALMOST SEEMS TOO EASY!

Chapter 4
THE RACE IS ON!

RACKLEFF IDIDNOTAROD START.

⇒BLARG!⇐

HEY!

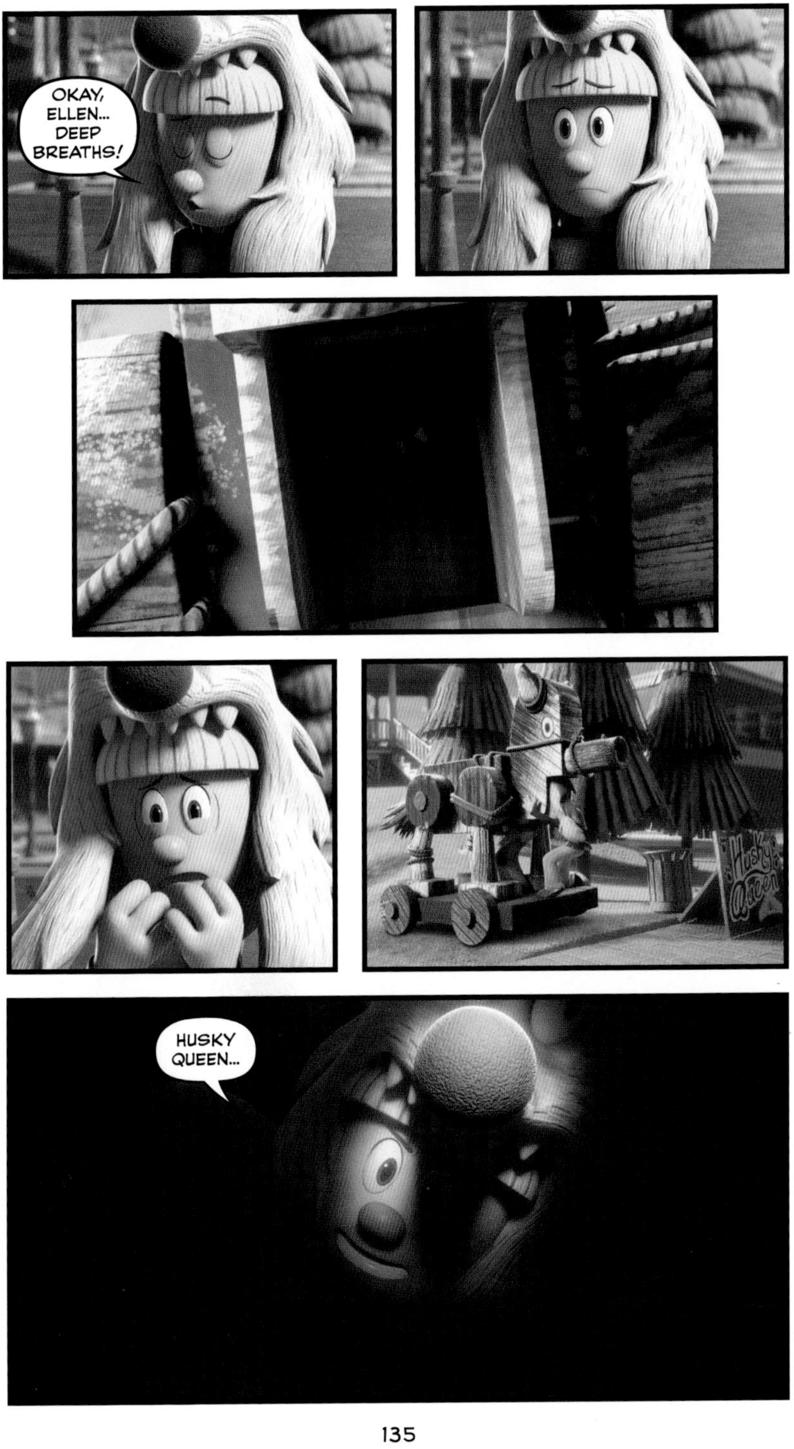
OKAY, ELLEN... DEEP BREATHS!
HUSKY QUEEN...

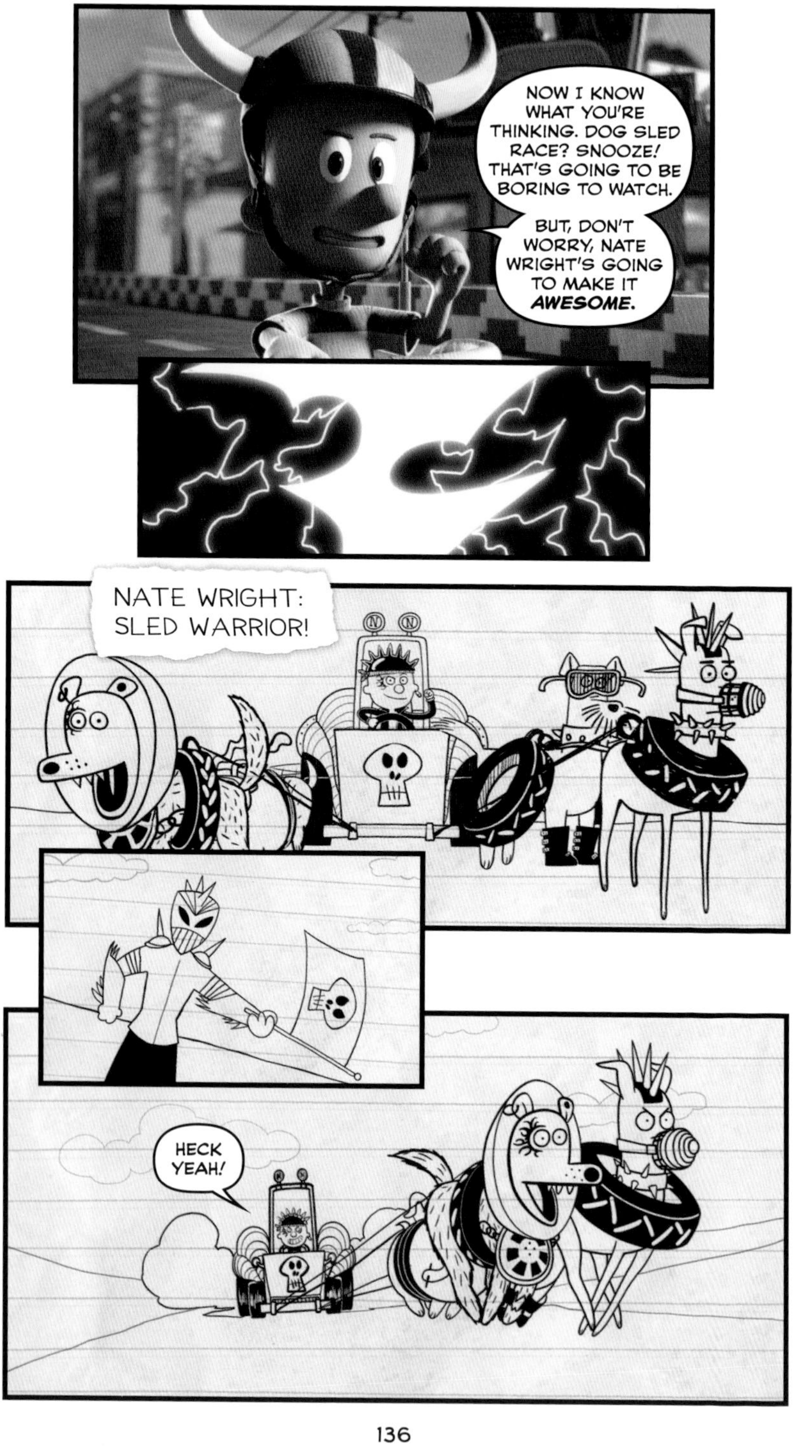
NOW I KNOW WHAT YOU'RE THINKING. DOG SLED RACE? SNOOZE! THAT'S GOING TO BE BORING TO WATCH.
BUT, DON'T WORRY, NATE WRIGHT'S GOING TO MAKE IT AWESOME.
NATE WRIGHT: SLED WARRIOR!
HECK YEAH!

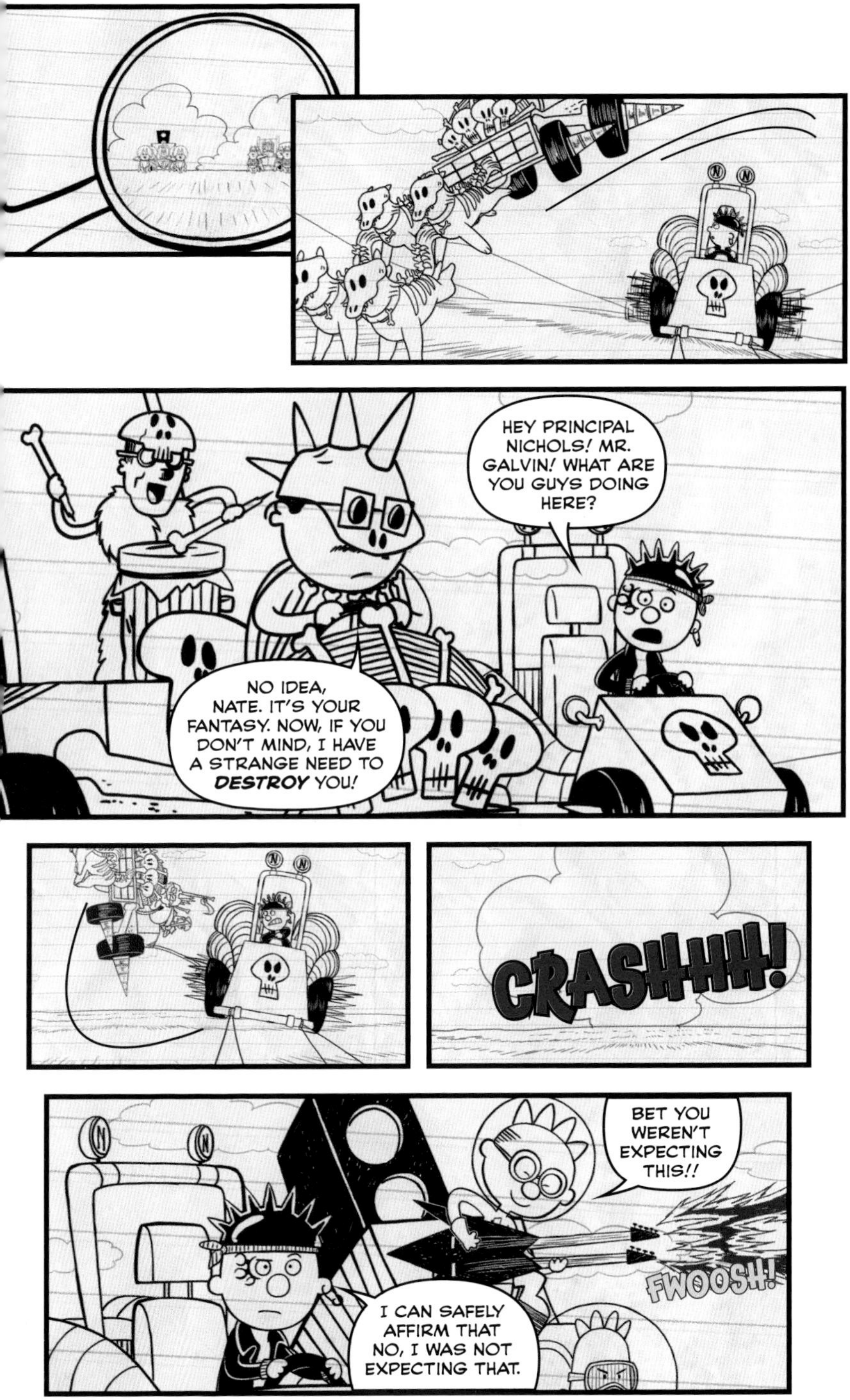
HEY PRINCIPAL NICHOLS! MR. GALVIN! WHAT ARE YOU GUYS DOING HERE?
NO IDEA, NATE. IT'S YOUR FANTASY. NOW, IF YOU DON'T MIND, I HAVE A STRANGE NEED TO DESTROY YOU!
CRASHHH!
BET YOU WEREN'T EXPECTING THIS!!
FWOOSH!
I CAN SAFELY AFFIRM THAT NO, I WAS NOT EXPECTING THAT.

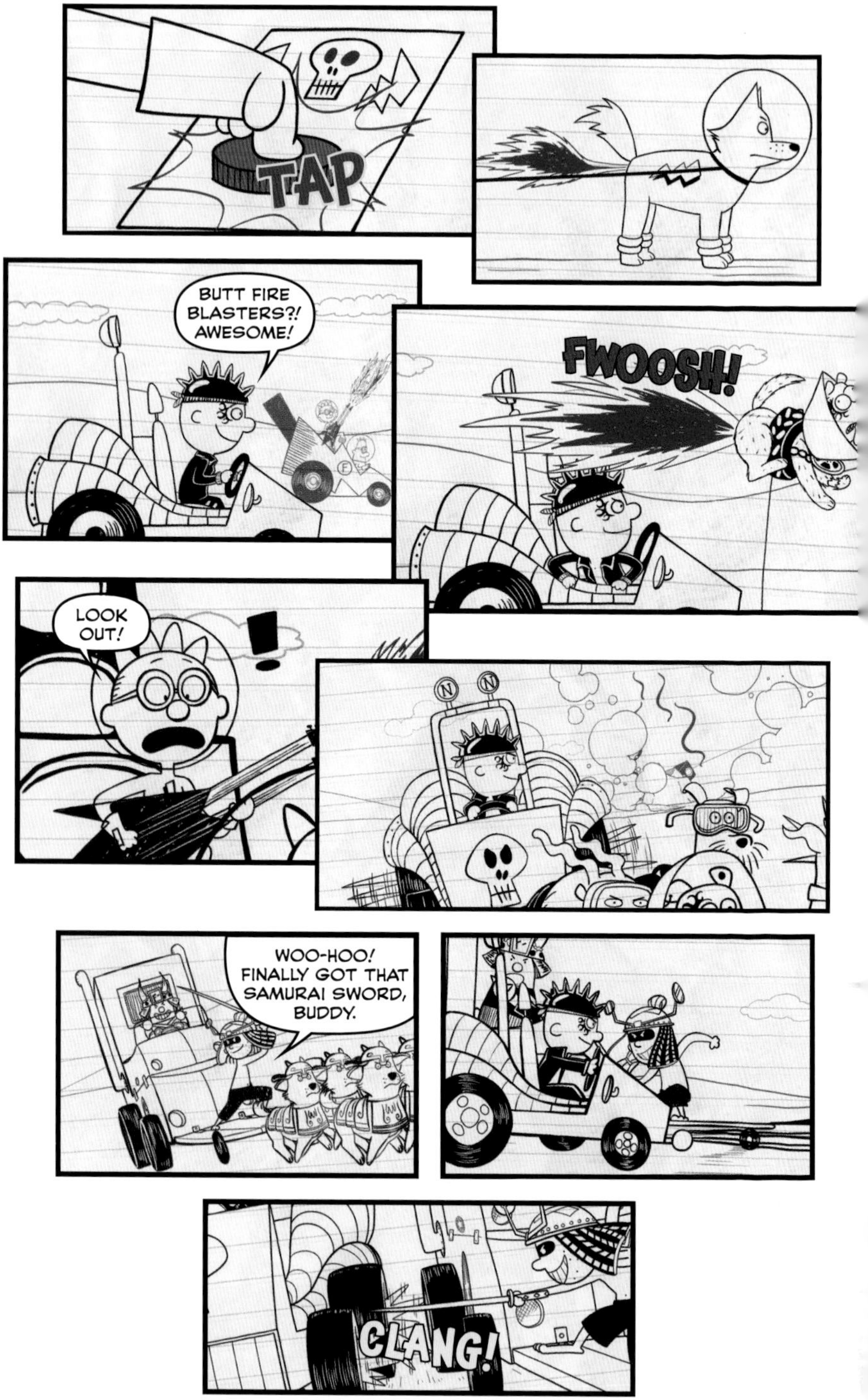
TAP
BUTT FIRE BLASTERS?! AWESOME!
FWOOSH!
LOOK OUT!
WOO-HOO! FINALLY GOT THAT SAMURAI SWORD, BUDDY.
CLANG!

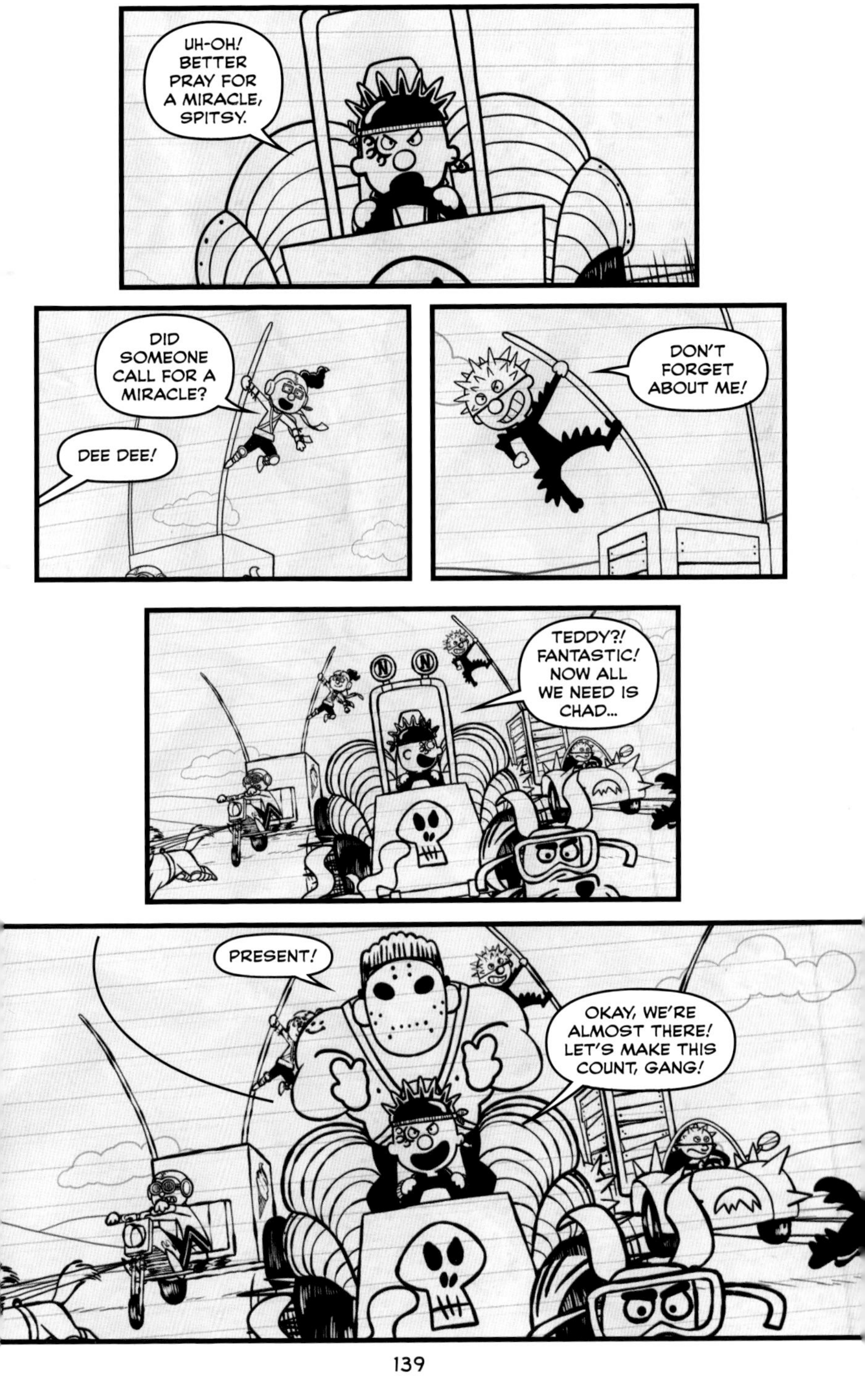

UH-OH! BETTER PRAY FOR A MIRACLE, SPITSY.
DID SOMEONE CALL FOR A MIRACLE?
DEE DEE!
DON'T FORGET ABOUT ME!
TEDDY?! FANTASTIC! NOW ALL WE NEED IS CHAD...
PRESENT!
OKAY, WE'RE ALMOST THERE! LET'S MAKE THIS COUNT, GANG!

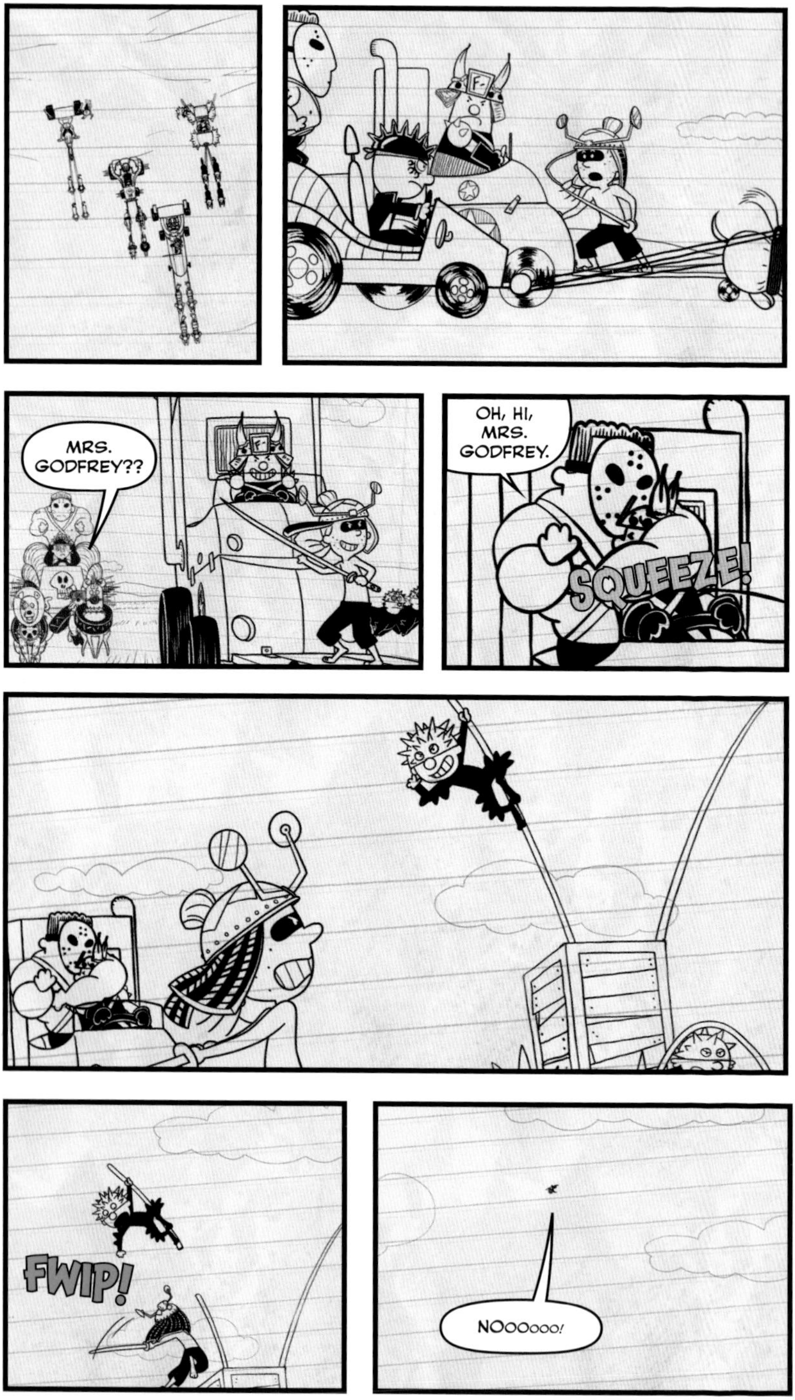
MRS. GODFREY??
OH, HI, MRS. GODFREY.
SQUEEZE!
FWIP!
NOOOooo!

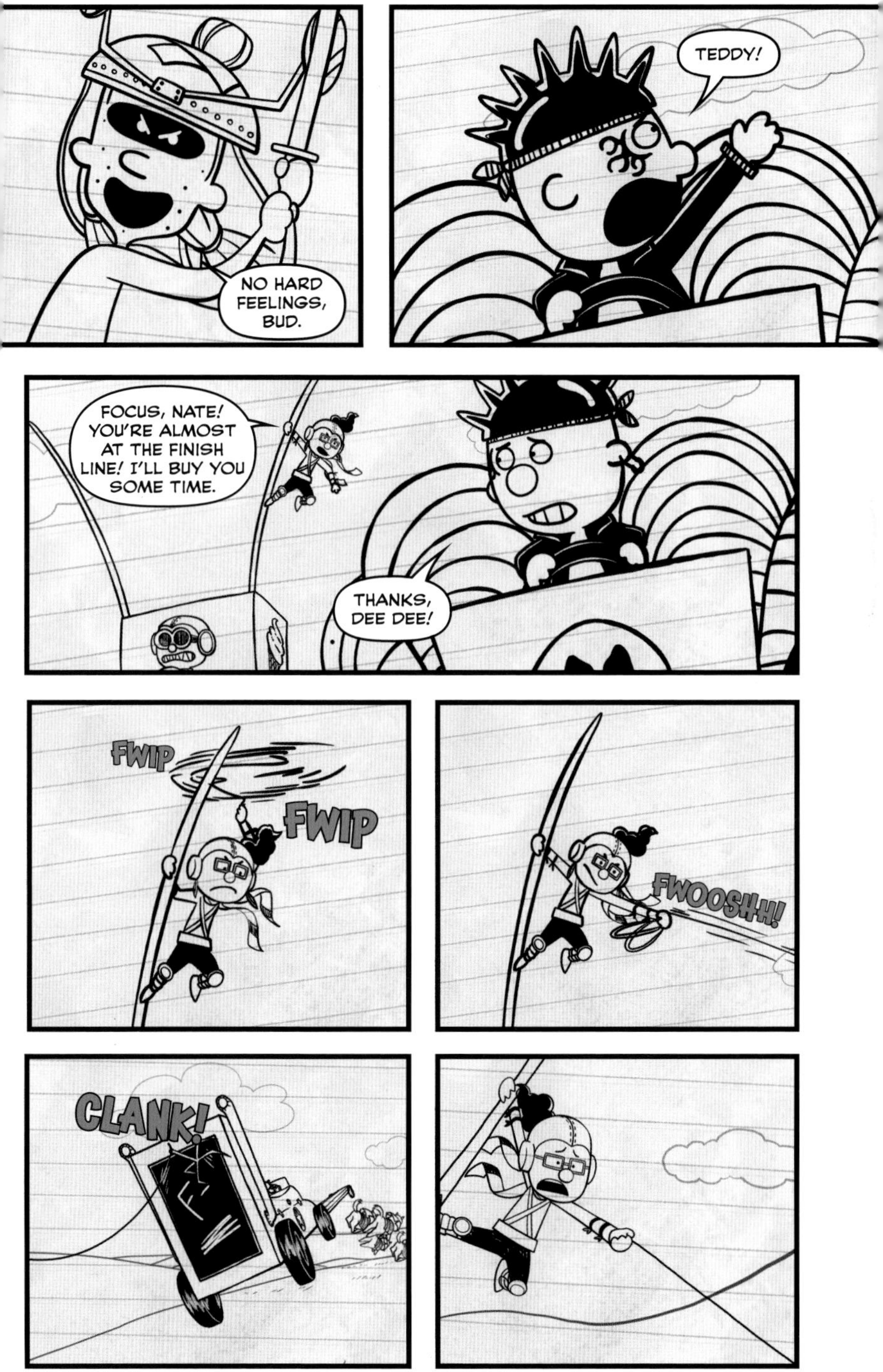
NO HARD FEELINGS, BUD.
TEDDY!
FOCUS, NATE! YOU'RE ALMOST AT THE FINISH LINE! I'LL BUY YOU SOME TIME.
THANKS, DEE DEE!
FWIP
FWIP
FWOOSHH!
CLANK!

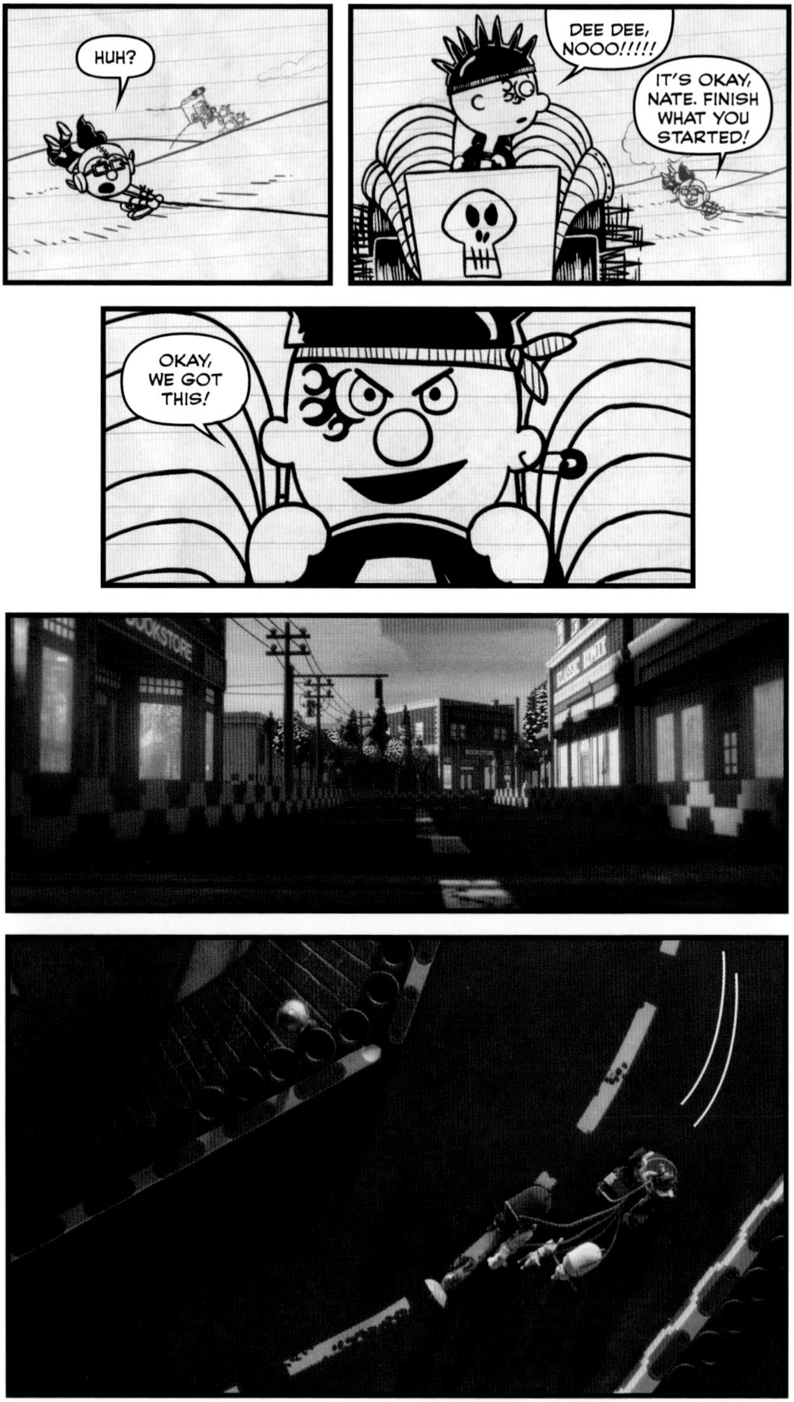
HUH?
DEE DEE, NOOO!!!!!
IT'S OKAY, NATE. FINISH WHAT YOU STARTED!
OKAY, WE GOT THIS!

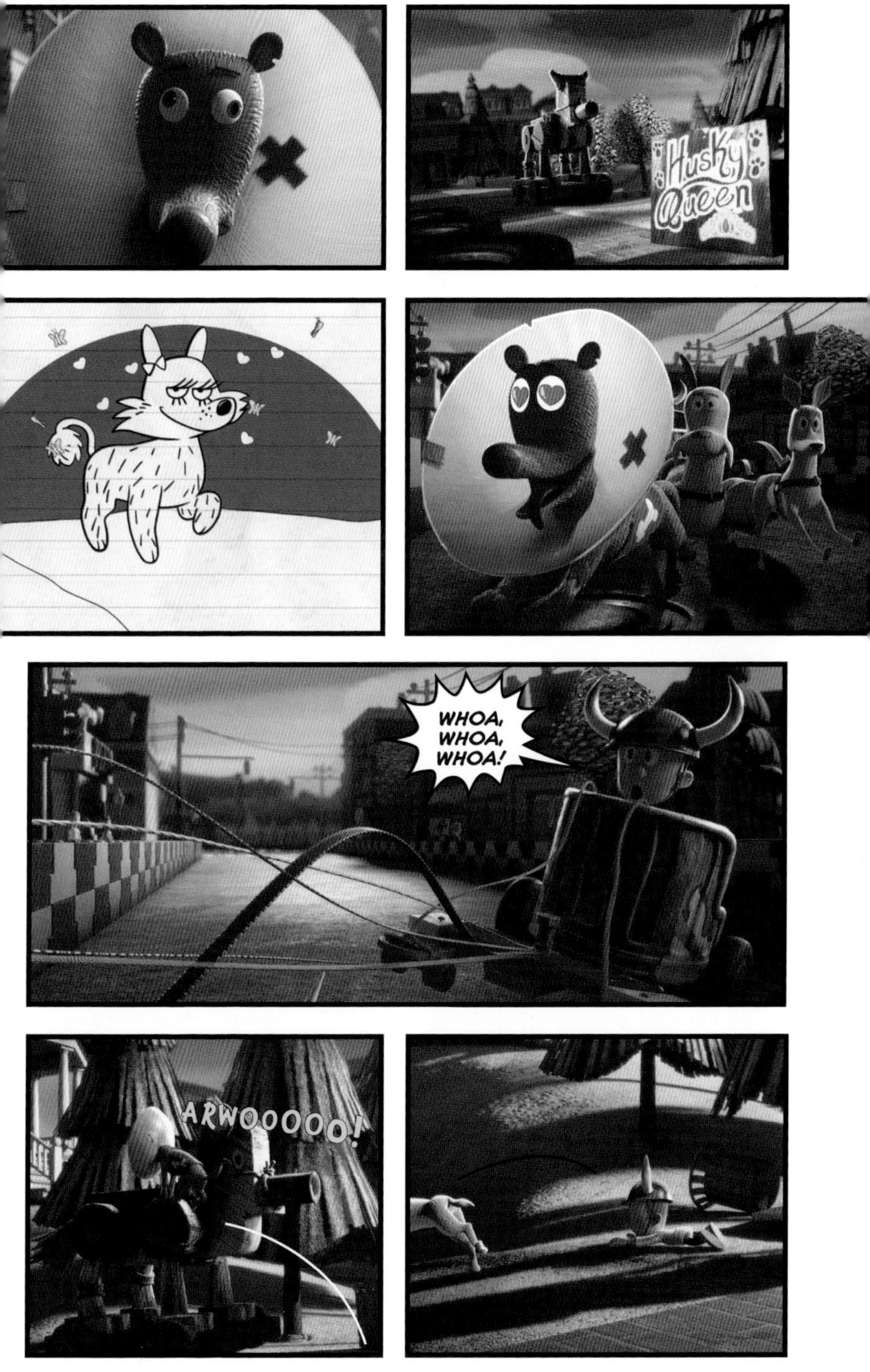
Husky Queen
WHOA, WHOA, WHOA!
ARWOOOOO!

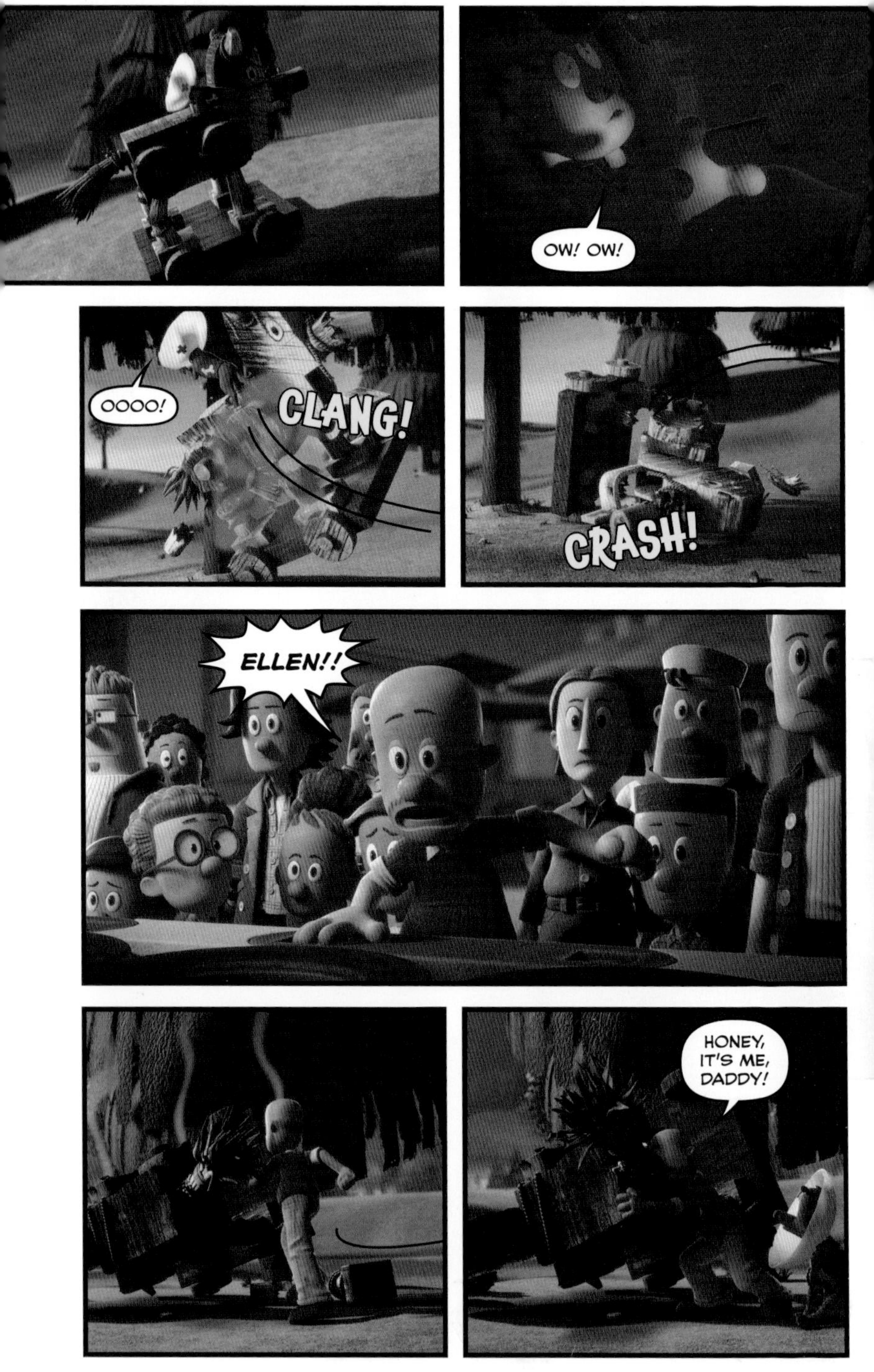
OW! OW!
OOOO!
CLANG!
CRASH!
ELLEN!!
HONEY, IT'S ME, DADDY!

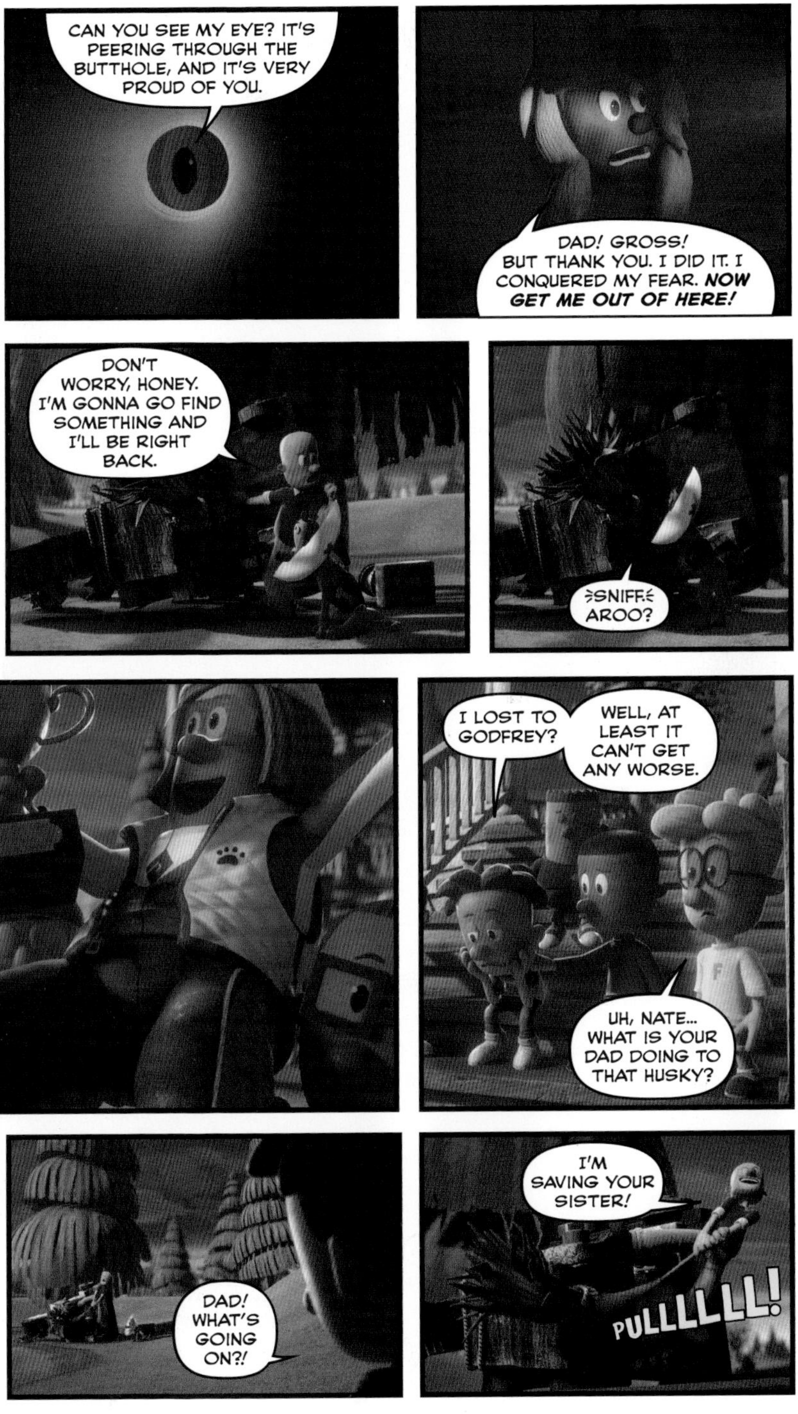
CAN YOU SEE MY EYE? IT'S PEERING THROUGH THE BUTTHOLE, AND IT'S VERY PROUD OF YOU.
DAD! GROSS! BUT THANK YOU. I DID IT. I CONQUERED MY FEAR. ***NOW GET ME OUT OF HERE!***
DON'T WORRY, HONEY. I'M GONNA GO FIND SOMETHING AND I'LL BE RIGHT BACK.
SNIFF AROO?
I LOST TO GODFREY?
WELL, AT LEAST IT CAN'T GET ANY WORSE.
UH, NATE... WHAT IS YOUR DAD DOING TO THAT HUSKY?
DAD! WHAT'S GOING ON?!
I'M SAVING YOUR SISTER!
PULLLLLL!

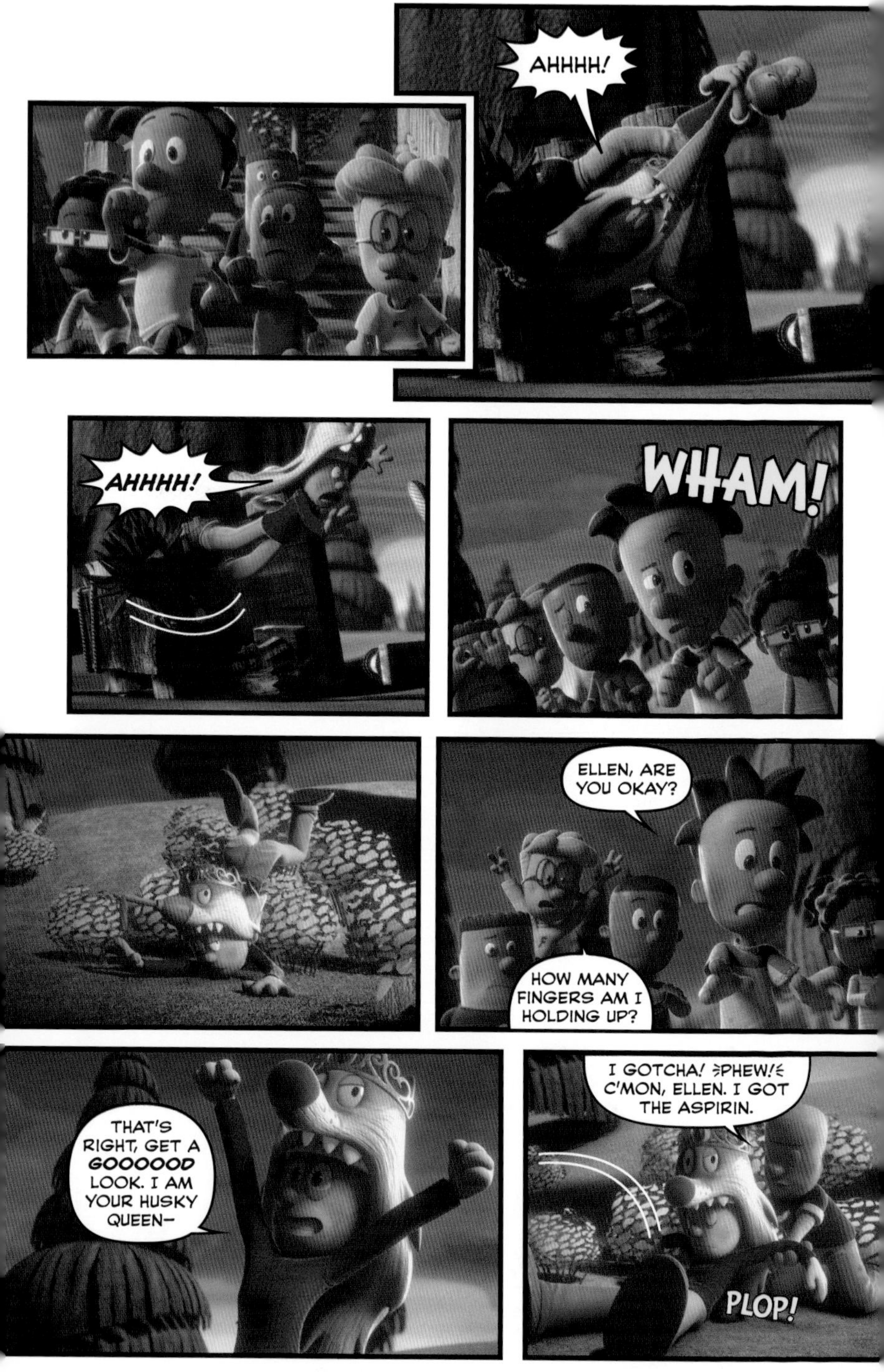
AHHHH!
AHHHH!
WHAM!
ELLEN, ARE YOU OKAY?
HOW MANY FINGERS AM I HOLDING UP?
THAT'S RIGHT, GET A GOOOOOD LOOK. I AM YOUR HUSKY QUEEN—
I GOTCHA! ⋟PHEW!⋞ C'MON, ELLEN. I GOT THE ASPIRIN.
PLOP!

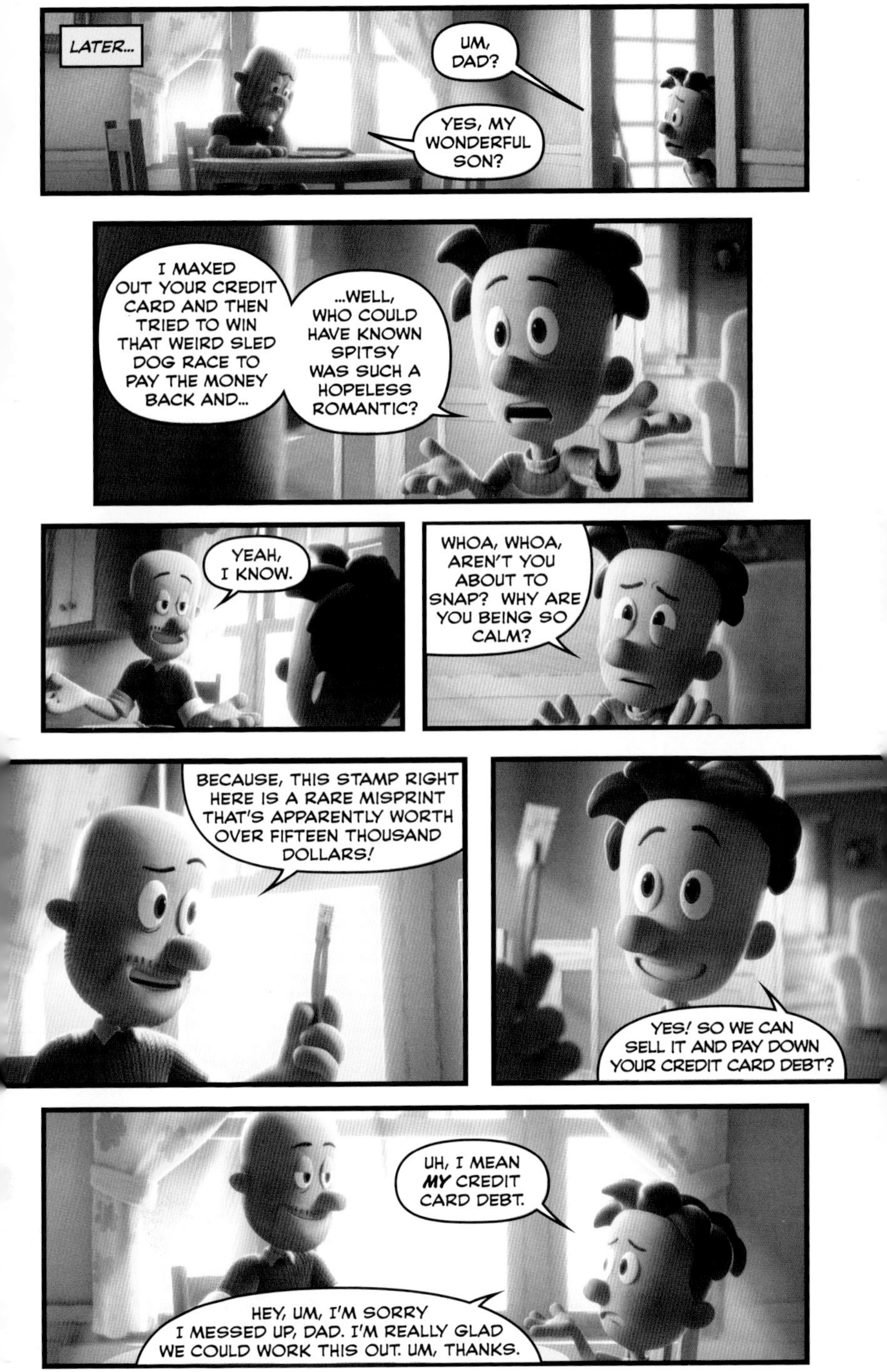
LATER...
UM, DAD?
YES, MY WONDERFUL SON?
I MAXED OUT YOUR CREDIT CARD AND THEN TRIED TO WIN THAT WEIRD SLED DOG RACE TO PAY THE MONEY BACK AND...
...WELL, WHO COULD HAVE KNOWN SPITSY WAS SUCH A HOPELESS ROMANTIC?
YEAH, I KNOW.
WHOA, WHOA, AREN'T YOU ABOUT TO SNAP? WHY ARE YOU BEING SO CALM?
BECAUSE, THIS STAMP RIGHT HERE IS A RARE MISPRINT THAT'S APPARENTLY WORTH OVER FIFTEEN THOUSAND DOLLARS!
YES! SO WE CAN SELL IT AND PAY DOWN YOUR CREDIT CARD DEBT?
UH, I MEAN ***MY*** CREDIT CARD DEBT.
HEY, UM, I'M SORRY I MESSED UP, DAD. I'M REALLY GLAD WE COULD WORK THIS OUT. UM, THANKS.

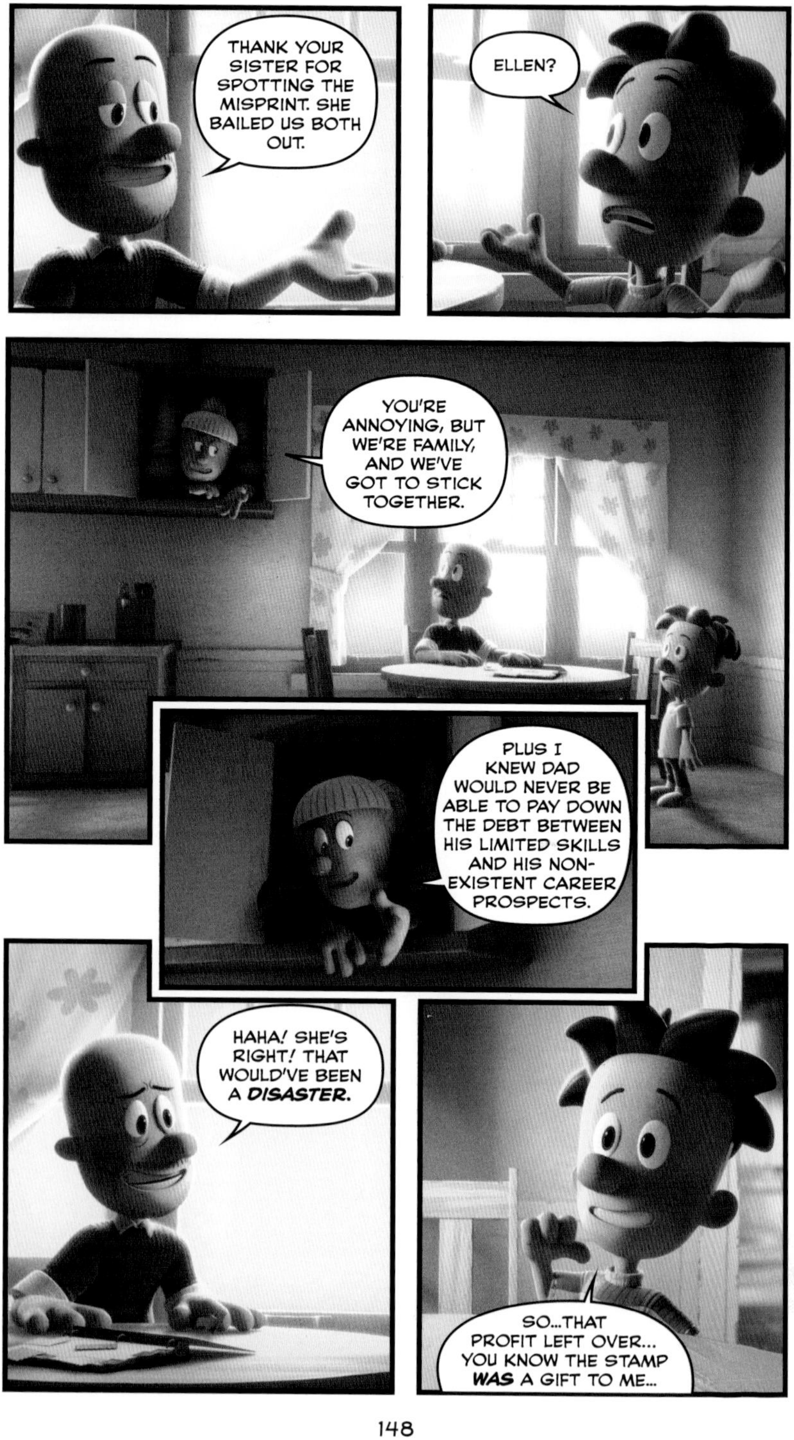
THANK YOUR SISTER FOR SPOTTING THE MISPRINT. SHE BAILED US BOTH OUT.
ELLEN?
YOU'RE ANNOYING, BUT WE'RE FAMILY, AND WE'VE GOT TO STICK TOGETHER.
PLUS I KNEW DAD WOULD NEVER BE ABLE TO PAY DOWN THE DEBT BETWEEN HIS LIMITED SKILLS AND HIS NON-EXISTENT CAREER PROSPECTS.
HAHA! SHE'S RIGHT! THAT WOULD'VE BEEN A ***DISASTER***.
SO...THAT PROFIT LEFT OVER... YOU KNOW THE STAMP ***WAS*** A GIFT TO ME...

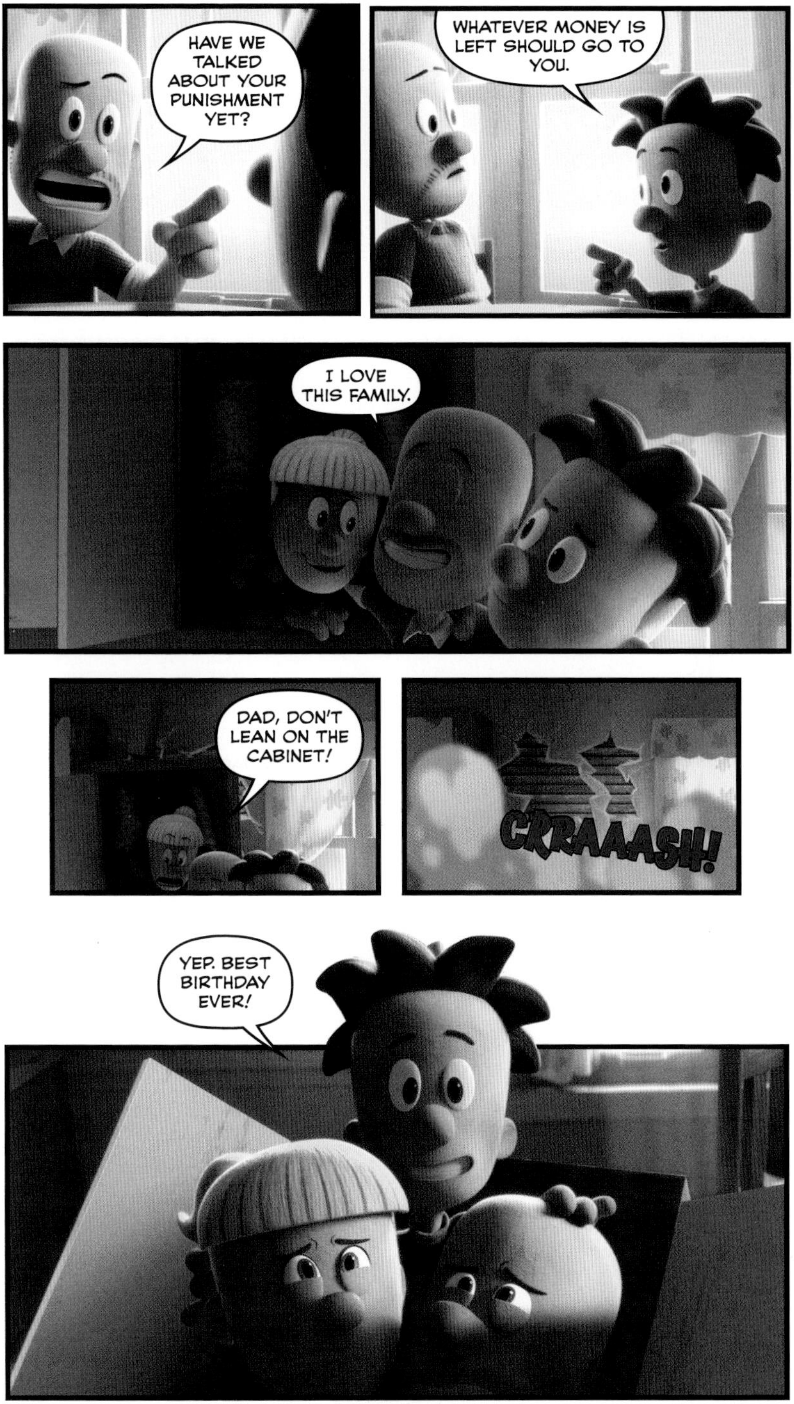

HAVE WE TALKED ABOUT YOUR PUNISHMENT YET?
WHATEVER MONEY IS LEFT SHOULD GO TO YOU.
I LOVE THIS FAMILY.
DAD, DON'T LEAN ON THE CABINET!
CRRAAASH!
YEP. BEST BIRTHDAY EVER!

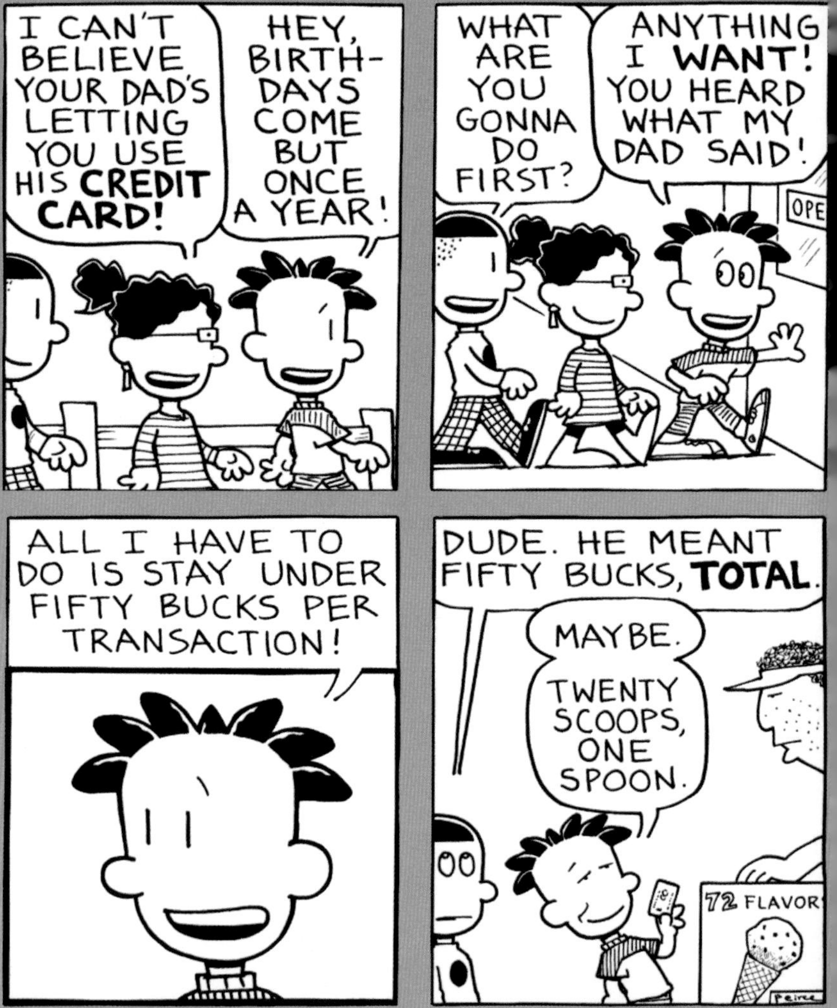
I CAN'T BELIEVE YOUR DAD'S LETTING YOU USE HIS **CREDIT CARD!**
HEY, BIRTH-DAYS COME BUT ONCE A YEAR!
WHAT ARE YOU GONNA DO FIRST?
ANYTHING I **WANT!** YOU HEARD WHAT MY DAD SAID!
OPE
ALL I HAVE TO DO IS STAY UNDER FIFTY BUCKS PER TRANSACTION!
DUDE. HE MEANT FIFTY BUCKS, **TOTAL**.
MAYBE.
TWENTY SCOOPS, ONE SPOON.
72 FLAVOR
Peirce

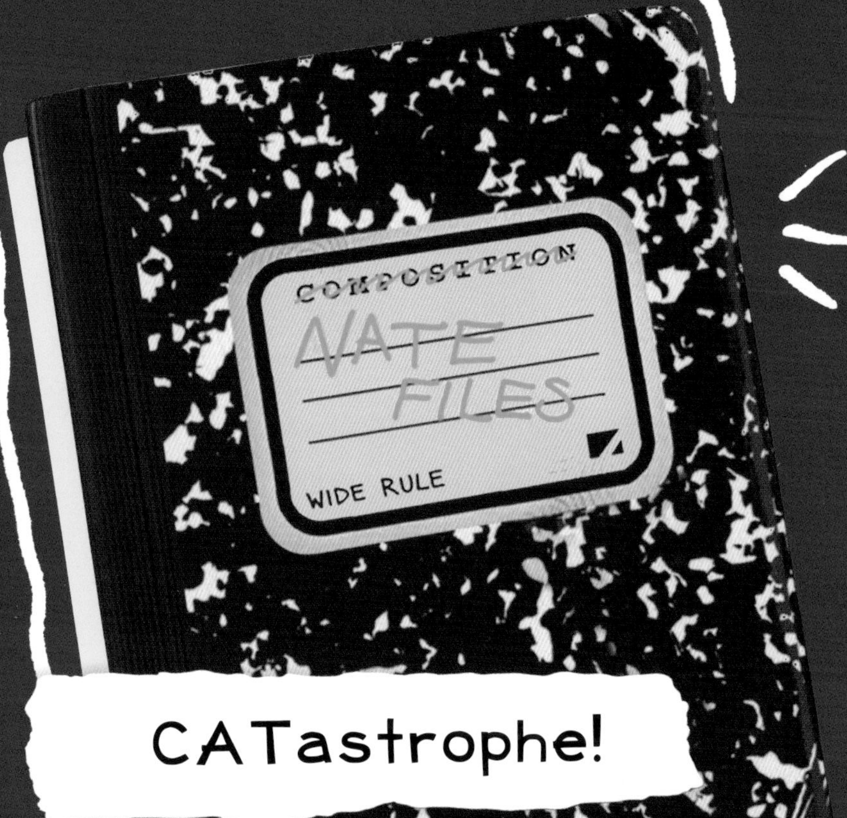
COMPOSITION
NATE FILES
WIDE RULE

CATastrophe!

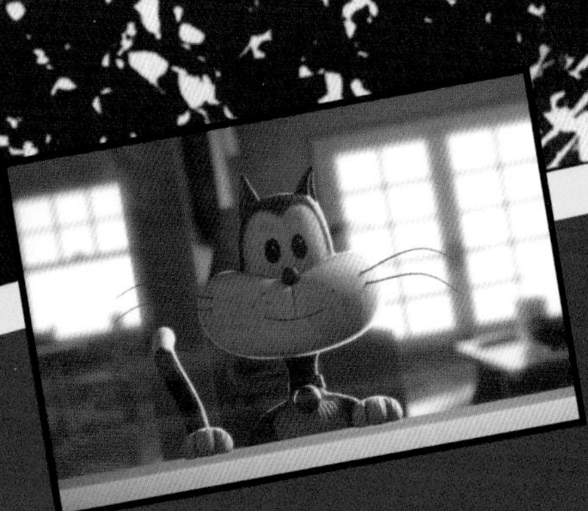

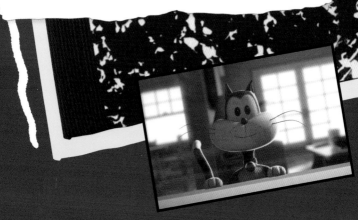

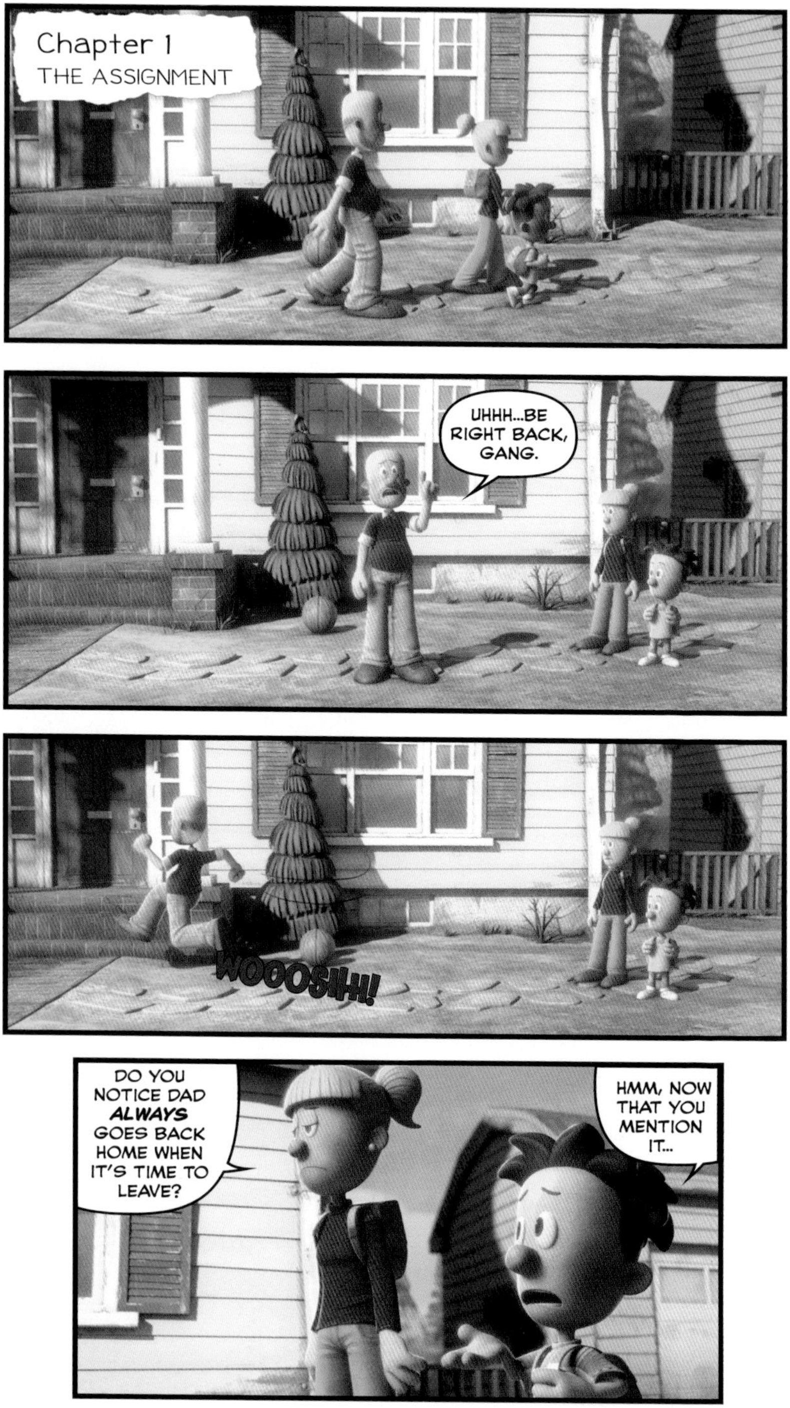
Chapter 1
THE ASSIGNMENT
UHHH...BE RIGHT BACK, GANG.
WOOOSHH!
DO YOU NOTICE DAD ALWAYS GOES BACK HOME WHEN IT'S TIME TO LEAVE?
HMM, NOW THAT YOU MENTION IT...

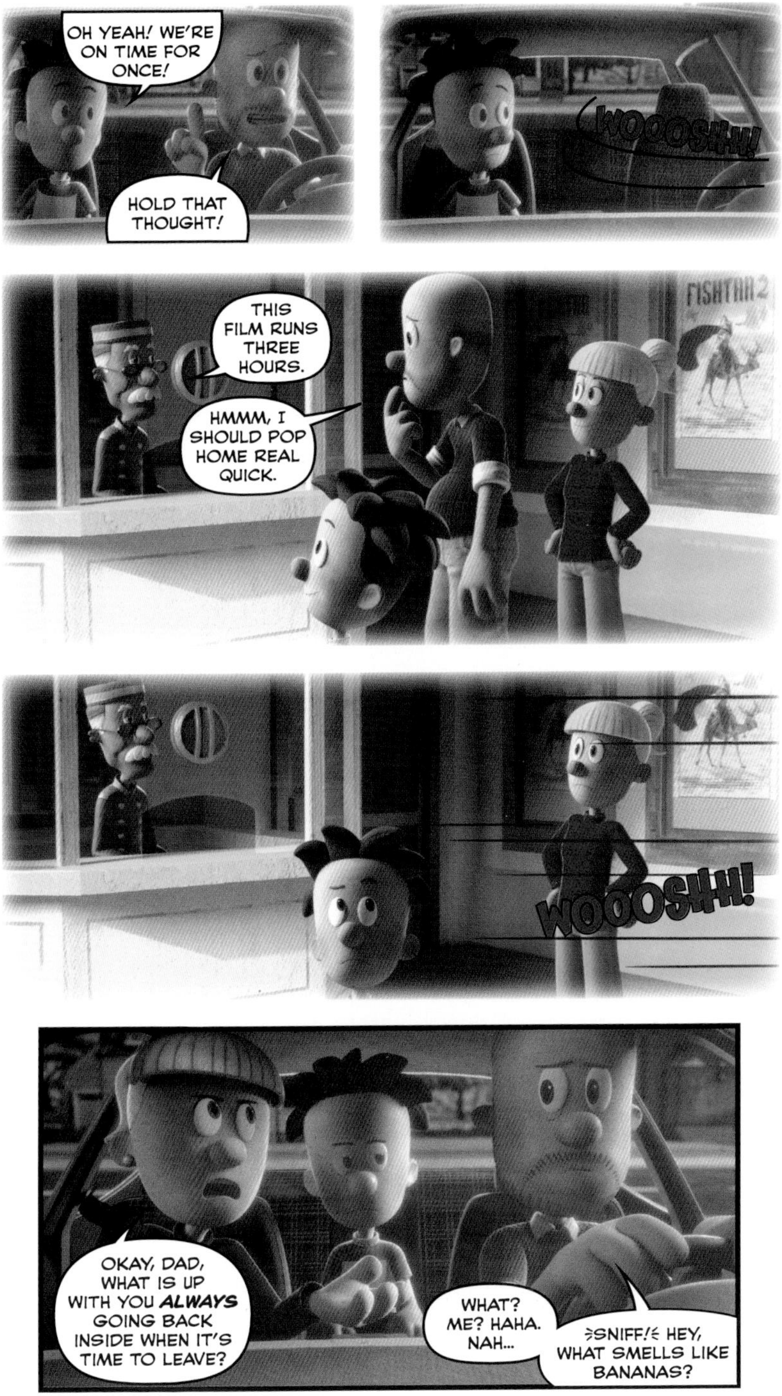
OH YEAH! WE'RE ON TIME FOR ONCE!
HOLD THAT THOUGHT!
WOOOSHH!
THIS FILM RUNS THREE HOURS.
HMMM, I SHOULD POP HOME REAL QUICK.
FISHTAR 2
WOOOSHH!
OKAY, DAD, WHAT IS UP WITH YOU ALWAYS GOING BACK INSIDE WHEN IT'S TIME TO LEAVE?
WHAT? ME? HAHA. NAH...
SNIFF! HEY, WHAT SMELLS LIKE BANANAS?

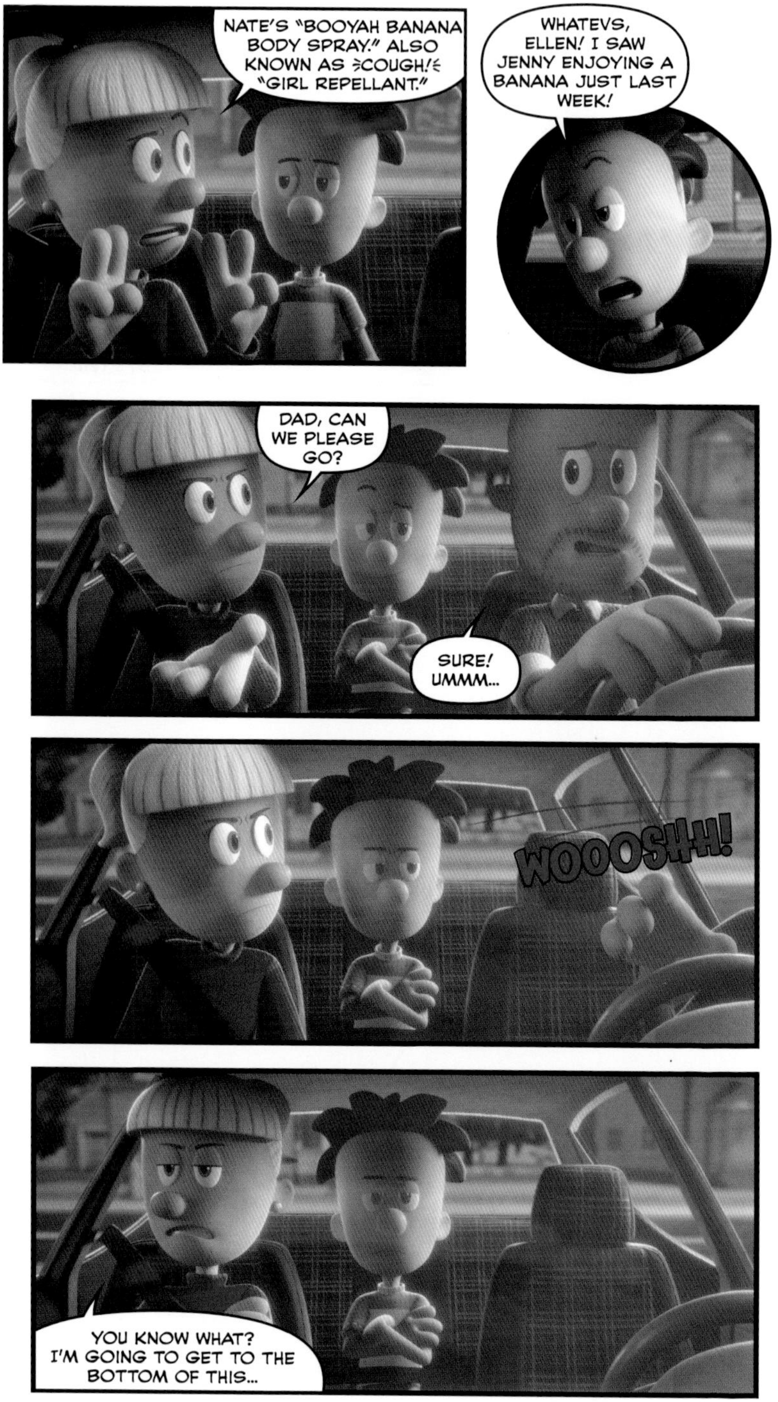
NATE'S "BOOYAH BANANA BODY SPRAY." ALSO KNOWN AS ≥COUGH!≤ "GIRL REPELLANT."
WHATEVS, ELLEN! I SAW JENNY ENJOYING A BANANA JUST LAST WEEK!
DAD, CAN WE PLEASE GO?
SURE! UMMM...
WOOOSHH!
YOU KNOW WHAT? I'M GOING TO GET TO THE BOTTOM OF THIS...

LATER, AT SCHOOL.

RUBE GOLDBERG MACHINES ACCOMPLISH A SIMPLE TASK IN THE MOST **OVERCOMPLICATED** AND **INEFFICIENT** WAY POSSIBLE, NOT UNLIKE THE DMV OR THE PUBLIC SCHOOL SYSTEM.

BEHOLD!

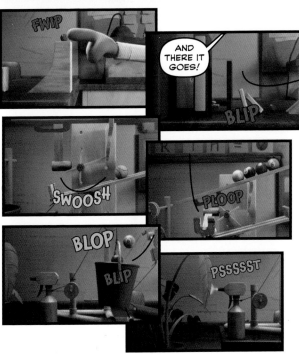

FWIP

AND THERE IT GOES!

BLIP

SWOOSH

PLOOP

BLOP

BLIP

PSSSSST

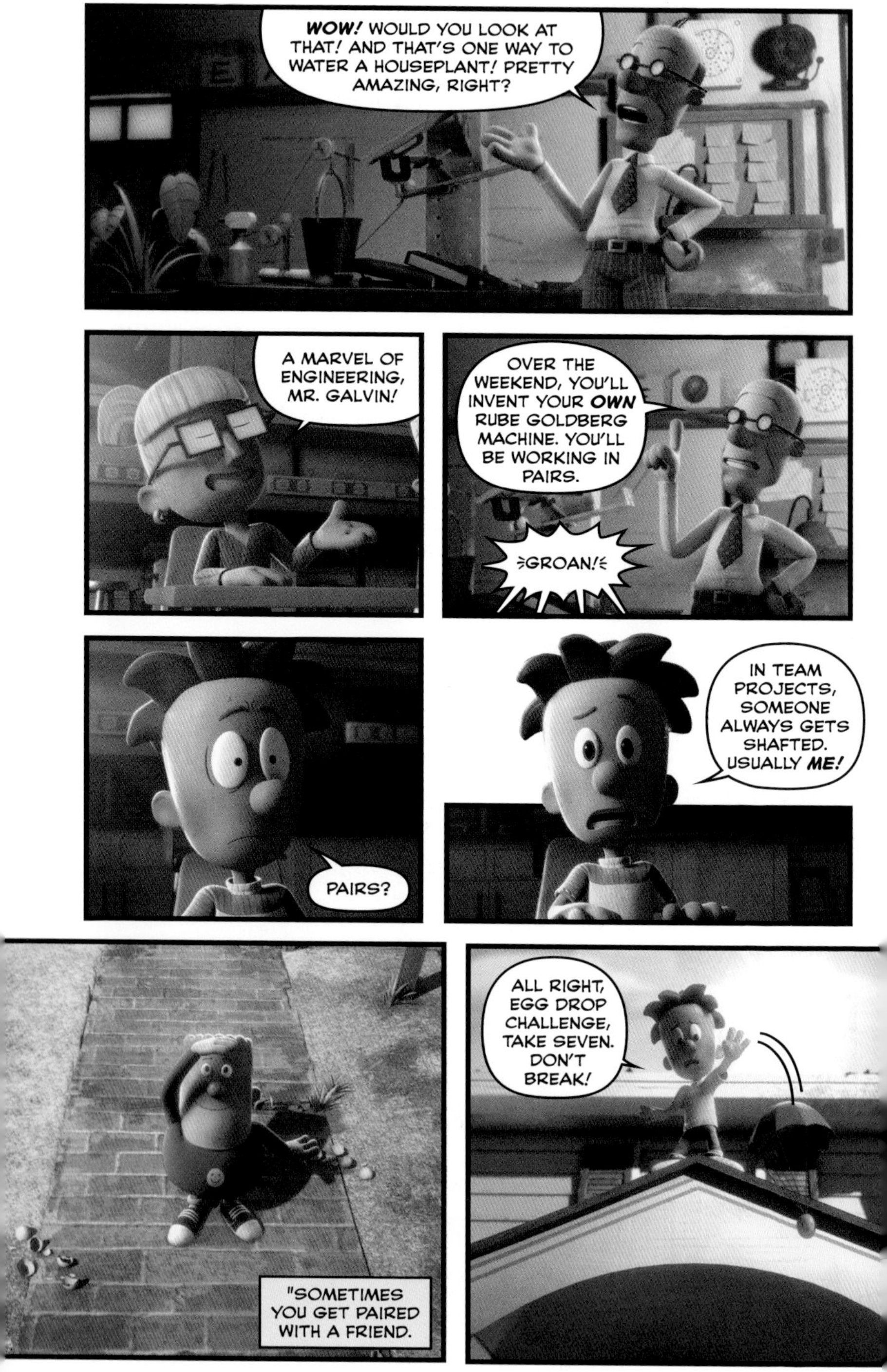
WOW! WOULD YOU LOOK AT THAT! AND THAT'S ONE WAY TO WATER A HOUSEPLANT! PRETTY AMAZING, RIGHT?
A MARVEL OF ENGINEERING, MR. GALVIN!
OVER THE WEEKEND, YOU'LL INVENT YOUR OWN RUBE GOLDBERG MACHINE. YOU'LL BE WORKING IN PAIRS.
GROAN!
PAIRS?
IN TEAM PROJECTS, SOMEONE ALWAYS GETS SHAFTED. USUALLY ME!
"SOMETIMES YOU GET PAIRED WITH A FRIEND.
ALL RIGHT, EGG DROP CHALLENGE, TAKE SEVEN. DON'T BREAK!

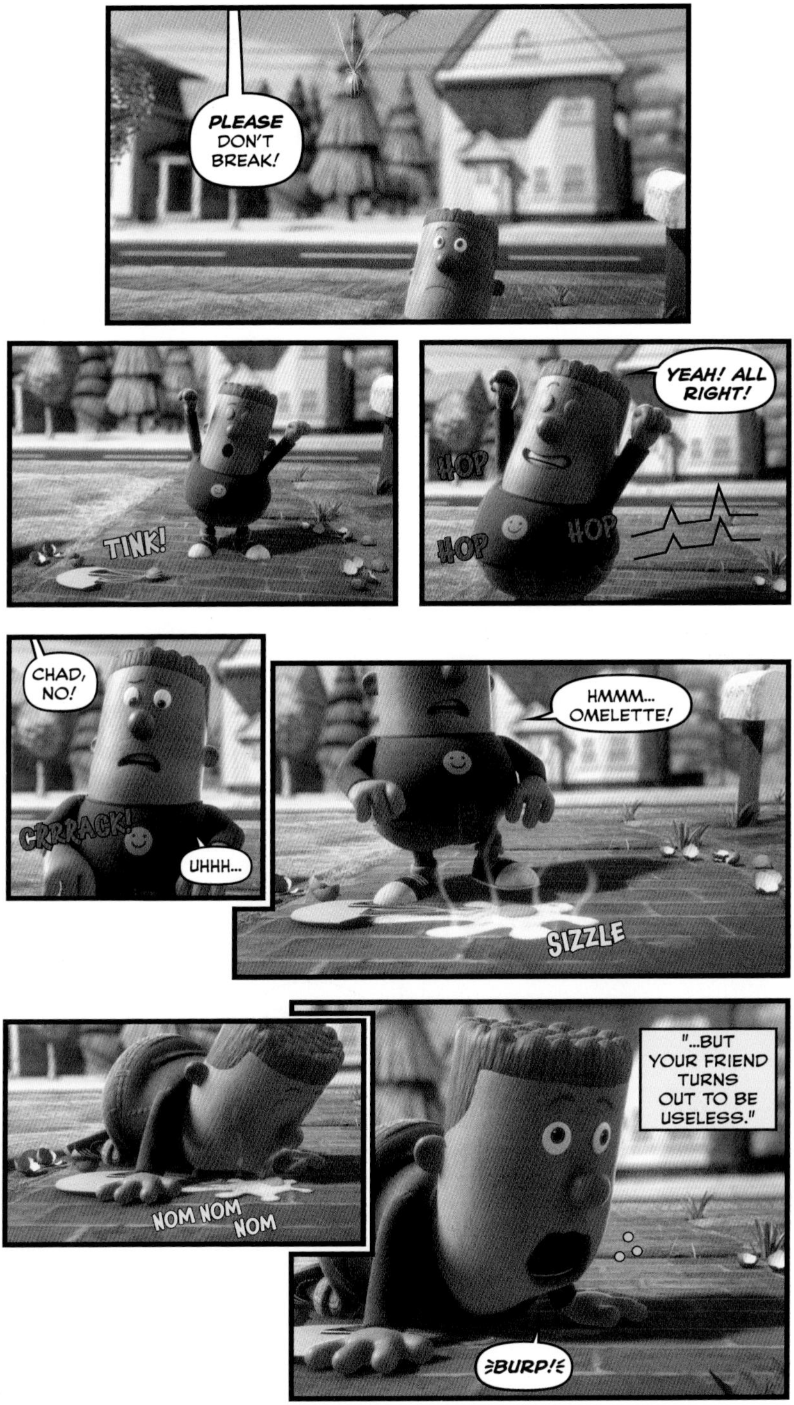
PLEASE DON'T BREAK!
TINK!
YEAH! ALL RIGHT!
HOP
HOP
HOP
CHAD, NO!
CRRRACK!
UHHH...
HMMM... OMELETTE!
SIZZLE
NOM NOM NOM
"...BUT YOUR FRIEND TURNS OUT TO BE USELESS."
BURP!

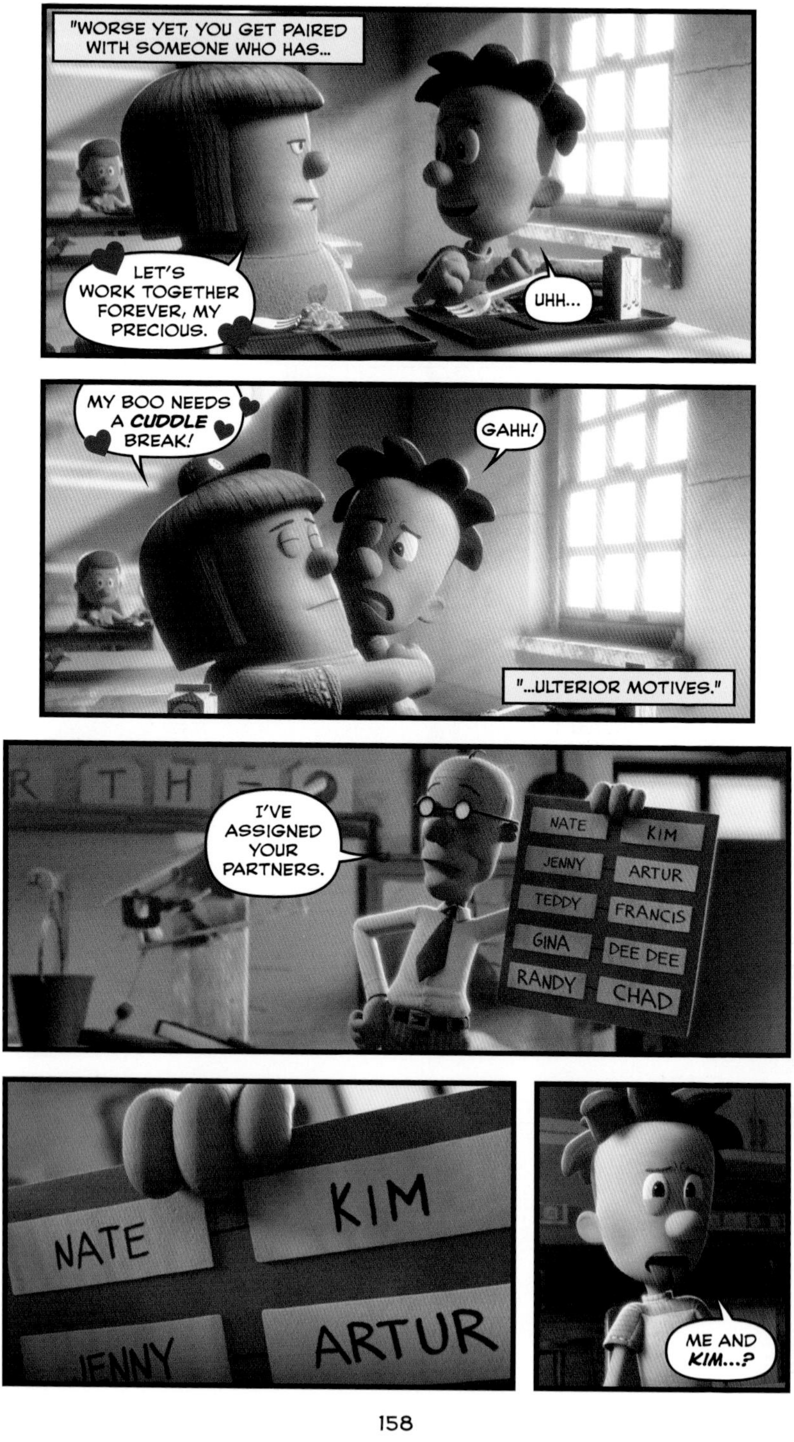
"WORSE YET, YOU GET PAIRED WITH SOMEONE WHO HAS...
LET'S WORK TOGETHER FOREVER, MY PRECIOUS.
UHH...
MY BOO NEEDS A **CUDDLE** BREAK!
GAHH!
"...ULTERIOR MOTIVES."
I'VE ASSIGNED YOUR PARTNERS.
NATE
KIM
JENNY
ARTUR
TEDDY
FRANCIS
GINA
DEE DEE
RANDY
CHAD
NATE
KIM
ARTUR
ME AND ***KIM...?***

MY PRECIOUS BOO...

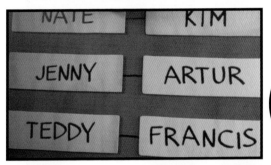

NATE — KIM

JENNY — ARTUR

TEDDY — FRANCIS

JENNY AND ARTUR? THAT'S *NOT* HAPPENING.

TEDDY, QUICK. DISTRACT GALVIN!

UHHH... HMMM...

HUH?

TUG

AHHH!

POOF!

HOLY CALCIUM!

COME BACK HERE, FERDINAND!

THUNK THUNK

≥SNICKER!≤

KIM

NNY — ARTUR

TEDDY — FRANCIS

GINA — DEE DEE

RTUR — KIM

NNY

ATE

FRANCIS

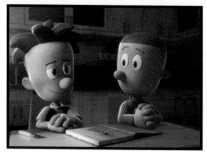

≥PHEW.≤

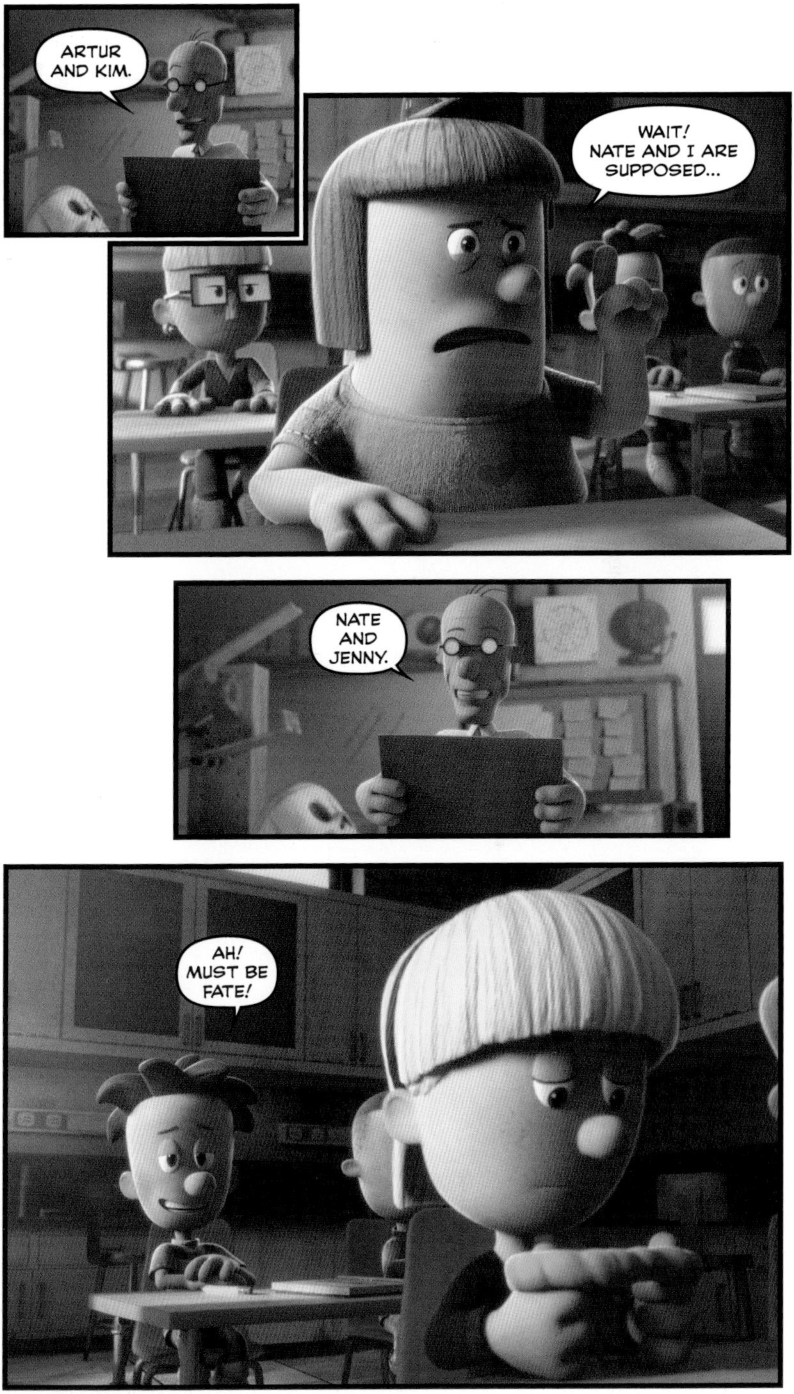
ARTUR AND KIM.
WAIT! NATE AND I ARE SUPPOSED...
NATE AND JENNY.
AH! MUST BE FATE!

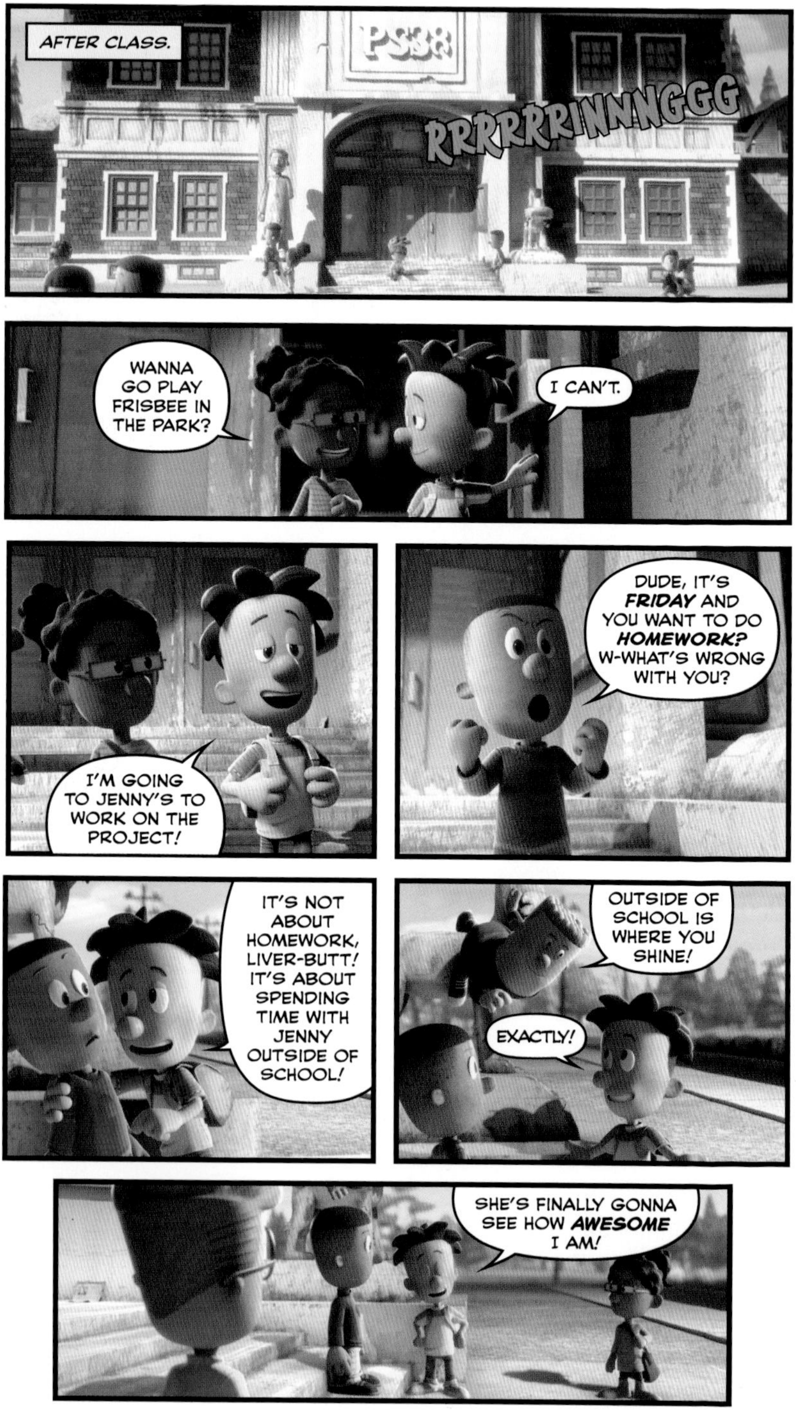
AFTER CLASS.
PS38
RRRRRRINNNGGG
WANNA GO PLAY FRISBEE IN THE PARK?
I CAN'T.
I'M GOING TO JENNY'S TO WORK ON THE PROJECT!
DUDE, IT'S FRIDAY AND YOU WANT TO DO HOMEWORK? W-WHAT'S WRONG WITH YOU?
IT'S NOT ABOUT HOMEWORK, LIVER-BUTT! IT'S ABOUT SPENDING TIME WITH JENNY OUTSIDE OF SCHOOL!
OUTSIDE OF SCHOOL IS WHERE YOU SHINE!
EXACTLY!
SHE'S FINALLY GONNA SEE HOW AWESOME I AM!

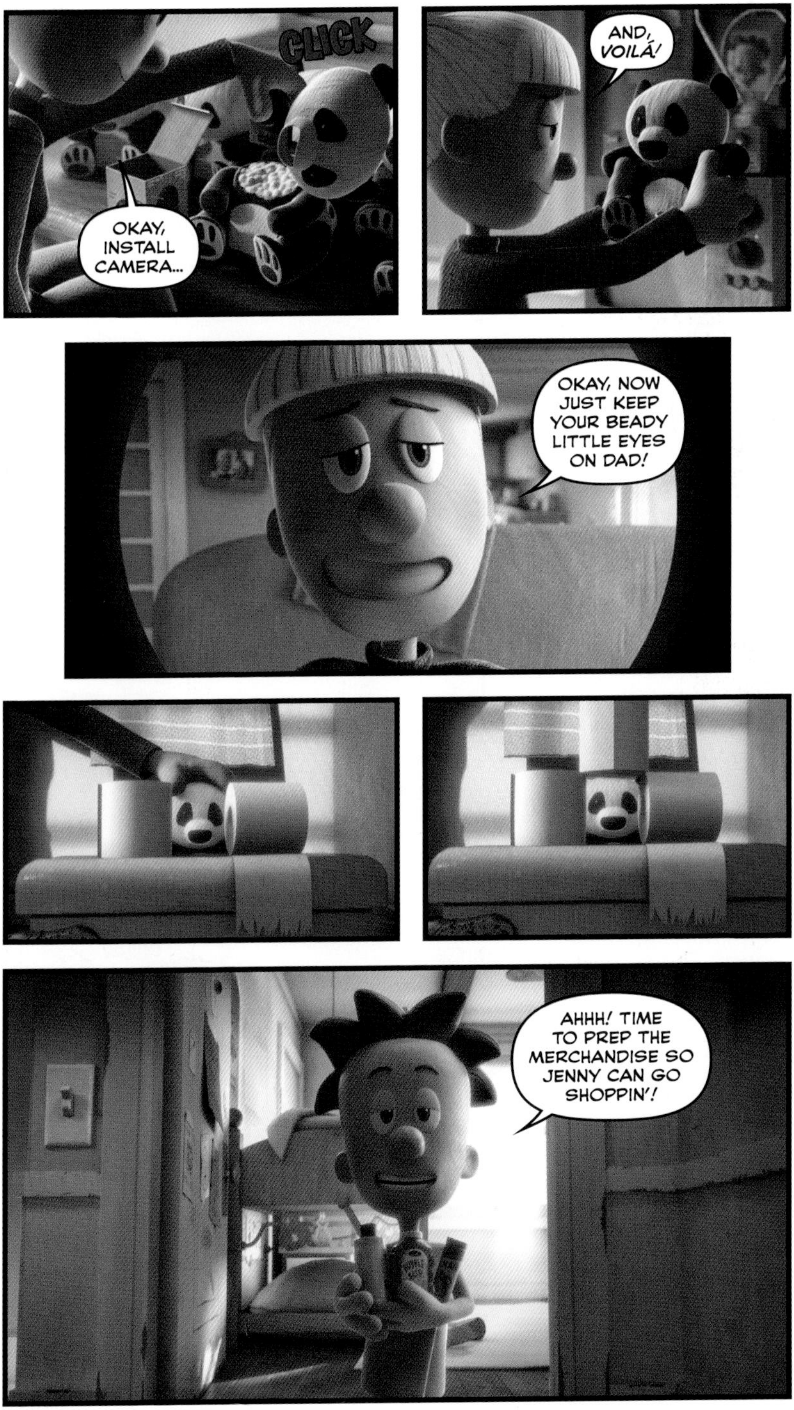
CLICK
OKAY, INSTALL CAMERA...
AND, VOILÁ!
OKAY, NOW JUST KEEP YOUR BEADY LITTLE EYES ON DAD!
AHHH! TIME TO PREP THE MERCHANDISE SO JENNY CAN GO SHOPPIN'!

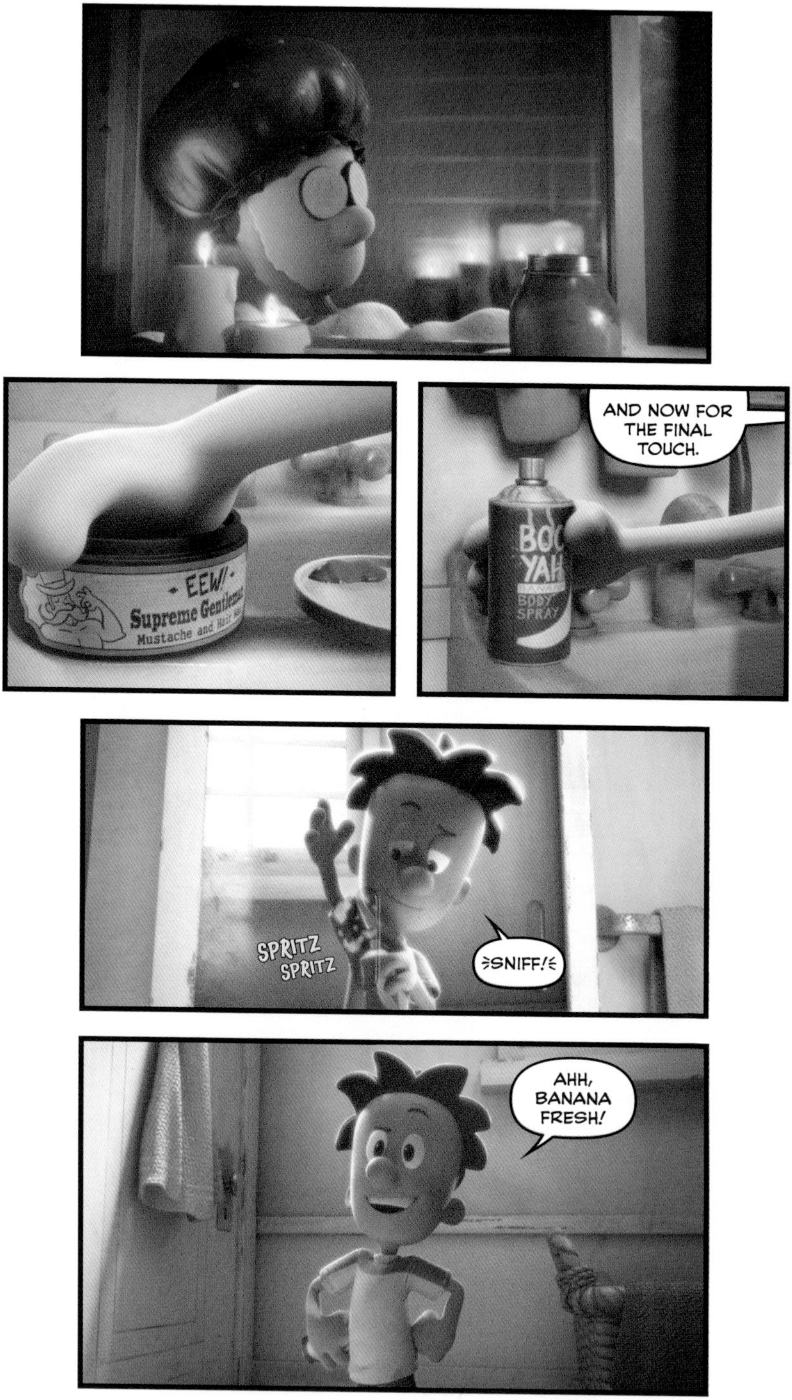
EEW!
AND NOW FOR THE FINAL TOUCH.
BODY SPRAY
SPRITZ SPRITZ
SNIFF!
AHH, BANANA FRESH!

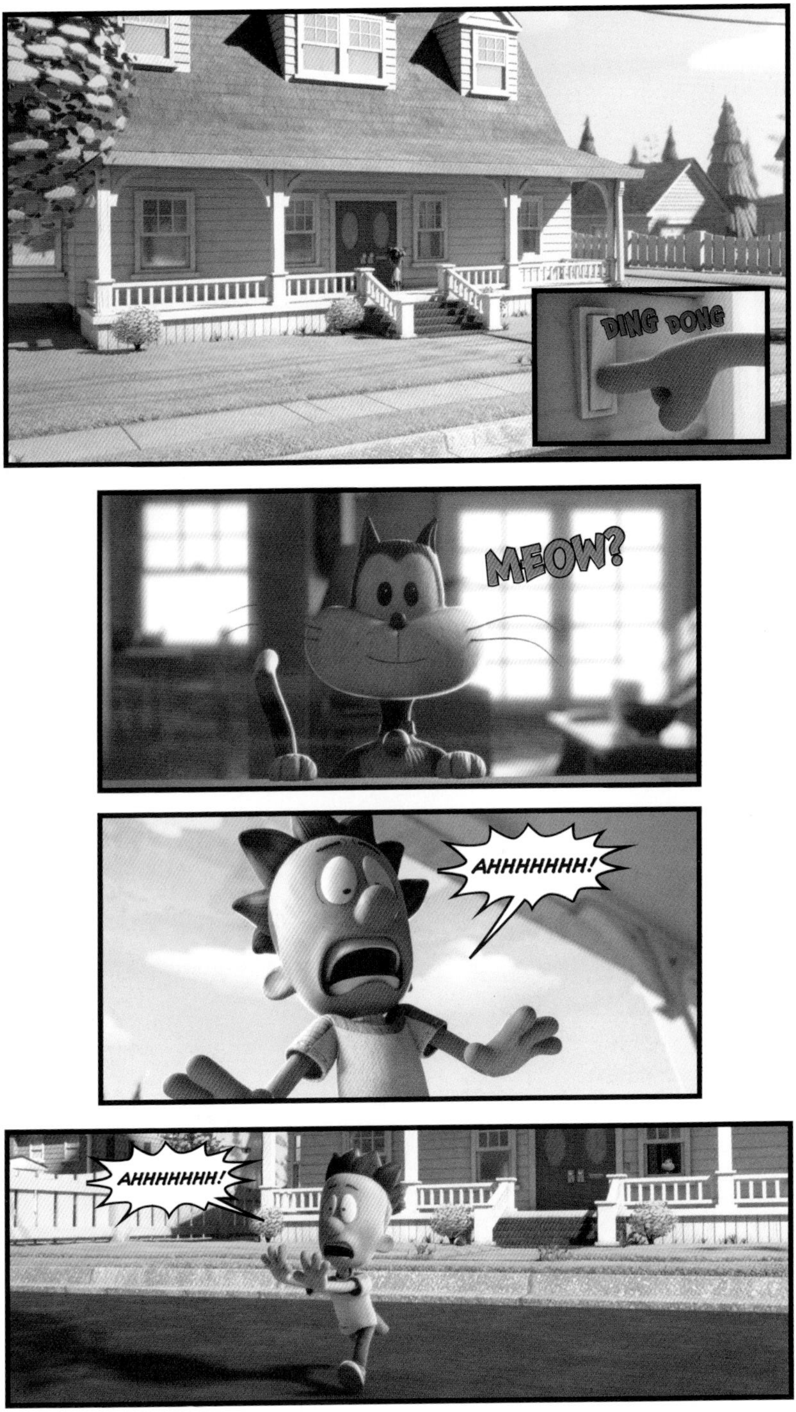
DING DONG
MEOW?
AHHHHHHH!
AHHHHHHH!

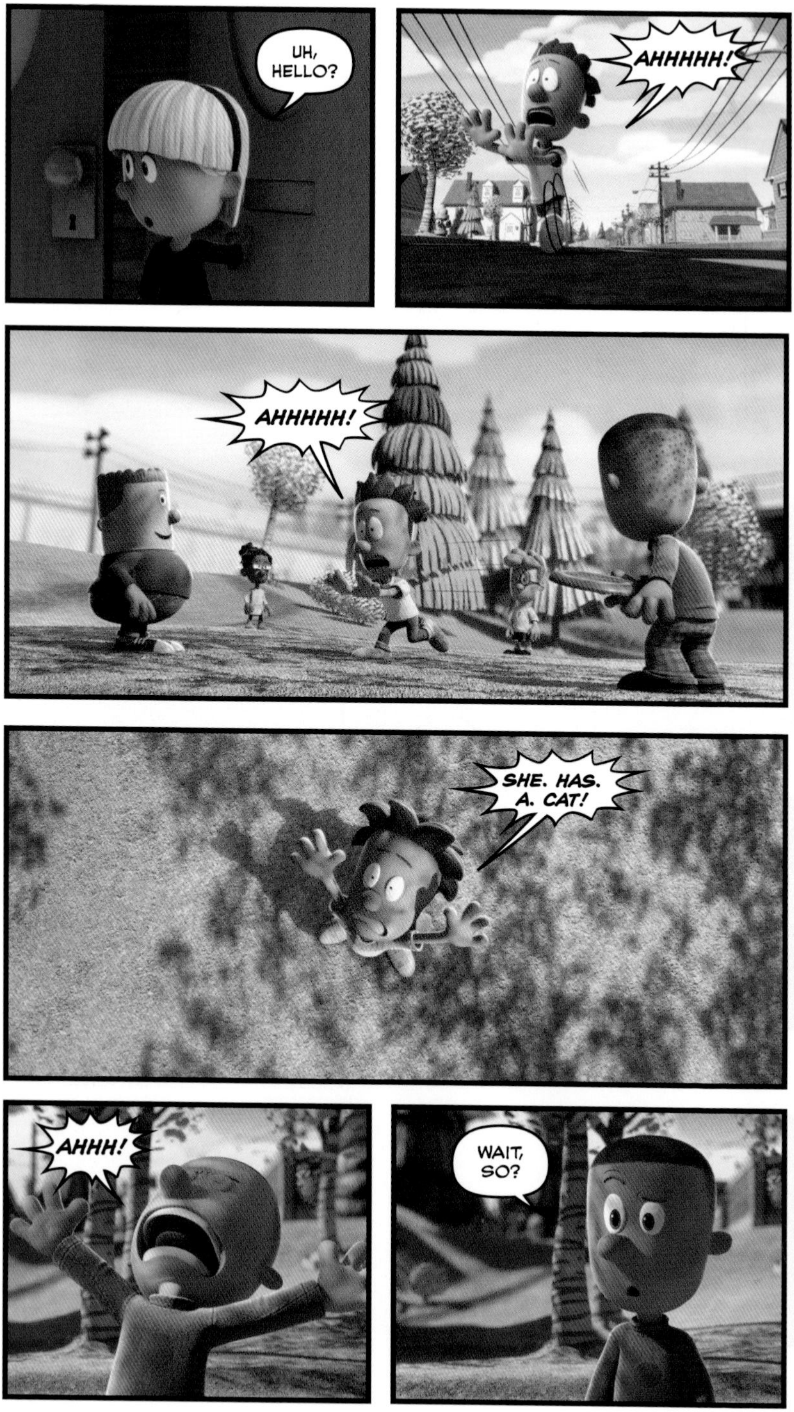
UH, HELLO?
AHHHHH!
AHHHHH!
SHE. HAS. A. CAT!
AHHH!
WAIT, SO?

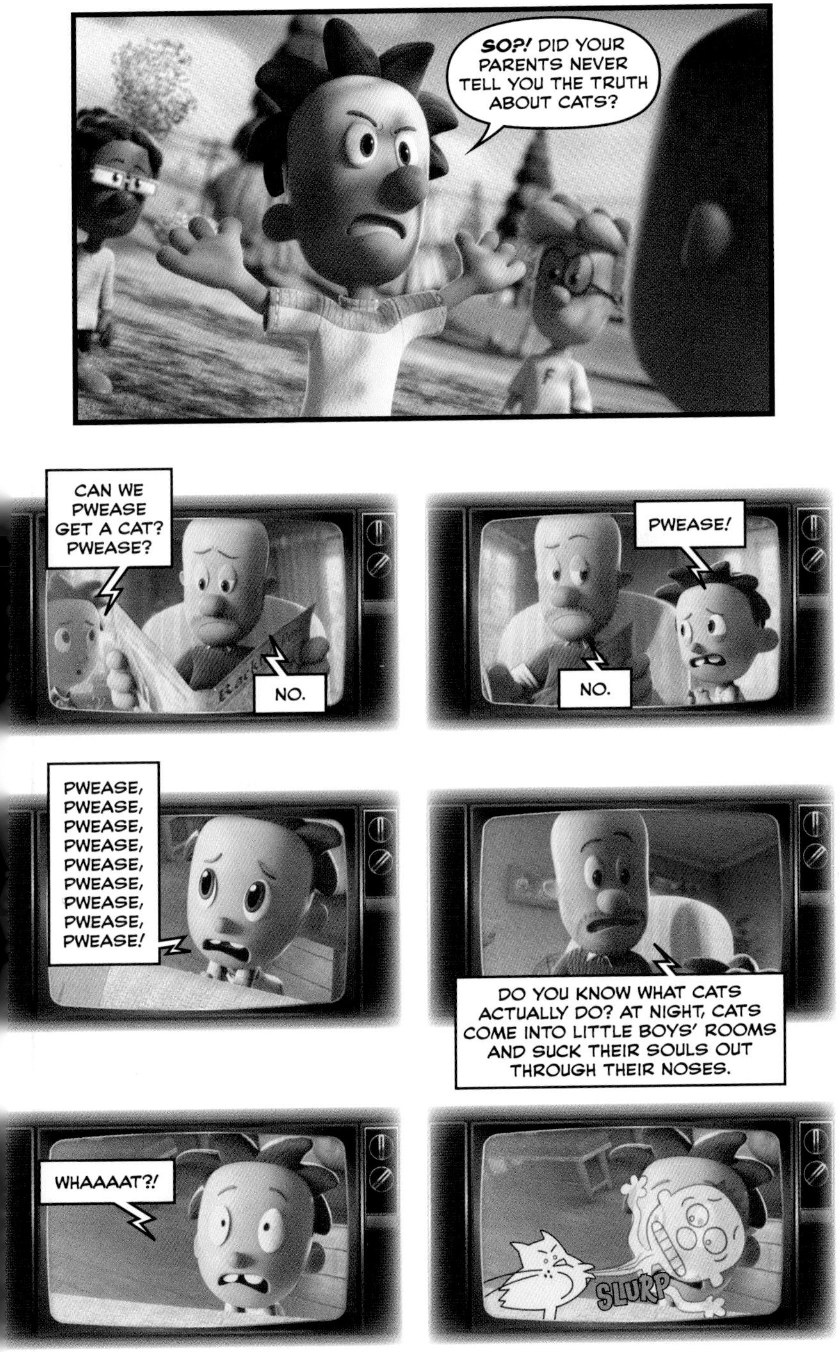
SO?! DID YOUR PARENTS NEVER TELL YOU THE TRUTH ABOUT CATS?
CAN WE PWEASE GET A CAT? PWEASE?
NO.
PWEASE!
NO.
PWEASE, PWEASE, PWEASE, PWEASE, PWEASE, PWEASE, PWEASE, PWEASE, PWEASE!
DO YOU KNOW WHAT CATS ACTUALLY DO? AT NIGHT, CATS COME INTO LITTLE BOYS' ROOMS AND SUCK THEIR SOULS OUT THROUGH THEIR NOSES.
WHAAAAT?!
SLURP

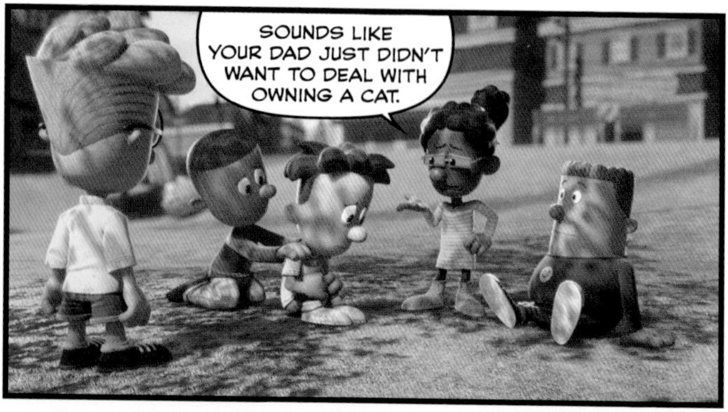
SOUNDS LIKE YOUR DAD JUST DIDN'T WANT TO DEAL WITH OWNING A CAT.

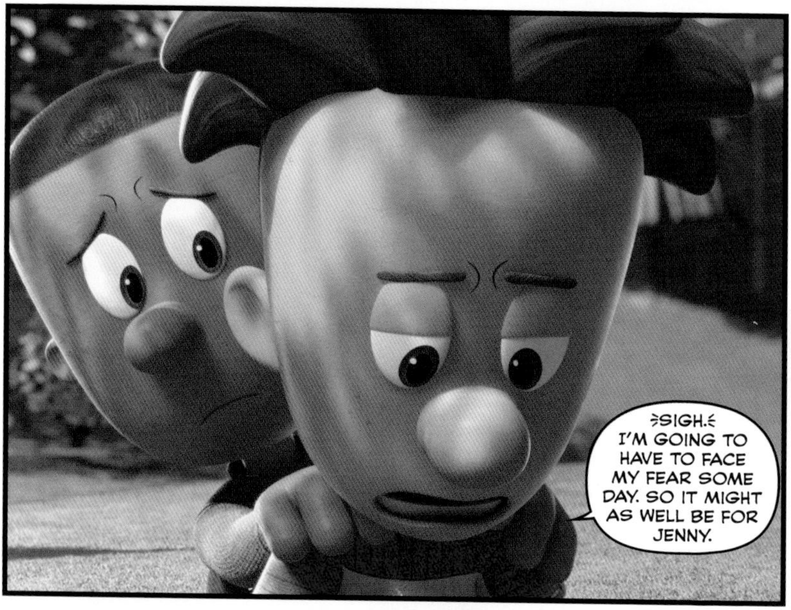
≠SIGH.≠ I'M GOING TO HAVE TO FACE MY FEAR SOME DAY. SO IT MIGHT AS WELL BE FOR JENNY.

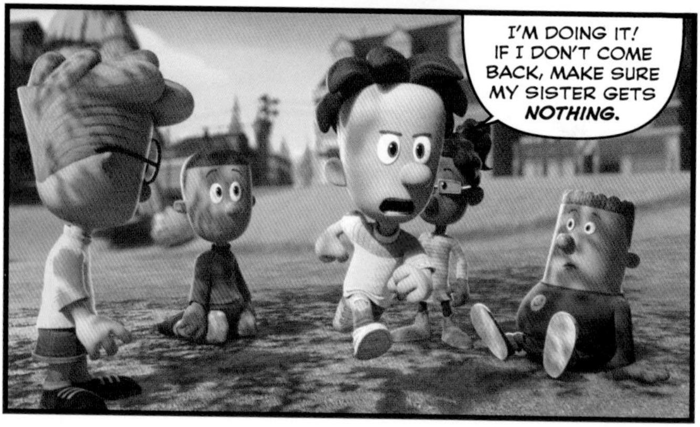
I'M DOING IT! IF I DON'T COME BACK, MAKE SURE MY SISTER GETS ***NOTHING.***

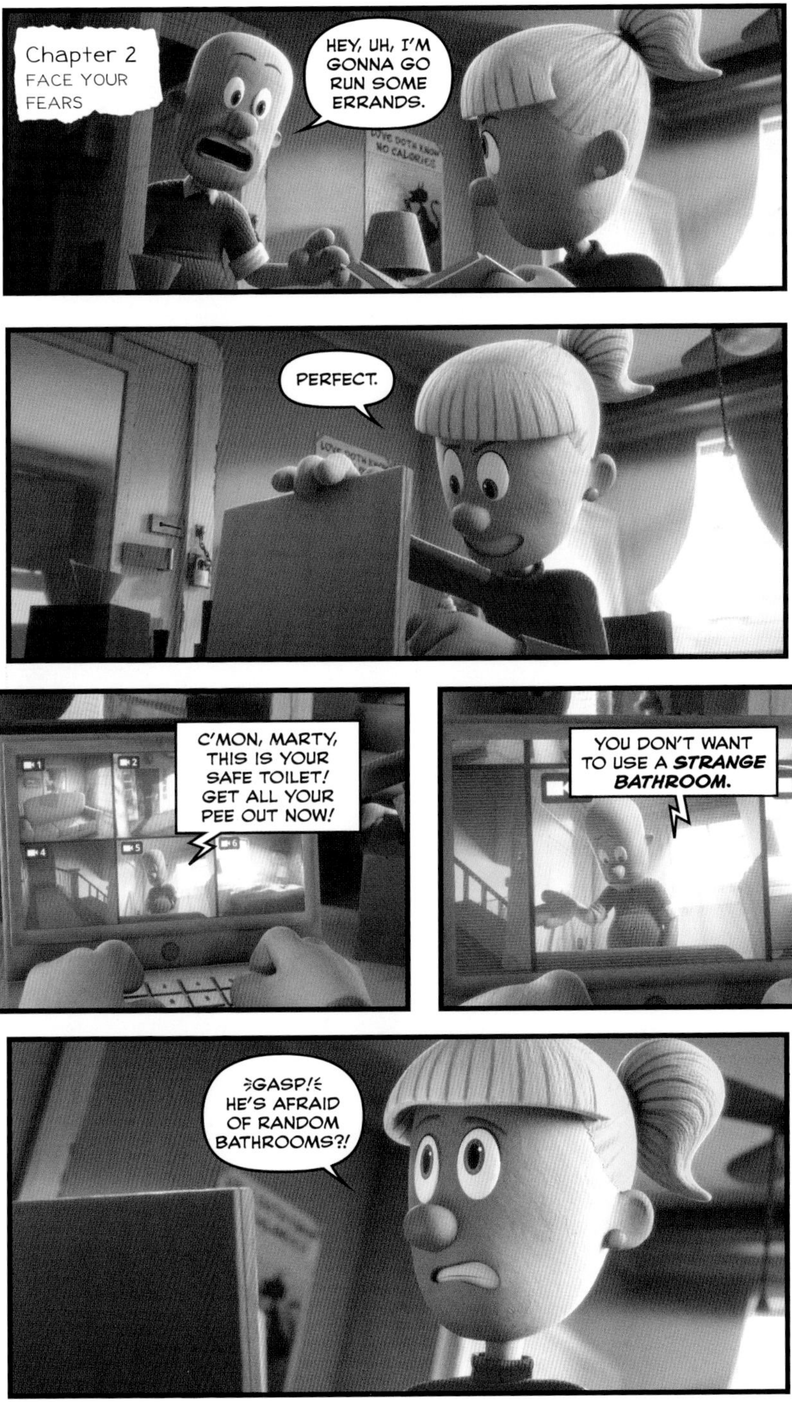
Chapter 2
FACE YOUR FEARS
HEY, UH, I'M GONNA GO RUN SOME ERRANDS.
PERFECT.
C'MON, MARTY, THIS IS YOUR SAFE TOILET! GET ALL YOUR PEE OUT NOW!
YOU DON'T WANT TO USE A ***STRANGE BATHROOM.***
GASP! HE'S AFRAID OF RANDOM BATHROOMS?!

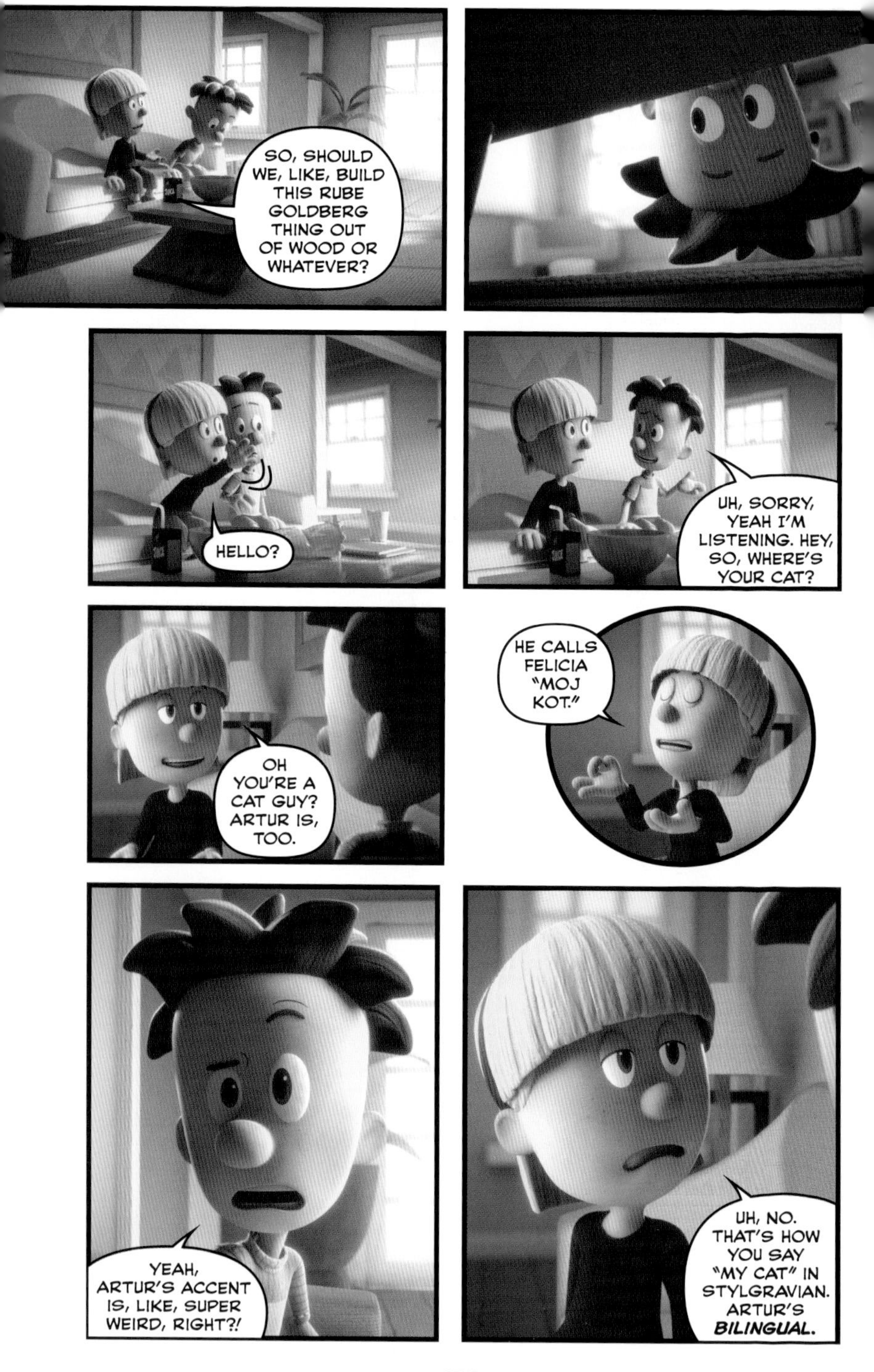
SO, SHOULD WE, LIKE, BUILD THIS RUBE GOLDBERG THING OUT OF WOOD OR WHATEVER?
HELLO?
UH, SORRY, YEAH I'M LISTENING. HEY, SO, WHERE'S YOUR CAT?
OH YOU'RE A CAT GUY? ARTUR IS, TOO.
HE CALLS FELICIA "MOJ KOT."
YEAH, ARTUR'S ACCENT IS, LIKE, SUPER WEIRD, RIGHT?!
UH, NO. THAT'S HOW YOU SAY "MY CAT" IN STYLGRAVIAN. ARTUR'S ***BILINGUAL.***

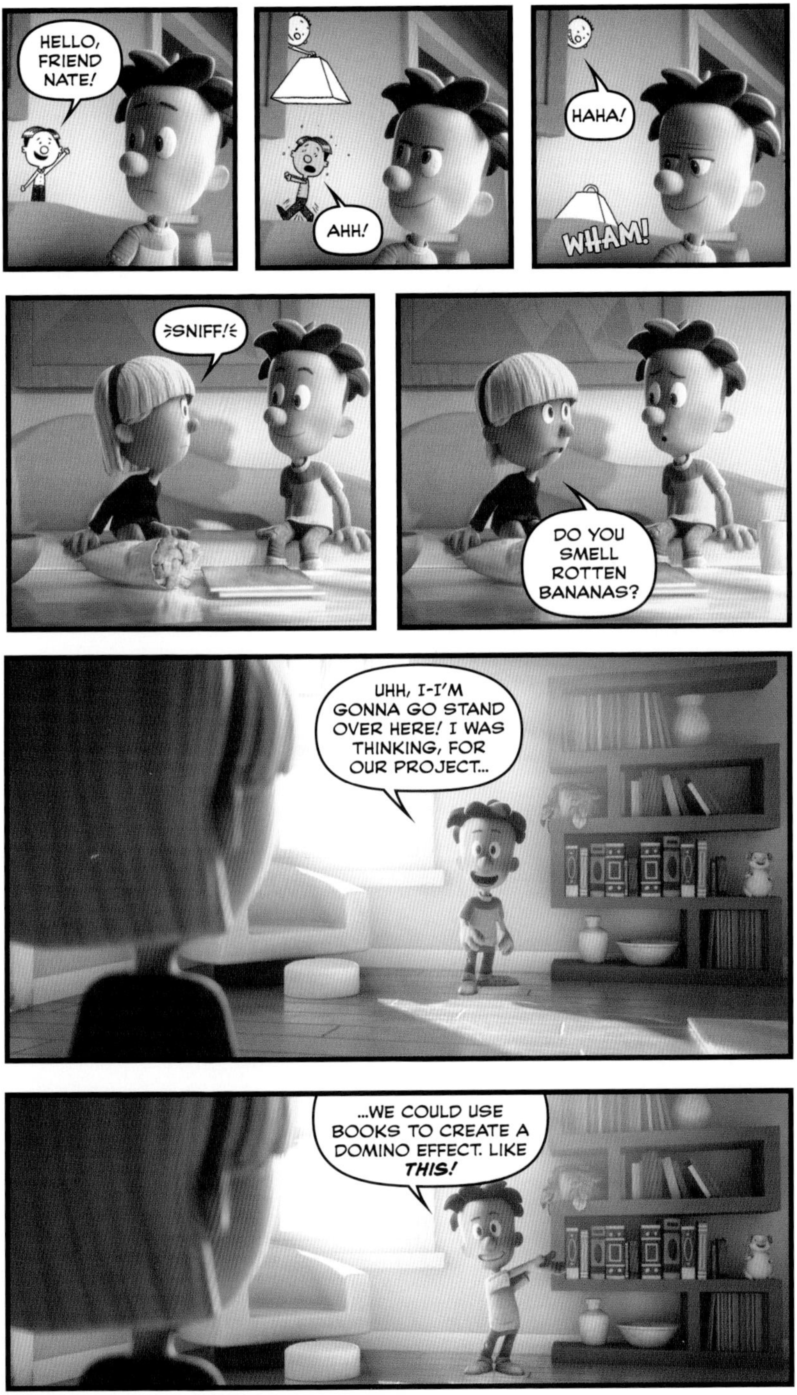
HELLO, FRIEND NATE!
AHH!
HAHA!
WHAM!
SNIFF!
DO YOU SMELL ROTTEN BANANAS?
UHH, I-I'M GONNA GO STAND OVER HERE! I WAS THINKING, FOR OUR PROJECT...
...WE COULD USE BOOKS TO CREATE A DOMINO EFFECT. LIKE *THIS!*

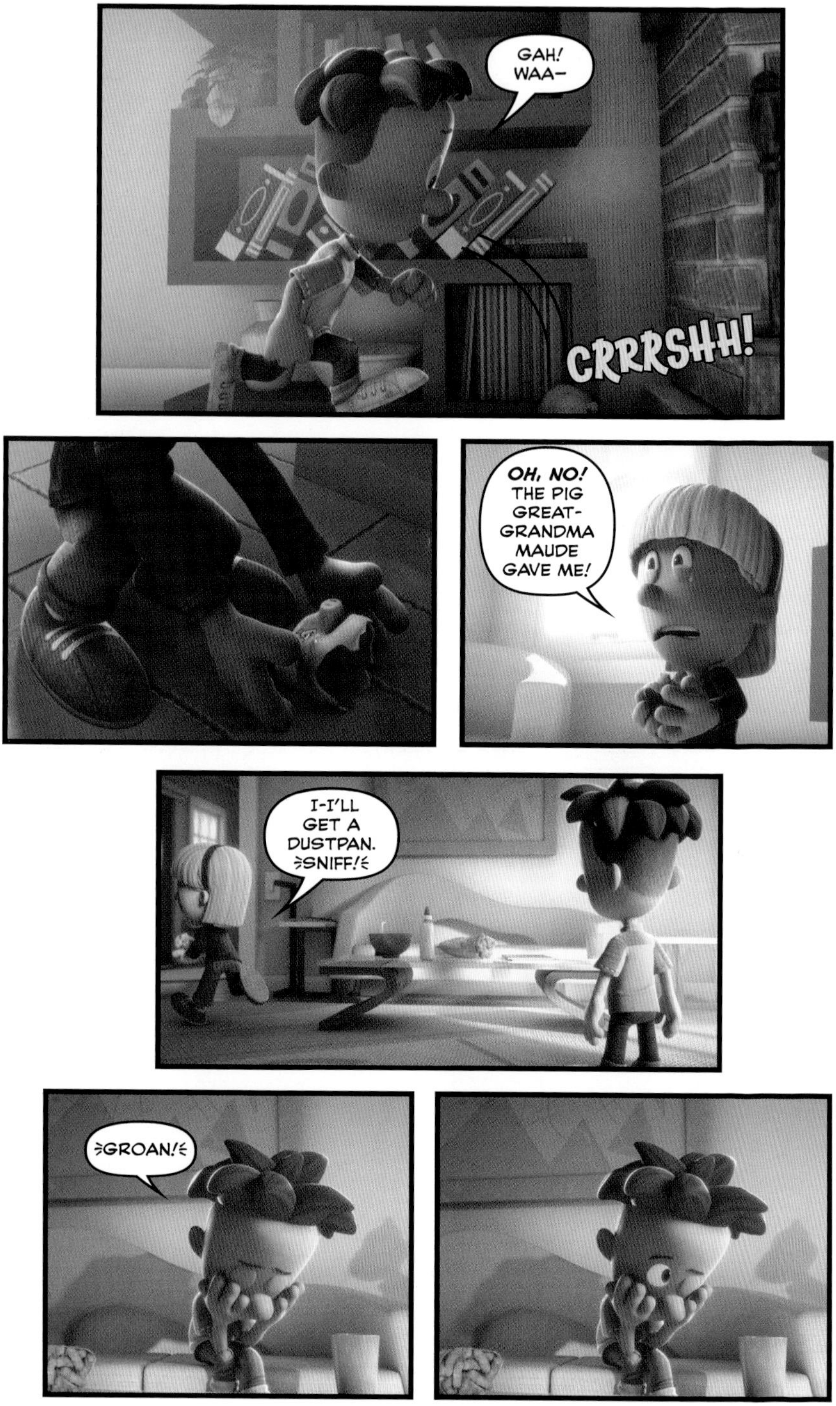
GAH! WAA—
CRRRSHH!
OH, NO! THE PIG GREAT-GRANDMA MAUDE GAVE ME!
I-I'LL GET A DUSTPAN. ⋟SNIFF!⋞
⋟GROAN!⋞

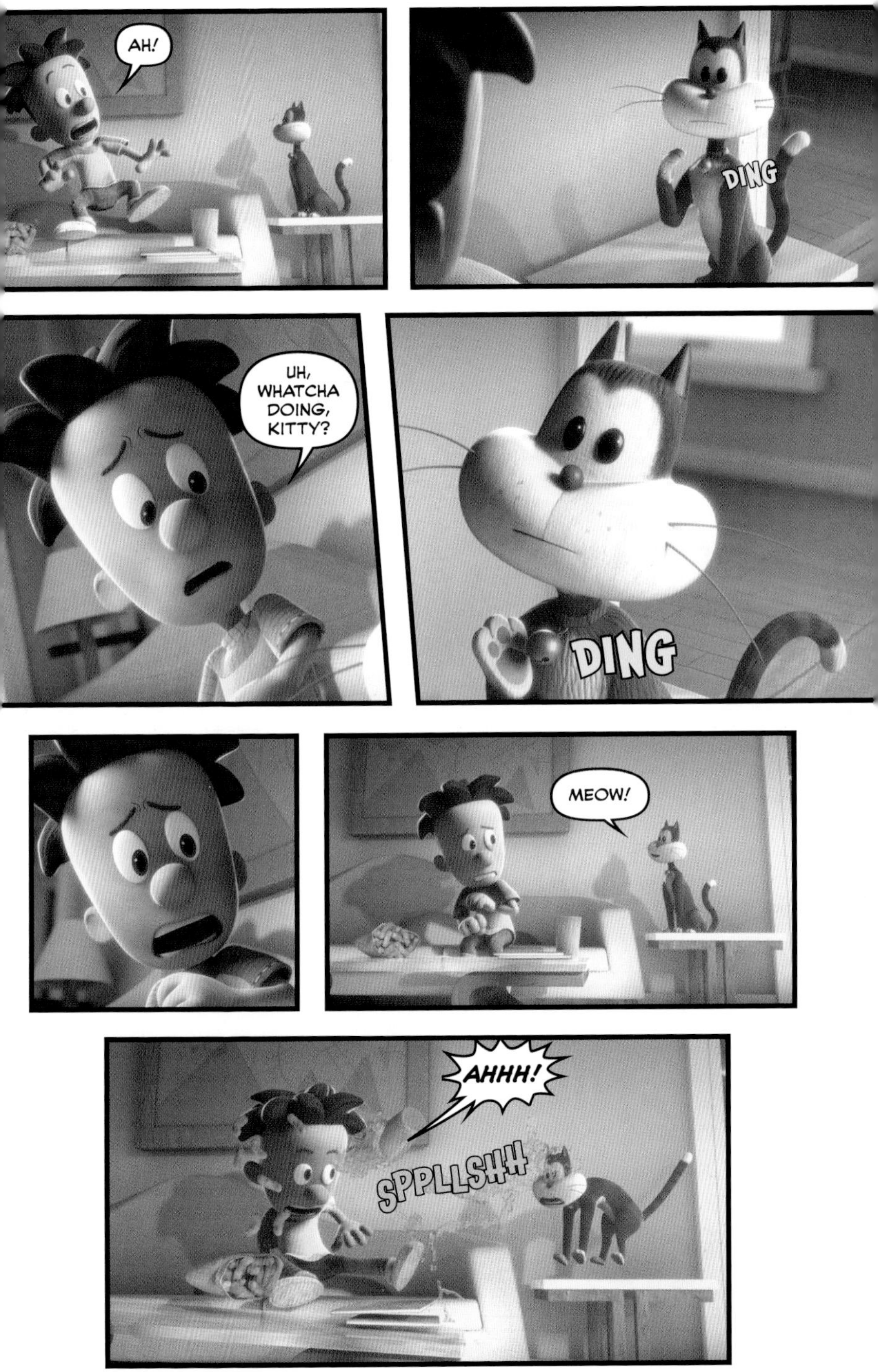
AH!
DING
UH, WHATCHA DOING, KITTY?
DING
MEOW!
AHHH!
SPPLLSHH

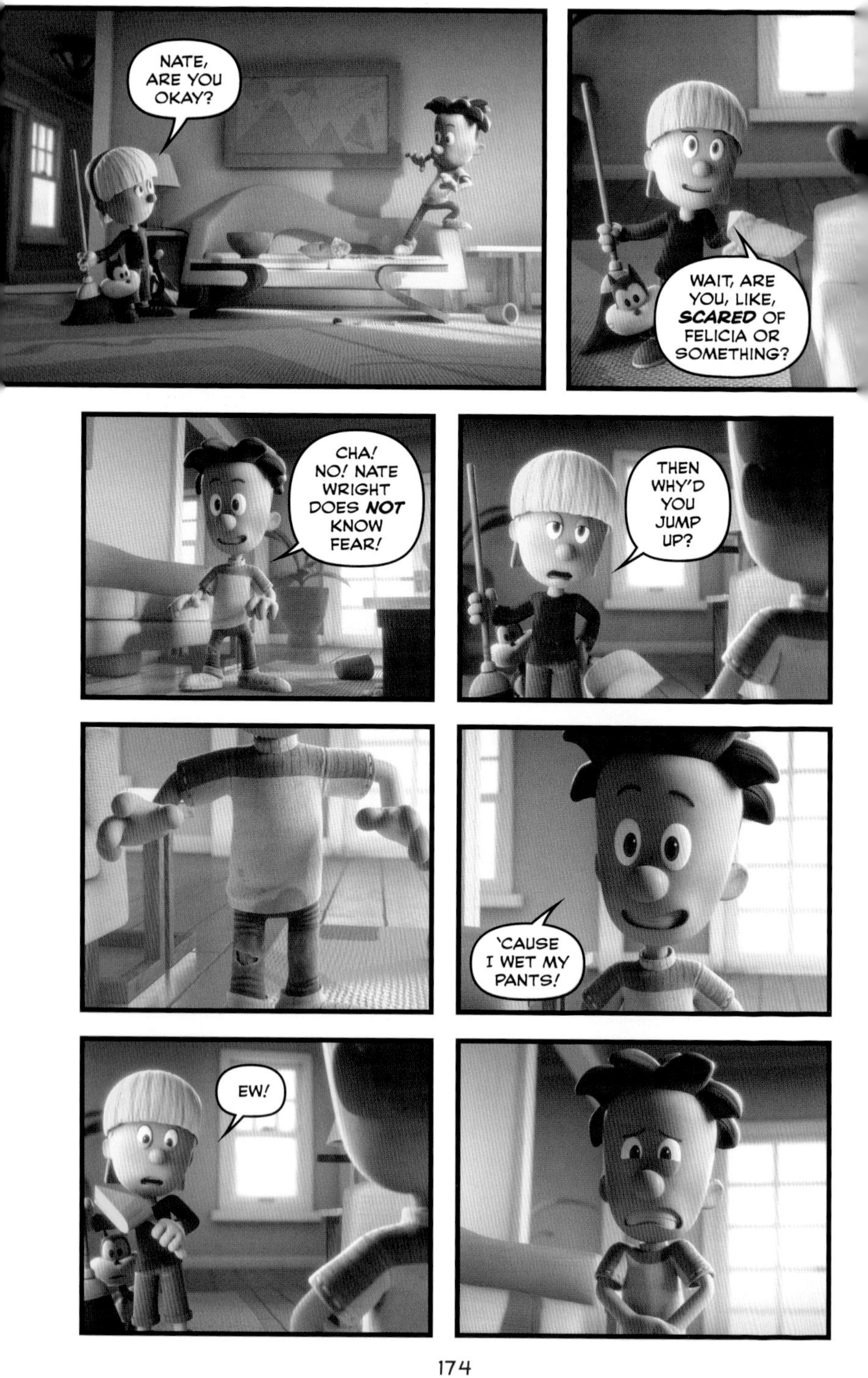
NATE, ARE YOU OKAY?
WAIT, ARE YOU, LIKE, **SCARED** OF FELICIA OR SOMETHING?
CHA! NO! NATE WRIGHT DOES **NOT** KNOW FEAR!
THEN WHY'D YOU JUMP UP?
'CAUSE I WET MY PANTS!
EW!

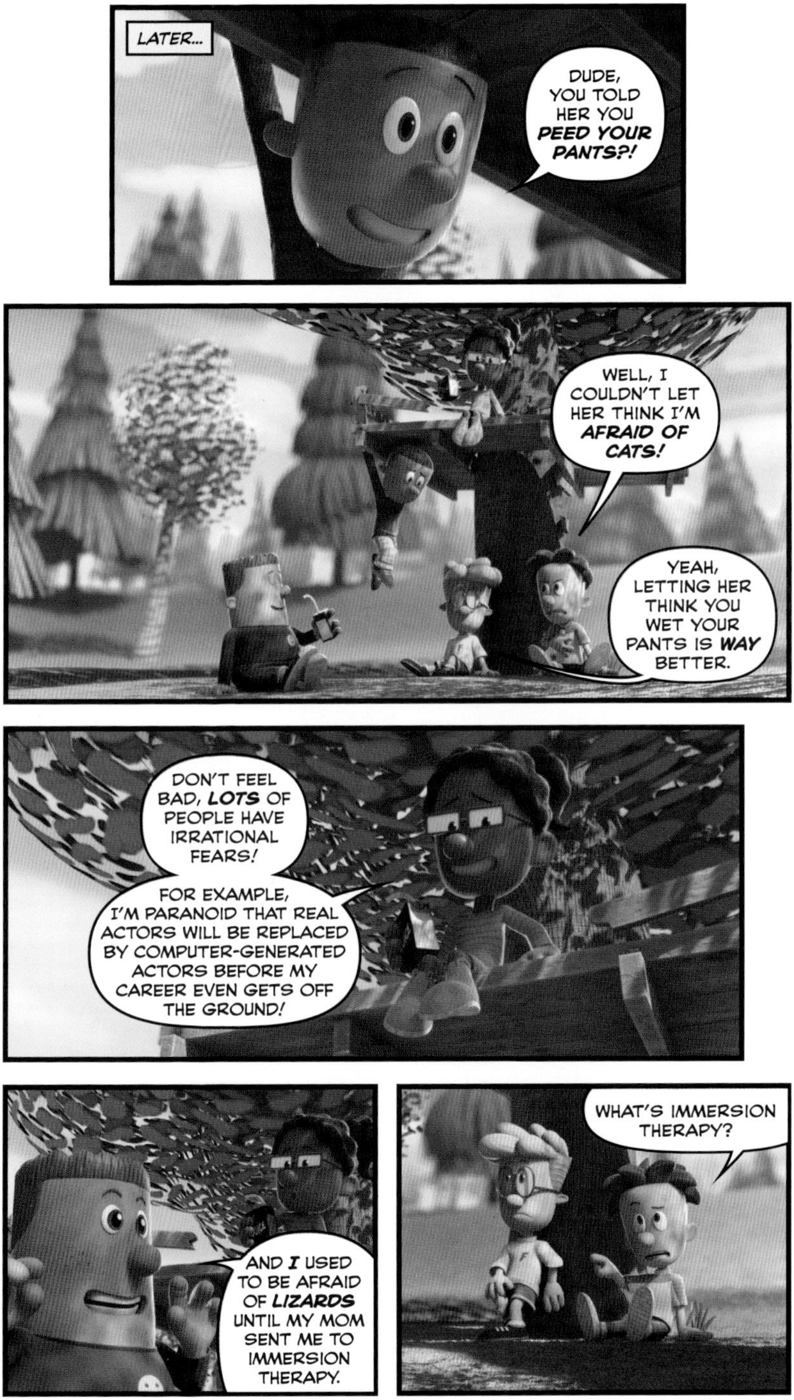
LATER...
DUDE, YOU TOLD HER YOU PEED YOUR PANTS?!
WELL, I COULDN'T LET HER THINK I'M AFRAID OF CATS!
YEAH, LETTING HER THINK YOU WET YOUR PANTS IS WAY BETTER.
DON'T FEEL BAD, LOTS OF PEOPLE HAVE IRRATIONAL FEARS!
FOR EXAMPLE, I'M PARANOID THAT REAL ACTORS WILL BE REPLACED BY COMPUTER-GENERATED ACTORS BEFORE MY CAREER EVEN GETS OFF THE GROUND!
AND I USED TO BE AFRAID OF LIZARDS UNTIL MY MOM SENT ME TO IMMERSION THERAPY.
WHAT'S IMMERSION THERAPY?

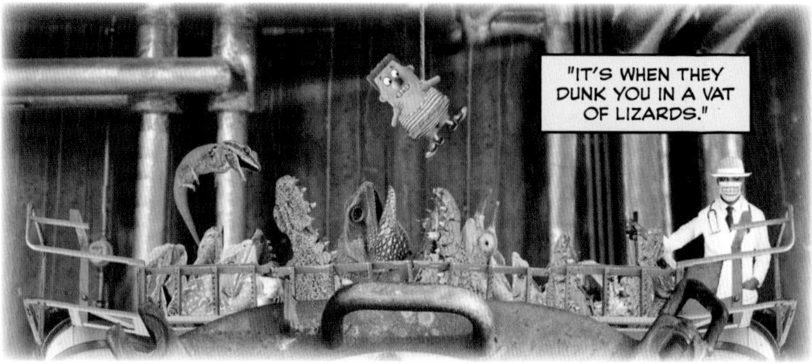
"IT'S WHEN THEY DUNK YOU IN A VAT OF LIZARDS."

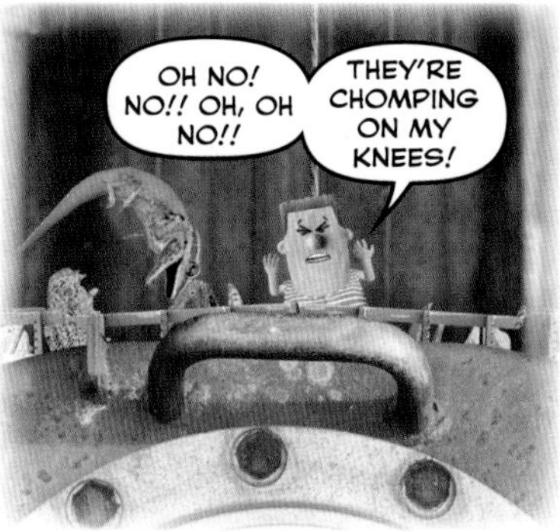
OH NO! NO!! OH, OH NO!!
THEY'RE CHOMPING ON MY KNEES!

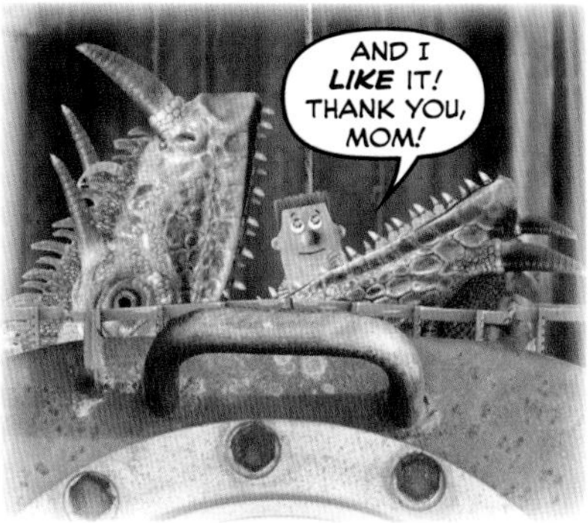
AND I LIKE IT! THANK YOU, MOM!

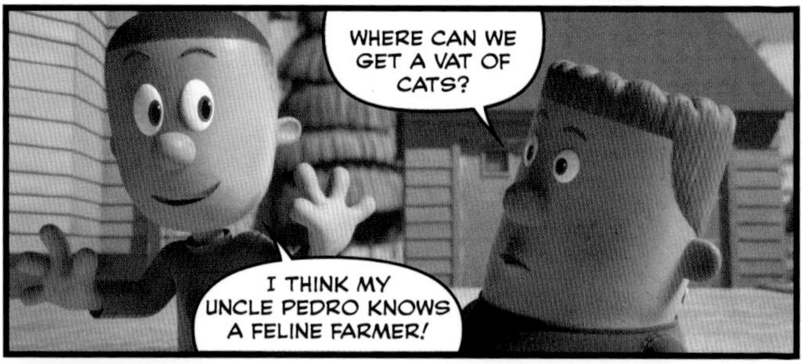
WHERE CAN WE GET A VAT OF CATS?
I THINK MY UNCLE PEDRO KNOWS A FELINE FARMER!

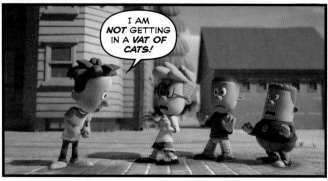

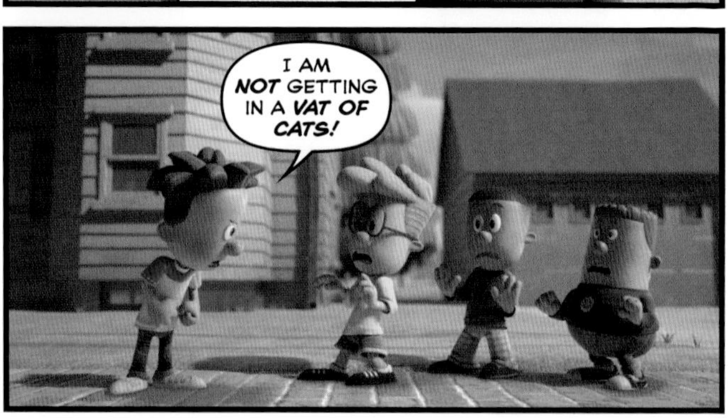
I AM NOT GETTING IN A VAT OF CATS!

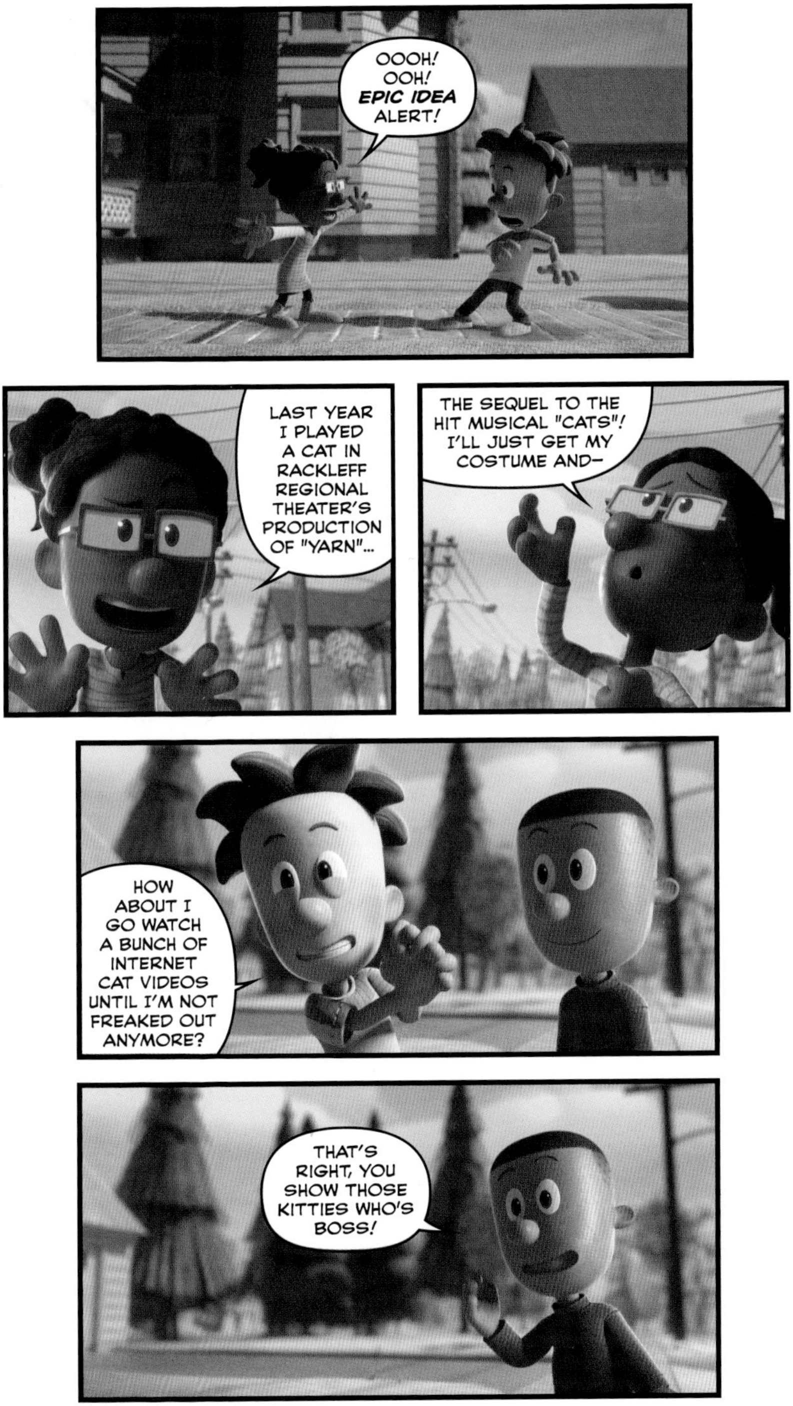
OOOH! OOH! EPIC IDEA ALERT!
LAST YEAR I PLAYED A CAT IN RACKLEFF REGIONAL THEATER'S PRODUCTION OF "YARN"...
THE SEQUEL TO THE HIT MUSICAL "CATS"! I'LL JUST GET MY COSTUME AND–
HOW ABOUT I GO WATCH A BUNCH OF INTERNET CAT VIDEOS UNTIL I'M NOT FREAKED OUT ANYMORE?
THAT'S RIGHT, YOU SHOW THOSE KITTIES WHO'S BOSS!

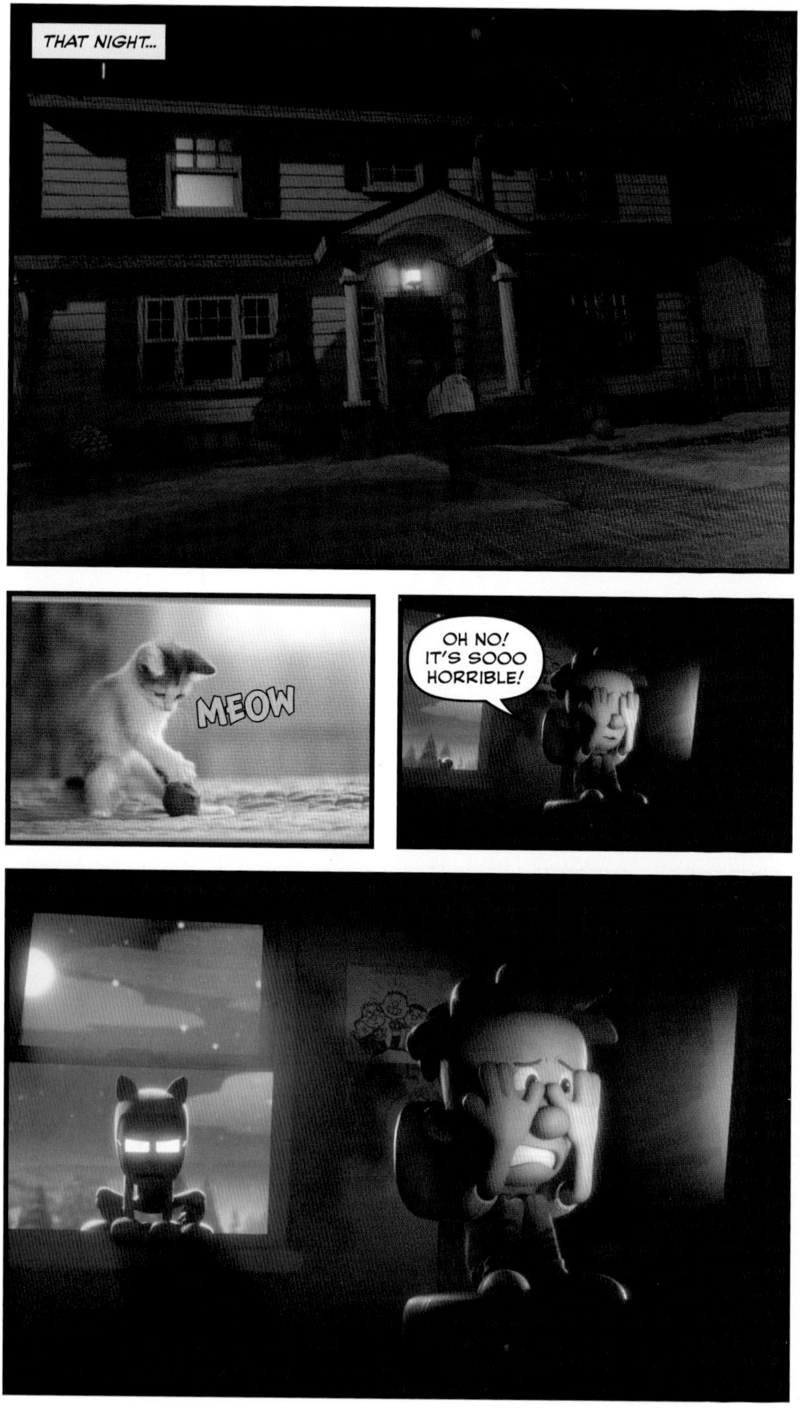
THAT NIGHT...
MEOW
OH NO! IT'S SOOO HORRIBLE!

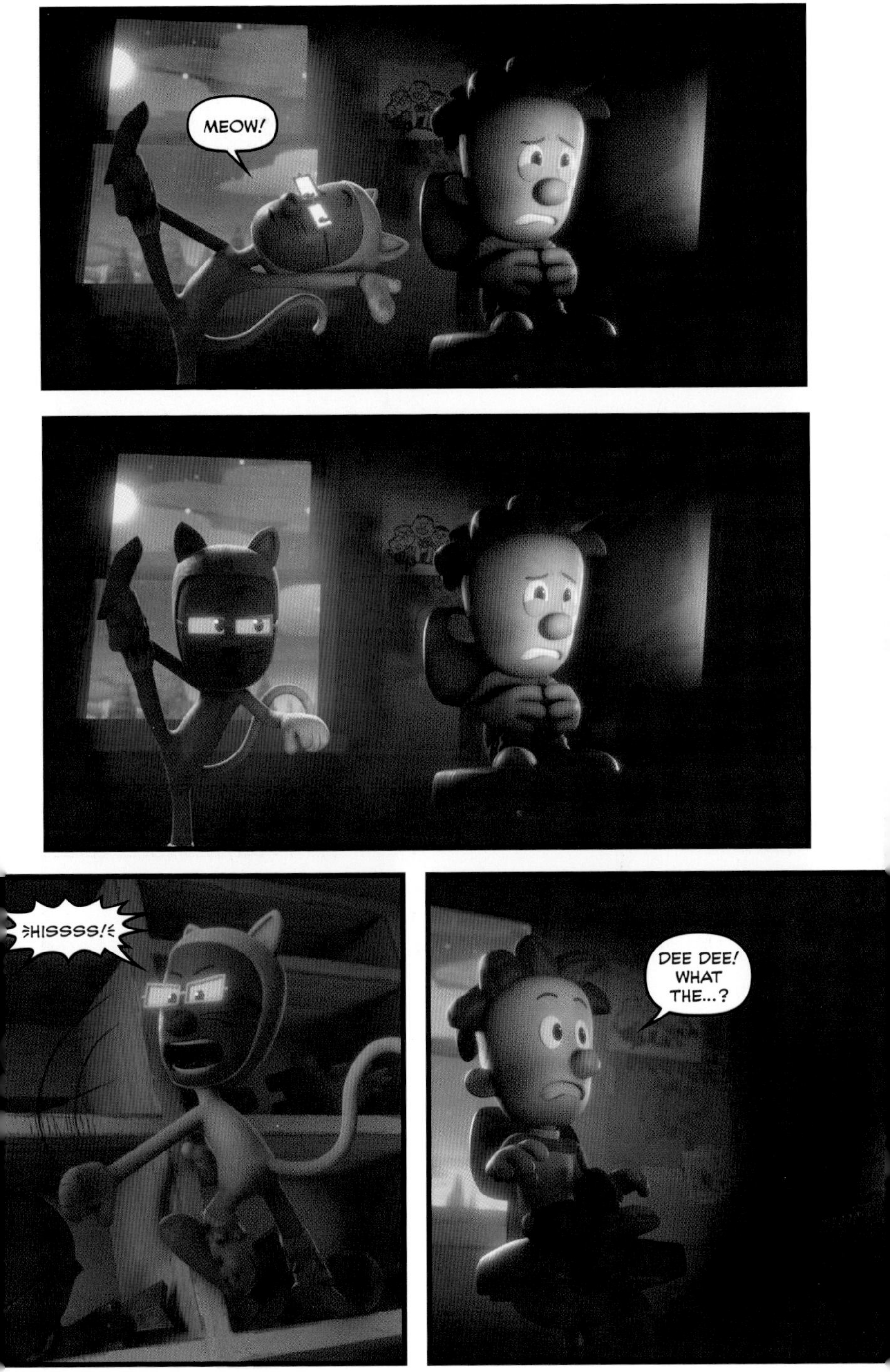
MEOW!
HISSSS!
DEE DEE! WHAT THE...?

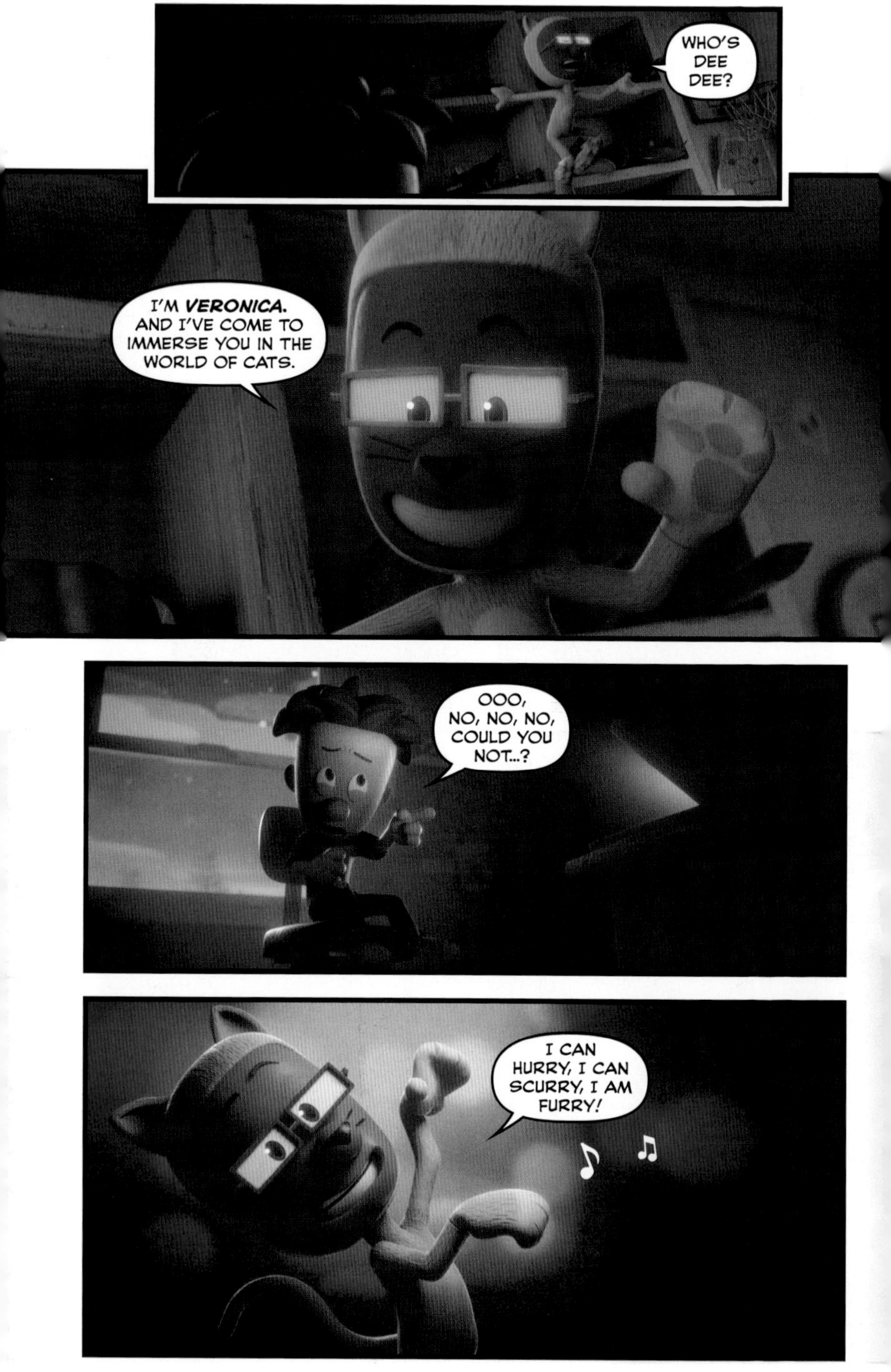
WHO'S DEE DEE?
I'M **VERONICA.** AND I'VE COME TO IMMERSE YOU IN THE WORLD OF CATS.
OOO, NO, NO, NO, COULD YOU NOT...?
I CAN HURRY, I CAN SCURRY, I AM FURRY!

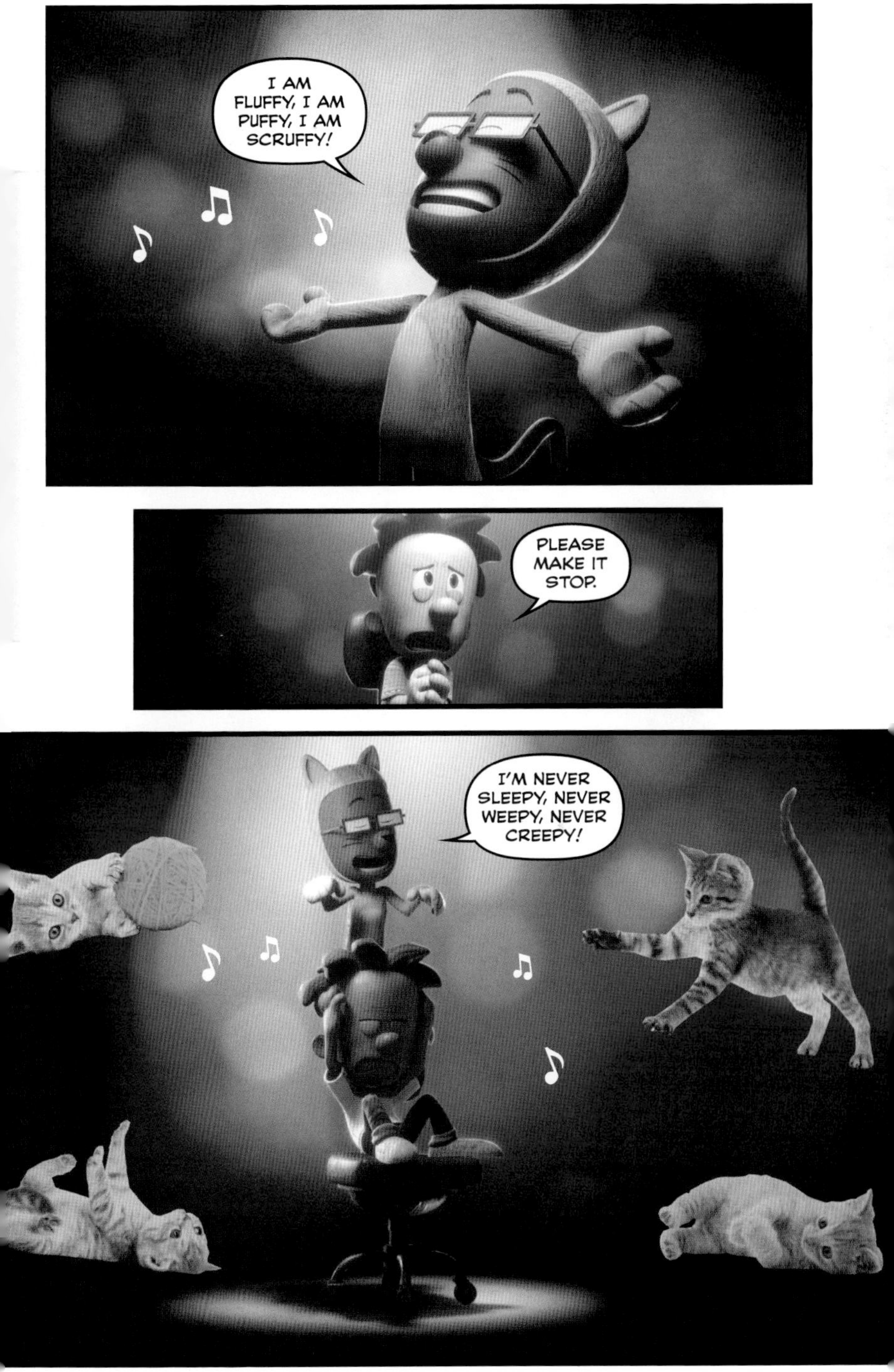
I AM FLUFFY, I AM PUFFY, I AM SCRUFFY!
PLEASE MAKE IT STOP.
I'M NEVER SLEEPY, NEVER WEEPY, NEVER CREEPY!

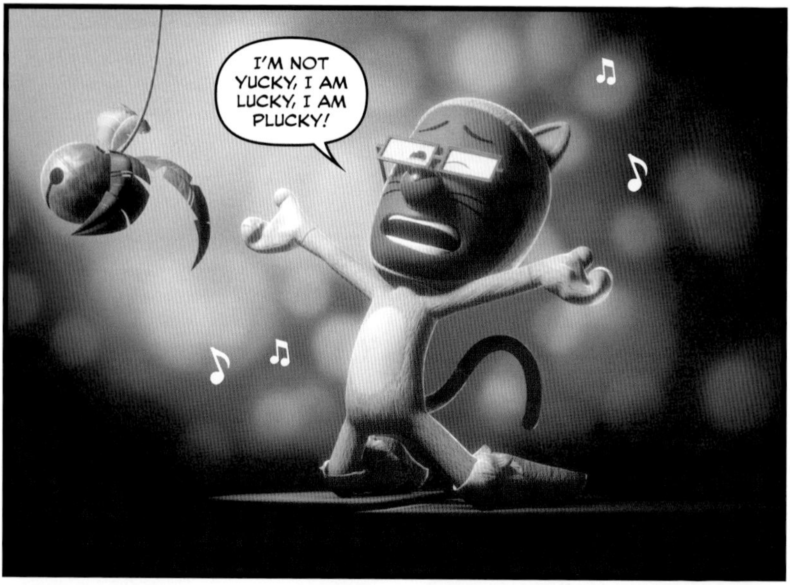
I'M NOT YUCKY, I AM LUCKY, I AM PLUCKY!

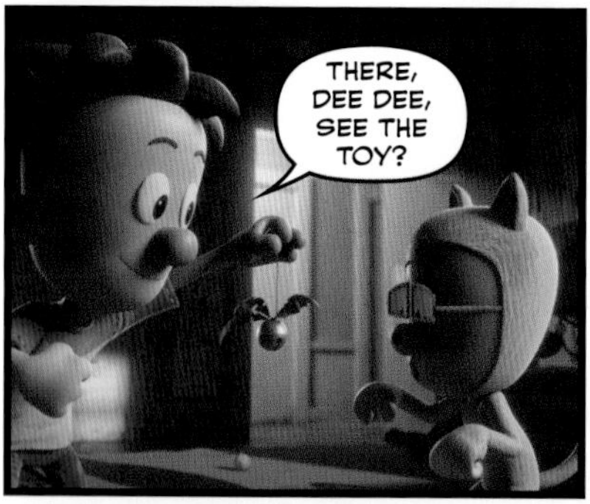
THERE, DEE DEE, SEE THE TOY?

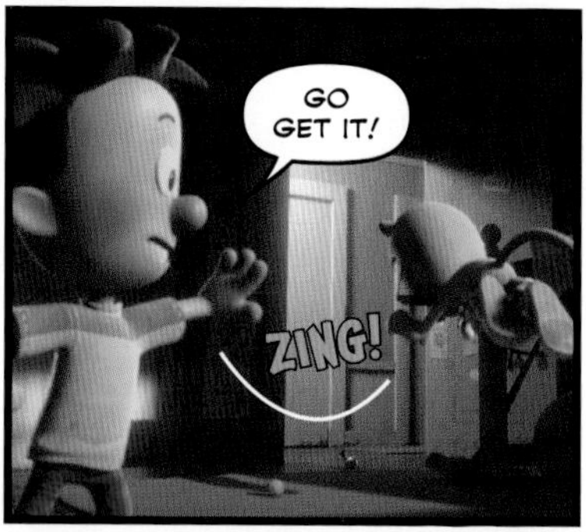
GO GET IT!
ZING!

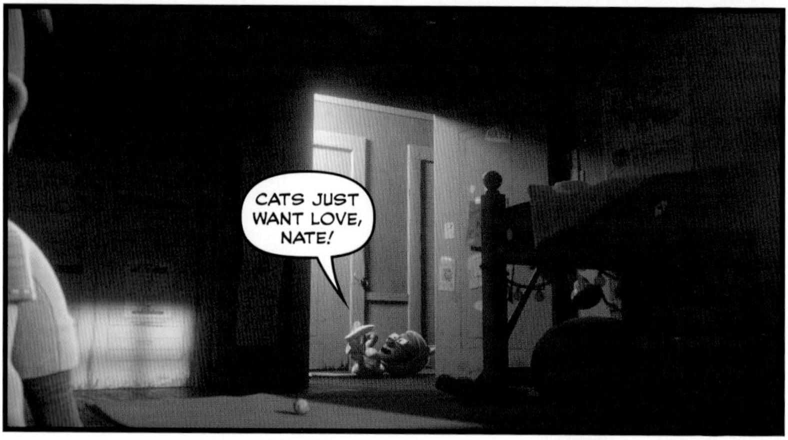
CATS JUST WANT LOVE, NATE!

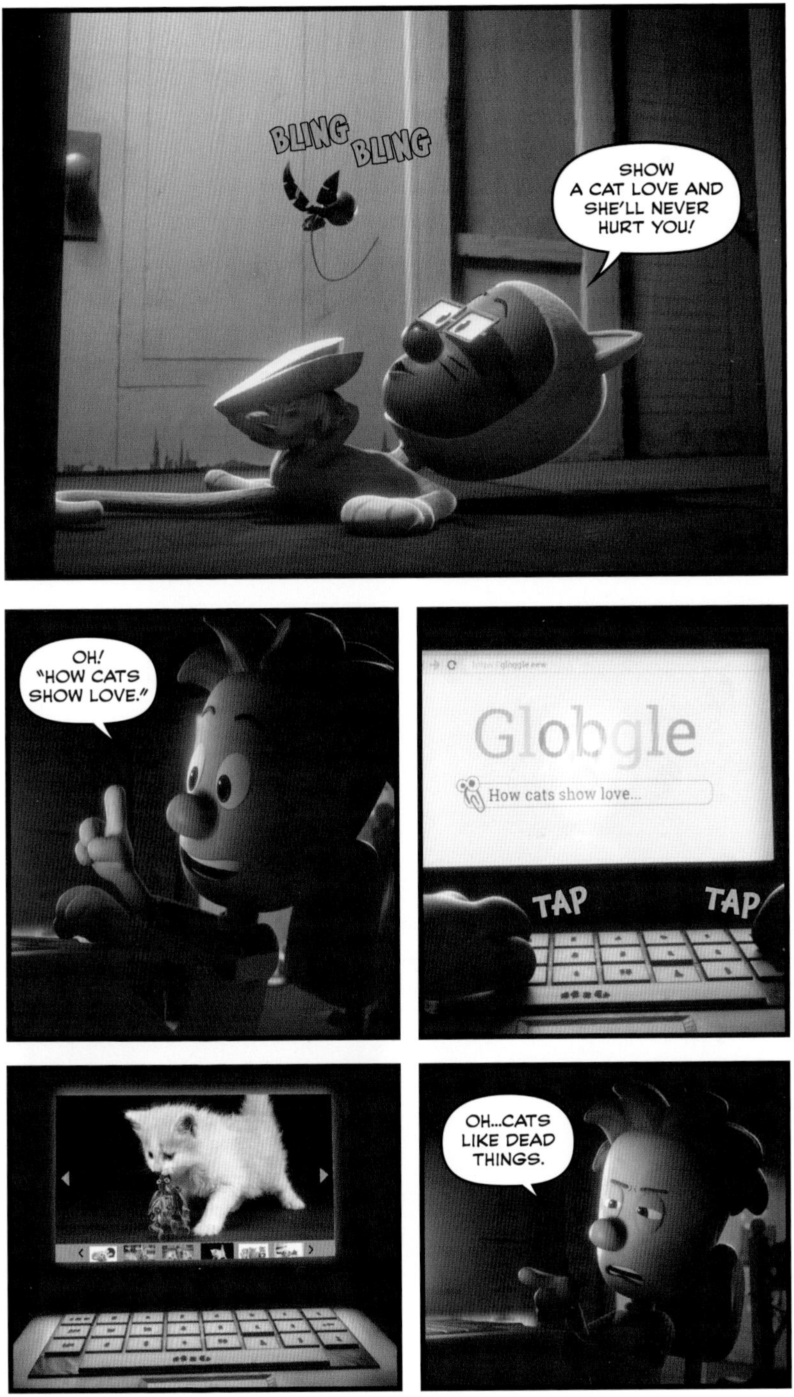
BLING
BLING
SHOW A CAT LOVE AND SHE'LL NEVER HURT YOU!
OH! "HOW CATS SHOW LOVE."
Globgle
How cats show love...
TAP
TAP
OH...CATS LIKE DEAD THINGS.

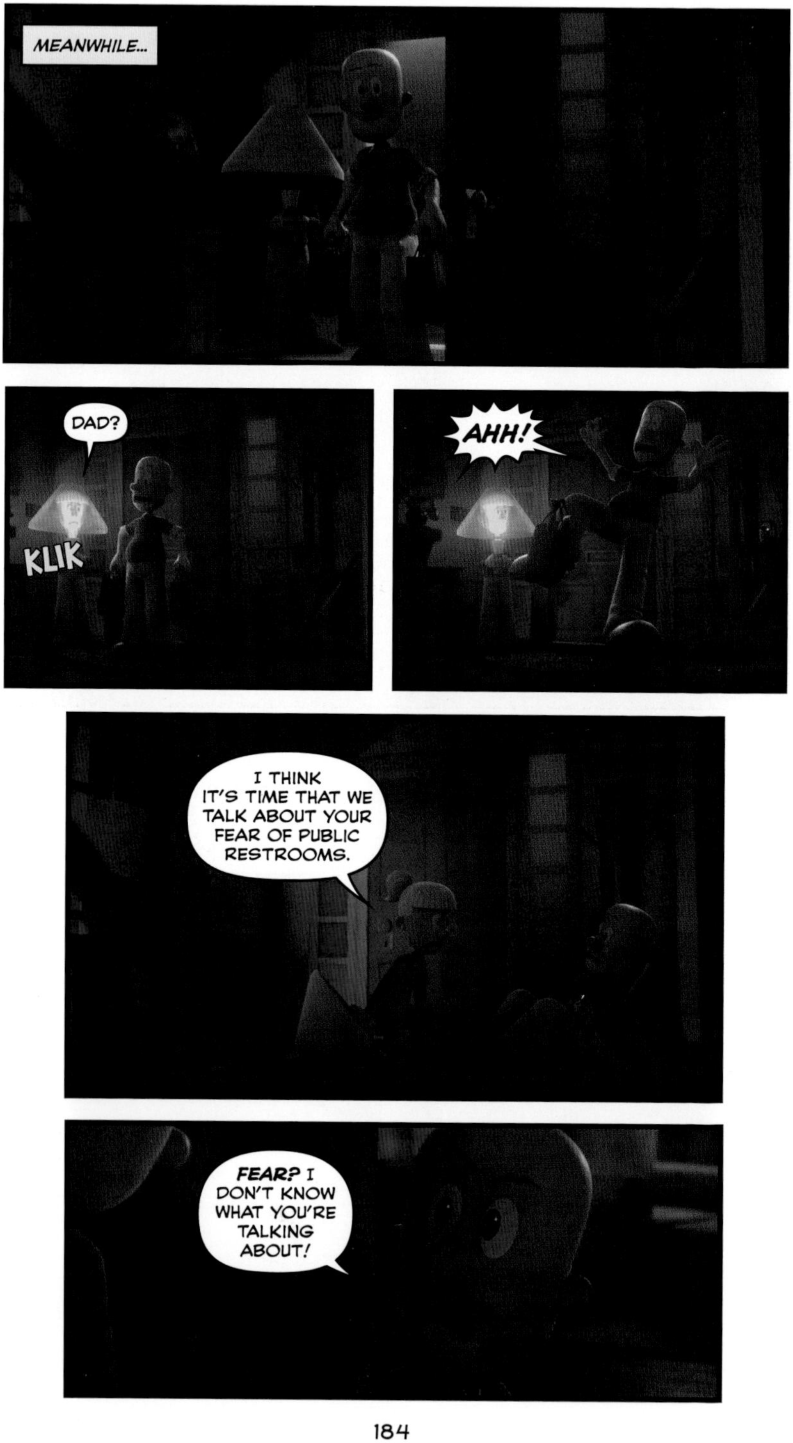
MEANWHILE...
DAD?
KLIK
AHH!
I THINK IT'S TIME THAT WE TALK ABOUT YOUR FEAR OF PUBLIC RESTROOMS.
FEAR? I DON'T KNOW WHAT YOU'RE TALKING ABOUT!

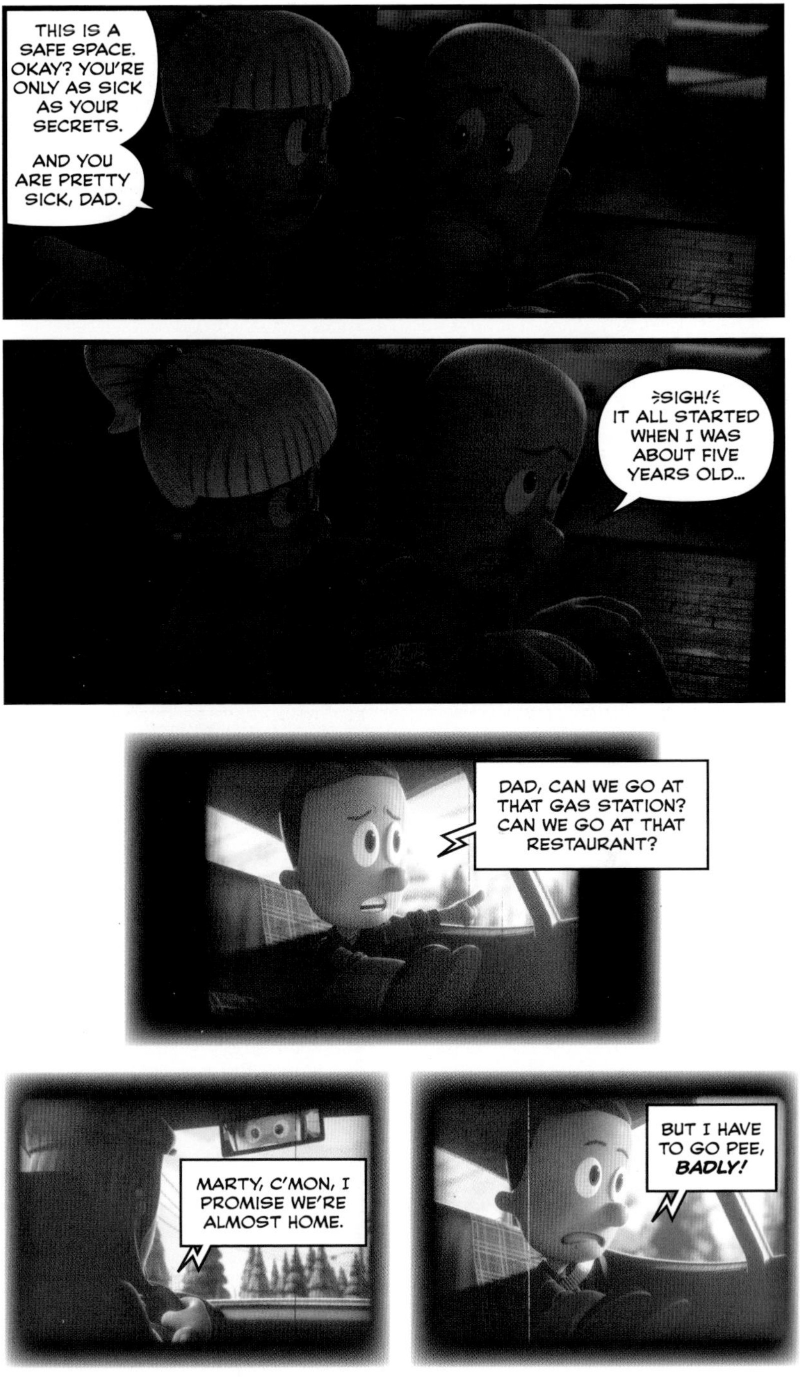
THIS IS A SAFE SPACE. OKAY? YOU'RE ONLY AS SICK AS YOUR SECRETS.
AND YOU ARE PRETTY SICK, DAD.
≥SIGH!≤ IT ALL STARTED WHEN I WAS ABOUT FIVE YEARS OLD...
DAD, CAN WE GO AT THAT GAS STATION? CAN WE GO AT THAT RESTAURANT?
MARTY, C'MON, I PROMISE WE'RE ALMOST HOME.
BUT I HAVE TO GO PEE, BADLY!

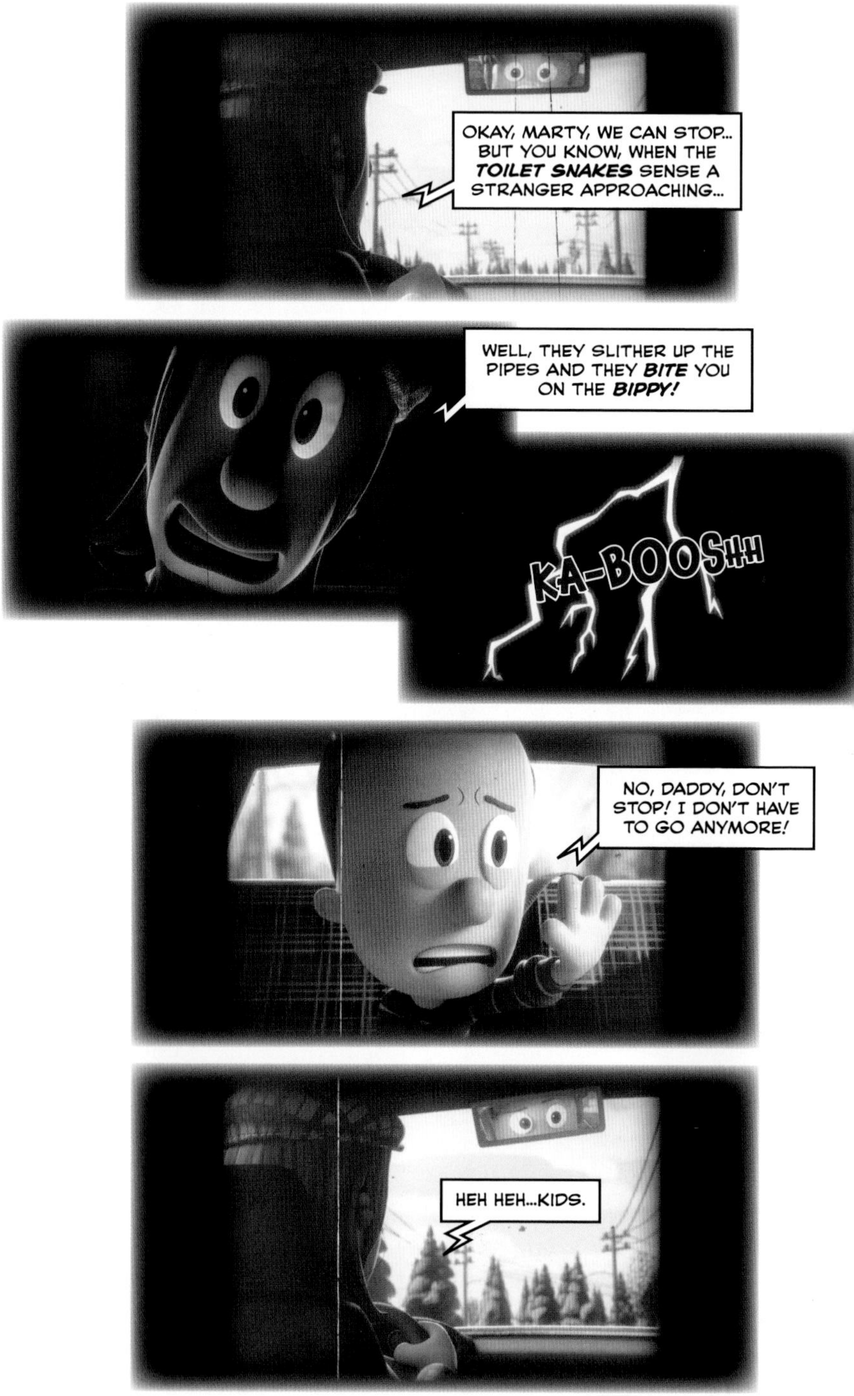
OKAY, MARTY, WE CAN STOP... BUT YOU KNOW, WHEN THE ***TOILET SNAKES*** SENSE A STRANGER APPROACHING...
WELL, THEY SLITHER UP THE PIPES AND THEY ***BITE*** YOU ON THE ***BIPPY!***
KA-BOOSHH
NO, DADDY, DON'T STOP! I DON'T HAVE TO GO ANYMORE!
HEH HEH...KIDS.

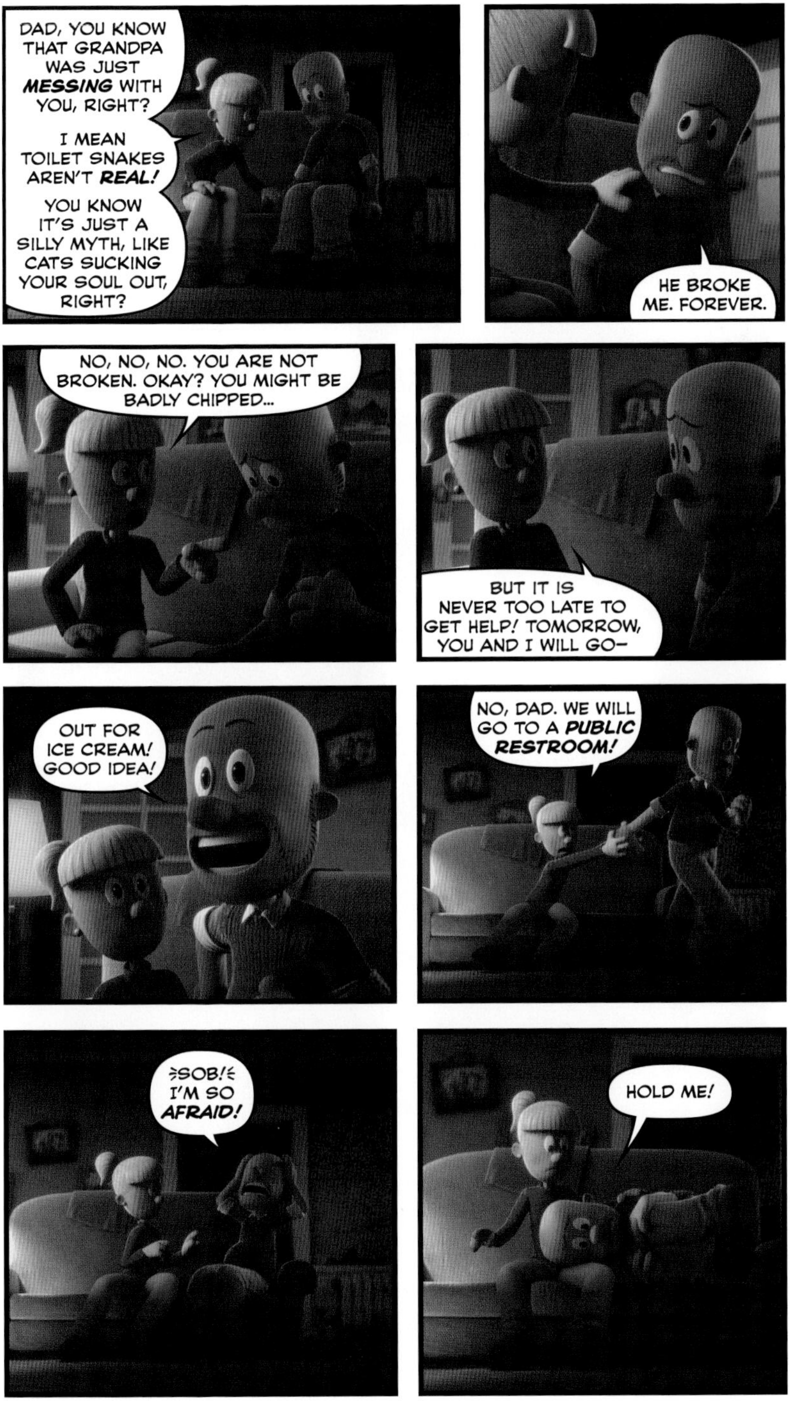
DAD, YOU KNOW THAT GRANDPA WAS JUST MESSING WITH YOU, RIGHT?
I MEAN TOILET SNAKES AREN'T REAL!
YOU KNOW IT'S JUST A SILLY MYTH, LIKE CATS SUCKING YOUR SOUL OUT, RIGHT?
HE BROKE ME. FOREVER.
NO, NO, NO. YOU ARE NOT BROKEN. OKAY? YOU MIGHT BE BADLY CHIPPED...
BUT IT IS NEVER TOO LATE TO GET HELP! TOMORROW, YOU AND I WILL GO—
OUT FOR ICE CREAM! GOOD IDEA!
NO, DAD. WE WILL GO TO A PUBLIC RESTROOM!
SOB! I'M SO AFRAID!
HOLD ME!

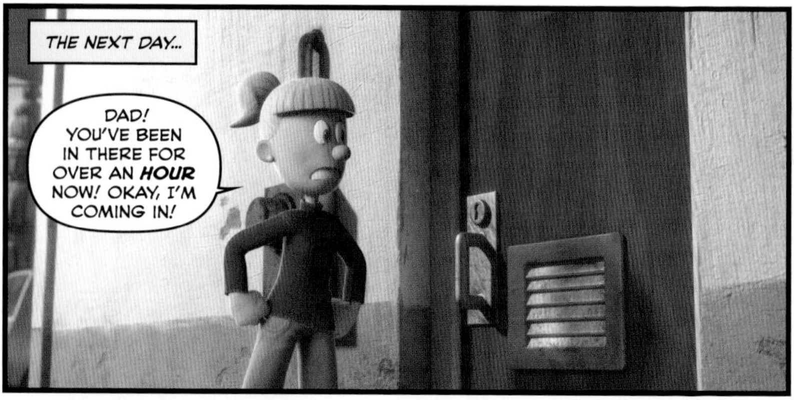
THE NEXT DAY...
DAD! YOU'VE BEEN IN THERE FOR OVER AN **HOUR** NOW! OKAY, I'M COMING IN!

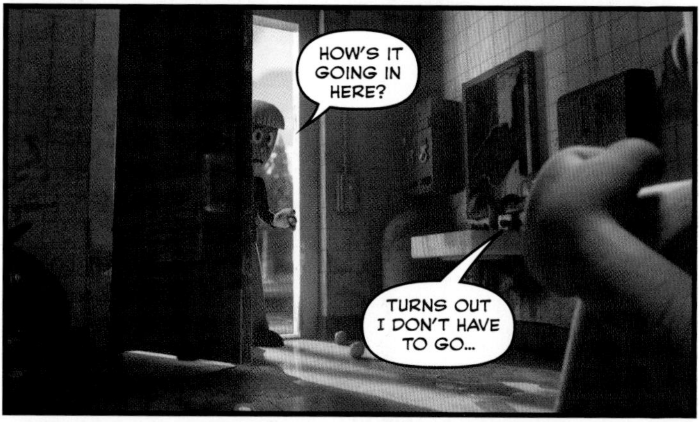
HOW'S IT GOING IN HERE?
TURNS OUT I DON'T HAVE TO GO...

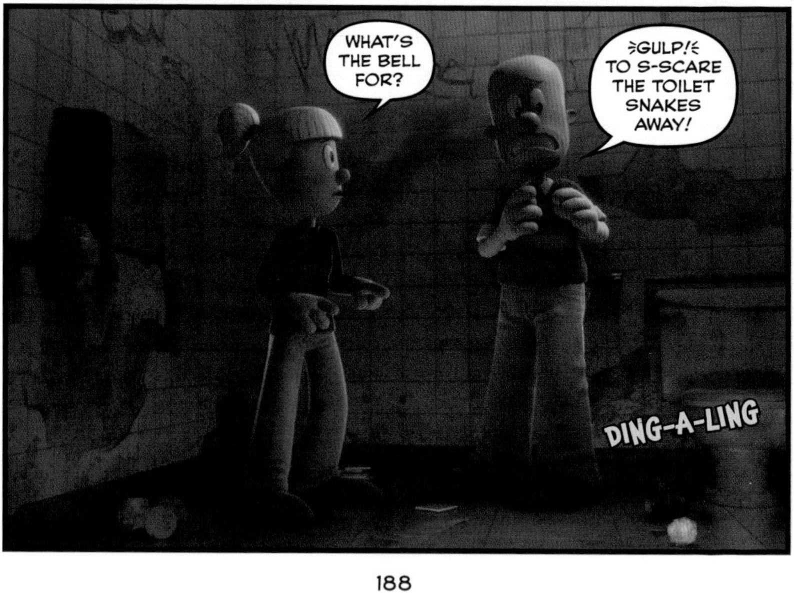
WHAT'S THE BELL FOR?
GULP! TO S-SCARE THE TOILET SNAKES AWAY!
DING-A-LING

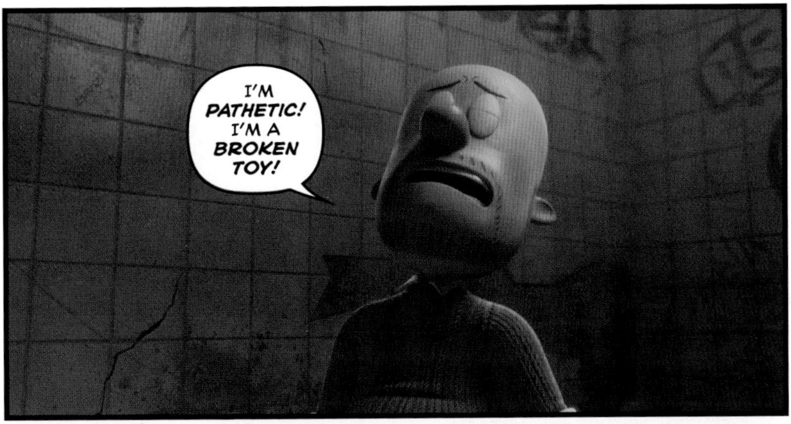
I'M PATHETIC! I'M A BROKEN TOY!

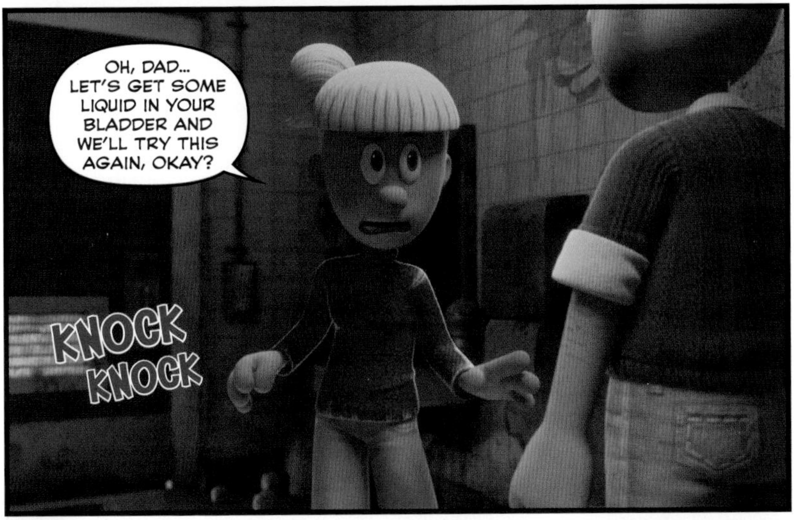
OH, DAD... LET'S GET SOME LIQUID IN YOUR BLADDER AND WE'LL TRY THIS AGAIN, OKAY?
KNOCK KNOCK

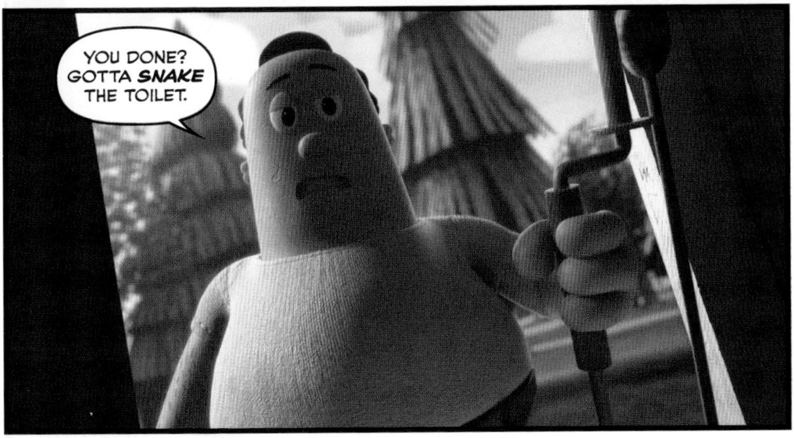
YOU DONE? GOTTA SNAKE THE TOILET.

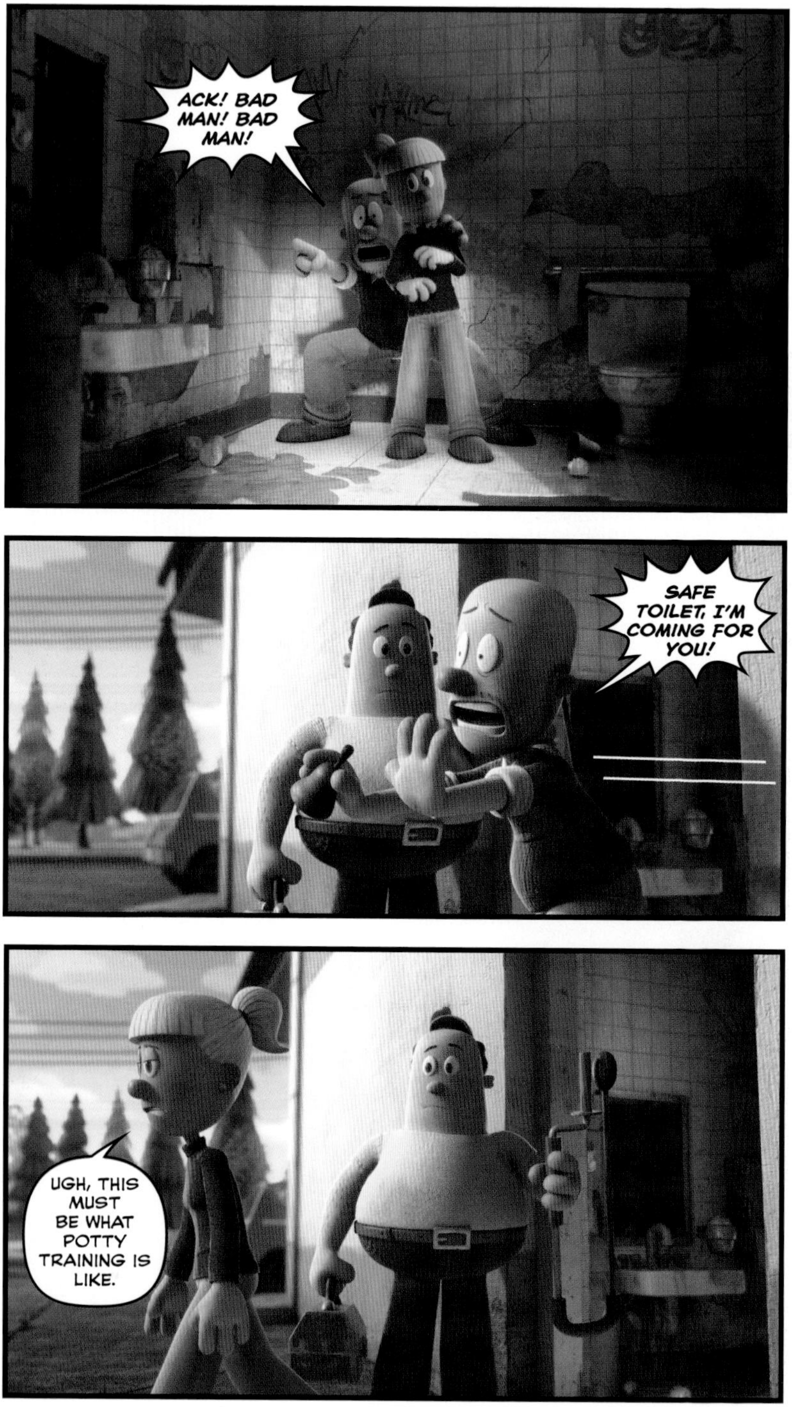
ACK! BAD MAN! BAD MAN!
SAFE TOILET, I'M COMING FOR YOU!
UGH, THIS MUST BE WHAT POTTY TRAINING IS LIKE.

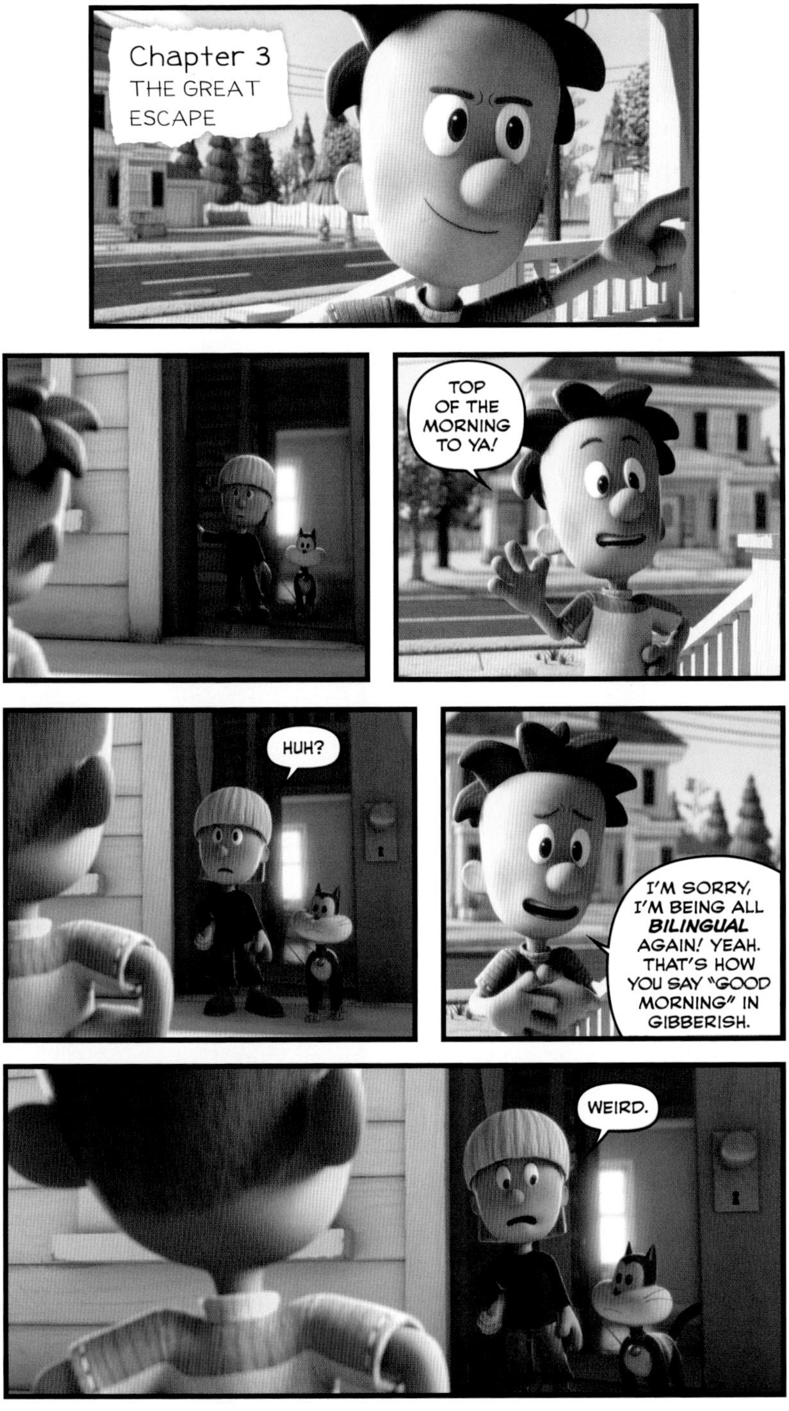
Chapter 3
THE GREAT ESCAPE
TOP OF THE MORNING TO YA!
HUH?
I'M SORRY, I'M BEING ALL **BILINGUAL** AGAIN! YEAH. THAT'S HOW YOU SAY "GOOD MORNING" IN GIBBERISH.
WEIRD.

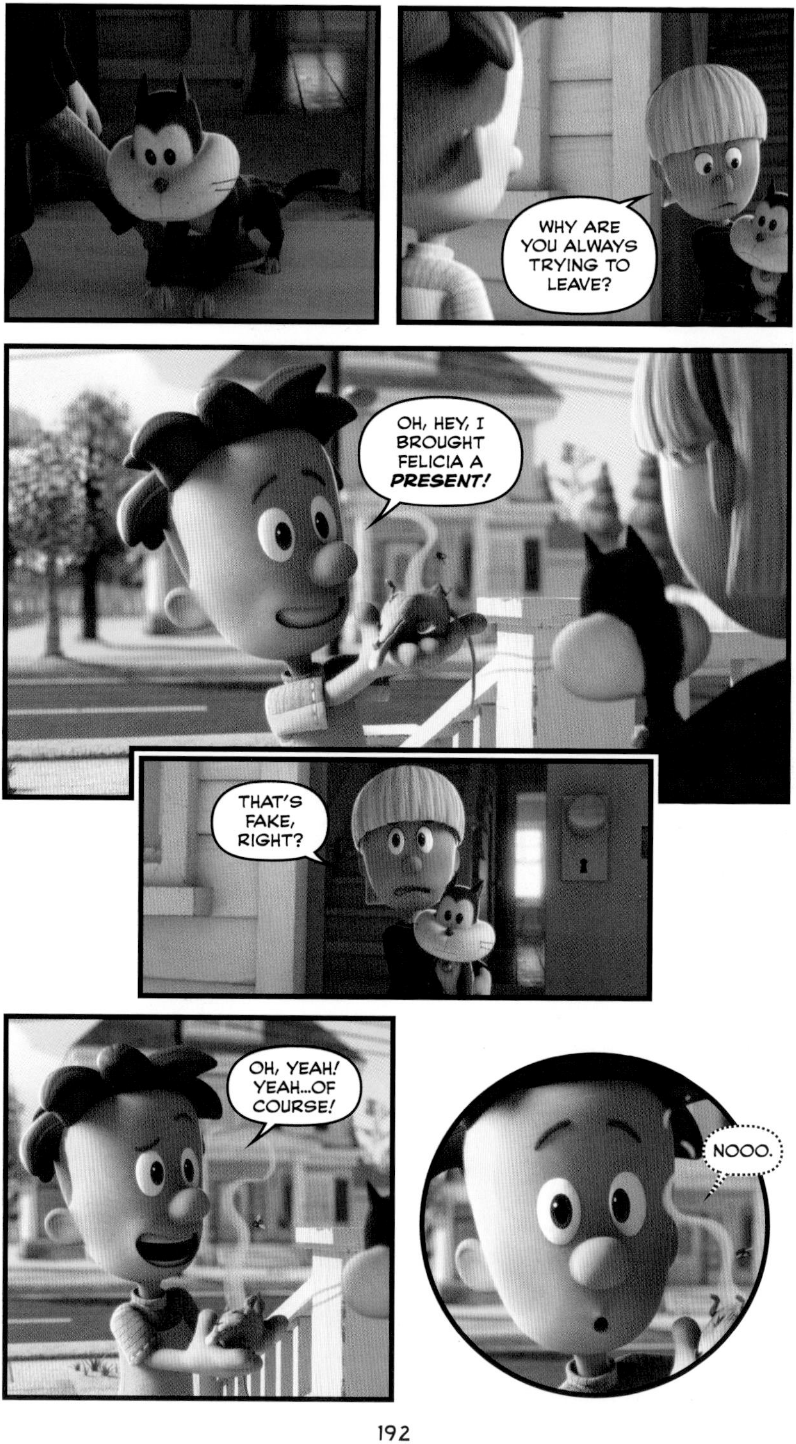
WHY ARE YOU ALWAYS TRYING TO LEAVE?
OH, HEY, I BROUGHT FELICIA A *PRESENT!*
THAT'S FAKE, RIGHT?
OH, YEAH! YEAH...OF COURSE!
NOOO.

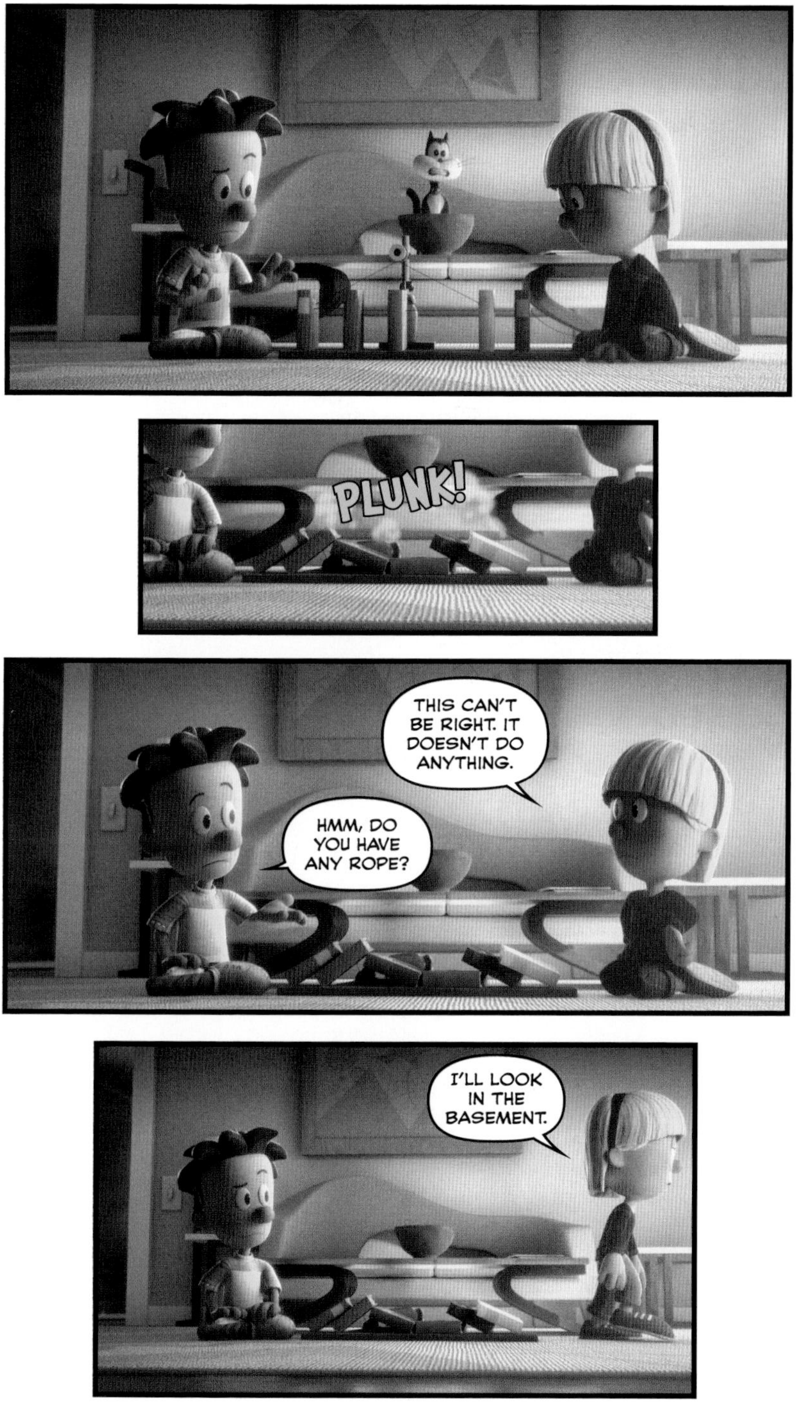
PLUNK!
THIS CAN'T BE RIGHT. IT DOESN'T DO ANYTHING.
HMM, DO YOU HAVE ANY ROPE?
I'LL LOOK IN THE BASEMENT.

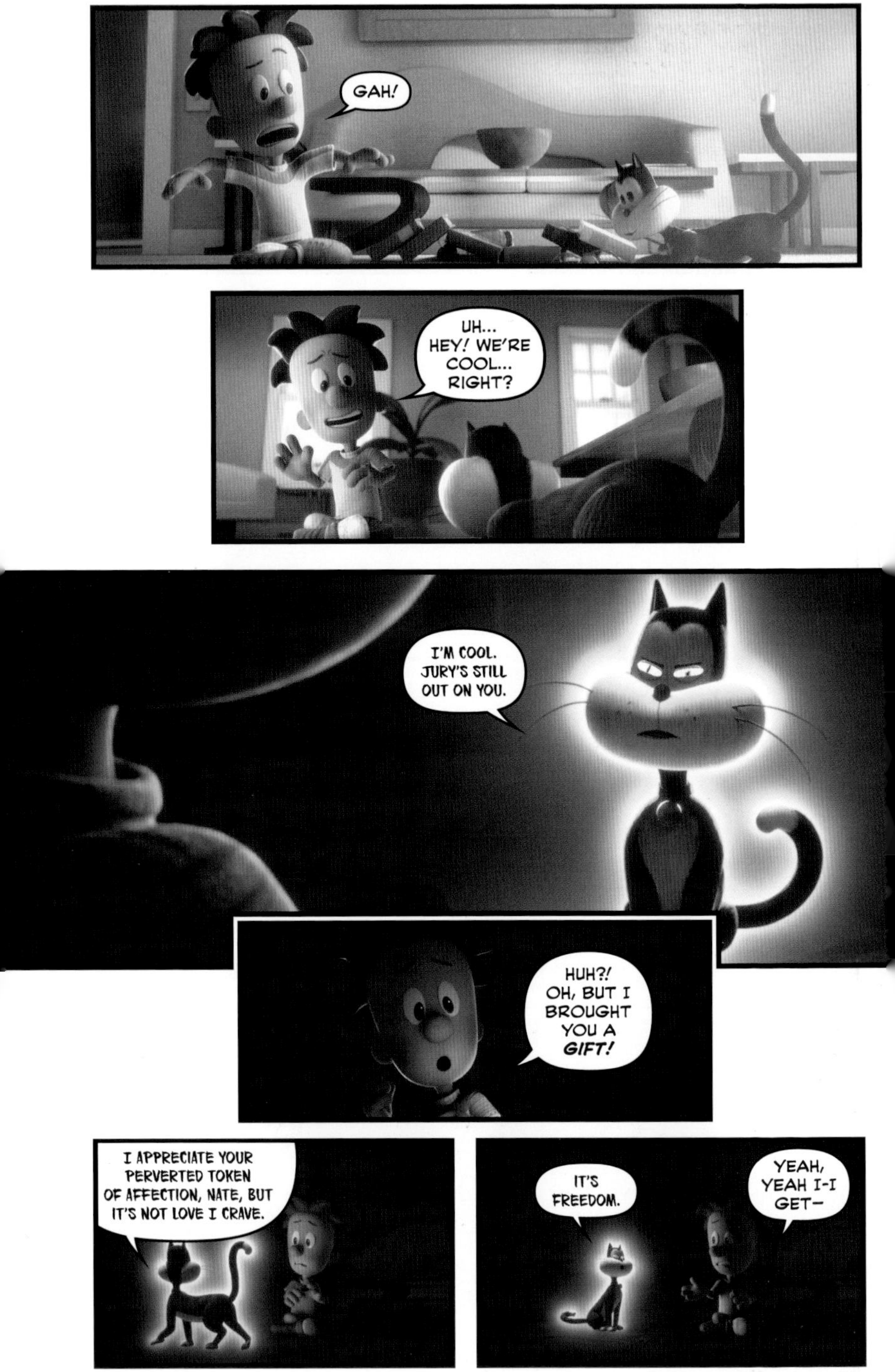
GAH!
UH... HEY! WE'RE COOL... RIGHT?
I'M COOL. JURY'S STILL OUT ON YOU.
HUH?! OH, BUT I BROUGHT YOU A GIFT!
I APPRECIATE YOUR PERVERTED TOKEN OF AFFECTION, NATE, BUT IT'S NOT LOVE I CRAVE.
IT'S FREEDOM.
YEAH, YEAH I-I GET—

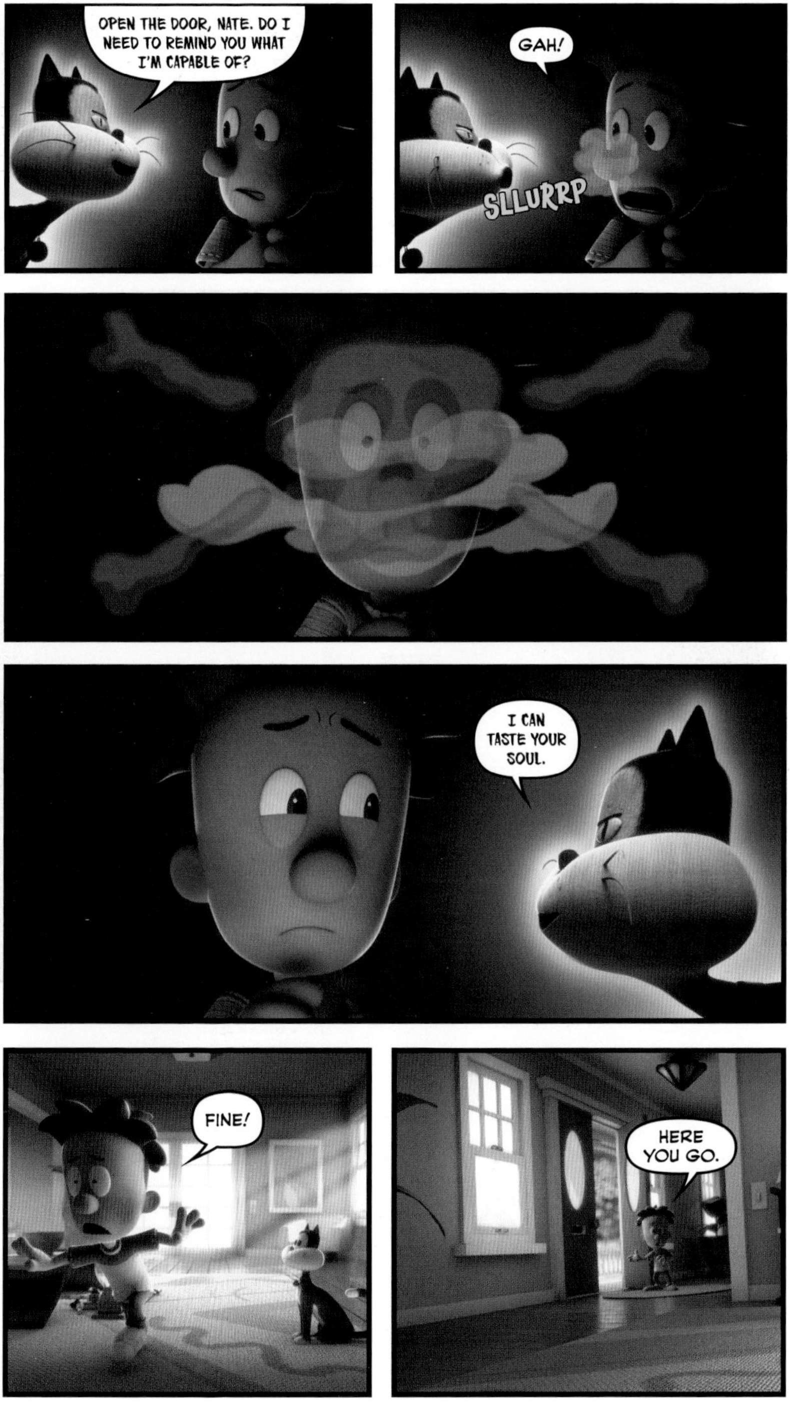
OPEN THE DOOR, NATE. DO I NEED TO REMIND YOU WHAT I'M CAPABLE OF?
GAH!
SLLURRP
I CAN TASTE YOUR SOUL.
FINE!
HERE YOU GO.

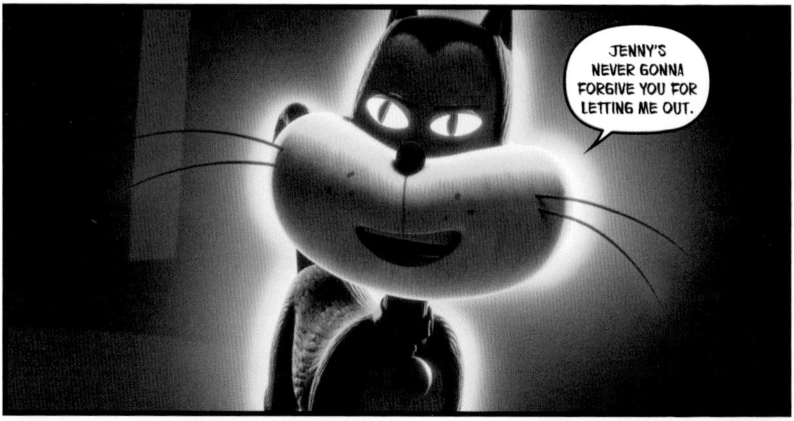
JENNY'S NEVER GONNA FORGIVE YOU FOR LETTING ME OUT.

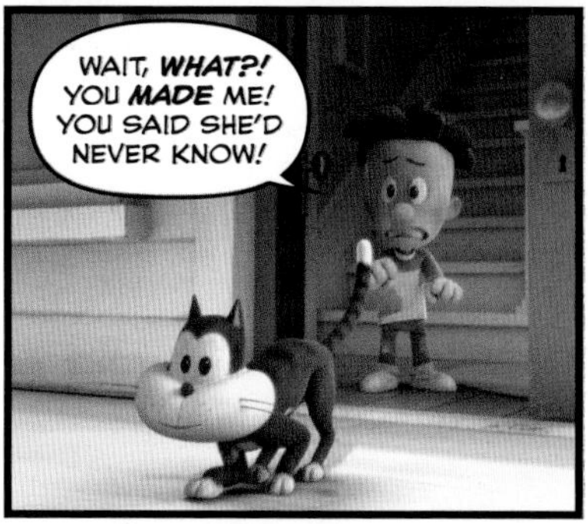
WAIT, ***WHAT?!*** YOU ***MADE*** ME! YOU SAID SHE'D NEVER KNOW!

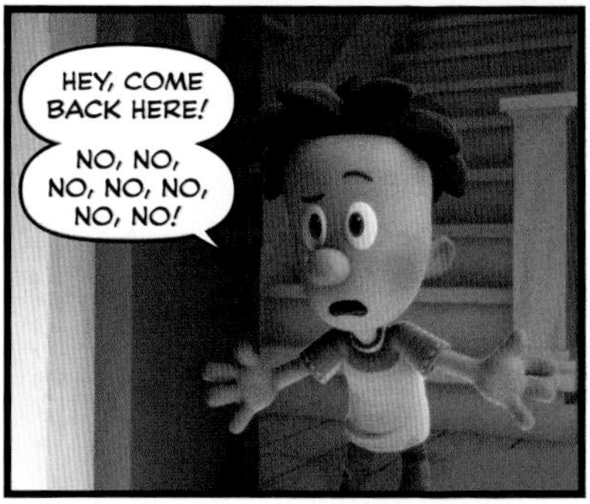
HEY, COME BACK HERE!
NO, NO, NO, NO, NO, NO, NO!

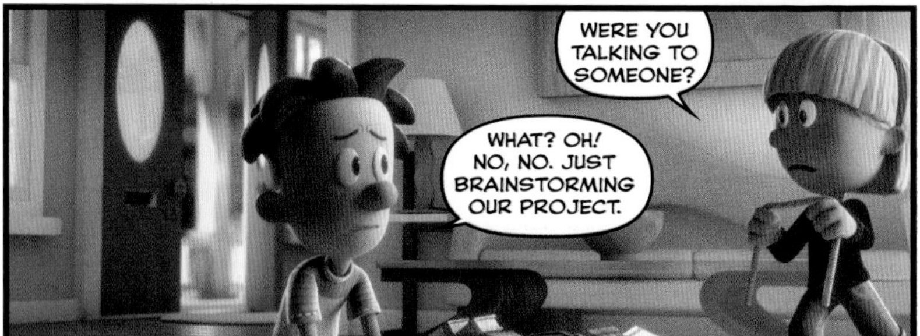
WERE YOU TALKING TO SOMEONE?
WHAT? OH! NO, NO. JUST BRAINSTORMING OUR PROJECT.

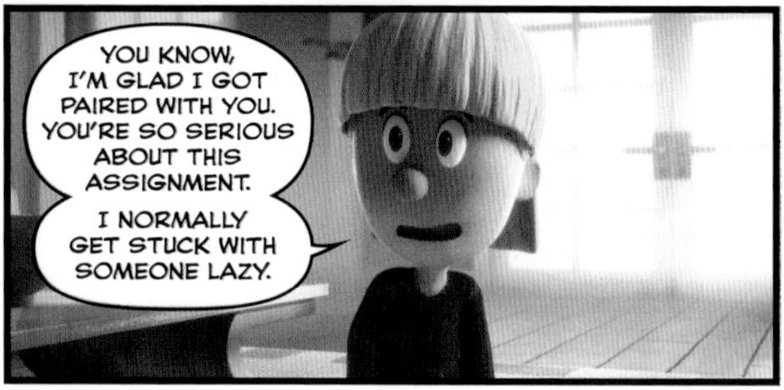
YOU KNOW, I'M GLAD I GOT PAIRED WITH YOU. YOU'RE SO SERIOUS ABOUT THIS ASSIGNMENT.
I NORMALLY GET STUCK WITH SOMEONE LAZY.

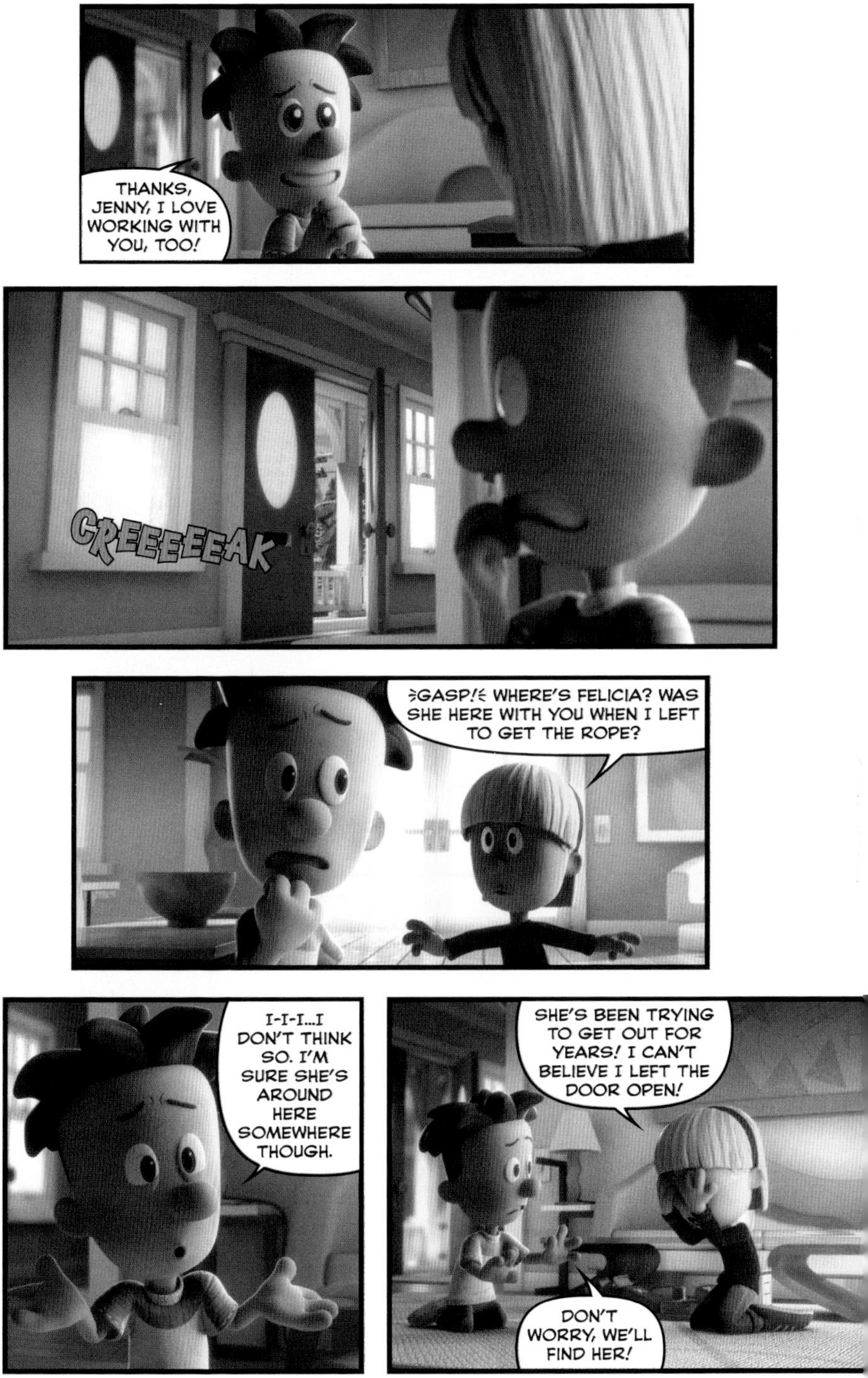
THANKS, JENNY, I LOVE WORKING WITH YOU, TOO!
CREEEEEEAK
⁘GASP!⁘ WHERE'S FELICIA? WAS SHE HERE WITH YOU WHEN I LEFT TO GET THE ROPE?
I-I-I...I DON'T THINK SO. I'M SURE SHE'S AROUND HERE SOMEWHERE THOUGH.
SHE'S BEEN TRYING TO GET OUT FOR YEARS! I CAN'T BELIEVE I LEFT THE DOOR OPEN!
DON'T WORRY, WE'LL FIND HER!

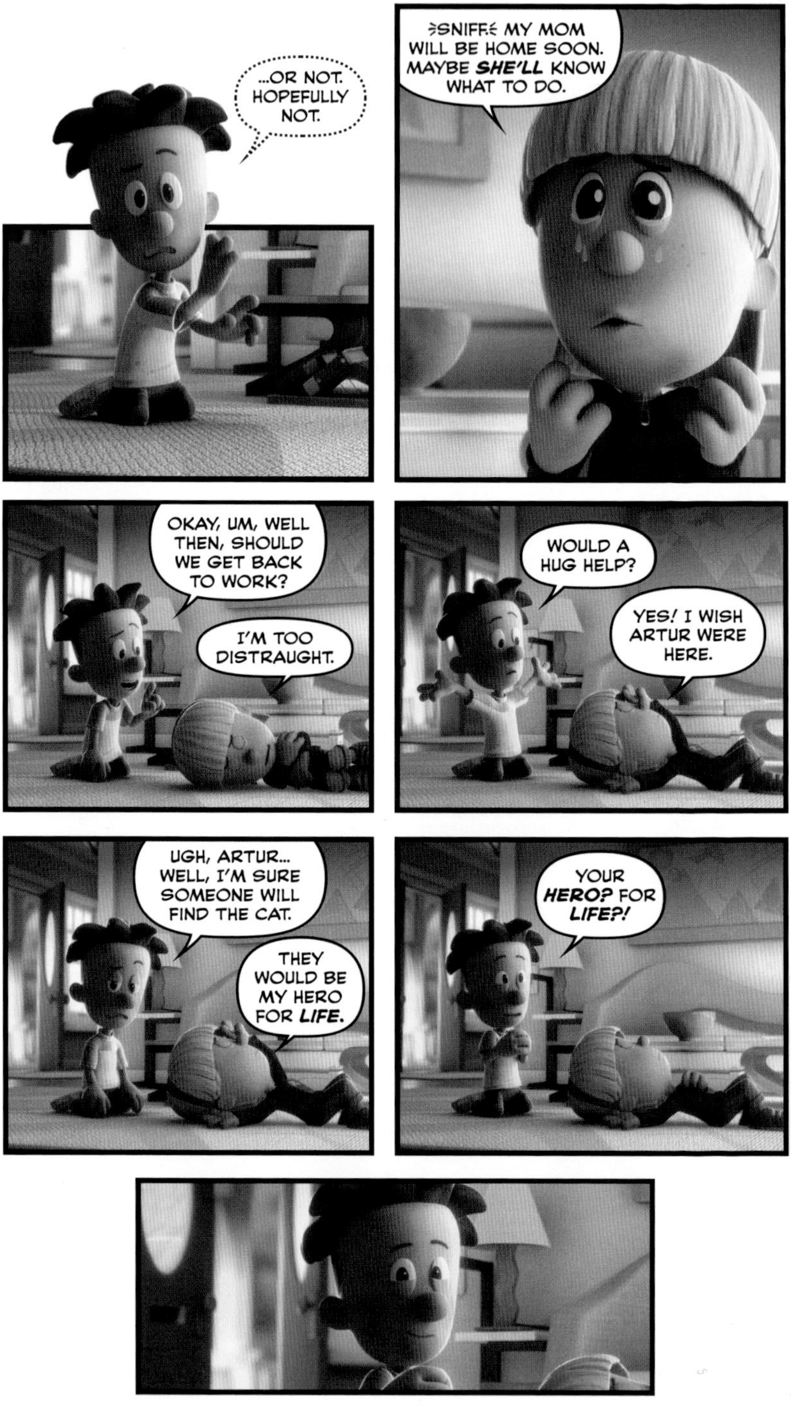
...OR NOT. HOPEFULLY NOT.
SNIFF MY MOM WILL BE HOME SOON. MAYBE SHE'LL KNOW WHAT TO DO.
OKAY, UM, WELL THEN, SHOULD WE GET BACK TO WORK?
I'M TOO DISTRAUGHT.
WOULD A HUG HELP?
YES! I WISH ARTUR WERE HERE.
UGH, ARTUR... WELL, I'M SURE SOMEONE WILL FIND THE CAT.
THEY WOULD BE MY HERO FOR LIFE.
YOUR HERO? FOR LIFE?!

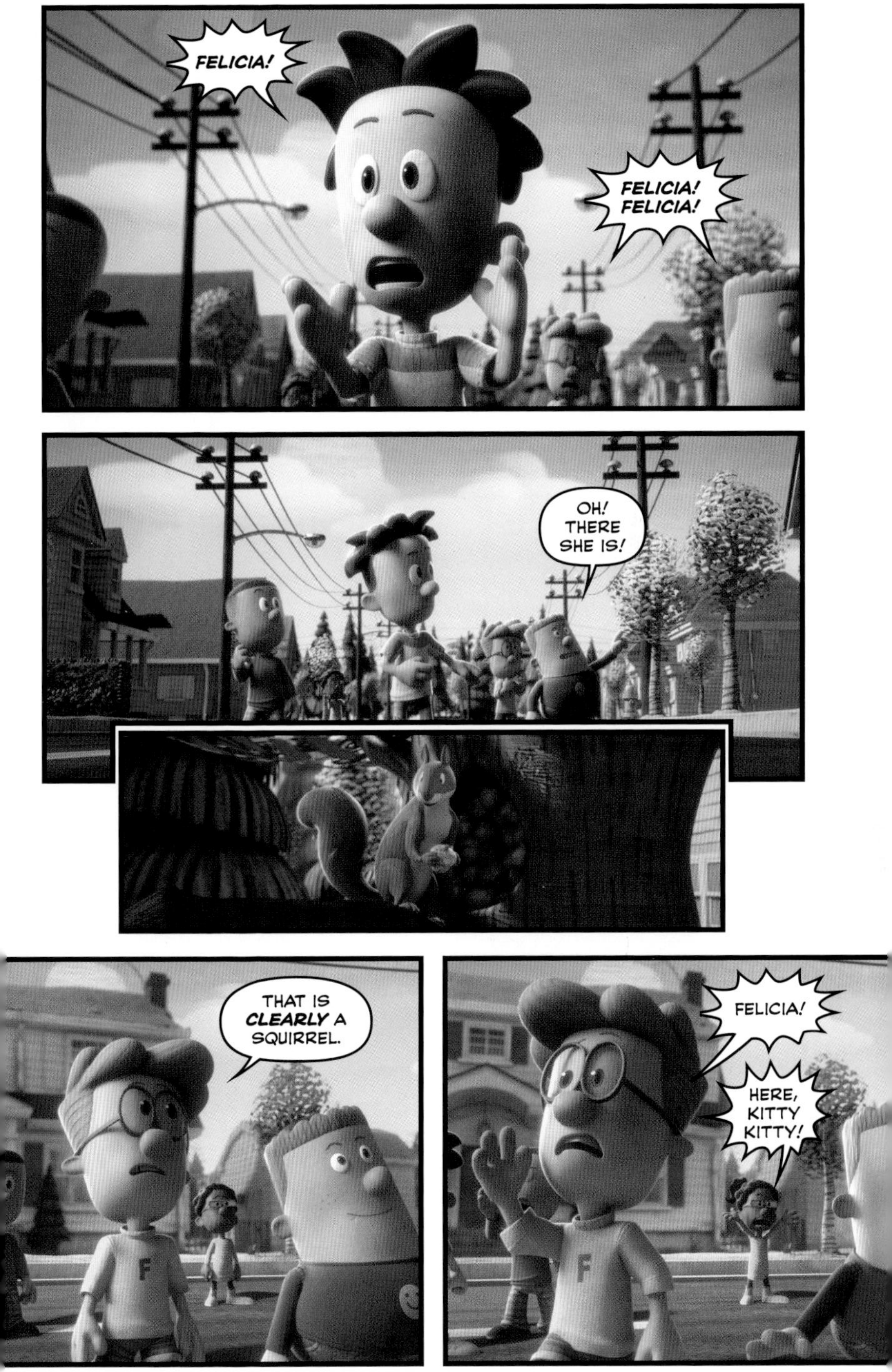
FELICIA!
FELICIA! FELICIA!
OH! THERE SHE IS!
THAT IS *CLEARLY* A SQUIRREL.
FELICIA!
HERE, KITTY KITTY!

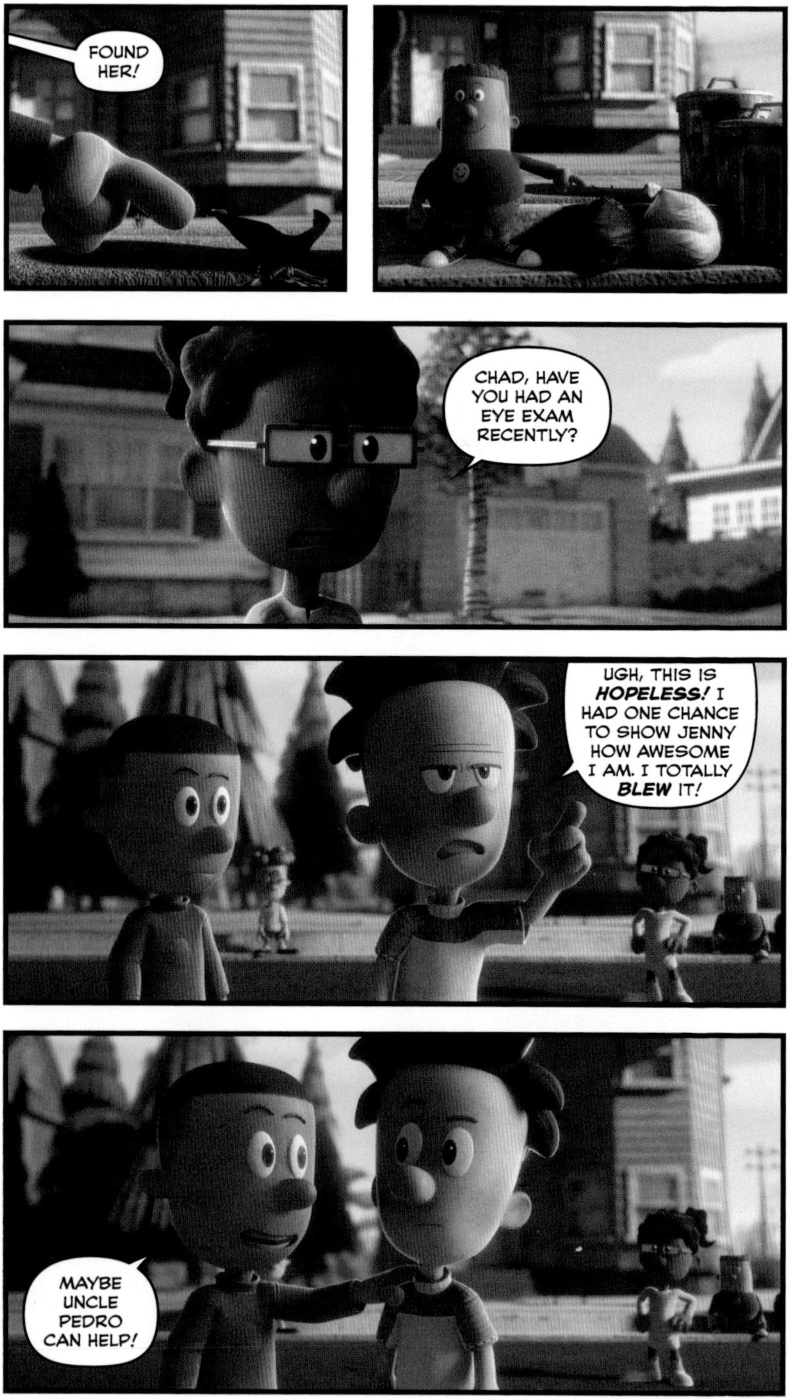
FOUND HER!
CHAD, HAVE YOU HAD AN EYE EXAM RECENTLY?
UGH, THIS IS **HOPELESS!** I HAD ONE CHANCE TO SHOW JENNY HOW AWESOME I AM. I TOTALLY **BLEW** IT!
MAYBE UNCLE PEDRO CAN HELP!

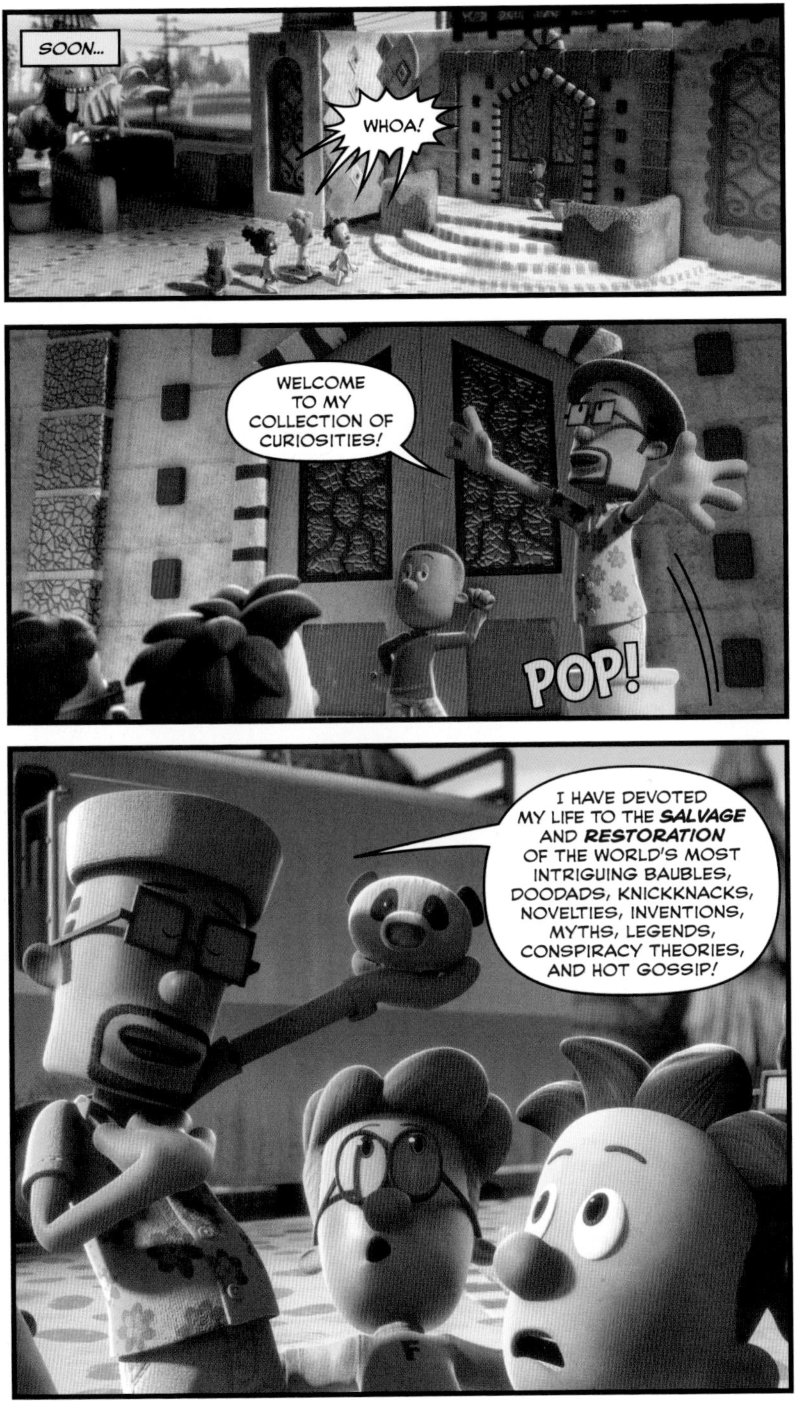
SOON...
WHOA!
WELCOME TO MY COLLECTION OF CURIOSITIES!
POP!
I HAVE DEVOTED MY LIFE TO THE ***SALVAGE*** AND ***RESTORATION*** OF THE WORLD'S MOST INTRIGUING BAUBLES, DOODADS, KNICKKNACKS, NOVELTIES, INVENTIONS, MYTHS, LEGENDS, CONSPIRACY THEORIES, AND HOT GOSSIP!

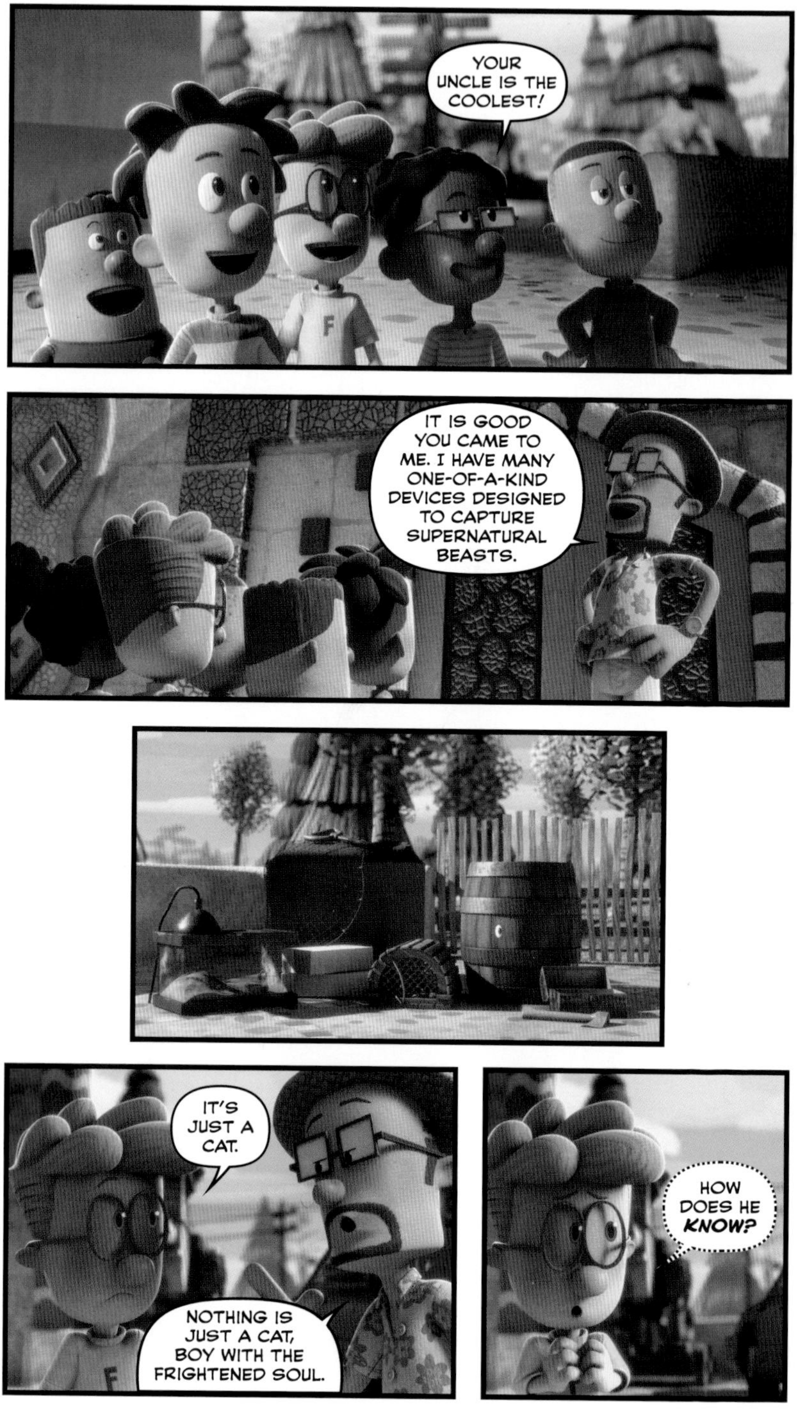
YOUR UNCLE IS THE COOLEST!
IT IS GOOD YOU CAME TO ME. I HAVE MANY ONE-OF-A-KIND DEVICES DESIGNED TO CAPTURE SUPERNATURAL BEASTS.
IT'S JUST A CAT.
NOTHING IS JUST A CAT, BOY WITH THE FRIGHTENED SOUL.
HOW DOES HE ***KNOW?***

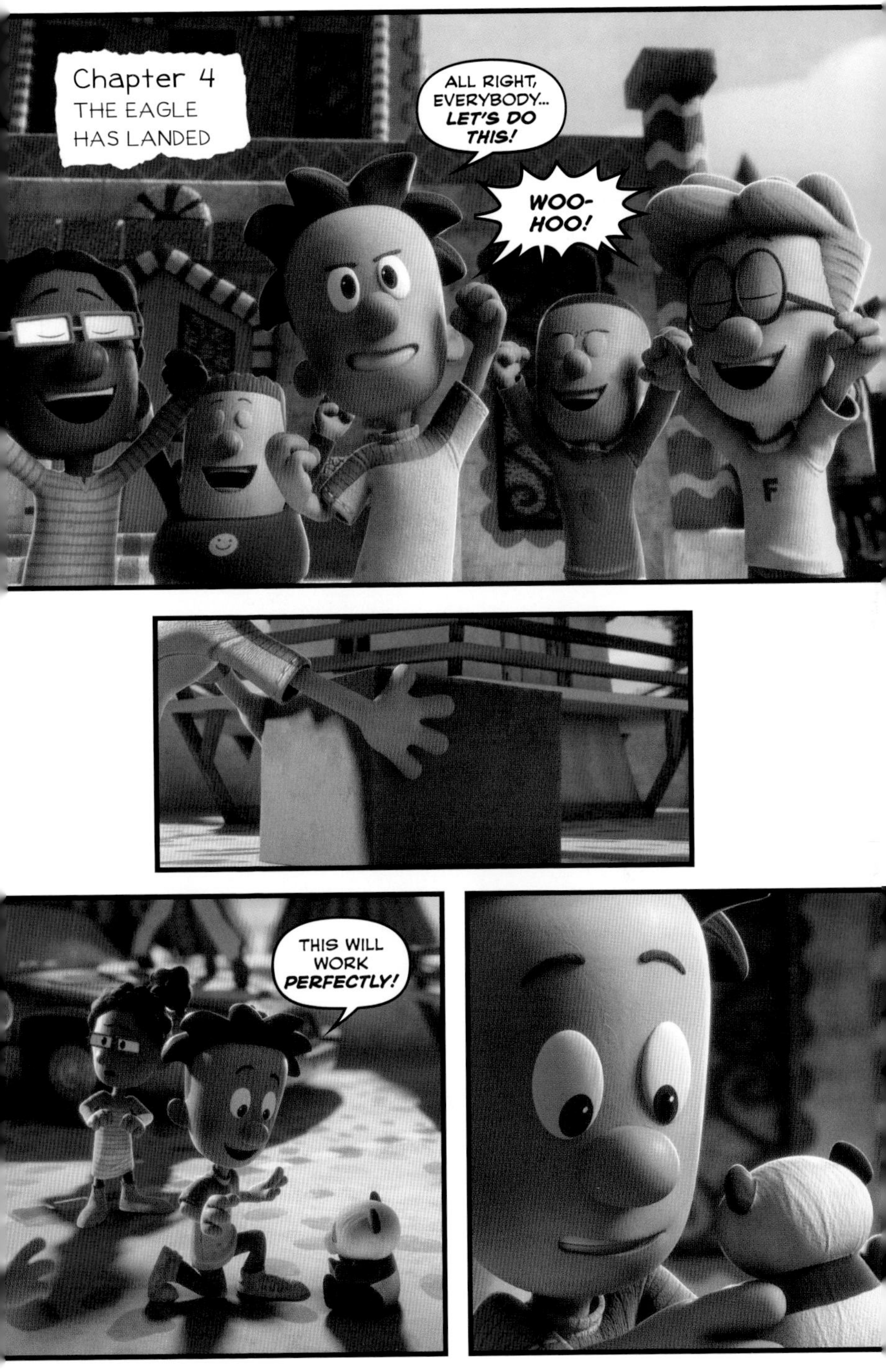
Chapter 4
THE EAGLE
HAS LANDED
ALL RIGHT, EVERYBODY... LET'S DO THIS!
WOO-HOO!
THIS WILL WORK PERFECTLY!

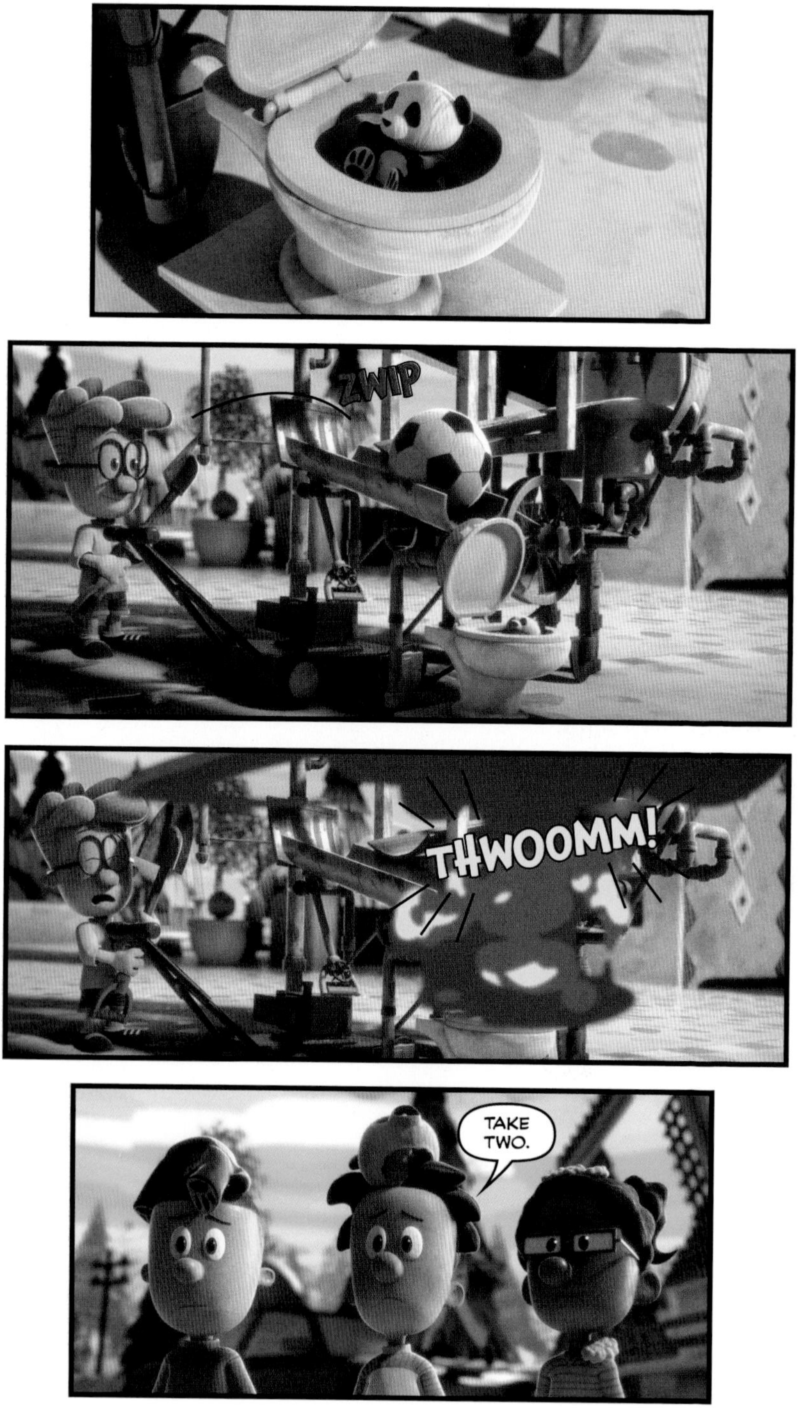
ZWIP
THWOOMM!
TAKE TWO.

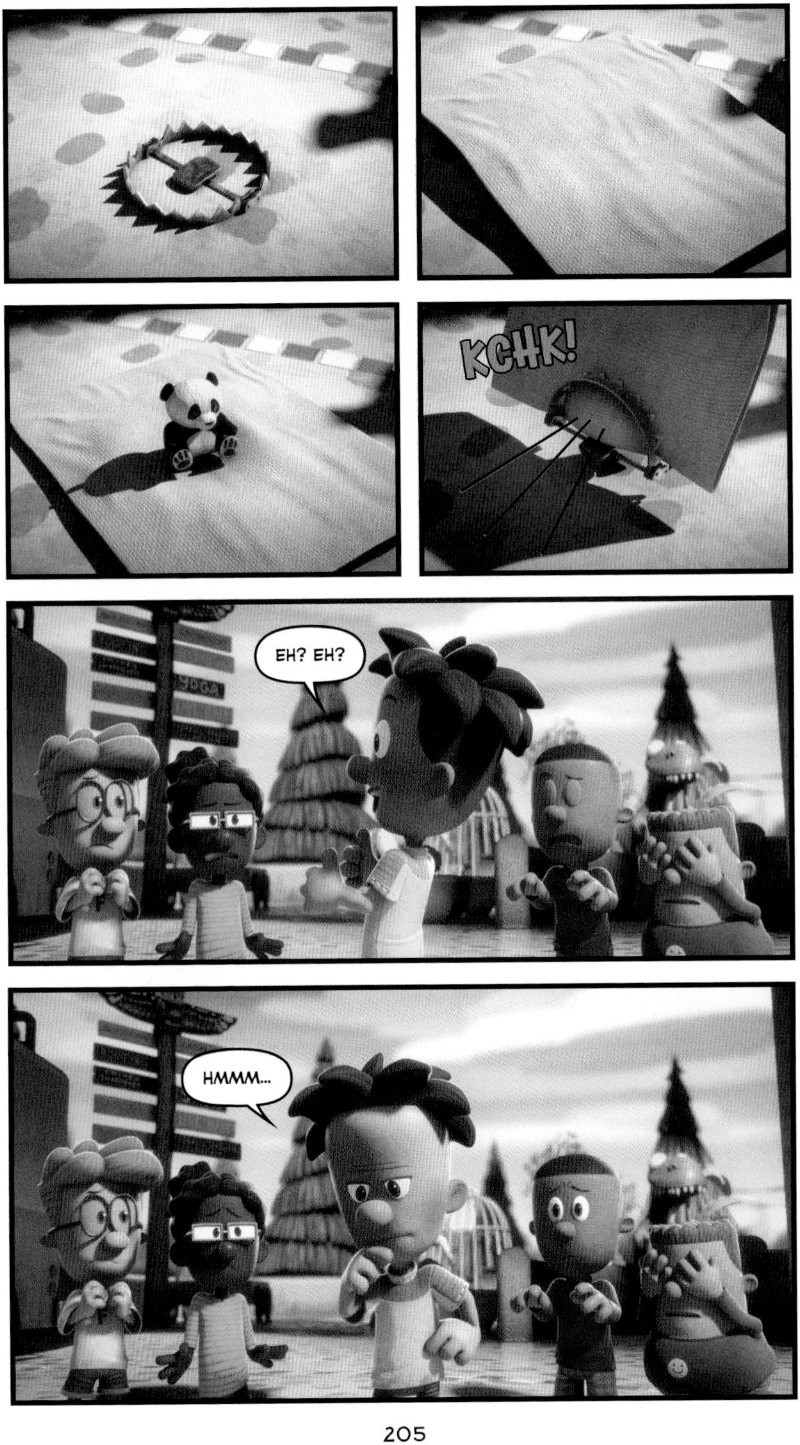
KCHK!
EH? EH?
YOGA
HMMM...

BING!

WOW! YES! IT LOOKS AWESOME! LET'S TEST IT. HEY, CHAD, PRETEND THERE'S FOOD THERE.

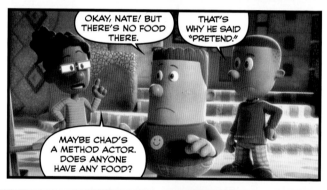

OKAY, NATE! BUT THERE'S NO FOOD THERE.

THAT'S WHY HE SAID "PRETEND."

MAYBE CHAD'S A METHOD ACTOR. DOES ANYONE HAVE ANY FOOD?

I HAVE A HARDBOILED EGG.

CLUCK!
CLUCK!

POP!

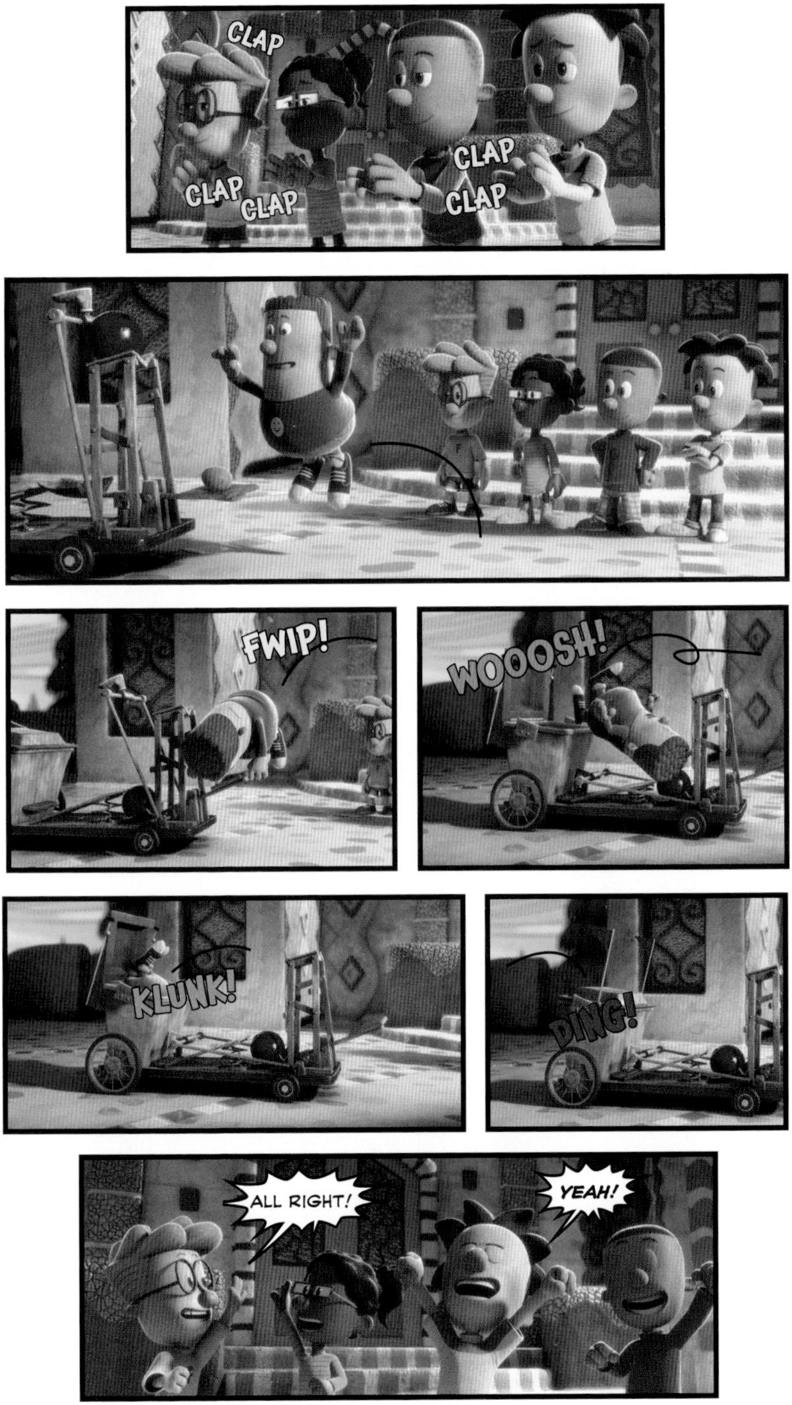
CLAP
CLAP
CLAP
CLAP
CLAP
FWIP!
WOOOSH!
KLUNK!
DING!
ALL RIGHT!
YEAH!

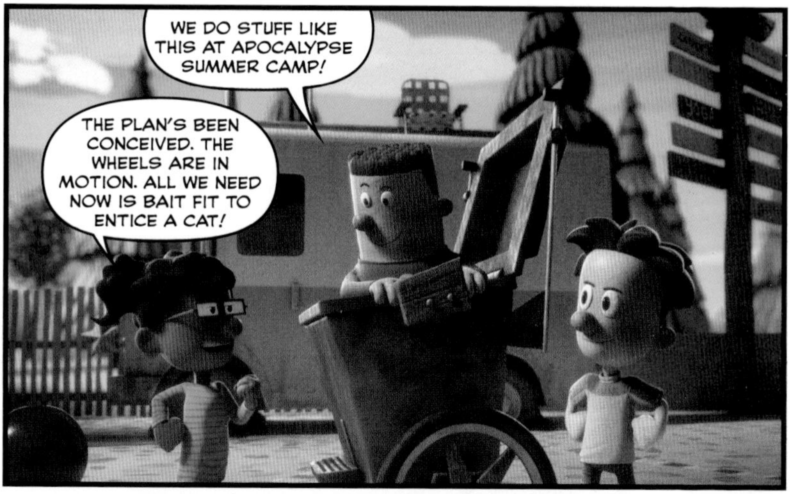
WE DO STUFF LIKE THIS AT APOCALYPSE SUMMER CAMP!
THE PLAN'S BEEN CONCEIVED. THE WHEELS ARE IN MOTION. ALL WE NEED NOW IS BAIT FIT TO ENTICE A CAT!

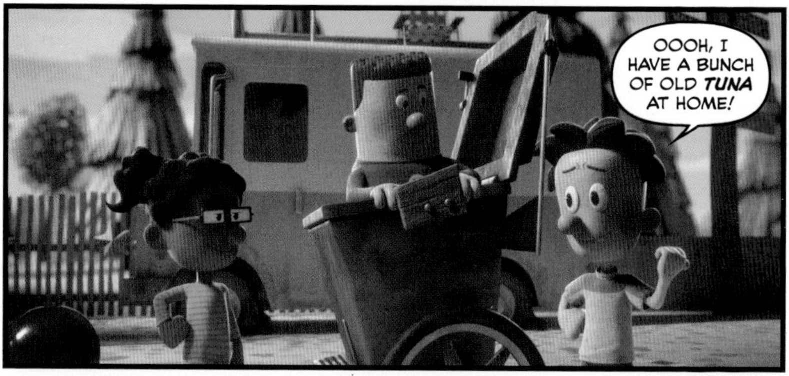
OOOH, I HAVE A BUNCH OF OLD *TUNA* AT HOME!

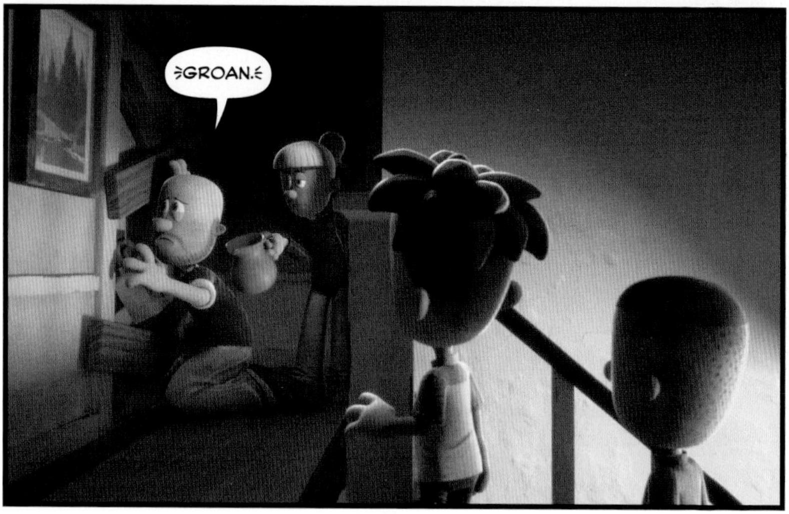
GROAN.

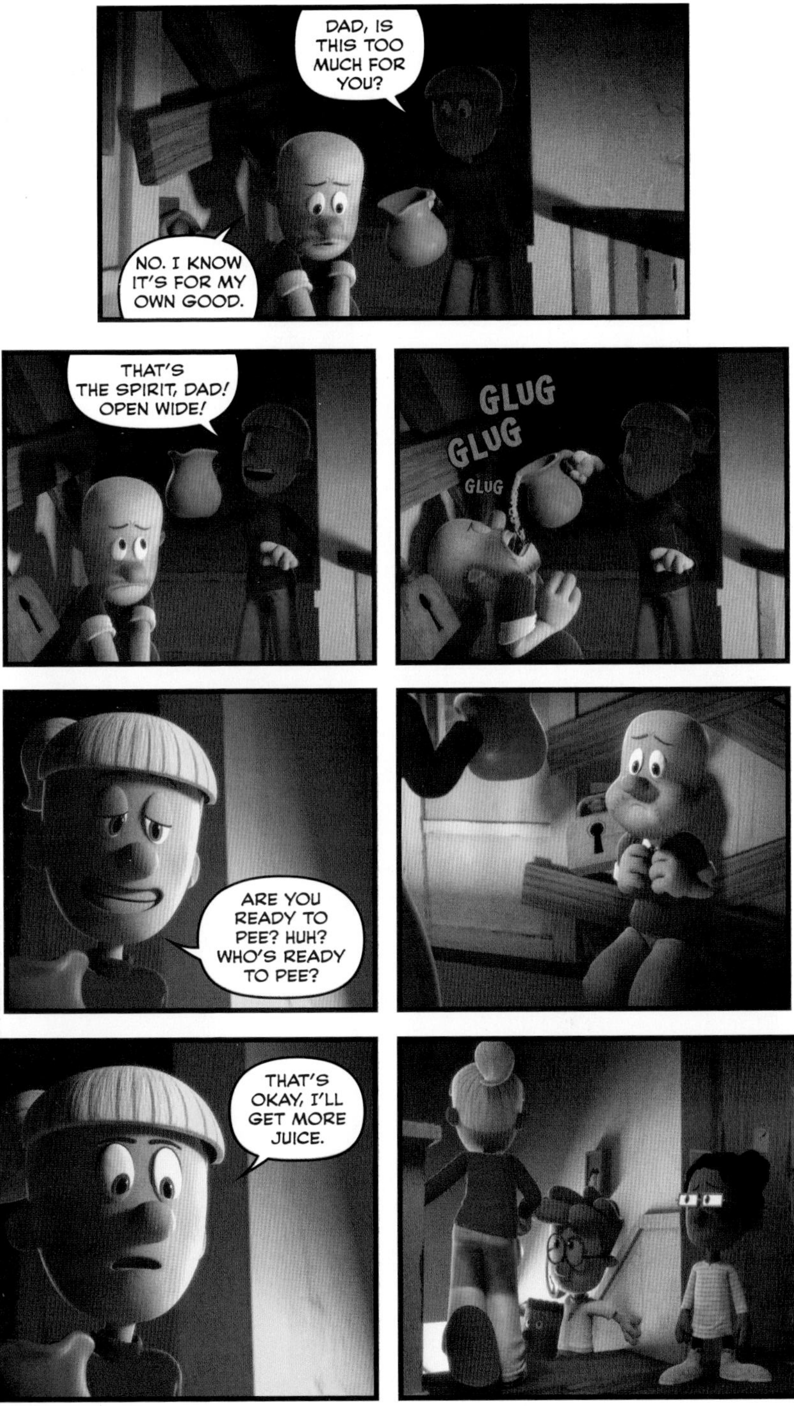
DAD, IS THIS TOO MUCH FOR YOU?
NO. I KNOW IT'S FOR MY OWN GOOD.
THAT'S THE SPIRIT, DAD! OPEN WIDE!
GLUG
GLUG
GLUG
ARE YOU READY TO PEE? HUH? WHO'S READY TO PEE?
THAT'S OKAY, I'LL GET MORE JUICE.

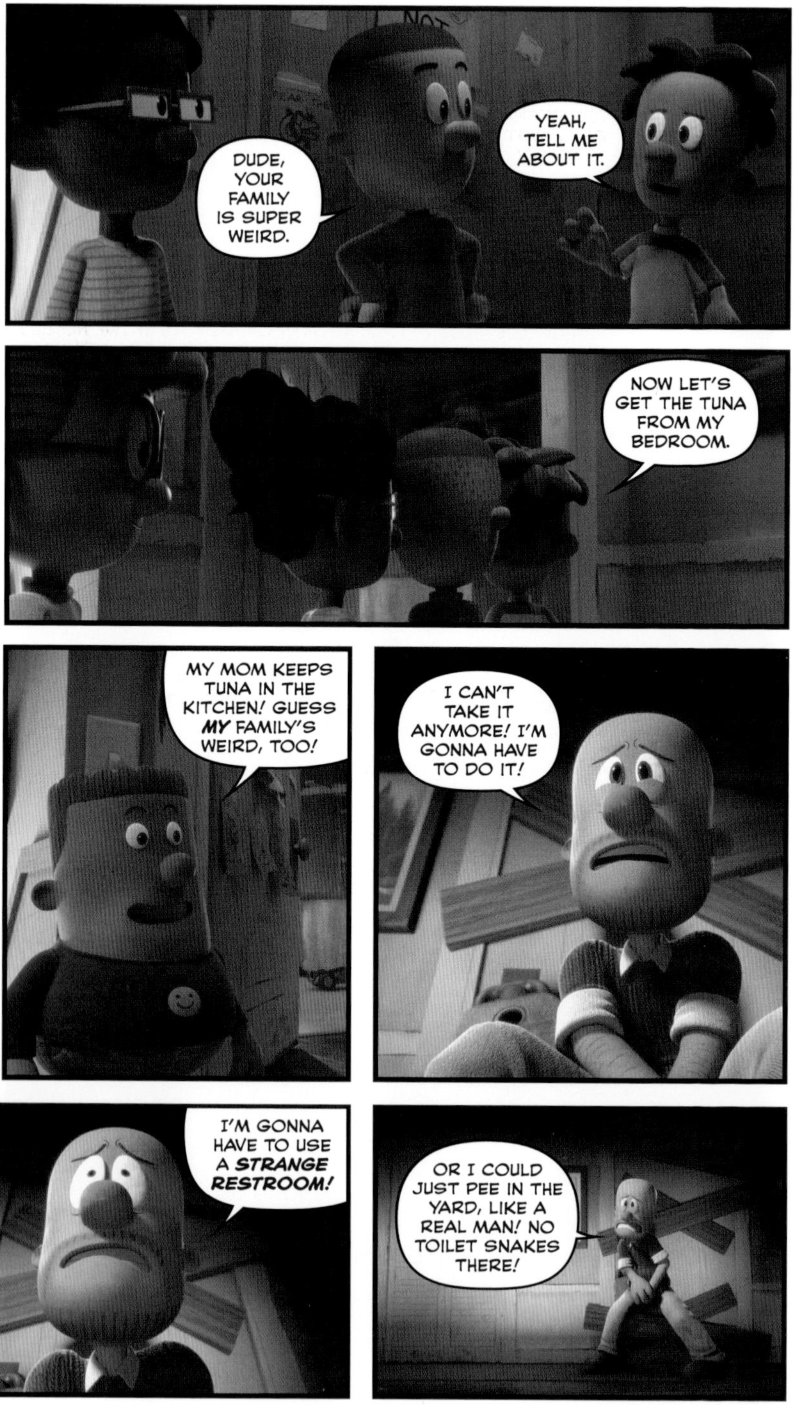
DUDE, YOUR FAMILY IS SUPER WEIRD.
YEAH, TELL ME ABOUT IT.
NOW LET'S GET THE TUNA FROM MY BEDROOM.
MY MOM KEEPS TUNA IN THE KITCHEN! GUESS MY FAMILY'S WEIRD, TOO!
I CAN'T TAKE IT ANYMORE! I'M GONNA HAVE TO DO IT!
I'M GONNA HAVE TO USE A STRANGE RESTROOM!
OR I COULD JUST PEE IN THE YARD, LIKE A REAL MAN! NO TOILET SNAKES THERE!

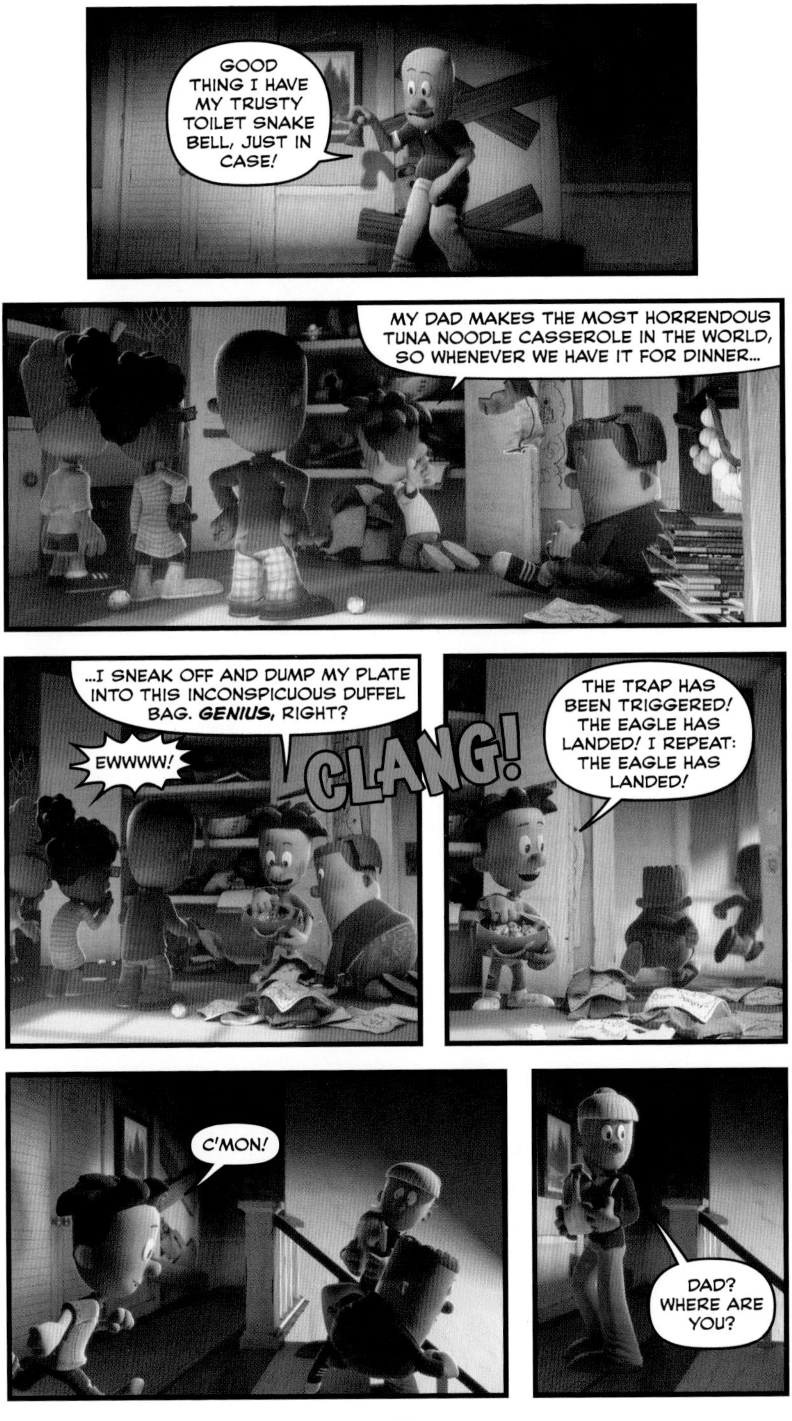
GOOD THING I HAVE MY TRUSTY TOILET SNAKE BELL, JUST IN CASE!
MY DAD MAKES THE MOST HORRENDOUS TUNA NOODLE CASSEROLE IN THE WORLD, SO WHENEVER WE HAVE IT FOR DINNER...
...I SNEAK OFF AND DUMP MY PLATE INTO THIS INCONSPICUOUS DUFFEL BAG. GENIUS, RIGHT?
EWWWW!
CLANG!
THE TRAP HAS BEEN TRIGGERED! THE EAGLE HAS LANDED! I REPEAT: THE EAGLE HAS LANDED!
C'MON!
DAD? WHERE ARE YOU?

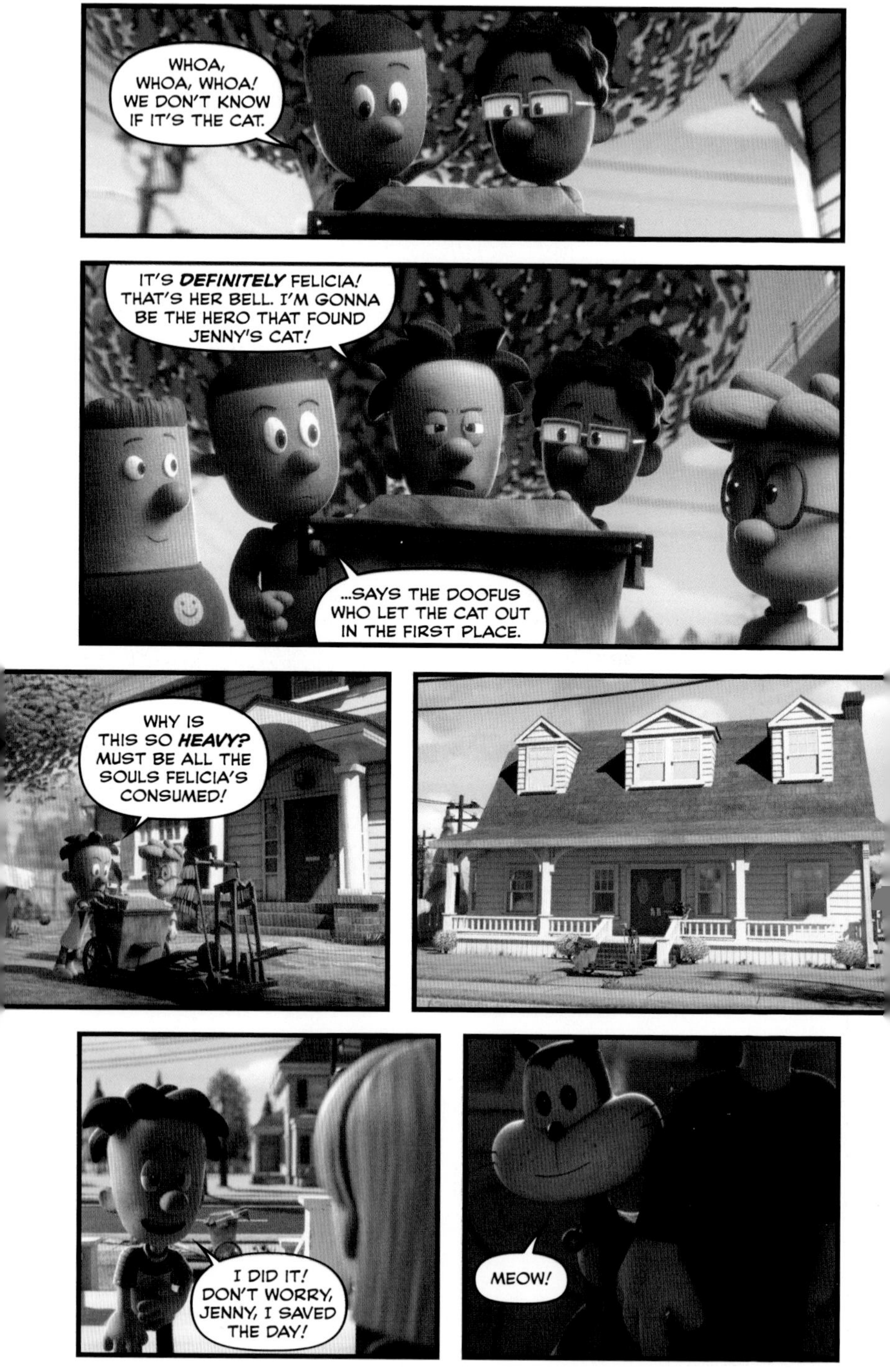
WHOA, WHOA, WHOA! WE DON'T KNOW IF IT'S THE CAT.
IT'S DEFINITELY FELICIA! THAT'S HER BELL. I'M GONNA BE THE HERO THAT FOUND JENNY'S CAT!
...SAYS THE DOOFUS WHO LET THE CAT OUT IN THE FIRST PLACE.
WHY IS THIS SO HEAVY? MUST BE ALL THE SOULS FELICIA'S CONSUMED!
I DID IT! DON'T WORRY, JENNY, I SAVED THE DAY!
MEOW!

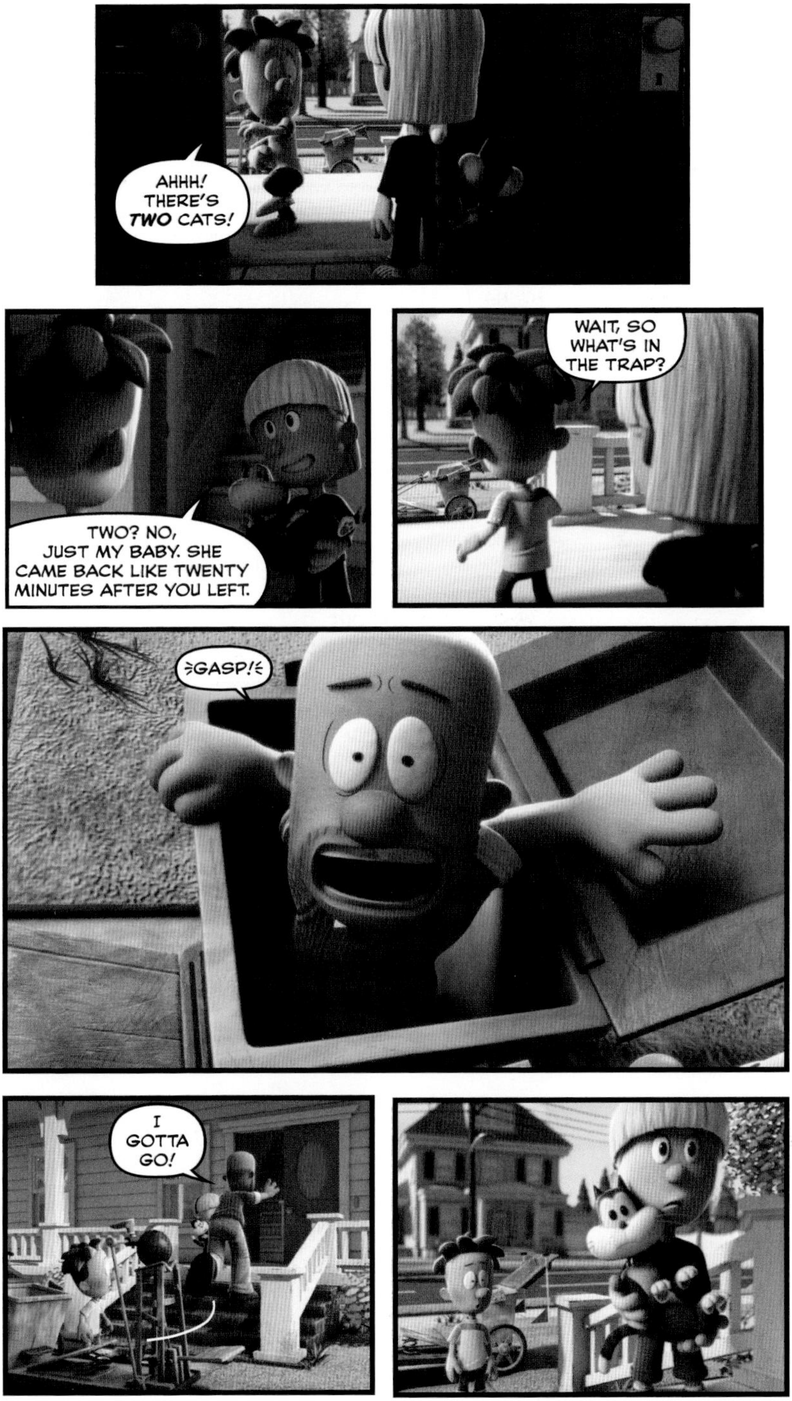
AHHH! THERE'S *TWO* CATS!
TWO? NO, JUST MY BABY. SHE CAME BACK LIKE TWENTY MINUTES AFTER YOU LEFT.
WAIT, SO WHAT'S IN THE TRAP?
GASP!
I GOTTA GO!

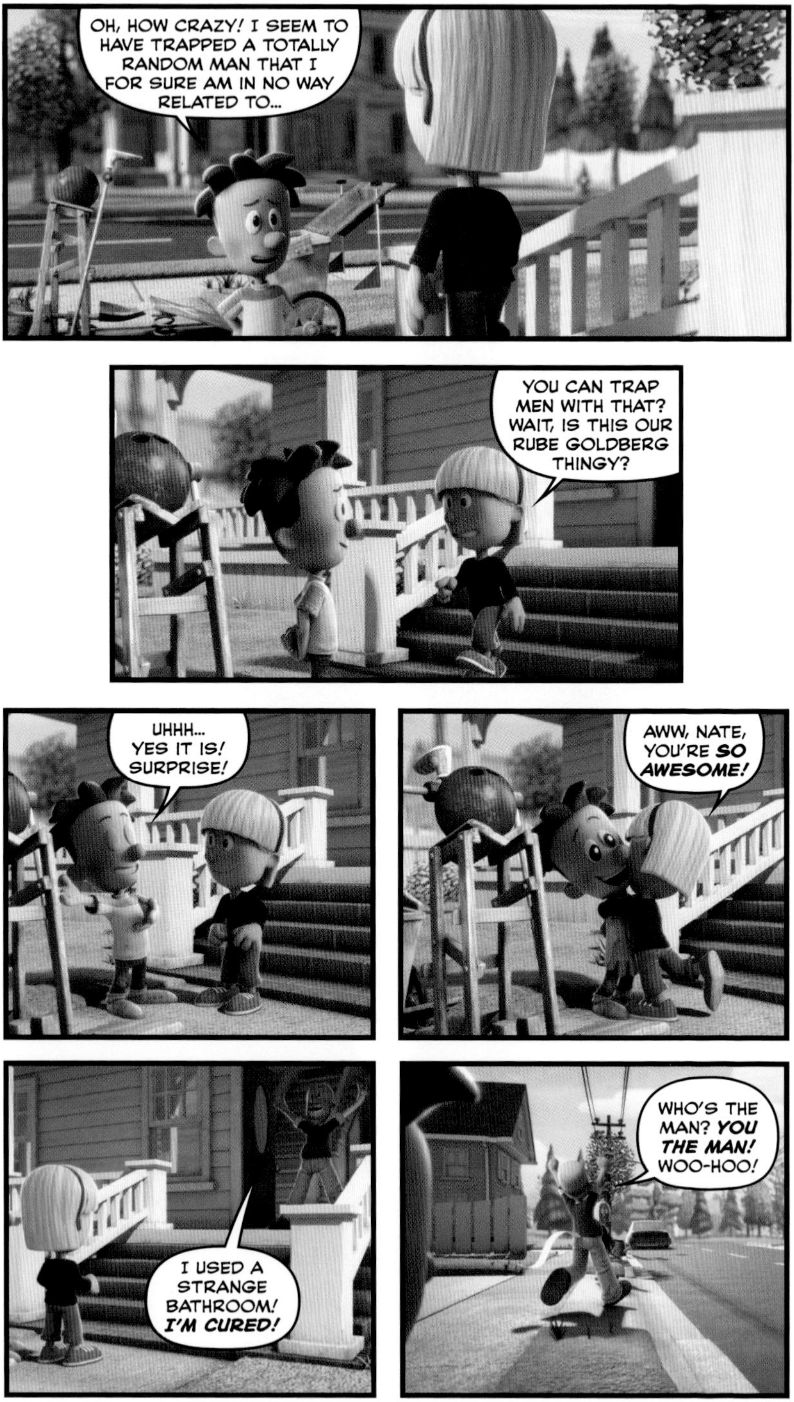
OH, HOW CRAZY! I SEEM TO HAVE TRAPPED A TOTALLY RANDOM MAN THAT I FOR SURE AM IN NO WAY RELATED TO...
YOU CAN TRAP MEN WITH THAT? WAIT, IS THIS OUR RUBE GOLDBERG THINGY?
UHHH... YES IT IS! SURPRISE!
AWW, NATE, YOU'RE **SO AWESOME!**
I USED A STRANGE BATHROOM! ***I'M CURED!***
WHO'S THE MAN? ***YOU THE MAN!*** WOO-HOO!

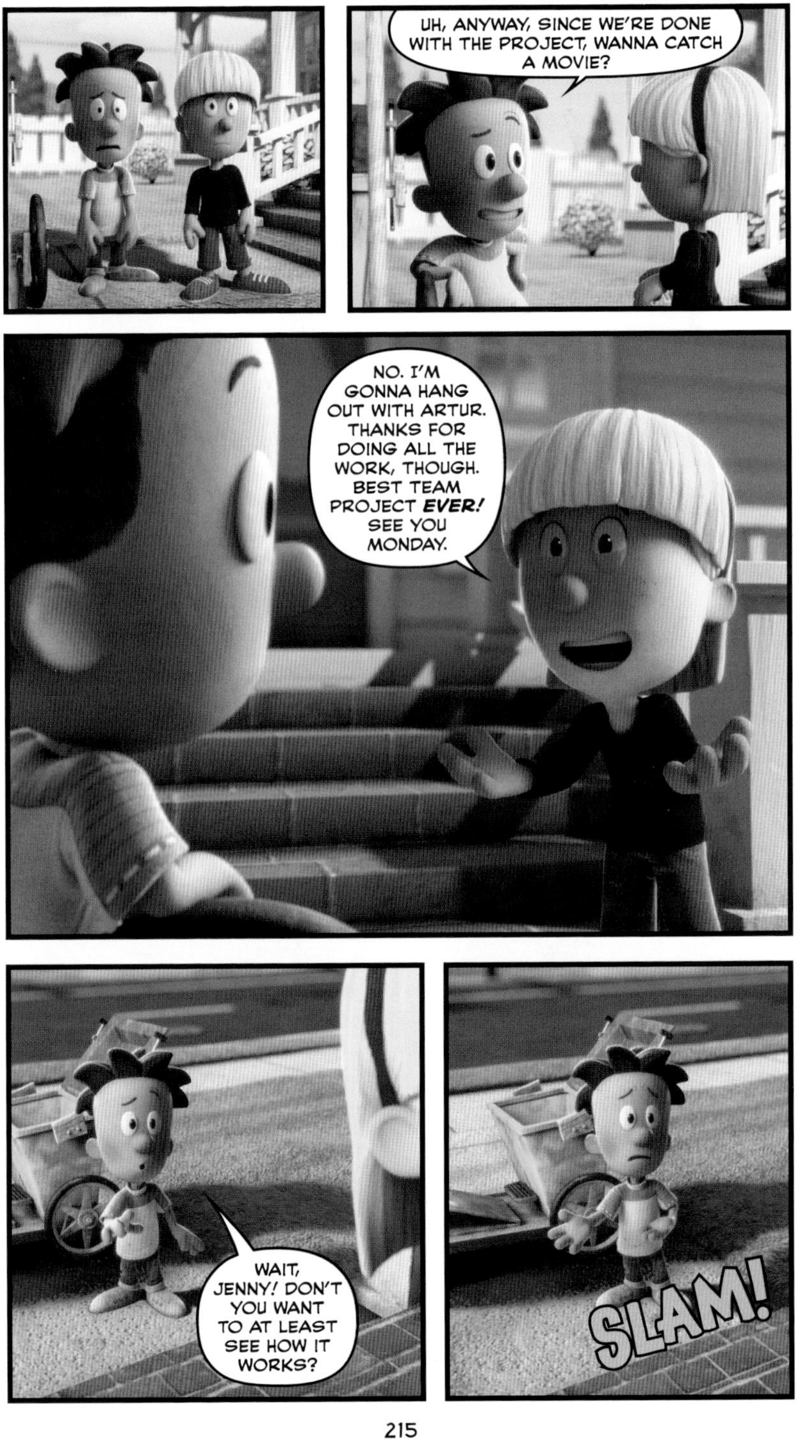
UH, ANYWAY, SINCE WE'RE DONE WITH THE PROJECT, WANNA CATCH A MOVIE?
NO. I'M GONNA HANG OUT WITH ARTUR. THANKS FOR DOING ALL THE WORK, THOUGH. BEST TEAM PROJECT ***EVER!*** SEE YOU MONDAY.
WAIT, JENNY! DON'T YOU WANT TO AT LEAST SEE HOW IT WORKS?
SLAM!

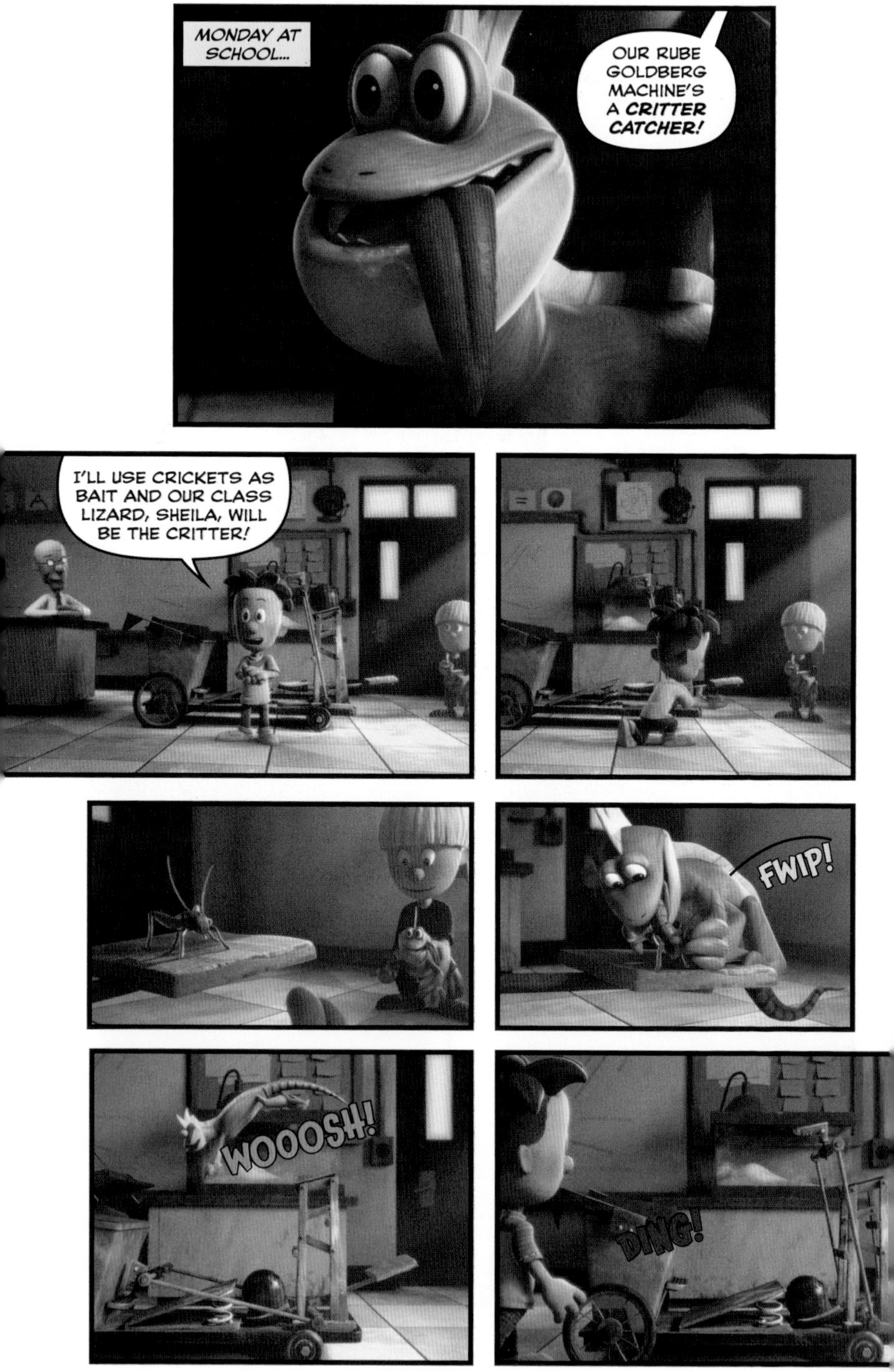
MONDAY AT SCHOOL...
OUR RUBE GOLDBERG MACHINE'S A CRITTER CATCHER!
I'LL USE CRICKETS AS BAIT AND OUR CLASS LIZARD, SHEILA, WILL BE THE CRITTER!
FWIP!
WOOOSH!
DING!

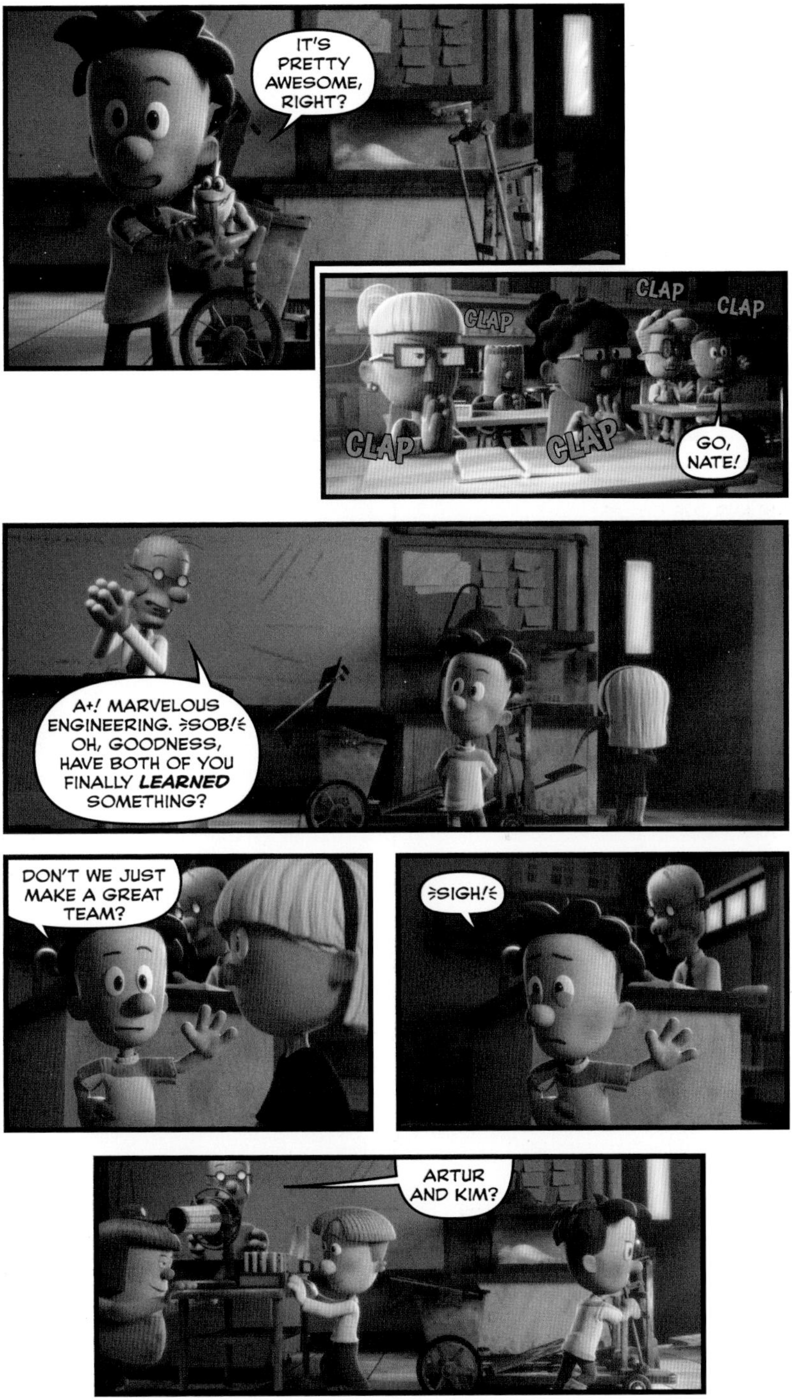
IT'S PRETTY AWESOME, RIGHT?
CLAP
CLAP
CLAP
CLAP
CLAP
GO, NATE!
A+! MARVELOUS ENGINEERING. ⋟SOB!⋞ OH, GOODNESS, HAVE BOTH OF YOU FINALLY ***LEARNED*** SOMETHING?
DON'T WE JUST MAKE A GREAT TEAM?
⋟SIGH!⋞
ARTUR AND KIM?

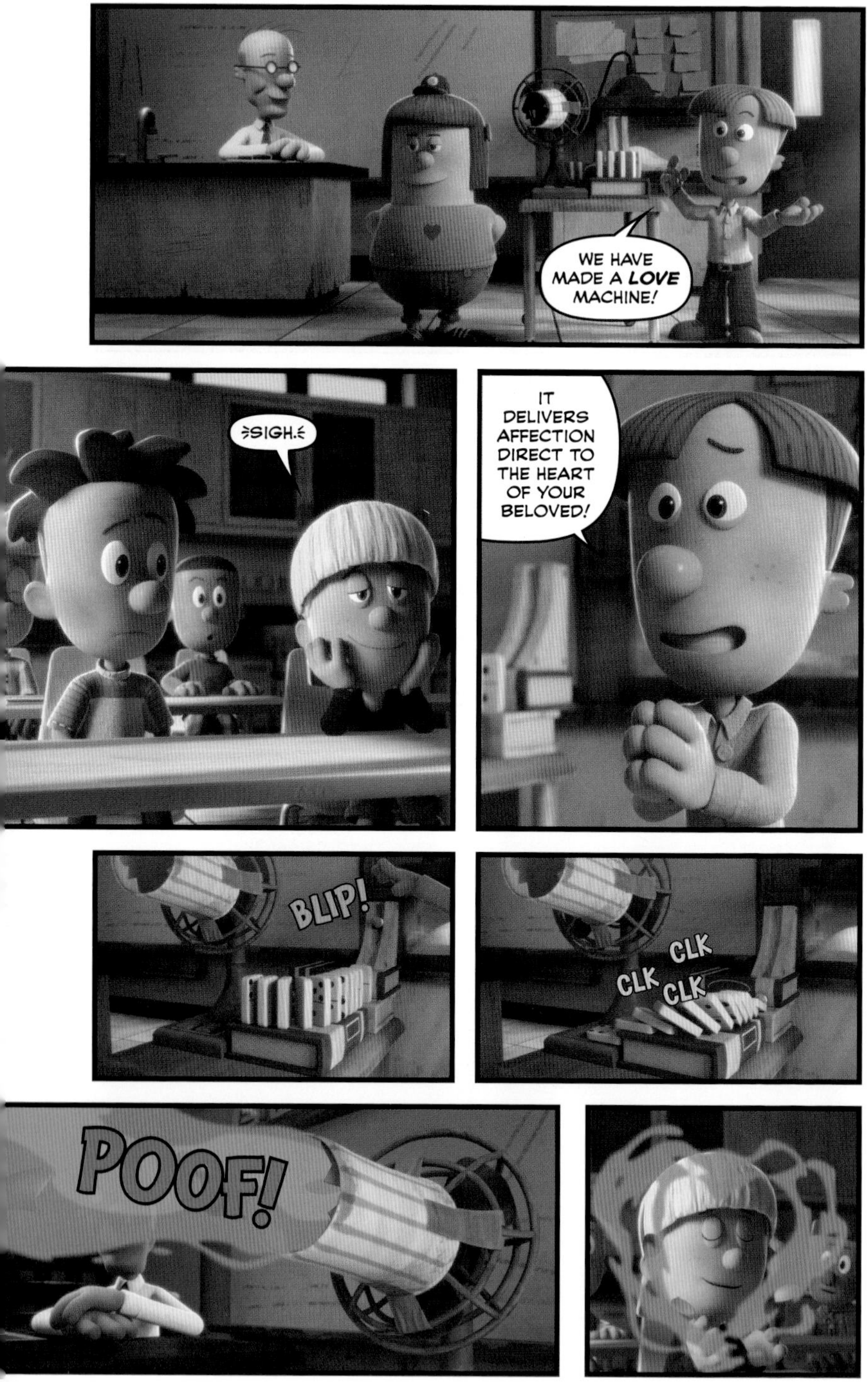
WE HAVE MADE A ***LOVE*** MACHINE!
⋟SIGH.⋞
IT DELIVERS AFFECTION DIRECT TO THE HEART OF YOUR BELOVED!
BLIP!
CLK
CLK
CLK
POOF!

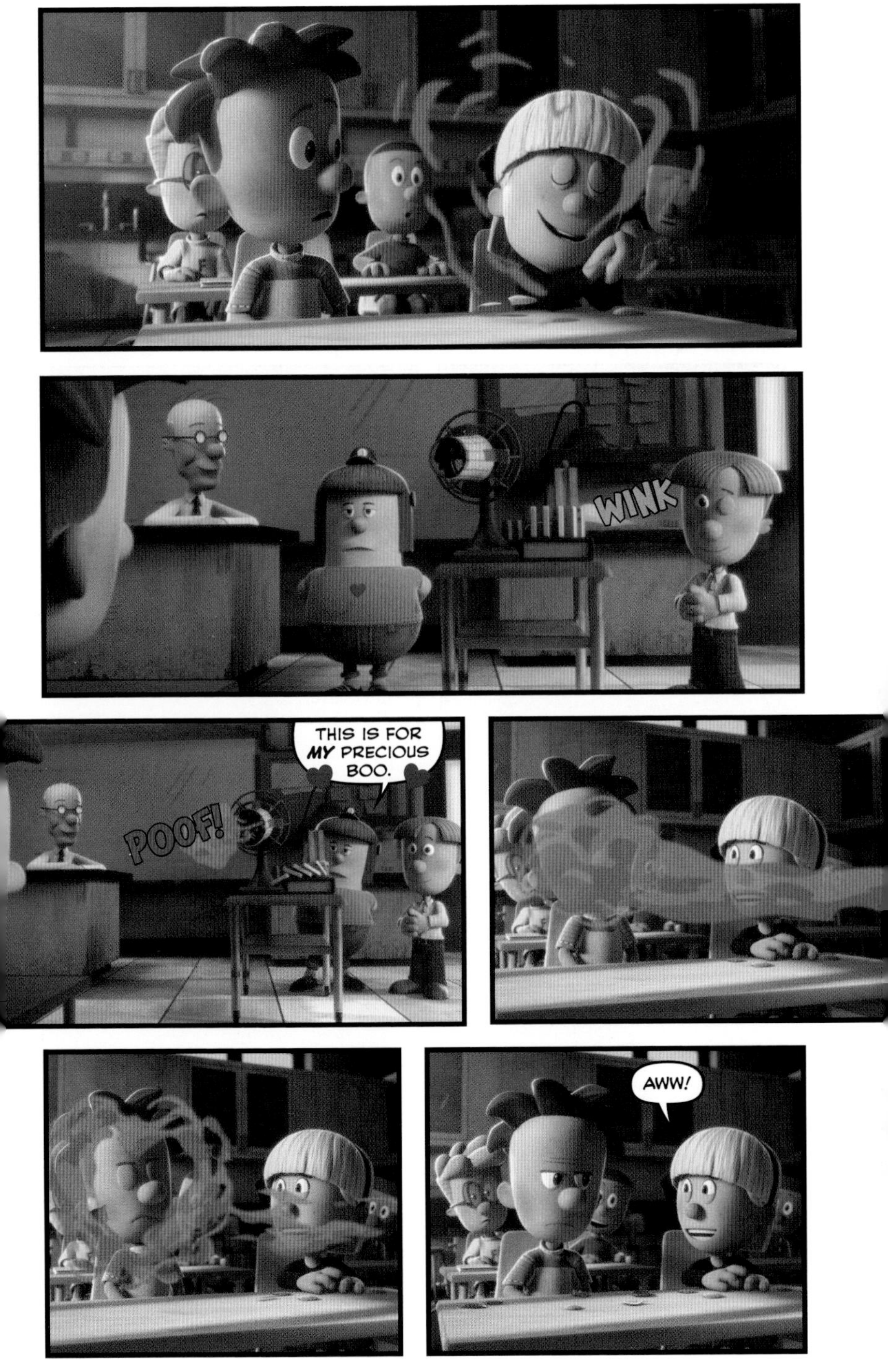
WINK
THIS IS FOR MY PRECIOUS BOO.
POOF!
AWW!

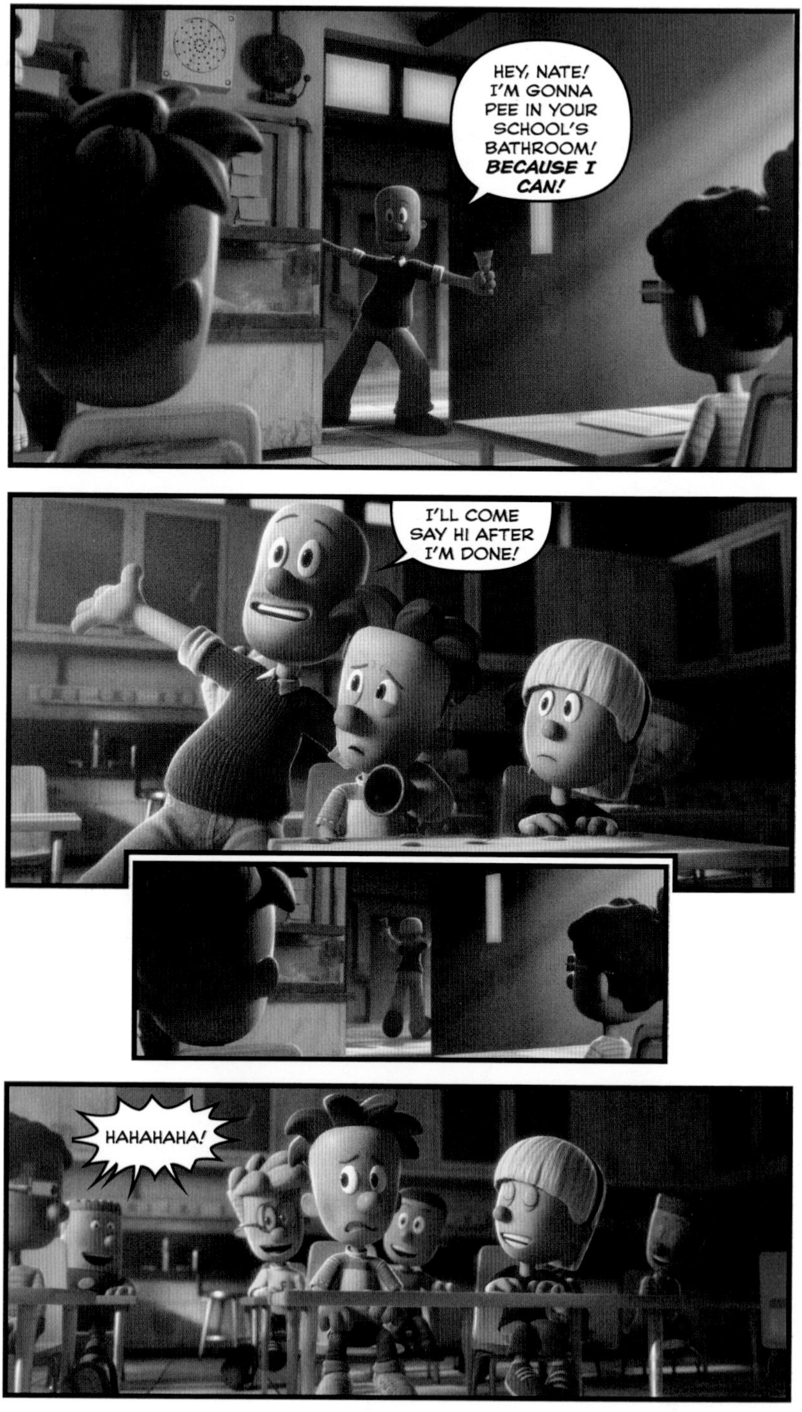
HEY, NATE! I'M GONNA PEE IN YOUR SCHOOL'S BATHROOM! BECAUSE I CAN!
I'LL COME SAY HI AFTER I'M DONE!
HAHAHAHA!

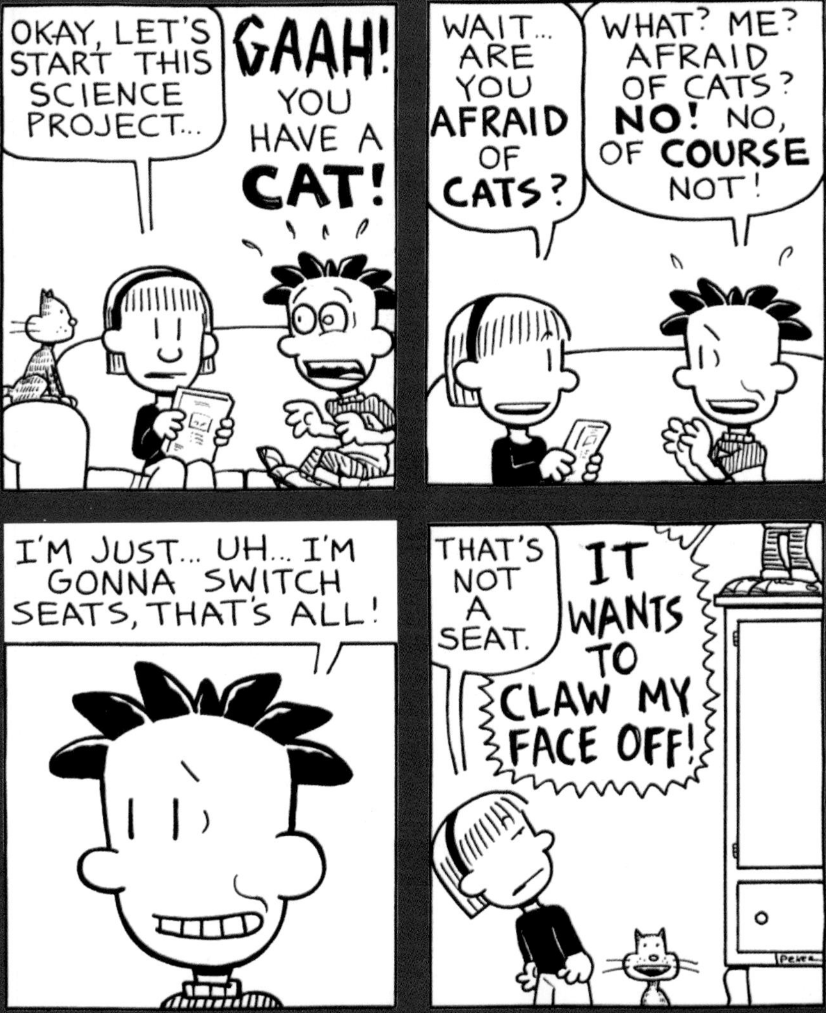
OKAY, LET'S START THIS SCIENCE PROJECT...
GAAH! YOU HAVE A CAT!
WAIT... ARE YOU AFRAID OF CATS?
WHAT? ME? AFRAID OF CATS? NO! NO, OF COURSE NOT!
I'M JUST... UH... I'M GONNA SWITCH SEATS, THAT'S ALL!
THAT'S NOT A SEAT.
IT WANTS TO CLAW MY FACE OFF!

SHOW CREDITS

WRITTEN BY
MITCH WATSON
ELLIOTT OWEN
SARAH ALLAN

STORYBOARD ARTISTS
KAT CHAN
LAKE FAMA
HEATHER GREGERSEN
KIMBERLY JO MILLS
JIM MORTENSEN
JEFF DEGRANDIS
BRADLEY GOODCHILD
ZOË MOSS
KYLE NESWALD
KEVIN SINGLETON
GREY WHITE
SEBASTIAN DUCLOS
RAY GEIGER
BRANDON WARREN
MARIANA YOVANOVICH

CONSULTING PRODUCER
LINCOLN PEIRCE
CO-PRODUCER
BRIDGET MCMEEL

ART DIRECTOR
DAVID SKELLY

CG SUPERVISOR
CHRISTINA LAFERLA

SUPERVISING PRODUCER
JIM MORTENSEN

PRODUCER
AMY MCKENNA

EXECUTIVE PRODUCER
JOHN COHEN

EXECUTIVE PRODUCER
MITCH WATSON
HEAD WRITER
EMILY BRUNDIGE
STAFF WRITERS
SARAH ALLAN
BEN LAPIDES

PRODUCTION MANAGER
TAYLOR BRADBURY

STORYBOARD REVISIONISTS
ANDREW CAPUANO
MISTY MARSDEN
JAZZLYN WEAVER

SCRIPT COORDINATOR
LISSY KLATCHKO
PRODUCTION COORDINATORS
BRANDON CHAU
CLAIRE NORRIS
CARLINA WILLIAMS
LOGAN YUZNA
ASSET PRODUCTION COORDINATORS
DIANA GRIGORIAN
SEAN MCPARTLAND

PRODUCTION ASSISTANTS
CYNTHIA CORTEZ
SARA FISHER
DARREN OJEDA
SIENNA SERTL
NATASHA SHIELDS
EXECUTIVE ASSISTANT
ALEX VAN DER HOEK

CHARACTER DESIGNERS
ROBERT BROWN
JUN LEE
JOCELYN SEPULVEDA
BACKGROUND DESIGNERS
PETER J. DELUCA
GRACE KUM
BECCA RAMOS
JOSH WESSLING
PROP DESIGNERS
ZACHARY CLARKSON
TYLER WILLIAM GENTRY
RC MONTESQUIEU
SHANNON PRESTON
2D DESIGNER
VICKI SCOTT
BACKGROUND PAINTERS
NATALIE FRANSCIONI-KARP
JONATHAN HOEKSTRA
QUINTIN PUEBLA
PATRICK MORGAN

LEAD CG GENERALIST
VYPAC VOUER
LEAD CHARACTER TECHNICAL DIRECTOR
AREEBA RAZA KHAN
LEAD LOOK DEVELOPMENT ARTIST
CANDICE STEPHENSON
LOOK DEVELOPMENT ARTIST
JUAN GIL

CG GENERALIST
THOMAS THOMAS III

ANIMATION DIRECTOR
DENNIS SHELBY
LIGHTING & COMPOSITING DIRECTOR
DARREN D. KINER
LEAD DIGITAL ANIMATOR
SAM KOJI HALE

2D ANIMATION SERVICES
XENTRIX TOONS
FOR XENTRIX TOONS
CREATIVE DIRECTOR
HARRIS CABEROY
PRODUCTION MANAGER
SHERYLEN CAOILI
FX SUPERVISOR
KERWIN OJO
PRODUCTION TEAM
ARA KATRIN LUDOVICO
JANILLE BIANCA TUDELA

SPECIAL THANKS
BRIAN ROBBINS
RAMSEY NAITO
BRIAN KEANE
ANGELIQUE YEN
DANA CLUVERIUS
CLAUDIA SPINELLI

ANIMATION DEVELOPMENT
NATHAN SCHRAM
LESLIE WISHNEVSKI

CURRENT SERIES MANAGEMENT
NEIL WADE

VICE PRESIDENT OF ANIMATION PRODUCTION
DEAN HOFF

EXECUTIVE IN CHARGE FOR NICKELODEON
NATHAN SCHRAM

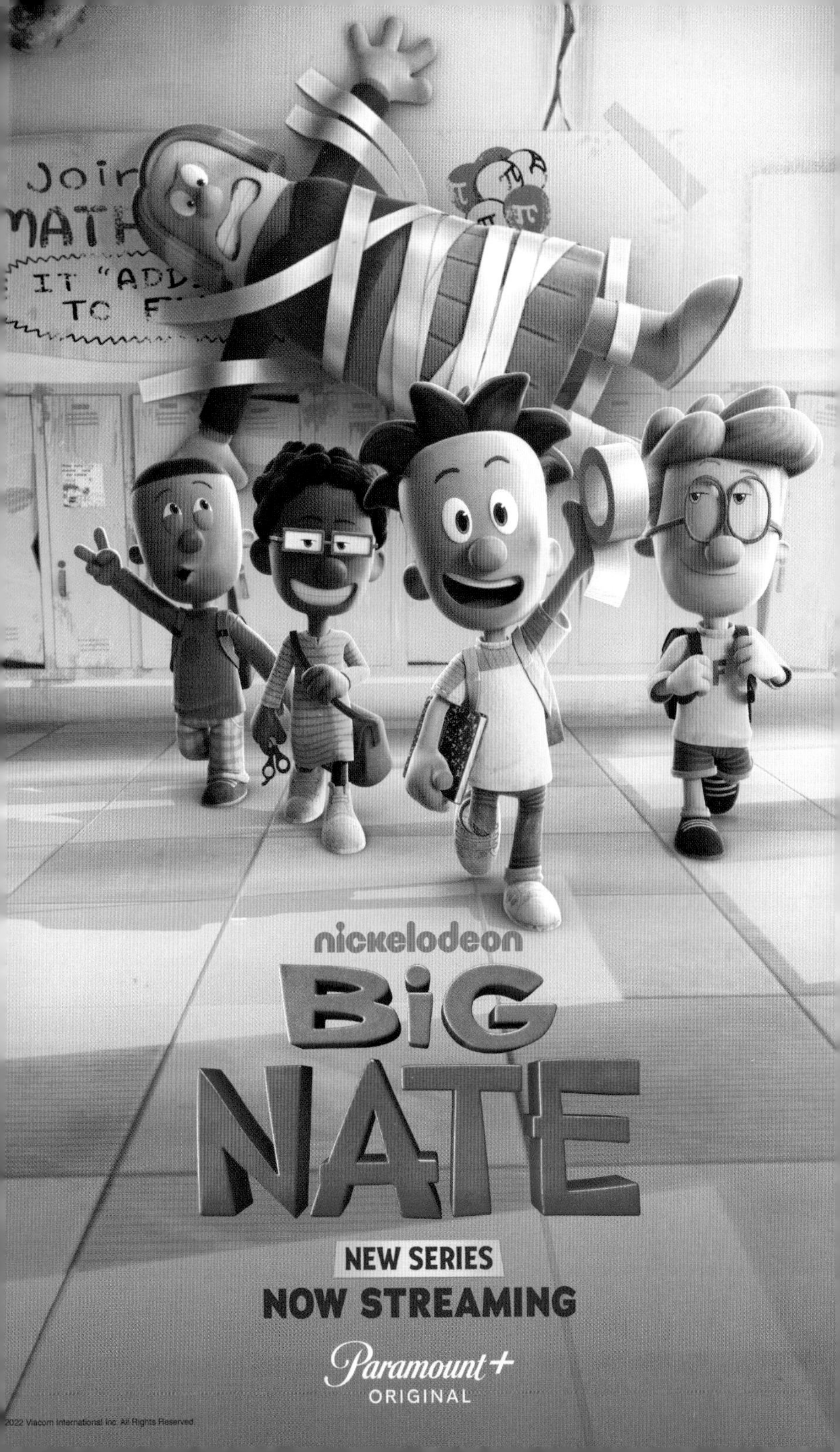
nickelodeon
BiG
NATE
NEW SERIES
NOW STREAMING
Paramount+
ORIGINAL
2022 Viacom International Inc. All Rights Reserved.

Complete Your *Big Nate* Collection

big NATE FROM THE TOP
by LINCOLN PEIRCE
big NATE OUT LOUD
by LINCOLN PEIRCE
big NATE AND FRIENDS
by LINCOLN PEIRCE
big NATE MAKES THE GRADE
by LINCOLN PEIRCE
big NATE GAME ON!
by LINCOLN PEIRCE
big NATE I CAN'T TAKE IT!
by LINCOLN PEIRCE
big NATE GREAT MINDS THINK ALIKE
by LINCOLN PEIRCE
big NATE THE CROWD GOES WILD!
by LINCOLN PEIRCE
big NATE SAY GOOD-BYE TO DORK CITY
by LINCOLN PEIRCE
big NATE WELCOME TO MY WORLD
by LINCOLN PEIRCE
big NATE THUNKA, THUNKA, THUNKA
by LINCOLN PEIRCE
big NATE REVENGE OF THE CREAM PUFFS
by LINCOLN PEIRCE
big NATE WHAT'S A LITTLE NOOGIE BETWEEN FRIENDS?
by LINCOLN PEIRCE
big NATE A GOOD OLD-FASHIONED WEDGIE
by LINCOLN PEIRCE
big NATE SILENT BUT DEADLY
by LINCOLN PEIRCE
big NATE GOES BANANAS!
by LINCOLN PEIRCE
big NATE PAYBACK TIME!
by LINCOLN PEIRCE
big NATE HUG IT OUT!
by LINCOLN PEIRCE
big NATE BLOW THE ROOF OFF!
by LINCOLN PEIRCE
big NATE THE GERBIL ATE MY HOMEWORK
by LINCOLN PEIRCE
big NATE IN YOUR FACE!
by LINCOLN PEIRCE
big NATE ALOHA!
by LINCOLN PEIRCE
big NATE BEWARE OF LOW-FLYING CORN MUFFINS
by LINCOLN PEIRCE

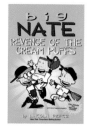

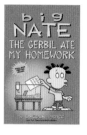

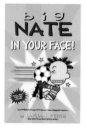